Praise for the novels of

ROBIN D. OWENS

"A multi-faceted, fast-paced gem of a book."
—*The Best Reviews* on *Guardian of Honor*

"This book will enchant readers who enjoy strong heroines."
—*RT Book Reviews* on *Sorceress of Flight*

"Fans of Anne McCaffrey and Mercedes Lackey will appreciate the novel's honorable protagonists and their lively animal companions."
—*Publishers Weekly* on *Protector of the Flight*

"Strong characterization combined with deadly danger make this story vibrate with emotional resonance. Stay tuned as events accelerate toward the final battle."
—*RT Book Reviews* on *Keepers of the Flame*

"A glorious end to the series."
—*Wild on Books Reviews* on *Echoes in the Dark*

enchanted no more

ROBIN D. OWENS

LUNA™

www.LUNA-Books.com

LUNA™

Recycling programs for this product may not exist in your area.

ENCHANTED NO MORE

ISBN-13: 978-0-373-80323-1

www.LUNA-Books.com

Printed in U.S.A.

To the Word Warriors and Lisa (Crash)

CHAPTER

1

A late January night, Denver

JENNI WEAVERS'S SKIN PRICKLED AS THE heaviness of ancient earth magic crossed her front boundary and marched up her sidewalk to her front porch.

A dwarf was at the door. The magical kind of dwarf, from the Lightfolk. He waited for her to acknowledge him. He could wait forever. She wasn't budging from her second-floor office.

The doorbell rang, a fruity ripple of notes that she'd gotten used to since she'd bought the house, and had begun to actually like.

She would not open the door. She'd been dodging phone calls from strange numbers for days.

The doorbell sounded again. She stared out the

window, nothing to see but dark, no moon tonight, and her neighbors' windows weren't lit.

The doorbell rang a third time. And the clear phone on her desk lit up and trilled. And her cell in her bedroom warbled "The Ride of the Valkyries." She was afraid if she answered the door the tune might become all too appropriate.

She set her teeth, turned up her computer speakers and continued typing. The final tweaks to the new little story line for the mass multiplayer online game were due *tonight*.

Her computer died an unnatural death.

A supernatural death.

A touch-of-fey death.

She stared at it openmouthed.

The ringing and ringing and ringing went on.

Stomping downstairs in her fuzzy slippers, she peered out the peephole and saw no one, not on the drafty covered porch or the stoop beyond. Definitely a full-blooded dwarf if she couldn't see him.

Another bad sign.

She shouldn't open the door, but didn't think the dwarf would go away or her computer would come back on until she responded to all the noise.

Her cell tune changed to "Hall of the Mountain King." She hadn't programmed that in.

Hard raps against the door—of course he wouldn't use the silver Hand of Fatima knocker.

Knowing she was making a mistake, she opened the door. Recognized and stared down at a dapperly dressed dwarf in a dark gray tux. Drifmar. "What part of 'never darken my door again' did you Lightfolk not understand?"

He smiled ingratiatingly, addressed her by her birth name. "Mistress Jindesfarne Mistweaver, we've found a pair of brownies who'd indenture themselves to you, despite your many cats. A token of our esteem." He swept a hand toward two small beings—shorter and thinner than the four-foot solidly built dwarf—shivering in the late-January cold. The long tips of their furry ears folded in for warmth. Both male and female were dressed only in white shorts and sleeveless tops.

Jenni looked at the goodwill offering. They were scrawny and wrinkled. Their triangular faces and equally large and usually triangular ears and small vicious pointy teeth made them look as mean as wet cats. They wrapped their arms around themselves and leaned together.

"I don't need household help," she said. "I am a productive member of human society, I have a cleaning team every month."

"You have a squirrel hole in your eaves above the door," Drifmar, the dwarf, pointed out.

"I like the squirrel hole," Jenni insisted. "I like the squirrels."

The brownies perked up.

The dwarf bowed. "Mistress Jindesfarne, we have great problems."

"Always great problems around. No." She slammed the door.

He stuck his foot in it and the door splintered. He smiled with naturally red teeth. "Now you need the brownies."

The brownies were looking hopeful, big brown eyes blinking at her, their thin lips turning black with cold.

Drifmar said, "You need the brownies and we need you. Let's talk."

"No."

"We will make it worth your while."

With just that sentence he ripped the scab she'd thought was a scar off the wound. Hot tears flooded her constricting throat. Her fingers trembled on the doorknob. "No. My family—my once happy, large family—*talked* with you fifteen years ago. Then we went on a mission to balance elemental energies while the royals opened a dimensional gate. My family died." All except her older brother, who blamed her for the fiasco, but not more than she blamed herself.

"They saved the Kings and Queens of the Lightfolk."

"I don't care. The Lightfolk did not save them." She didn't control her magic, let her eyes go to djinn blueflame. The brownies whipped behind the dwarf.

She got a grip on herself. It was Friday night and the sidewalks had people coming and going. Besides, losing her cool with a chief negotiator of the Lightfolk was not smart. "Most of my family is dead in the service of the Lightfolk. I have no responsibility to the Lightfolk at all."

"Your parents taught you better." There was a hint of a scold in his voice.

Since Jenni felt like shrieking again she kept her lips shut on words, breathed through her nose a few times, then managed to say, "Go away. Never come back."

"You are the only one with the inherent magic to balance elements left."

Her gut clenched. The dwarf didn't have to remind her that her brother was crippled physically and magically. She remembered that every day and prayed for him.

She stared into Drifmar's pale silver slit-pupil eyes. He could have no power over her, her own eyes were sheened with tears. "I am well aware of that. Go away. Never come back and if I say it three it *will* be."

"Wait! We will make you a Princess of the Lightfolk, you will lack *nothing* for the rest of your life, your very long life. We need you for just a small job, and it's time sensitive so the mission would be for a short time, only two months."

Harsh laughter tore from her throat. "You can't make a half blood a princess. Against all your rules. A small job for a great problem? I don't believe you, and two months is eighty-four thousand, nine hundred and fifty-nine minutes more than I want to spend in Lightfolk company." She looked down her nose. "That left you with one minute. Time's up."

"You'll have power and status and money and love, whatever your heart desires."

"I desire to be left alone by the Lightfolk." She flicked her fingers. "Go away and that makes *three!*" She put her fury in it, hurled the magical geas at him, but drew on no magic around her. Not to use on such as he.

He vanished.

The brownies remained.

The male squealed, "What to do? What do we do now?"

Jenni stared at the pitiful couple. "You can come in for the night, I suppose, but just one."

They stepped on the stone hearth, then clapped their fingers over their rolled ears and ran back to the far side of the porch. The woman looked at her reproachfully. "You have a nasty-sound scare-mouse machine."

Jenni didn't like the sound, either, but she'd been able to ignore it.

The man appeared interested. "You have *mice*. They said we would have to suffer many cats. Why do you have mice?"

Jenni sighed. "I have one old, fat, toothless calico cat."

The brownie woman—browniefem—bustled back, stared up at Jenni with determination. "Go turn off the scare-mouse sound machine."

Giving them a hard look, Jenni said, "You will guard this door and let no Lightfolk in."

"We promise." They bobbed their heads. "Please leave the door open for the warmth," whined the man.

Jenni muttered a swear word under her breath—a *human* word—and tromped back to the kitchen. Sighing, she removed the sonic mouse repellers. In the summer she could live-trap the mice and relocate them, but in the winter and the bitter cold…no. If her cat, Chinook, had caught them and eaten them, that was different, that was natural. But she had too many advantages over mice to destroy them. Stupidity.

By the time she reached the entryway, the brownies were in and the door propped shut.

Chinook, always curious, descended the stairs two

paws at a time. When she got three steps from the bottom she saw the brownies and her fur rose, her tail bottled and she hissed.

The male hopped into her face, bared his fangs and hissed back.

Jenni went to Chinook and picked her up. "She's lived here for years, you're overnight guests. As long as you're here, you must treat Chinook with respect. She responds well to pampering."

Before she'd petted Chinook twice the brownie couple had zoomed to the kitchen. Jenni followed.

The browniefem looked around, nose in air. "You need us. I am called Hartha and this is Pred."

Pred grinned. "Mousies!" He disappeared into the crack between the stove and the counter.

"The cleaning team comes Monday, only three days from now," Jenni said. The house didn't look too bad to her.

Hartha was suddenly wearing an apron made from two of Jenni's dish towels. That had been in a drawer. "Go sit down and I'll make you some nice tea. You've had a shock." Another sniff. "We must have the house warmer, but we will do it with magic, lower your heating bill."

Jenni hesitated.

"We need the positions." The woman lit the gas oven without turning the knob. She met Jenni's eyes and her own were not pitiful but shrewd. "Those new shadleeches have nested in our home. We had to leave or they would drain our magic dry."

Brownies were mostly magic. But Jenni didn't want to hear their long, sad story.

Music filled the house, her computer was back on. She hoped she hadn't lost much work.

Chinook wriggled and Jenni set her down. The cat sat and stared at the brownie. The woman went straight to the dry food container and filled the cat's bowl. Chinook hummed in greedy pleasure.

Magic filled the atmosphere along with the lavender scent of home spells that Jenni recalled her mother using. She didn't want to think of her family or the brownies or the dwarf. She let Chinook crunch away and went back upstairs to work.

Soon she'd turned in the leprechaun story and was in the depths of email consultation with the game developers about its debut the second week of March, only six weeks away. The scent of sweet-herb tea wafted to her nose. More memories of her mother, her five siblings, whipped through her. The browniefem set the pretty patterned cup before Jenni, twisted her hands in her apron.

So Jenni picked up the tea and sipped.

It was perfect. Just sweet enough.

Naturally. Hartha would have sensed her preferences.

The brownieman, Pred, appeared in the doorway, grinning. "There is no more mouse problem."

Jenni let the brownies have the back storage room, messy with piled boxes, computer parts, cables, extra clothes, mailing materials, old software and broken appliances. She had a feeling it wouldn't be untidy in the morning.

* * *

Grief and ghosts and guilt haunted her dreams.

She should have known that the arrival of the dwarf and the brownies would stir up the old trauma, but had worked that night until her vision had been fuzzed with static from looking at the screen. Then she'd fallen into bed and slept, only to watch the fight around the dimensional gate with the Darkfolk, and be too late again.

Her family had died in that fight fifteen years before. Jenni had been late to help her family magically balance energies as a portal to another dimension was opened. She'd been more interested in her new lover and loving. Hadn't been there when the surprise ambush had occurred. A fatal mistake she was unable to fix, so she had paid the price every day since.

She would never forgive herself for her mistake.

Neither would her elder brother, the only other survivor of her family.

She awoke weeping and curled into a ball, and knew from the soft and muffled quality of the air outside her windows that snow fell in huge, thick flakes. She felt the silent coming and going of the female brownie, Hartha, but kept her back to the woman until the smell of an omelette and hot chocolate made with milk and real liquid cocoa teased her nostrils. She rolled over to see her best china on a pretty tin tray along with a linen napkin and tableware.

As she ate, Chinook hopped onto the bed, onto her lap, and purred, accepting bits of ham and cheese from the omelette. The cat was her family now, old and scruffy as she was.

Only one old cat.

As she stared out the frosted window, she accepted that the Lightfolk would not leave her alone.

They'd send others to negotiate.

They'd send *him*.

Her ex-lover.

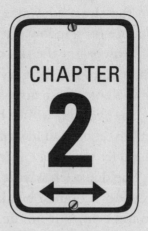

CHAPTER
2

DURING THE NEXT THREE WEEKS, KNOWING the Lightfolk wanted her to go on another "time-sensitive mission" for them niggled like a sliver deep in Jenni's skin. A splinter she could sometimes ignore, but sometimes would jar and send pain shooting through her.

She didn't want anything to disrupt her steady life, didn't want to recall her past or actively use her magic. She did fine living in the mortal world.

Missions for the Lightfolk were deadly.

Jenni stayed inside, hermitlike, avoiding any world beyond her computer, until she yearned for fresh air. So one bitterly cold morning when the snow had melted and the sun was high and yellow in the crystal sky, she left the house. She walked briskly from the Mystic Circle cul-de-sac toward the local business district a few blocks away, circling around the green spaces dotted with skeletal aspens and lush evergreens.

It was good to hear the slap of her leather boot soles on the clean sidewalks, to see shafts of golden sunlight bounce off window glass. The trees and grass were shades of brown, but the sky was blue and gold with sunshine and white with frost crystal clouds and she inhaled deeply of the cold, fresh air.

She was out of her house, away from the brownies' earthy energy. They had made her life so much easier, she'd let them stay. Life might just be okay.

She'd just left Mystic Circle when she heard the sharp crack of a branch breaking. Her shoulders tensed. That sound echoed from the past…when her ex-lover wanted her to know he'd arrived. Stopping in her tracks, she turned back and looked. Aric Paramon stepped out of a huge evergreen tree.

The sight of him jolted her down to her bones. She hadn't seen him since the evening of the ambush, the failed mission. She'd left after her brother Rothly had thrown salt and silver at her, disowning her.

Aric was as gorgeous as ever. He was a tall man, like the California redwoods he lived in, about six feet four inches to her five-eleven. His skin was ruddy-copper. The sun accented the faintest tint of green in his long black hair. The deep green of his eyes would be ascribed to contact lenses by humans. Wide shoulders tapered to a muscular torso. His mother was a dryad and his father an elf.

He wore a raw silk shirt the same color as his eyes, brown slacks and a long, dark brown leather trench coat.

Jenni gulped, and her heart thumped heavily in her

chest. She should have anticipated Aric would arrive that way—he was half Treefolk and could travel the world through any tree.

"I knew they would send you," she said, and the heat of her emotions dried her throat, "the kings and queens of the elements, the Eight, to convince me to go on that mission. I don't want to see you. Go away."

Aric rolled his shoulders, the gleam of pleasure she'd thought she'd seen in his eyes vanished. His face went impassive, then he said, "I've wanted to talk to you for a long time." His voice lowered. "I hoped you would be done mourning."

He didn't add that it had been fifteen years. Aric was nearly immortal and she—half human and quarter djinn and quarter elf—was very long lived.

Fifteen years was like three years to a mortal. "Oh? How long do you think a person grieves for the loss of two brothers and two sisters and both parents?" She wanted the words to be sarcastic, but they also were laden with sorrow. She stiffened her spine and lengthened her stride. Aric wouldn't accompany her to a busy human area.

He kept up with her, glanced down. "I wouldn't know how long your grief lasts," he said. "But I have had losses, too." He looked away. "I am sad when I think of my lost friends. Your father, your brothers."

She didn't care. Sometimes she had moments when wild grief tore at her from the inside.

"You didn't say goodbye," Aric said.

The sentence was a blow that stopped her breath. She struggled for air. She understood, then, that though Aric might grieve as she did, he felt none of her guilt for making love instead of being with her family for their mission.

That was a wide gulf between them that she couldn't cross, didn't even want to think about. Didn't want to think about that time at all, only could speak one sentence of her own to reply. "I thought Rothly throwing salt and silver at us, showing we were dead to him, was enough." Again her voice rasped from her throat.

She turned away, ready to hurry back to her house, her home, her sanctuary. A place untouched by any magic save her own and the brownies'.

His wide, warm fingers curled around her wrist, touching her skin, and she experienced an unwelcome shock of attraction. While she was dealing with that, he said, "You could be a Lightfolk *Princess,* that's what the Eight are offering you as payment for this mission."

She snorted. "Unlikely." Then she shrugged. "I don't want to be a princess." But she felt the vibration of yearning in his body, saw the ambition in his eyes. When had he become interested in Lightfolk status? He hadn't been much before. He'd been as easygoing and laid-back as any Treefolk man she'd known. She wouldn't ask. None of her business.

"There is nothing you can offer me that would make me help the Lightfolk. My parents—family—wanted to be accepted, like most half humans. They're dead and I've made my home in the mortal world. Leave me be." She tugged at her hand.

"It's not just the Eight, the Lightfolk rulers. The entire

magical community needs you, fast. Just for a month and a half—through March."

"I don't need the magical community!"

His jaw flexed. "My family needs you."

"My family needed *you* and you failed them." Her anger poured out with the words, her hair charged with her temper, lifted and nearly sizzled in the cold air.

Aric dropped her wrist, stepped back.

Ugly emotions seethed between them. Jenni couldn't take the words back. She swallowed and pressed on. May as well lance this festering boil. "When you and I ran to the ambush at the dimensional gate, I went to my family to try to help—to balance the energies—to save them from the Darkfolk warriors. You went to the royals and fought." Another thing she didn't think she could forgive him for.

He paled, and replied steadily, "I knew if the Eight fell, all would fall. The loss of the greatest elemental leaders would be such a blow, cause such an imbalance, that the Lightfolk wouldn't recover for centuries. Easy for the Darkfolk to kill us, take us over."

Her smile was cold. "And my brother and I struggled with all the elemental energies in the interdimension. A huge mass of energies that my *whole family* had called, stabilizing the magic, releasing it slowly so magic would not destroy *everyone*. Knowing if we stepped out of the gray mist we would be attacked and killed." She found she was grinding her teeth.

A huge shudder shook Aric. "I didn't know."

He would have if he'd thought about it instead of springing to help the royals. Jenni trembled, too, then cut her hand through the air. "Past is past. But the disaster was such that I have no love of the magical community, no reason to help, no wish to help."

His nostrils flared. He set his feet as if settling into a solid balance, braced to give or take a blow. "I have news of your brother."

Jenni flinched, caught sight of birds circling in the blue sky and realized they were talking of matters in the open where wind could take words to Lightfolk—or Darkfolk. She was glad Aric hadn't said Rothly's name.

Her chest tightened but dreadful hope spurted through the constriction. She hadn't bothered Rothly since he'd disowned her on his sickbed the night of the ambush. Jenni would have known if he'd forgiven her—a lightness would have infused her spirit. He'd have come to her, or sent a message asking that she return home.

Home. Home was not in Northumberland, England, anymore, would never be there again. If she walked in the hills the shadows would flicker and she'd think her parents were there. If she walked along the shore the tide pools would reflect the images of her lost family, the endless waves of the restless ocean would carry their voices. She couldn't live there.

She stopped, could not take another step. Trapped.

By love, as Aric had trapped her before.

This time not for him, but for her beloved brother who now hated her. Rothly had been coldly, flayingly acid to Aric, too, but maybe he'd forgiven Aric. If he had, maybe there was a chance he'd forgive her, too.

"What news of my brother?"

"Must we speak of this on the street?" Aric asked.

"I don't want you in my house."

He winced and only a twinge deep in her heart regretted hurting him. She'd spoken the truth after all.

His breath soughed in and it seemed as if the trees on the street bent toward him in sympathy. He straightened to his full height and Jenni got a feeling of implacability. "There's a commercial area a few blocks down, yes?"

She blinked. That didn't sound like the Aric she'd known, ready to mingle with full humans. "Yes." She smiled briefly. "There's a coffee shop. It's very busy. I agree, we must speak of matters." She had to know about Rothly. Aric wouldn't lie to her.

He angled his head then waited until she came parallel to him, though she kept a good two feet from him. "Calm your djinn nature," he said. He swept a hand before them and the bare branches of the trees shivered as if in a wind. The needles of the evergreen trees whispered against each other.

Aric lowered his voice so that his words were covered by the sound, murmuring so only Jenni's magical hearing had her understanding him.

"Listen. There's been plenty of change since the old Air and Fire couples went through the gate and new ones took their place." He paused, then said even lower, "The sacrifice you and your family made to stabilize the dimensional gate was not for nothing." His gaze was set straight ahead, his expression impassive.

Jenni's laughter mocked. She'd been over every instant of the ambush, the fight, the frantic effort to save her family and everyone at the gathering from wildly unbalanced magic. She no longer thought the "mission" had been important. "All occurred just because two of the kings and queens had reached the height of their power and wanted to move into a dimension richer with magic than poor Earth." She laughed again and it was dissonant.

Once more his jaw tightened, released. "The decision to open a portal to another dimension was the Eight's, not yours or your family's. Your family equalized all four elements so the gate could be made and stay for the time it took for two of the four couples to leave."

"We were so flattered as halflings to be asked to help." She shook her head. "Pleased that we could invite guests to such an important ritual and gathering." Sarcasm. Aric had been her guest. "All the family was close to the portal, the target of the Darkfolk, and *died*."

"Not you, or your brother," Aric said.

"Has my brother's crippled magic and arm been restored?"

Aric was silent.

Jenni hissed out a steamy breath of anger. She wanted to turn back, to hole up and hide again in her house, but she needed to know about Rothly.

She swept her senses around her, glanced over her shoulder toward the entrance to Mystic Circle. In the entire cul-de-sac and all its houses, earth was equal to fire to air to water. Her doing by just living there. The natural magic within her made it so, a comforting thought. All the strongest magic and spells worked better when all elements were equally balanced.

Aric followed her stare, his glance lingered. "Wonderful place," he said. His gaze slid over her, then he looked forward again and began walking. "The old Kings and Queens of Air and Fire left, and new couples ascended to their rank, and change began," Aric said smoothly, as if he was telling a tale. He hadn't been much of one to tell stories before, preferred to listen.

He continued, "The new Kings and Queens of Air and Fire are progressive. More, human technology is catching up with our magical energies enough that we might be able to merge the two. Lightfolk could live easier with mortals, and mortals could stop harming Earth for their fuels." He glanced at her. "As you know, you use a little of that in your work to develop that game you write."

"Fairies and Dragons." Jenni's mouth twisted. He knew more about her than she'd thought. "Neither of which exist anymore. I just finished working on a leprechaun story line. They are gone, too."

"And shadleeches have become." The tone of his voice was grim and laced with hurt.

Jenni didn't know much about shadleeches, they were a relatively recent phenomenon, appearing in the time since she'd turned her back on the Lightfolk. She knew they gnawed on magic.

They reached the coffeehouse, the Sensitive New Age Bean, and Jenni pulled the door open. Human noise and luscious scents emerged, along with warmth. Her mouth watered. She wanted to taste something hot and fiery and jolting down her throat. Espresso and cinnamon.

There was a line at the long wooden counter and she stopped at the end. The icy cold had the humans bundled up in puffy coats, scarves and hats. Jenni was wearing her red leather trench and Aric a brown one—unbuttoned and open. She hadn't felt so inhuman in years, especially in a place she loved, and it unnerved her.

They waited in silence. Her body felt starved for the ineffable essence of standing near Aric, a purely magical being who carried elven blood, and she despaired of herself.

He wasn't manipulating her through active control, he couldn't do that, not as one with Treefolk blood, but he was tempting her with what she shouldn't want and now discovered that she did—news of her brother. That would remind her of all that she'd been and lost.

But she longed for news of Rothly.

Aric leaned on the counter, absently stroking the smooth finish with his fingers, and charmed the women. He ordered hot chocolate with whipped cream and made it sound manly. Of course a male who topped six-four and was built on muscular lines would automatically make whatever he did "manly."

When the logo-etched glass mugs were slid toward them, he casually paid and had Jenni staring. He appeared as if he knew mortal money and was accustomed to using it. Before she could comment, he lifted a glass in a half toast and she followed his gaze to the top of the bookshelves in the other room. "You kept the brownies."

The brownie couple was there though they had been home when she'd left. They were dressed in their best colorful patchwork made from Jenni's fabric scraps and old clothing. Small round upright hats glittering with tiny mirrors sat on their heads between their huge ears. They both had little leather slippers of bright red that

Jenni thought were made from one of her old and shabby purses.

Their eyes were locked on Aric's drink. Like every being in the Folk world, they loved chocolate. Jenni's liquid cocoa had disappeared within hours of their arrival.

Jenni didn't keep chocolate candy in her house. She couldn't. The minute she touched solid chocolate, it melted, a tiny physical idiosyncrasy of her and her mother and sisters. Her lost family.

The espresso burned her throat but it wasn't as hot or as bitter as the taste of tears she'd thought were all gone. Or the memories that Aric and the dwarf and the damn brownies stirred up.

Aric took his mug and two small paper sample cups of cocoa in his other hand. He crossed to a corner surrounded by bookcases, an alcove with a wooden table that was painted in colorful green and blue swirls. He sat sideways in the wooden-runged chair, his arm across the top, angled toward her. His perfectly "pressed" linen trousers couldn't hide the long, thick lines of his thighs, the narrowness of his waist. His silk shirt emphasized the broadness of his shoulders, the proportional length of his arms. His expression was studious as he examined her, but a sad wistfulness was in his pretty eyes. Yes, he was beautiful. But not for her ever again.

His whisper—a sound more like the rustling of leaves than a voice—came to her. "We can talk here, no magical creatures can eavesdrop, and the brownies are loyal to you."

Jenni stared. How could they be after only three weeks?

He gestured the "currently invisible to human eye" brownies down to the table, where they perched on two corners. Blocking the view of humans, he poured cocoa in the sample cups for the brownies. When they took the pleated paper cups, the vessels "vanished."

"We like you, Jenni," Hartha said after she'd taken a sip of her drink.

"Your basement and the house and the cul-de-sac are wonderful," Pred said.

"We do not want to live anywhere else, such as in trees," Hartha said, glancing at Aric.

"Or in a tall building with steel and fake rock, high above the ground in downtown Denver," said Pred.

"Thank you, Hartha, Pred." Jenni managed courtesy, but her yearning to hear about her brother slid like a fever under her skin. She stared at Aric. "What of Rothly?"

Though Aric didn't change his casual pose, she felt tension radiating from him. He'd promised to tell her of Rothly and now had to deliver.

A dreadful anticipation seeping into her blood told her she was going to lose in this struggle with the Folk.

As she'd lost before.

Lost too much when her family had answered a previous summons. Aric was going to win.

She hunched over, curving her fingers around the heat of her glass mug, the same warmth as her hands. She looked at the dark espresso, not at Aric.

Skinny, long, four-jointed fingers were laid across her knee. Hartha had hopped from the table to stand beside

Jenni, her big eyes sad. "Do not keep us if it makes you indebted to the Eight. The Treeman can arrange another place for us."

Pred hissed and she snapped at him in words that thunked in Jenni's ears, but she couldn't understand.

"Rothly," Aric breathed on a sigh. He shook his head, straightened in his chair, met her eyes. "The dwarf Drifmar made him the same offer he'd made to you. If Rothly did the mission for the Lightfolk, he'd become a Prince of the Lightfolk."

Jenni stood. Her chair slammed on the floor. "No." Silence for ten rapid heartbeats. "Tell me that's not true. Rothly is crippled. Physically and magically. He can't work *any* of his once natural elemental balancing magic without peril."

"Crippled in mind and heart emotions, too," Aric added, "not to be able to forgive."

"Tell me that isn't true about Drifmar." Jenni's strident voice overrode Aric. "Tell me you *Lightfolk* did not send my brother to his death." Fury and terror dried her eyes so she experienced everything with an awful clarity— the human gazes focused on them, the trembling of the brownies, the small muscles of Aric's hand flexing around his mug.

"I can't tell you that."

"Is Rothly in danger?"

Aric looked away, his jaw clenched.

Jenni's blood heated. Could she manage to save Rothly without the help of the Lightfolk? They'd said it was time sensitive. How long would she have? Especially since she hadn't practiced any large magic, like stepping into the interdimension, for years.

She locked gazes with Aric, his eyes looked like chips of deep green emerald…but not even as soft as emerald. Again she was facing a man she didn't know, who had changed in fifteen years.

He had his own agenda and he—and the Lightfolk—would keep up the pressure on her.

Standing slowly, Aric said, "Your brother promised on the Mistweaver honor that the mission would be fulfilled."

Jenni flinched, as she knew that wording had been just so. If she didn't consider herself a Mistweaver, was really just Jenni Weavers and not Jindesfarne Mistweaver, she could walk away.

But Rothly had disavowed her, she hadn't abandoned him.

She felt tears gush to the back of her eyes, her chin tremble. She firmed it, swallowed and watched Aric's eyes. "You win."

CHAPTER

3

"I DON'T WANT TO BE HERE WITH YOU," JENNI said steadily, "or listen to you." She didn't sit. "But once again the Lightfolk have given me no choice, have they? They've endangered my brother."

"Jenni—"

Without looking at him, she said, "Tell Drifmar and whoever else needs to know that I will take care of this 'little mission' with the 'terrible problem' for them." Those had been Drifmar's words. Without letting herself think, she said the words that might lead to her death. "I'll finish what my brother tried to do. Uphold the family honor. You've done your job." She'd never heard of a mission for the Lightfolk that wasn't dangerous. "Now tell me of Rothly."

Aric raised his brows. "You'll commit to the whole mission? Not just try to rescue Rothly yourself?"

Jenni's lip curled before she answered. "Would I be

able to rescue Rothly myself? And would Lightfolk help me with that with no strings attached?"

Aric hesitated and she knew the answers were what she'd feared. No help at all from the Lightfolk without conditions.

"Don't—"

"I won't break my Word or Rothly's Word on a contract with the Folk. I haven't lived in the human world so long that I turned stupid."

"You're one of the smartest people I know," Aric said.

"Tell me of Rothly."

"Your brother is missing. From what we know of your family's natural magical gift, you are not totally in this reality when you weave magic."

Aric knew that, he'd been a friend of her brothers' for years. How much had he told the Eight who ruled the Lightfolk? He was obviously loyal to them.

Jenni said nothing, but thought of the half step into a different reality, the gray misty place where the only colors were the elemental energies she could summon— the gold of earth, flaming red-orange of fire, frosty blue-violet of air and the rolling waves of green-blue water. Mystical as the northern lights.

Aric said, "We think Rothly is stuck in what your father called the interdimension...." He stopped as if he felt the flames of anger licking her insides, nearly causing her to lose control of her eye color. If she wasn't careful they'd heat to the blue-white mortals found threatening.

Steam was just below her skin. She needed to cool

down before it issued from her pores. A steaming woman was also a cause for concern in the human world. And why was it that a half hour with one of the Folk could make her forget all her years as a mortal?

"Then I will find him, damn you all," she said.

"Let's discuss this fully somewhere else," Aric said. He gestured back toward the cul-de-sac and her house.

Jenni shot up her chin. "I'm not inviting you into my home."

His skin darkened from light copper to dark. He stood and clamped a hand around her lower arm. "We know Rothly isn't dead, just…caught. We can monitor him."

She yanked her arm away and he let her go. "So you can monitor me, too? How reassuring. You go report to your people. But I get Rothly home first, before anything else."

Aric's fingers clenched. His gaze met hers, his eyes taking on that deep brown rim around his irises that appeared when he felt strongly. He was angry with her because she didn't want him in her home. Well, she could care less what Aric Paramon felt for her. Keeping his gaze locked on hers, he reached into the pocket of his coat and held out a little greenish-white business card.

She stared at the human thing. He dropped his hand and it floated in midair, so she snatched it. This was her neighborhood and she wanted to continue living here. Automatically she glanced down on it. In forest-green ink it said *Aric Paramon, Consultant, Eight Corp,* with an address in the downtown Denver business district. In a high-rise of all places.

Mind-boggling.

"I am your liaison on this matter, Jenni." His voice lowered. "I volunteered for the mission. We go together. We live or die, together. Get used to the idea."

Sounded like something he was repeating from TV, but the Folk didn't watch television, didn't move in the mortal world. Humans were sometimes good for sex, that was all. Like most full-blooded Folk he'd once had a great deal of scorn for the mortal and human. But fifteen years ago the Lightfolk hadn't had a corporation or business cards. She had no clue what was going on.

Aric smiled a knife-edged smile. "Like I said, there have been changes in our world. Considerable changes. And I'm not the man you knew. You will be briefed by one of the royal Eight. Two p.m. Be there."

He'd never been a man to give orders. He was half-dryad-Treefolk, half-elf. He'd been mellow as a Treeman descended from flighty dryads would be, and taken the generally optimistic nature of the elves.

Jenni shrugged all the strange things off. She wasn't about to show ignorance—that led to manipulation. "I'll be ready for our afternoon meeting, make sure you are, too, and that you and the royal will exactly and completely tell me the truth." Her nostrils pinched. She didn't trust any of the Lightfolk, especially the Eight. "Otherwise we'll both die, and whatever terrible problem the Lightfolk have will be worse." She glanced at Hartha. "Looks like you two will be staying to take care of the house while I'm gone."

Hartha nodded. Pred made a small sound of glee. "We will have the *whole* house to ourselves!" His toes curled and he vanished in a small, excited spark of golden topaz.

"I'll get your luggage from the basement," Hartha said, her head tilted toward Aric, so Jenni figured he was telling her what Jenni would need for wherever she was going—besides the step into gray mist, which she would traverse alone since only she had the intrinsic magic to do so.

She turned on her heel and left him, striding out of the coffee shop into the frigid air. With gritted teeth she suppressed her emotions so steam didn't trail her as she marched home.

As soon as she entered her house, she smelled espresso with cinnamon and Hartha was there, holding Jenni's drink from the coffee house out to her in one of her own cups.

"You will need this," Hartha said.

Jenni knew she would need a lot more, and not just caffeine or clothes.

She'd need all her courage, all her skill.

What she didn't need was Aric Paramon going with her. Not a man who reminded her of her own failure. But he was her "liaison." A disgusted sound escaped her.

She inhaled the scent of the coffee, then handed the mug back to Hartha, looked the small brownie in her big brown eyes, which were tinted with gold flecks. The tips of her ears were curled inward, defensively. "I'll set my hand to paper giving you and Pred house-rights to stay here while I'm gone." Jenni sucked in a breath and added, "Currently the house goes to my brother if I die. If we both perish you might as well have it. Those who live here in Mystic Circle will make it so. My next-door neighbor, Amber Sarga, will file the right papers with the human world, and the halfling Harmony Windrose will keep a sworn document for the Lightfolk."

Hartha tipped her head back and stared at Jenni. "We might have this wonderful house in the cul-de-sac where all four elements are present and balanced!" The mug floated as she squeaked and fell to the ground to roll around in excitement, clapping her hands.

Pred joined her. "We can extend the basement tunnel and make a common room for the whole cul-de-sac!" They tumbled in brownie-joy-dance together.

A tingle along Jenni's spine told her that the brownies had already done stuff to the basement. Not that she—or anyone in Mystic Circle—would or could have stopped them.

She kept her eyes on the blurred brownies. How much would they know of the problems and changes in the Lightfolk world? Changes so extreme to break with the many traditions that they actually were following mortal rules—the Eight had a mortal corporation. Changes that pure-blooded Folk would make a half blood like Jenni a Lightfolk Princess?

Hartha wouldn't be in the confidence of the highest circles of the Eight, which, apparently, Aric was. A flash of anger-heat slipped through Jenni.

No reason to interrogate the brownies, not with all that must be done right now.

She had to verify Aric's statements, look for her brother in the interdimension, a half step away from true reality.

She prayed that she would be able to sense him there. Taking off her coat, she hung it on a hook by the door.

The brownies had stopped and stood before her, curtsying and bowing. "We thank you, we thank you, we thank you."

They flicked their fingers at her and she felt herself coated with dust that sunk through her skin. Hartha said, "We bless you on your journeys and may you return safely. You gave us sanctuary and did not indenture us. We like taking care of you and this house. We are loyal."

Pred added, "Blessings and return safely. It is not good to inherit from nonrelatives who are cut down in the midst of life and meet an untimely death."

Jenni winced, shrugged off renewed dread and addressed Hartha. "I must use the kitchen." She'd barely stepped into it since the brownies had come. Hartha considered it her domain. But Jenni needed the herbs that would help her transition from the reality of Earth to the gray mist of the interdimension.

If she'd practiced her craft—entered the interdimension every day—she would've needed very little tea, but she hadn't. She went to the small pantry area between the kitchen and the basement stairs and reached for the red tin on the highest of the built-in shelves. The shelves were spotless, of course, and the contents had been moved around, but the tin was still there.

Ignoring Hartha, Jenni lifted the top of the tin and inhaled deeply, let the scent waft and spiral through her. Potent. Good. Despite the fact that she'd rarely used her magical gift in the last fifteen years, she was dedicated to keeping the special mixture of herbal tea for her talent ready, as her mother had emphasized.

"Do you want me to make the tea?" Hartha stood next to her, twisting her hands in the frilly bright yellow skirt of her apron she now wore over work clothes of a brown blouse and skirt.

Jenni looked down at the brownie. Of course the woman had noticed the tea, probably discerned the ingredients and the quantities of the herbs. "No, thank you, family secret." The brownie flinched, the tops of her ears rolled tight down to the cartilage near her head.

Jenni tried a smile, the corners of her lips curved, and that was enough. "I'm the last uninjured person with Mistweaver magic, so the secret will be archived with the Lightfolk if I die, but until then I prefer it to *be* secret."

Hartha vanished.

With a sigh, Jenni spooned out a teaspoon of the special mixture: the finely ground black Ceylon tea, long, thin and twisted leaves of tringle and green shoono herbs, three minuscule rare moon-crescent blossoms. She dropped the spoonful into a pottery mug made with a special clay that enhanced the power of the herbs. Then she placed the tea tin back onto the top shelf, not shoving it deep this time. She'd need it in the future.

Why had she figured she could ignore or outwit the great Lightfolk, the Eight? If she'd been practicing her craft…if she'd been practicing, surely she'd have sensed Rothly caught in the interdimension? Maybe, maybe not…but if she'd been practicing and he *was* there she might have been able to pull him out…if she knew where he'd stepped into the mist.

Right now, even if he were here in Denver instead of Northumberland, England, she wouldn't have the strength to get him out, would barely have the strength to enter and leave herself. She'd let her natural magic ability to step into the gray mist atrophy. The skills it took to call up the interdimension, go in, stay in for a time, leave—those were all rusty.

She'd have to use the tea, all the mind-body-emotion preparation rituals her family had developed to successfully enter the gray mist. And that was here—in her own home, in Mystic Circle that she'd balanced. She'd be lucky to last fifteen minutes, enough to orientate herself and find him. She *should* be able to find him...but hadn't searched for him for fifteen years.

He had disowned her, cut ties to her. Yet he was her brother. She should still have at least one small bond to him. She hoped.

She didn't dare attempt to save Rothly without more practice...at least three times in the mist, balancing elements—and she'd have to rest in between times. A day would be good.

But the pressure of inner dread made her think that she wouldn't have a day to rest between attempts.

If she didn't get it right, have the skill and strength to pull him from the mist, she'd kill them both.

Her stomach sank as she frowned at the tea. For a quest to save her brother in the interdimension and a mission after that, she should make a fresh mixture. She gritted her teeth. A process of two weeks that couldn't be hurried or even started when the moon was waxing instead of waning.

Unless Rothly had made a fresh batch before going on *his* mission. Which meant returning to her family home in Northumberland to find out.

She poured water into the mug, then set her hands around it and let the heat of her turbulent emotions bring the water to a roiling boil, counting down the necessary seconds, then stopped. As she walked to her bedroom she kept track of the time needed for the infusion. Finally, she whispered a small spell and the leaves whisked up and disintegrated, leaving a tang on the air.

She could grab a ten-minute shower using the proper soap while the tea cooled. It was always better to go to the interdimension cleansed and with clear mind and intentions.

Usually Jenni would heat her skin as she showered in cool water, or heat tub water with her own magic before she bathed. But she must conserve her personal energy. She'd need all her power to enter the interdimension and search for Rothly. If she got stuck herself she would fade away, die.

So she let hot water spatter against her and began the process that would ensure a successful trip into the mist. She thrust away the notion that Rothly was trapped. The Lightfolk could be wrong. Thinking of Rothly snared, that she might be stuck trying to save him, could lead to panic.

As a human and elf, she liked the water, her djinn part not so much. So she let the human enjoy the liquid slipping against her skin, and hummed. Then she let the elf part twirl in the shower, and sang. Then she stepped from the tub and let her djinn heritage flash her dry.

She put on a raw silk orange robe and stepped in a particular rhythm to her bedroom, closed the door. She walked around a large tapestry bag that Hartha had brought from the basement.

Jenni reached for the mug on her bedside table, saw her hand trembled. Chinook, who'd been snoozing on the bed, strolled over and rubbed against Jenni. Sucking in a deep breath, Jenni picked up the heavy cat. Chinook purred. The cat loved elemental energy.

Holding Chinook, Jenni rocked back and forth, comforting them both. "It's just been you and me, but you know I have a brother, Rothly." She'd cried enough tears while calling out for all her lost family.

Chinook just purred.

"I'm going into the gray mist, the interdimension. I haven't done that for many years. But I have to go now. I think I'm the only one alive who can survive the interdimension. Because I can balance the energies. The greatest magical Folk—Light and Dark—are usually only one element…and I'm babbling. Dammit, Rothly shouldn't have tried. He had enough Mistweaver talent to get in, but not out!"

Chinook swept a quick tongue under Jenni's chin and she dragged in a breath. "I'll have to be careful, not move a step in there lest I lose my way. Not stay too long or I'll be trapped like the Lightfolk say Rothly is." She let a nervous heat wave shudder through her. Chinook butted her head against Jenni's arm, stroking them both.

"Yes, I know you like magical energies, especially balanced." Jenni set Chinook back down on the bed.

"Since I haven't done this for so long, you can be

my anchor, so I don't lose my bearings, unable to exit."
Another deep breath at the thought. With the lightest
of touches, she connected to the cat's energy, linked
them, let some of hers cycle to Chinook. The cat's purr
revved.

"I won't be gone long." She hoped. "Just need to find
out if I can sense him. I should, even if he's at home—I
mean in Northumberland. *This* is home now. Ready?"

Chinook sat on the bed, tail curled around her paws.
Jenni snagged her mug from the bedside table, then
turned to face south and began her energy cycling. She
must match her own energies to the vibration of the
interdimension. She drank the tea and let the magical
essence of it flicker through her like tiny flames, igniting
her nerves so she'd be prepared to enter the gray mist.
Make sure the timing was right, longer than if she'd
been practicing often. Cool her energy for two minutes.
Warm for six. Then *hot!*

She set the empty mug aside, walked beyond the end
of her bed and into the middle of the room, faced south
once more. She checked that she was completely balanced
magically, saw the gray mist rise before her and chanted
an entrance to the interdimension open. Taking one step
forward on the carpet, she also moved a half step away
from the dimension of Earth and into the gray mist that
was the space between the reality of Earth and other
planets, other places, other Earths.

She didn't have the talent to open a temporary portal
or establish a gateway to another dimension, but she *knew*
that there were other worlds just beyond the mist.

It was quiet here, and it felt like she stood on solid

ground, but if she looked down, she wouldn't be able to see her feet. She could see nothing but flashes and sheets and twists of the elemental, magical energies, bright against the sky like the northern lights, the aurora borealis.

The real geographical landscape had faded, the house, the mountains in the west, the skyscrapers downtown. Slowly she turned in a full circle, checking the immediate area around her. All magic was balanced, the land around her imbued with equal amounts of fire and air and earth and water. Because she, an elemental balancer, had lived here in Mystic Circle for fourteen years. Her innate power did that. Slight tendrils of the equally mixed energy steamed upward.

Narrowing her eyes, she stared toward the south and the small business district that held the coffee house, the Sensitive New Age Bean. Since it was close to her influence, the elements were more equal than those in other directions. Yet there were still more flares of earth and fire.

Farther south the blue-green of water elemental energy swirled in a pool, spiraling from the "ground" that Jenni couldn't see, tingeing the mist with color. That denoted Sloan's Lake several miles away. One of the reasons she'd chosen this neighborhood was to be near Sloan's and several other minor lakes. Water in Denver was at a premium and having lakes relatively close made it easier for her to call that element.

There was a slow, slight echo of a mew and she knew Chinook was near her feet in the real world. Dear Chinook, the being closest to her in the last few years, her remaining cat. The cat who liked magical energy best.

A tingle on Jenni's skin prompted her to turn east and she faced that way, saw huge streams of magical elemental energy near downtown. They looked as if they were *directed,* not the random flares of naturally occurring magic. Not balanced, though. The blue-violet of air predominated. This was Lightfolk crafting.

Her eyes widened. She'd never seen anything like that in her seventy-five years. That phenomenon hadn't been there when she'd moved to Denver.

So this Eight Corp that the Lightfolk ran was not a small deal. Not if it was messing with the magical energies like that.

She'd allowed them to sneak up on her, hadn't been paying attention, hadn't known they'd established a base in Denver. Why Denver? She shivered. Chinook mewed again and Jenni tore her gaze from downtown.

She was here to find her brother. She swallowed hard.

The Lightfolk believed Rothly was lost in the gray mist of the interdimension.

How long? A person died after a period of time...Jenni wasn't sure of the length. But she wasn't the scholar of the family. Another reason to return to Northumberland, for information.

Since she'd never spent more than forty-five minutes in the mist, the time it took to die had seemed long to her as a youngster. Now she thought it was under three months. *How long had Rothly been gone?* She'd been too angry, too frightened for her brother, to ask the right questions.

Maybe she could sense him. She wouldn't be able to see him, or move in the mist without becoming lost, but she might know.

She hoped. A lot of hoping and praying going on. As usual when involved with the great Lightfolk.

She wanted to save him more than anything else in her life.

He'd be the only other person in the mist.

She sent her energy probing through the interdimension, searching, searching. There! Somewhere, north? Northwest? Geographically she couldn't tell…but there was a pulsing human-and-Lightfolk-elf-djinn aura… Rothly.

If she stilled enough, breathed shallowly, she could *feel* the faintest touch of his fractured energy against her skin.

She closed her eyes, and *visualized* an image from the sensations she felt. His aura was damaged—his magic didn't envelop him evenly. It was ragged, uneven, with a couple of splintered spots.

A sound broke from her, a keening in this silent place. She couldn't tell how far it echoed, how long.

His aura pulsed slowly, too slowly, like he was dying. Trapped in the interdimension without the magic to save himself.

How could she find him and retrieve him? Love poured from her toward him and she thought his aura throbbed slightly stronger. How aware was he? She waited but he said nothing, not mind-to-mind, not aloud.

"Rothly!" she screamed. Still nothing, not even a flinch. She thought he'd have moved, yelled, *cursed* if he were conscious.

She didn't know enough about this deadly dimension, would have to research family records to save him. But she'd have to be where he was to haul him out.

Shivers ran through her. She couldn't bear this. Bad enough that only one of her family had survived the battle. Horrible that he'd been maimed. Worst of all that he'd condemned her as she had blamed herself, bitterly lashed out and cut her guilt deep.

She couldn't lose him. Not the very last of her family. She *must* save him.

Then she sensed something else around him. A flickering, fluttering blip. How could that be?

Jenni's breath stopped as the *thing,* some *other* magical being—a shadleech?—swarmed around Rothly, blocking his aura, hung on him batlike. It was *here* in the interdimension. It—perhaps more than one initially—had trapped him as much as his own crippled power. The shadleech sucked away his magical energy.

Worry gnawed on her like the shadleech on Rothly. She must find out exactly when he'd entered the mist, started so ill-fated a mission. Find him!

She lifted her foot. Another mew and a tug from Chinook, Jenni's tiny anchor, reminding her that she didn't dare step away from the place she'd entered.

Time to leave the interdimension, search and find where Rothly had entered the gray mist. Haul him out.

Hope she could save him and not die herself.

CHAPTER 4

JENNI DREW IN A BREATH, STICKY WITH THE strange misty atmosphere of the interdimension, said the spell to leave. Her limbs trembled and her legs gave out and she stumbled until she fell onto the soft bed. She shook not only from the exertion, but also from fear for Rothly.

Fear for herself, too. She couldn't save Rothly herself, needed to have the help of the Lightfolk to battle the shadleeches. The last time she'd trusted the Lightfolk her whole family had died.

Chinook hopped onto the bed and settled onto her stomach and it was even harder to breathe.

There was a knock on the door.

"Come in, Hartha." Holding Chinook, Jenni panted as she scooted up against the headboard.

The brownie woman set a laptop tray of thick and

hearty stew before her. There was more herbal tea, the stuff to build up her energy.

"You weren't gone long," Hartha said, some curiosity in her voice. "Less than a quarter hour."

"Long enough," Jenni said. There was fresh bread and not from the local deli. Hartha had baked it the night before. Fresh sweet cream butter that didn't come from the cheese shop. More and more the magical way of doing things was overtaking the human customs Jenni'd lived by for so long.

"We have thought how to repay you for all your kindnesses. We know you want a sunroom and will add one to the house when you are gone," Hartha said.

Jenni stared, thought of all the permits, shrugged. The sunroom might very well go up overnight. When they noticed, none of her neighbors would say anything to the authorities. People with magic gravitated to Mystic Circle. Not that she'd ever spoken openly about magic or magical heritages with her neighbors. "Sure." She cleared her throat, did a half bow. "Thank you."

It took Jenni the rest of the morning to arrange for time off and the journey—first to save Rothly, then to complete the mission for the Lightfolk.

She told the game developers she worked for that she was going on a research trip for the next big expansion issue that they were designing and that would go live in the autumn. She also suggested the idea of including flying horses as optional mounts for players. That made the devs dither enough about the work it would take that they'd be glad she was gone.

The brownies and she discussed her mission and she

drew up documents, then she inspected the house from attic to basement. The squirrel holes in the attic were gone, the eaves repaired. In the basement she found that her half crawl space was no longer "half." There was a new and suspicious-looking polished wood door set in the wall fronting the cul-de-sac.

Jenni decided not to dress in a professional suit; instead she tried an arty look for her appointment with the Lightfolk, feeling more comfortable. Feeling like she might be able to hold her own.

She finally finished the espresso from the coffee shop just before she hopped the bus to downtown. She could transport herself magically with great effort, but she sure wouldn't be able to handle a meeting with manipulative Lightfolk afterward and she wanted all her wits as keen as an elven blade.

As the bus wove the five miles into downtown Denver, the sky darkened from the crystalline blue of bitter cold to thick clouds of bruised gray. Humidity spread through the air with the taste of snow and Jenni shivered. Wet cold sank into her like nothing else.

She disembarked with many others in LoDo, lower downtown, at the stop for the free Sixteenth Street mall shuttle toward the business district and the Capitol.

"Got any change, lady?" Coins rattled in a paper cup. Jenni glanced at the guy, her hand dipping into her red trench-coat pocket, pulling out change. She swallowed hard. He was…grotesque, with disproportional head and limbs, growths on his face and hands, a yellowish bad-kidney tinge to his skin. The scent of stale bubblegum rose from him.

She shouldn't stare, but couldn't help herself. He grinned a broken-and-missing-toothed smile and Jenni's fingers opened, dropping coins. He caught them deftly with his cup. People streamed around her.

Jindesfarne. It was less the audible sound of her name than a feeling, not quite a mental touch on her mind. Not from the homeless man before her.

She looked across the street and saw a...tall, broad-shouldered being of gray shadows watching her. Magic surrounded him so she knew no one else noticed him.

A hood obscured his features, though she thought they were fine—as fine as the most beautiful Lightfolk. Frissons slithered down her spine and she knew she wasn't looking at an elf, but a great one of the Darkfolk. Her throat tightened. She would not answer.

You should reconsider this mission for the Lightfolk. Now that he spoke more than a word, Jenni heard rich undertones in the gorgeous voice, seduction. She was glad she couldn't see his eyes, a gaze that would snag and seduce her into anything.

She couldn't reconsider. She had to save her brother. No Darkfolk would understand that. They cared for nothing more than their personal plans, one and all. But her inner alarms were sounding. Don't contradict him. *Maybe,* Jenni mentally projected.

The figure laughed, showing white wicked teeth. *You lie.*

To her horror he broke apart before her eyes, into tiny flittering beings that had comprised him. Shadleeches! Most winged away, but one came and fastened on her wrist, claws piercing her skin, hurting! Sucking her magic from her. She flung it off, stopping a cry by clamping her hand over her mouth. Her heart thumped so hard it was all she could hear. People walked by her faster.

The man had not been real, but a construct. How? Clawlike fingers clamped around her ankle. The beggar. *He* was the real Dark one. He'd created the other, distracted her.

She looked down into wet orbs of eyes, wrenched her gaze away. Shudders ran through her.

My shadleeches are pretty things, the great Dark one said, in that beautiful voice. His fingers tightened, grinding into her flesh and against her bone.

Fear flared and she used it, used her magic to flash heat to her ankle, burn, burn, burn!

The "beggar's" shriek was beyond regular hearing. She was free! She stumbled, limped, saw the bronze doors of a nearby bank and rushed to them. She barreled through the doors and as they slowly shut, a glimpse revealed the Dark one's ungainly body cloaked in an "invisible-to-mortals" illusion hanging in midair. His bulbous stomach drooped, his eyes blazed red. "Mistweaver blood is like the finest wine." A long tongue swept his slashlike mouth. He vanished.

Inwardly quivering, she sank onto a marble bench in the bank's atrium. His words drummed in her ears. He'd hurt her family, perhaps killed them, and he was back.

Since people were staring at her here, too, she sat stiffly, regulating her breathing from ragged panting. She studied the marks on her wrist from the shadleech. The beggar-Dark-one referred to *his* shadleeches. Were they all his, or only that bunch? She thought the latter.

And the more she thought of him, the more power she gave him. Fear coated her mouth.

She still had the Lightfolk to deal with, had to decide how much to tell them—about a lot of things. She couldn't afford fear. Sending adrenaline energy and a touch of fire magic to her wrist and her ankle, she let the marks fade away, scanned her body for any dark poison and found nothing except a small weakness in her magic.

It had not been a strong attack. Too many mortals around for that—since she sensed he'd wanted to gut her and feast on her blood and magic. His voice had lost the illusion of beauty, too, crackling and breaking and screeching. He might have been beautiful in all ways once, but evil magic worked on a being.

But he was a great Dark one and she was a halfling. Nothing could change that. She would need the Lightfolk to fight him. So much for the vague idea of saving her brother and refusing to consider the rest of the mission, though breaking her word could kill her and her brother just as dead.

She was truly trapped, and she'd better think smart.

Her pocket computer chimed. Half an hour before her appointment…she'd left very early. She could spare a few minutes to gather herself, sink into a little meditative trance. She *had* to push the attack aside or the Lightfolk would easily manipulate her at their meeting—she'd have no control over the quest to save Rothly.

So she centered herself and breathed and felt magic surrounding her. Significantly more magic in downtown Denver than there had been six months ago. Good, concentrate on that.

She left the bank and walked, stretched all her senses, let loose the extra one that gauged magic, *tasted* it, and knew magic rippled like minor waves from a central point.

All the stray molecules in the atmosphere of magic were being *pulled* to one source, then emanated from it, like a recycling pump…her nose and tongue and skin and scalp told her that the new magic emanating from that point was just a little richer than it had been.

Walking close to a concrete wall, she trailed her fingers. As she'd suspected, the building was soaking up magic. It was penetrating into the electrical system. Fascinating.

After skirting a winter-dry fountain, she crossed to the doors of one of the tallest buildings in Denver, hesitated as she put her hand on the door pull, which sparked energy against her palm. She suppressed fear that sparked with the magic—fear for her brother, for facing great Lightfolk who assigned missions that only caused her hideous loss.

But she had to save her brother and the Lightfolk had information and the quest was the price.

With one last deep breath, she entered the building and approached the security desk. There she showed her human ID that stated her birth date was fifty years later than it had been. She would be twenty-five for a while yet.

As the guard scanned her ID against the computer's appointment list, Jenni studied the directory. Eight Corp was the only business on the thirty-second floor. The guard murmured "Good afternoon," and indicated the correct elevator, not that she could have missed the bay. The magic was much stronger there.

During the elevator ride, she breathed in a calming rhythm, checked that her natural fire was banked. Losing control in these negotiations would be disastrous.

The door opened and Jenni stepped out onto moss. To humans it might look like a dark green sculpted rug, but it was true moss. Her toes wiggled in her shoes.

She faced a gray-blue marble wall that framed a large granite desk with a top-of-the-line computer system. Fountains bubbled somewhere near.

The female dwarf receptionist—dwarves traditionally guarded entrances—didn't stand when Jenni swished in, the layers of her filmy, multicolored skirt rustling. But the receptionist gave her outfit a glance and frowned at the bright gold blouse Jenni wore, easily seen since her red leather trench coat was open.

The dwarfem's wide nostrils flared, "Djinn and elf," she stated, then, "half-breed human."

Dwarves responded well to rudeness. Jenni showed her pointy incisors. She could be ill-mannered, too. She scanned the female with all her senses. "Full dwarf, ancient fem." She didn't meet the receptionist's gaze. "And I am an elemental balancer." A quality that no one else now in this world could claim. "Why would anyone choose a dwarf as a greeter?" She let the question hang. "Surely one of elven blood would be much better." But pure elves wouldn't see the job of greeting others as important.

The receptionist grunted, a sound like pebbles rolling down a rocky slope, then said, "My apologies, Jindesfarne Mistweaver."

A full-blooded dwarfem apologizing to her. Things certainly had changed. Jenni curled her tongue to the bottom of her mouth, letting the taste of magic coat it. The best, finest kind of magic, all four elements in nearly equal measure.

Then the atmosphere *changed* and the tang on her tongue turned to honey. More elves had entered the suite. Odd to even think of elves in a modern office building...any of the Lightfolk.

"Djinnfem?" The receptionist was prompting a reply to her apology.

Jenni didn't know the dwarfem's name and the scrolled-and-engraved brass nameplate on the granite stated Mrs. Daurfin. Jenni snorted. No Lightfolk would ever put a real name out for anyone to see. Jenni narrowed her eyes but did the proper thing, naming the dwarfem's heritage as she did so. "Apology accepted, Dwarfem of the Diamond clan."

The receptionist narrowed her eyes, too. They became glinting slits of black between brownish curves of flesh. "Mistweaver, Desertshimmer, Cirruswisp," she rumbled again, defining Jenni's ancestry.

"I'm Jenni Weavers in the human world."

"Please wait," the dwarfem instructed, and gestured with a stubby hand to two semicircular groupings of furniture in the space between the elevator and the desk. Both were black and cushiony, one side was leather, the other looked like leather but was actually made from the hide of naugas.

Jenni was not early enough to sit down. They were making her wait. Her inner fire simmered. She heard the tiny clicks of multikeystrokes from a nearby room and tasted another wave of magic. With a smile, she headed for a corridor off the lobby. She found what appeared to be a smooth wall with a bespelled door behind the illusion. Jenni waved and the spell vanished.

"You can't go in there," snapped the dwarfem.

Jenni shrugged a shoulder, opened the door to ripe swearing of the minor Waterfolk kind. The room was long and narrow, painted a stark white that none of the eight Lightfolk and Treefolk workers would appreciate. There was a long counter holding eight computers, a mixture of desktops, laptops, tablets and pockets, according to the size of the beings.

Just in front of her was a naiader—a minor Waterfolk male—who was slender with a bluish tinge to his skin and natural spiky green hair. He stood next to a chair, shoulders hunched as he typed. A mug of hot chocolate made with real cocoa steamed on the desk as if he'd just gotten it.

Programming lines rolled across his screen.

Jenni stepped near him to look at the code on his monitor without him being aware, as he was so caught up in his own irritation.

Orange symbols, *magical* symbols, lit the screen along with regular white human programming lines and mathematical formulas. She nearly choked on her tongue.

Magic.

And technology.

These Folk were writing spells on the computer to draw magic into...into what?

She frowned. She knew this spell, but it was an old and slow and limping one when they needed a big, gliding one to...store electricity? A magical and electrical battery?

Snared by the problem and the knowledge that she could flick it and fix it, she slid into the waterman's—the naiader's—seat, stared at his strange keyboard, memorized it, nudged his fingers away. She moved to the middle of the poorly constructed line, erased the spell he was trying to write and encoded a spell she'd developed and recorded in her spellbook a while back...with a shorter, elegant twist that came to mind. Now this spell would do what they'd intended better than the one that had been on the screen.

There was a wet sucking of breath. "Damned djinn," the guy muttered. "Whole project is fire, electricity, why did it have to be *djinn?* Fluidity should be the key. Flexibility." He squatted and bumped her hip with enough force that she had to stand or fall. He took his chair, brows down, staring at the screen. Then his fingers flew to the end of the spell as his mind engaged and he began writing code.

"I'm plenty flexible, and you're welcome," Jenni said.

He stuck out his lower lip. "Irritating."

She studied the rest of the full-blooded Lightfolk in the computer room. They lounged, watching her, like a tableau of the beauty of the Folk.

There was the water naiader that she'd displaced, a Treefolk dryad with a tinge of green in her skin and her body encased in a black fake-leather catsuit, a dwarf with a heavy scowl and long beard that marked him as one of the older generations—what was he doing here? At the end was a small red fire sprite perched on the ledge of a monitor, wearing a merry grin. He-she winked at Jenni, but remained stationary.

"Jindesfarne, we did not bring you here for your computing skills," Aric said coolly from the open doorway.

At the sight of him, Jenni felt a melting inside. That didn't stop her hair from lifting in individual shafts as her aggravation transmuted into static electricity.

"Dampen spell!" The naiader flung his arms wide, scowled at Jenni, his face beading with drops of distress. "That's why I hate djinn. Should know better than to release static electricity around all these computers."

She did, but she wouldn't apologize. "I'm excellent with computers, and I know a little something about business ergonomics, too." She looked down at the computer counter. "This is a pitiful working space."

The tree dryad perked up.

Aric's brows lowered. The dwarfem receptionist, half his height but nearly as broad, joined him, tapping her foot.

"Everyone should have individual spaces," Jenni said.

"Rounds and semiround rooms," breathed the dryad.

Jenni cast her a sympathetic look. "Or cubes, and those

of like elements grouped together, or those working on congruent inquiries—"

"Enough." Aric glanced down at the receptionist. "Please note what Jindesfarne Mistweaver advised."

A rock pad and a tiny chisel appeared in the dwarfem's hands. She scritched on it, glaring at Jenni. "You're keeping the Air King waiting," she said, "and I'll tell him a lot." She showed red pointed teeth before marching back to her desk.

"Du-u-ude," breathed the water naiader, his round eyes getting wider and more orblike, staring at her. He must be a baby…born in the last thirty years or so.

The palm-sized red fire sprite whizzed to Jenni, buried itself in her hair. "Ver-ry fun plac-s-s-se," it hissed. "Glad to s-see you, Mis-stweaver energy balanc-ser. You s-smell *fine*." It nuzzled her head, nipped her ear, took off to prance along the top of watery guy's monitor.

Aric prompted again, "Jindesfarne."

"The light is all wrong, too, should be tailored to each element," Jenni said.

There was a low murmur from the workers.

"Come, Jenni," Aric said, holding out his hand.

Jenni didn't want to leave these kindred spirits to talk to the Air King about a mission she didn't want to do. But that was the price to save her brother. When she recalled Rothly caught in the mist because of the eight kings and queens, anger roiled through her. She tamped down her temper, but couldn't stop one statement. "Sounds as if Air King Cloudsylph picked up the manner of an Eight fast," she said. "He ascended to royal fifteen years ago, right?"

"You have no idea," murmured the dryad like the whisper of new leaves in spring. "But the changes in the Lightfolk community have been incredible." She beamed and her pewter eyebrow rings shone in the light.

Jenni nodded to the workers, waved a jaunty hand and strode to the doorway. When she reached him, Aric stepped away, then touched her elbow to indicate direction. His fingers were warm and steady.

They strolled by the receptionist dwarf, who was standing on her granite desk, hands on hips, mouth a straight line of disapproval.

The hallway they took was all glass, showing open offices that appeared to be occupied, obviously a set stage for any human clients. But the rooms wouldn't fool a mortal for a minute. Jenni shook her head. Maybe the Lightfolk were finally beginning to try to live—work— side by side with humans, but they weren't doing a very good job yet. They needed to consult the half mortals among them, those who'd lived among humans, integrated into their culture.

But not her.

The sooner she rescued her brother and finished her business with these Folk and got on with her own life, the better.

Aric was wise enough to say nothing as he ushered her into a glassy corner office that was all light and grace.

The Air King sat behind a large, pale green, art deco glass desk. He might not have learned how to handle subordinates in a business setting exactly right, but he had "intimidation" down well.

He was thin and elegant and fascinatingly beautiful.

The elf, Air King Cloudsylph. One of the four kings. Her mouth dried.

She hadn't been in the presence of a full elf for fifteen years, let alone a royal. His magic washed over her and her lips trembled at the sweetness of it, the way his energy brushed away the vestige of fear from the Darkfolk, the faintest weariness from the step into the gray mist.

She avoided eyes that she knew would be ice-blue, set in an unlined heart-shaped face with a deep widow's peak of silver hair. His hair was manelike and flowed to his shoulders, covering his pointed ears.

He wore an exquisitely built suit of pale gray silk, a white linen shirt that was only slightly paler than his skin and a light blue tie. Everything in her shuddered—he was dressed as a human and mortal. Her world tipped.

Jenni reminded herself that they needed her.

His first words emphasized how much *she* needed the Lightfolk. "We have the best elemental healers on call to repair whatever trauma or physical problems that your brother might have endured in our service…his service to the Lightfolk and the Eight."

Jenni hunkered into her balance. "So there are rewards for being injured in service for the Eight. I hadn't noticed."

The king's gaze went cold. "The Eight issued formal thanks and paid a rich reward to the proper Mistweaver after the incident at the dimensional portal fifteen years ago."

Jenni inclined her head. "To Rothly, and I suppose you mean that you tried to heal or help him." She smiled as cold a smile as she could manage. "Yet I never sensed he was complete, as I would have." She inhaled deeply. "When I checked on him in the mist this morning, he was still crippled."

Since she couldn't look the elf in his eyes without being caught by his glamour, she stared at the perfectly formed pale pink elven lips. "And you must not have rewarded him so well before, since he risked his life for a title of 'Prince of the Lightfolk.' You tempted a maimed man and sent him to die."

The air went still and thin, too thin to breathe.

CHAPTER
5

ARIC STEPPED NEXT TO HER, GRASPED HER
hand. Bonds she'd thought were ruptured between
them—mental, emotional, magical—snapped back into
full being.

Do not anger the king! he warned her telepathically.

Sensations flamed through her with his touch. She
couldn't grasp Aric's emotions, didn't dare stop to consider them. He was right, she'd said something stupid,
but she couldn't take it back.

Aric continued his mental scolding. *It was the King of
Water, the merman, who sent the dwarf to you and Rothly. The
King and Queen of Earth, the dwarves, approved. The older
couples. They did not tell the Cloudsylphs or Emberdrakes.*

Great, now she knew more about the Eight's internal
politics than she'd ever wanted, and was tangled in them
like in seaweed.

"I will accept an apology for that," the king said, each word a bullet of ice.

Jenni risked a fleeting glance in his eyes. They remained light, and she thought she'd seen a flash of pain. "Then what I said was not the truth. I apologize."

"Questioning the actions of the Eight is not wise," Cloudsylph said with absolutely no emotion in his voice.

Jenni felt all too human, all too vulnerable. A lifting of his finger could remove all the air from the room and she would die…except that Aric's warm hand was wrapped around hers and he could live without air for a time, and could keep her alive.

She looked out the window at the city, gray-block buildings diminishing in size to the brown-yellow plains. "Yet you seem to think that the Eight need me."

He tapped his fingertips together. Once. Jenni thought it was a mortal gesture he was trying to mimic. "As you need us to save your brother."

Again her chest constricted, this time from emotion. She dragged in a breath, wet her lips. "Do I?"

The elf's brows lifted in the faintest arch. "You may be able to find your brother, but will you be in time to save him? Your father told me once that staying in the interdimension decays the life force. Can you travel through the interdimension to him?"

Jenni figured the king knew the answer was no. Her lips were now cold and she didn't want to use energy to raise her body temperature.

After a minute-long silence, the king continued.

"I didn't think so. And you can't tell where he is, geographically?"

"I can't pinpoint his location." All she knew was that Rothly was to the northwest.

"We know he is in your 'gray mist,' but not where in the real world he stepped into it—geographically. It is my understanding that the closer you are to where he might be in this world, the easier it will be for you to bring him from the interdimension into reality. We sense he is not alone in the interdimension, but shadleeches feast on him, draining his magic." The king's fingers curled in a tiny flex. "Can you separate him from his pursuers and pull him out without bringing them, too?"

A shivery breath sifted through her. The elf's phrasing sounded as if it had come directly from one of the Mistweaver family journals, one she'd thought had been personal. How many journals did they have transcriptions of? How many of the Mistweaver secrets did the Eight know? And how many of the Eight had read them?

"Your father was my friend," Cloudsylph said.

Jenni didn't remember that. Didn't recall Cloudsylph being in their lives. He was of a royal line and the Mistweavers were "mongrels."

"I can send warriors to protect you and him," the king said.

"A little late for that."

For the first time he showed anger. "I was not responsible for the deaths of your family. I fought and suffered. We all suffered."

"But you survived, became a new royal and part of the Eight. All of the Eight survived and four of the old

Eight got to transfer to another, richer dimension. My family paid for your survival and that portal with their lives. You did not save them."

"You do not know all that occurred. You were not with your family when the Darkfolk attacked. Nor did you save them."

Jenni went up in flames. Literally.

She let the heat of her fury burn her clothes away, flash her being into fire, then smoke. She shot through the air vent, melting the grate, hurtled out of the building. There was a snow-fat dark cloud in the sky and she grabbed energy from it, drew electricity around her and became a lightning bolt. She concentrated and snapped onto the ground—

—into an icy stairwell. A rectangular concrete hole in the alley six blocks from her home, a basement access to a business.

She collapsed into a heap, so completely drained she wouldn't be able to move for hours.

She hadn't been smart.

And she was naked.

And a shadleech separated itself from a brick building and fluttered close.

The gray magical being-scrap bent itself. Jenni's human sight saw a large crow tilting its head and hopping toward her. Its claws scritched on the stairwell's concrete. The thing came close enough that she smelled old bubblegum. She shuddered. It would take only a wisp of thought for that dark thing to call others…and the great Dark one, who would feast on her.

If she got a second chance, she would work on anger

management. Work on growing beyond grief and guilt.

Another hop and the shadleech's sharp beak pierced her wrist. Hurt! Like a nail had been driven into her, pinning her. Then she felt an awful tug, as if it drew magic from the very threads of her muscles, the marrow of her bones. She thrashed in pain, but still heard the thing's clicking noise as if disappointed in the thin trickle of her magic.

She was cold, colder than she'd been in Cloudsylph's office. Snow and ice coated her back and butt and legs.... Focus! Use the fear, the short adrenaline rush.

She *reached* to the earth below the concrete, to the air, for any magic. Earth energy, air, water from the ice. It began to snow.

Slowly magic coalesced inside her. The shadleech gurgled in pleasure. A race now. Could she use the magic before the shadleech drained it? She sent heat sizzling down her nerves, zapping the thing off, flung herself up to sit, stand, zombie-lurch to the stairs.

There was a door close, but no one in the basement. Another back business door was at the top of the stairs. People behind it.

"You filthy thing!" Hartha's voice, thick with fury and loathing.

Jenni pitched forward, noodlelike arms barely breaking her fall. She cranked her head sideways, saw the brownie whipping the shadleech with her apron. It cringed, wisped to nothingness under the onslaught of earth magic, died.

"Humph." Hartha dropped the apron, stamped on the

very end of the string and the shadleech disintegrated. Snow fell faster. The browniefem flicked her fingers and glitter imbued the flakes falling on the apron with cleansing magic. Nothing would take harm from the once-cloth or the vanished shadleech.

Hartha turned and Jenni saw the survey of herself—her state of nakedness, skinned hands and knees, more-than-pale magically drained skin.

The brownie tsked, shook her head. "Translocated, did you? Those royal Lightfolk can rile a body fast." The small woman hopped forward and grabbed Jenni's thumbs. Then her head tilted back and her nostrils flared as she sniffed the air. Her eyes widened to huge orbs and her ears rolled against her head. "Must go. Something big and bad and *Dark* coming. We be safe in Mystic Circle."

The great Dark one. Jenni hunched.

There was a brief moment of gritty blackness, then Jenni was falling down onto her very own bed in her pretty and *warm* coral-colored room. She flailed and flopped over onto her back. An instant later Hartha had pulled a gold silk comforter over her…covering even her head. Chinook hopped on the bed, found Jenni's stomach and curled her substantial self on her. The blessing of the cat's heat and energy made Jenni moan.

She'd nearly died—mostly due to her own temper, but a Dark one was on her already and the mission hadn't even begun.

"I will bring a strengthening tonic," Hartha said in a no-nonsense tone.

Jenni huddled, fatalistically knowing that in this

moment the power in the household had shifted to Hartha. Jenni was now a person on a deadly quest and Hartha was the stable person.

A busy-mind thought to keep Jenni from actually thinking hard about what she'd done—her out-of-control temper—and the consequences of her actions, both to herself and to Rothly. No one could save him from the interdimension but her. There could even be consequences to Aric.

No, Cloudsylph wouldn't blame Aric for Jenni's reaction. But that elven lord would know he'd won the skirmish with Jenni. He'd kept his control and she'd lost hers. He knew her weakness. Her guilt was one hell of a hot button.

Guilt was just one of her weaknesses. Right now she felt like she was a messy heap of nothing but weaknesses. Far too emotional. She grieved for her family and was eaten by guilt. She was angry at the Lightfolk for not protecting her family and for manipulating them in the first place. She was angry at Aric for choosing to save the Eight instead of rushing to her family and saving her brothers...his friends.

Then there was the Dark one. He—*it*—had killed her family. It had posted a shadleech in her neighborhood to watch for her. Another reason she would need the Lightfolk, and that was as bitter as the rest.

She'd suppressed so much anger and grief and guilt. Now the emotions burst through her as if her skin crackled then iced and split and all she was left with was emotion. Thought fled.

Jenni wept, then she slept.

She awoke in dim light, with the scent of a potion that still steamed, though Hartha must have left it hours ago. A sensing of the neighborhood atmosphere told her the sun had set and it was past rush hour. People were home from their jobs.

Testing her power and energy, she knew even with Hartha's tea she didn't have the strength to do anything more than small magics. Not tonight, not until tomorrow. And she'd need to be more skillful—go into the mist several more times—before she could save Rothly. Her stupidity had cost her time.

Curling into a ball, she thought of the shadleech attacks and whispered a prayer that Rothly stayed unconscious until she retrieved him.

She had the night to rest, to prepare for the missions, and couldn't afford to lie about doing nothing. Struggling to an elbow, she realized Chinook snored gently beside her. Her old cat, a cat she'd gotten as a kitten a year after she'd moved into the house, was now her only family. A cat who was in indifferent health that Jenni would be leaving to brownies who didn't particularly like cats.

All the gloppy sentimentality in her nature swamped her as she cuddled Chinook. "I love you. I'll miss you."

The cat spared a lick on Jenni's hand then grunted and slipped from Jenni's loose grasp to walk over to the table and investigate the drink. She made a disgusted noise then thunked to the floor and waddled from the room.

Chinook would be fine when Jenni left. The brownies would take care of her.

Jenni rubbed her face. She needed another shower, this time to rehydrate herself.

Stretching aching kinks from her body, she found a tiny amount of elemental energies had dribbled into her while she had slept. Too many earth particles—the brownies must have been concerned. After she drank Hartha's potion, she was able to equalize her own small store of energy and discovered she was ravenous. Too much magic spent wastefully.

With a deep breath, she set down the mug, shifted her shoulders. Her house felt odd, the balance off—more air and tree...Aric was here.

She'd have to tell Aric about the Dark one.

As she stood under the shower, she let the atmosphere of her home envelop her. It was odd to *feel* Aric in this place that she'd made her own. Obviously the brownies had let him in, and since he was her contact with the Eight—and between the choice of the Eight and Aric, she'd choose her ex-lover—it was efficient that he was there.

She dressed. Much as she'd like to avoid the home she'd grown up in, she would have to go to Northumberland to get more tea. She was hoping that Rothly had left notes about the mission. She cringed to think of him trying to practice his craft as a cripple.

Her childhood home would haunt her, she knew that. It would hurt.

Being with Aric there would hurt her more. They'd become lovers there. Every second would remind her of her guilt.

She took a big breath, and checked the tapestry bag

with wooden handles. It was full of clothing from natural fibers—hemp, wool, cotton, even silk shirts and her two cashmere sweaters. For an instant she mourned her long red trench. Her own damn fault it was gone.

From her closet shelf, she pulled down a padded cloth backpack.

Nothing that was synthetic could pass through the trees on her journey with Aric. Odd and strange and sad all the little habits that came back from when they were a couple. It would only get worse.

So she just walked down the stairs and didn't look back.

Aric was seated on the couch in the living room. Chinook was on his lap, purring. "Beautiful cat," he said, stroking her.

"Yes, she is," Jenni said. "And very loving." Her mouth pruned. "Not very discriminating, though."

Aric's jaw flexed. He inhaled deeply, blinked. "This place is wonderful, Jenni, very powerful."

Jenni swallowed as the compliment touched her, narrowed her eyes. "Don't think of doing any great casting here."

Aric gave Chinook a last stroke, then carefully placed her on the sofa beside him. "I wouldn't, and you should know that. Are you going to snipe at me all the time we're together on this mission?"

Jenni's nostrils flared as she inhaled. "I *don't* know you. You've changed. I have changed. And I don't think that my anger is unreasonable. The Lightfolk sent my crippled brother on a mission he couldn't hope to fulfill, just to manipulate me to save him, to be in their debt and do the mission myself." Her voice still had the roughness of fear and sleep and tears.

Aric stared at her. The light was dim, the brownies only had a couple of glow globes going, so Jenni couldn't make out the expression in his eyes.

Finally, he inclined his head. "It's the truth that I have changed. As we all have, since that day of the opening of the portal and the Darkfolk attack. Your anger may not be unreasonable, but it is uncontrolled."

Well, she deserved that. "Yes. Obviously I have issues—psychological problems to work on."

"I know the word *issue,* and I'm not the only one. We are trying to integrate back into the mortal world." He gestured in the direction of downtown. "When magic and technology fuse, humans may be ready to accept us."

"Much as that appeals, that's not the point. The point is saving Rothly, then doing this mysterious mission for the Lightfolk," Jenni said. She squared off against him and silence pulsed.

Hartha walked in with a tray holding two large pottery bowls of steaming stew. She put down a bowl at Jenni's place at the dining room table. A table now clean of books, papers and laptop, and set with another mat, bread plate and silverware. She put down the second bowl there.

Frowning, Jenni said to Hartha, "You invited Aric into my home when you knew I didn't want him here."

"A great Dark one is after you," Hartha said. "Safety is more important than tender feelings."

Jenni flinched.

"You knew?" Aric asked.

Jenni didn't look at him and said, "A recent development."

He stood tall, his stance set but balanced, and Jenni knew that he now had more than the minimal fighter training for a Lightfolk male. Jenni's middle brother had surprised them all in apprenticing himself to a great Lightfolk as a soldier. Her throat tightened. Stewart's body had been covering her mother's. He'd been the first to defend and the second to die. She'd never had the chance to say goodbye. Like all the others.

She rubbed her eyes.

Aric said, "I won't eat the offered food and I will leave if you do not wish to discuss this now." His soft tones backed with steel slid through her. She'd never heard such from him before that morning. She was too right, he'd changed.

She hadn't changed enough. Today's events had made that painfully clear in so many ways. "You're going with me."

He nodded, no muscle of his face soft. "I remain your liaison."

She shook her head, gestured to the place setting Hartha had made for him. "Then we should speak of saving Rothly." Before she sat, Jenni extended her senses for any negative energy in her home or Mystic Circle— and discovered the area was better shielded than ever. The brownies and Aric had helped…and her neighbors were reinforcing it a bit. There also seemed to be some dryad Treefolk magic from the parklike center of the cul-de-sac. "We must go to Northumberland first."

Aric flinched.

So he didn't want to relive memories there, either? Too bad for both of them. After a deep breath that brought no relief, Jenni said, "I must see if Rothly left any notes about where he was going, and discover if he made any of the special tea that helps me enter the interdimension." She let stew broth dribble from her spoon.

Frowning, Aric dipped his bread in the stew and ate, then said, "You didn't need the tea often...before."

He meant all of them, the Mistweavers, and when she lived with her family.

"The tea can be helpful even when one steps into the interdimension daily." She scowled. She was talking as if there was more than one whole elemental balancer in the world. There wasn't. There was only her. Hunching a shoulder, she shrugged the reality of the thought away, met Aric's eyes. "I haven't been traveling to the interdimension much."

"Then it is all the more impressive that Mystic Circle and Denver are so well balanced with the four elemental magics," Aric said softly.

A compliment. It made her throat tighten with longing for the past. Which she had to put behind her or doom them all with her uncontrolled emotions.

"Northumberland, eh?" Aric asked.

"Yes."

He spooned up more stew, ate. When he met her eyes, his own were resigned. A corner of his mouth twisted. "A journey to Northumberland before a quest to save Rothly before a mission to help the whole magical community—"

"The Lightfolk," Jenni corrected.

Aric's gaze was stern. "The whole magical community, and benefiting humans, too. A mission you don't want to know about."

"After we save Rothly." She managed a bite or two. Her mouth savored rich beef, but her stomach remained tense.

"About this Dark one—"

Hartha appeared, shook her finger at Aric's nose, rumbled something in her own language, gestured to Jenni.

Aric nodded. "The browniefem's right, such talk will definitely upset your digestion."

Another bite before Jenni replied, "Her name is Hartha."

"That I know, but she hasn't given me leave to use it."

Quiet sifted through the room, and the quality of it— gold from the brownies' homey glow globes and the soft shades of summer green that Aric brought with him— soothed Jenni. As if this was a standard meal among family instead of two people ready to embark on a dangerous adventure. In that quiet lilted by Chinook's purr, Jenni ate her entire meal. As soon as she put her spoon down, Hartha whisked the remains away with invisible speed.

Aric stood, turned slowly in the room as if testing the elemental energies, shields and threat. He nodded. "The Dark one can't come nearer than that business district in the south."

Jenni shivered at the recollection of what had happened

there, expected Hartha to show up and reveal all the circumstances of her save. Leaving Jenni as emotionally naked as she had been physically and energy-wise when Hartha had found her earlier. But Hartha remained in the kitchen, actually making a little noise to show she wouldn't be interfering. Jenni had to tighten a slack jaw at that. The brownies *were* loyal.

She stood and angled her body toward Aric's again, but this time not in a face-off, this time her legs moved her almost in reflex to how she'd stood near him...before... but she didn't step back.

He did.

That hurt but she mixed the pain of it with the renewed fear of the Dark one when she met Aric's eyes, and got out the most important aspect of the attack first. "I believe he was the one who killed my family."

CHAPTER
6

ARIC'S SUCKED BREATH CARRIED THE NOTE of a gale tossing leaves. He swept his arms in circles, vertical and horizontal, adding a layer of muffling spells, then said, "Kondrian."

The inner, heavy plastic storm windows trembled with clicks as the air pressure changed and Jenni shivered as her fine hair rose. She whispered, "Kondrian."

With an effort she kept her voice conversational, but scooped up the purring Chinook, liking the heavy weight of the cat. "It said it liked…um…Mistweaver essence." Words—though not quite the sentence—that she'd used often here at home. They wouldn't be singled out. She couldn't stop her question. "They know who killed my family?" She'd thought the melee of the Dark-folk ambush had been chaotic. It had seemed chaotic to her, but she wasn't a fighter. She'd thought several beings had killed her family.

"Yes," Aric said. "I must tell King Cloudsylph this. Mystic Circle will not let the Dark one in...or rather, it would hurt him more to attack you here than it would benefit him. You are safe for tonight." Aric looked at Hartha, who stood shifting from foot to foot, twisting her hands in her apron as tiny sparkles of brownie glitter fell to the floor. "And I think that once Jenni is gone the neighborhood will be free of any shadleech or Darkfolk activity."

"The Dark one had shadleeches, from its 'estate,'" Jenni said. "They seemed to be under his control."

Aric's brows rose and the light caught them and showed the deep green. He'd look great with a silver brow ring.

He bowed to Hartha and Pred, who stood in the dining room, arms around each other's waists. Then Aric bowed to her. "I must leave. Since we're heading to Northumberland first, we'll leave at dawn. Seven hours' time difference between here and Northumberland."

Dawn wasn't that early, a few minutes after 7:00 a.m., but it would be another bright and cold day here...and probably a dim and weepy afternoon in Northumberland. Not helping her dread.

She made herself smile at Hartha and Pred. They looked right, here in her living room, as if they should always stay. "You'll be safe here."

The brownies nodded.

Aric donned his trench and paced from dining room to living room and back, the tail of his coat lifting. He wasn't suppressing any of his magic around her. Jenni wondered if that was a good or bad sign.

He said, "We may be able to travel to Northumberland and save Rothly without the Dark one interfering. He will be expecting you to start the mission for the Light-folk immediately, believe that the Eight would coerce you into that."

"Instead of just manipulating me."

"Give your anger up at that, Jenni. Dispose of that to-night, or it will work against us and Rothly." Harsh again. "We are not always bad. The Eight are not *Darkfolk*."

"I suppose not."

With no more than another nod he was gone out of the house, moving faster than any mortal or half mortal.

Jenni turned to the brownies. "Chinook and I are glad you are here."

The brownies bowed together, once again flicking luck at her and murmuring a spell. Hartha glanced at Pred and said, "We prefer not having an empty house. Looking after a family." She glanced at the front door, and Jenni felt her ears heat. The brownies knew she and Aric had been lovers and seemed to be hinting…something Jenni didn't think she wanted.

Pred's upper lip lifted as he stared at Chinook, still purring in Jenni's arms. "We will take care of the feline."

"Thank you." Her shoulders felt stiff, there was tension in her body she hadn't known she carried. "I'll see you tomorrow morning."

"Would you like a hot toddy?" Hartha asked.

"Sure."

Before the word was out of her mouth, a mug of choc-olate laced with rum was floating before her. Trapping a small sigh in her mouth at all the magic and the loss of her human lifestyle—nothing would ever be the same—Jenni turned and let the mug bob with her to her bedroom.

She drank it, set alarms on her chiming clock and her pocket computer as if she were alone—one last attempt at normalcy—then drank the toddy and slipped into sleep.

Dreams did not come and even in sleep she was grateful.

She woke before her alarms rang and dressed in the dark. Slipping on the clothes of natural fabrics, comfortable undies with thin drawstrings instead of elastic, sewn by Hartha. More would be in the tapestry bag.

With a soft word Jenni summoned a glow globe, made her bed awkwardly around Chinook, who moved immediately to the middle. "I'm going bye-bye." It was what she said when she stepped out for groceries, to run errands, informing Chinook she'd be the only one in the house. Not that Jenni knew how much Chinook understood.

Such innocuous words. Jenni petted Chinook, rubbing her head, as she always did. "I'll be back." Usually when she was going on a trip she would tell Chinook the length—five days, a week. "As soon as I can."

She bent down and kissed Chinook between the ears. "I love you." Always the last thing her family said to each other before going anywhere. *I love you.*

There was a slight shifting in the atmosphere, then Aric knocked at the front door and was admitted to her space. Jenni slipped into her wool coat, shouldered on the pack, lifted the tapestry bag and walked downstairs.

He stood in the entryway and looked up. Pain seemed to flash over his features before his expression became impassive again.

"You don't have any bags?"

He shrugged. "We won't be in Northumberland long today, then we'll go to the Earth Palace where I have rooms." He seemed to close in on himself. "Warriors travel light. Ready?" he asked. He held out a hand for her again. Another step from the mortal world into the Lightfolk and Jenni knew it. She took his warm hand.

A soft "hmm" came and Jenni turned to see Hartha and Pred standing together in the arch from the entryway to the living room.

More emotion flashed through Jenni. She wanted to bend down and hug them both, but something in their manner prevented it. So she nodded to them. "Thank you for taking care of Chinook and the house."

"We are honored," Hartha said in a muffled tone.

Aric opened the door and she left with him. The sound of the door shutting and the locks being flipped were metallic clicks of her old life ending.

They walked to the round park in the center of the cul-de-sac. Then he stepped into a pine not wide enough for him and pulled her after.

There was the smell of resin and the harsh caress of bark. Jenni didn't know how the trees—and the dryad's homes—were larger on the inside than the outside. Some sort of inner space that the Treefolk called greenspace or greenhome, just as the Mistweavers had called the misty place the interdimension.

Greenspace was still on Earth—if you considered living in the spaces between atoms as solid reality. Jenni just accepted it as magic.

So they went through the tree into the greenspace and Jenni caught a brief glimpse of a dryad's living room. Aric angled his body and there was a whooshing sound and a feeling of rushing.

They stepped out of the ring of beeches in the patch of forest and into a gray, early afternoon. Before them was the long, low house against the hill, and Jenni's heart lurched into her throat. Her eyes stung. She hadn't seen her childhood home for over fifteen years. It was so dear.

For a few seconds, she couldn't get her feet to move, she just stood and stared at the two-story house of gray stone, long side facing her and two wings on each side angled back toward the hill, forming a small courtyard in the back. A courtyard where the family spent most of their time, usually noisy with their talk and shouts.

She found wetness on her cheeks. Not tears, rain. She shivered. The day was cold and wet and she wasn't used to the humidity of a relatively near ocean. Now she lived in the middle of a huge continent. The air wasn't as thin as a mile high, either. Clamminess coated her skin, tightened her hair until she thought she could hear a *twang* as individual strands curled.

The breath she dragged in was thick and the damp seeped into her skin until she shivered again. So different than Denver, this humid cold, this dense air. How had her half-djinn mother and her half-elf father and all her brothers and sisters managed?

Because it had been home, and was in a land steeped in magic, richer and more ancient than that of Denver, a mixture of Lightfolk races who had lived there for centuries and worked magic.

Aric's fingers touched the small of her back as she shivered again. "I'm here with you. Let's go in." She thought she heard him gulp, but disregarded that notion because the smooth, in-control guy that he'd become wouldn't do something so nervous.

She was glad of his touch, the touch of a pure magical being, of a man who hadn't been raised here, wouldn't cherish this place more than Denver.

This wasn't home anymore.

Her particular fire and air—and human—nature preferred where she lived now, a bustling city with towering mountains in the distance instead of huddled against a hill in a bit of forest with the ocean an hour and a half away.

Aric's hand flattened against the small of her back and she realized she hadn't moved, so now she did, to get away from that warmth sending sensual tendrils unfurling through her. He kept pace with her, his fingertips still in contact with her, and she wondered at it.

She stepped up to the house. Would Rothly's silver-and-salt spell that disowned her keep her from opening the door? Or would the house spells still recognize her as family?

The door was blue-gray with a tarnished brass knocker.

The tint had faded from glossy to flat. It hadn't been repainted in a long time.

Jenni braced herself before she put her hand on the ornate brass knob that was covered in fire runes...from her mother.

More hurt, deeper hurt, welled through her.

"We need to find your brother," Aric said.

The knob was warm under her hand and it turned easily. Jenni stepped inside her old home.

Anger slammed against her, pushing her back into a solid Aric.

Rothly's anger, both directed at her that she dared to come into *his* space, and a long-term ire that pervaded the place.

Jenni panted through the constriction of her chest, striving to pull a trickle of air into her lungs. An air-and-fire spell directed at them! The spell tightened over them like a net, choking, heating, burning.

Aric shuddered behind her and she turned. He was against the closed door and she was against him. His skin had darkened, taken on a coarser texture more like bark. He was half elf, half-dryad Treefolk, he didn't need as much air as she.

Faint steam radiated from him, the ends of his hair crisping. She hadn't felt the fire as much as the air.

Aric was turning browner. His hair became greener, and he'd lost a sizzling inch that sent a fragrance like burning redwood needles into the air.

Rothly had tailored a spell to both of them, to his sister and his friend. Disowning all friendship, all bonds. She and Aric could die!

Jenni widened her stance, struggled to inhale. Any spell Rothly had crafted, she should be able to unravel.

Time was too short to step into the gray mist. She wasn't prepared. She couldn't push through Rothly's spell to reach the older ones that the rest of her family, and she herself, had crafted.

She only had a few seconds.

So she visualized her new home—high, dry Denver, with the thin air of altitude—stripped the humidity from the air of Rothly's spell and pulled enough in to survive. She leaned against Aric's solid strength, twined her fingers with his and heated his cooler body to her own skin temperature, sharing the protection of her fire nature. As his temperature equalized to that of the spell, he stopped burning.

Good. She *looked* at the spell. It was frayed in one corner. Rothly's magic was crippled. Jenni mentally *reached* for a loose thread and yanked. The net vanished.

A tremor went through Aric, starting at his feet and raising his hair, accompanied by the sound of rattling leaves. Jenni realized she was still measured against his full length, righted herself and stepped away. She made a show of looking around the living room that hadn't changed at all as Aric settled.

Something else hit her...but not with a slam, more like a whisper that coated her, sank into her, alerting all her senses. This was not the home she remembered. Her tapestry bag fell from limp fingers.

Scent came first. The fragrance of elf and djinn and human wasn't as rich, nor were there any individual scents of her brothers and sisters, her parents. Only Rothly, and a crippled Rothly. Anger-fear-despair sweat. The slight hint of decaying magic, the astringency of healing herbs kept as potpourri, burnt as incense, used in bath and on wounds.

He was still crippled, then. Somehow Jenni had had a lingering hope that his wounds weren't as bad as the last time she'd seen him—on a pallet in the triage area after the ambush. That his arm and magic might have healed a bit.

She grieved and this time the sharp grief wasn't for her lost siblings and parents, but was for her remaining brother. As she stepped through the house, she understood that she had accepted the deaths of her family. It only needed her to come back here to this empty place for her to understand that.

"It's not the same," Aric said. He hadn't touched her again and she was contrary enough to wish that he still did. "It's so quiet. I've never heard quiet in this place."

Jenni kept her flinch inside. She'd been ignoring the silence, focusing more on the unwholesome feelings that writhed through the atmosphere.

"Your sisters and brothers…even your parents were always cheerfully loud."

Jenni gritted her teeth. "That's right."

Aric frowned and lines she hadn't noticed before appeared in his forehead. He was maturing. A small tremble went through her as she did a quick calculation. He was two hundred years old, his seed would be viable soon, and he'd look for a mate. She brushed the thought aside as she feathered her hand over her coat, though the last of the rain droplets had disappeared minutes ago.

"Quiet and smells funny and…it's out of balance." His voice had lowered and deepened on the last. He lifted his feet one at a time and the action was slow, as if he pulled invisible roots from the ground below the shabby oriental rug and the flagstones beneath.

Jenni stilled. She'd been concentrating so much on her human senses that she hadn't noticed. But he was right. From before she'd been born, for a century before that, this land—this house—was equal in all four elemental energies. Now there were equal parts of air and fire, but earth was about a quarter less than it should be. Water was a good two-thirds less than air or fire. The very thought of it shocked her.

After a quick breath, she nodded. "Yes. I'll fix that before we leave." The best practice she could have to build her skill set to save Rothly. She needed three balancings at least, with rest in between. But no resting here. "I don't want to spend the night here. This is Rothly's home."

Aric grunted. "Not much of one." He turned up his hands, spreading his fingers, testing the magic and atmosphere of the place in the way of Treefolk. "Feels like he's just existing." Aric's mouth turned down. He shook his head. "Full of anger and grief." There was a pause. "Like you, though worse than yours."

"I'm not crippled," Jenni said.

"Not physically or magically," Aric agreed.

Jenni stomped away from him—through the house to the kitchen. It was clean and soulless, though it appeared the same as when her mother and sisters were alive. Jenni and her mother and one of her sisters—the one with more djinn than elf nature—had loved cooking. Together. Jenni's throat closed and she pushed through the kitchen to the pantry. Her mouth twisted as she recalled that she'd painted her own kitchen the same creamy yellow.

She stopped in the large pantry, turned to the glass-fronted cabinets on her left that were for magical ingredients—and found it full of both the makings for the special tea and the tea itself. Pounds of it, stored in large tin containers. It appeared as if Rothly had made enough for her whole family for a decade—or enough to boost his crippled magic for a vital, dangerous mission?

Her heart simply ached. The tins had been labeled with the date...no more than two and a half weeks ago. After Jenni had refused the dwarf at her door and the mission of the Lightfolk.

Thrusting that thought and guilt away, Jenni flicked her fingers to let the steam roiling within her out and banish negative emotions. She took off her backpack and flipped back the flap, then opened the cabinet. The canister was a large, squarish tin with rounded edges. She took it, pried open the top and sniffed.

A wave of dizziness engulfed her. The edges of her vision grayed and thinned to mist.... This was a prime mixture of the tea. Better than Rothly had ever made before. He'd taken more care with it. He'd had to. He was lucky even a nonmagical human could make the tea...the magic was in when the herbs were cut, how they were dried and the processing itself.

With an impatient shrug, Jenni poured the concoction

into a smaller tin, plenty enough to see her through a couple of years of intense daily balancing.

She'd brew the potion to balance this place before she left, as well as filling a few travel vials for emergencies.

Aric watched from the doorway but said nothing. She glanced at him. "Maybe you could check the library." She cleared her voice. "And Dad's study to see if Rothly left any notes?"

Nodding, Aric left and Jenni let out a relieved breath. She didn't think Aric had the nose or the magical sense or training to sort out the mixture of herbs, but she felt better keeping him away from the family secret.

They should have separated the moment they walked into the place. Why had he followed her to the kitchen, the heart of the house when her family had been alive? Maybe he, too, missed them.

The thought insinuated itself into her emotions and she couldn't rid herself of it. He'd told her that he'd grieved, hadn't he? She hadn't allowed herself to believe him. Was she so selfish in her grief? As selfish as Rothly had been. Calming her feelings, she settled into her own balance, unfocused her eyes and murmured the proper words over the tea mixture to reinforce Rothly's arrhythmic and limping spell. This would boost the magical properties of the herbs, keep them fresh.

When her tin was stowed in her pack, she went to see if Aric had discovered anything. As she entered the hallway bisecting the house, she comprehended that he wasn't on the ground floor that held the library and den. He wasn't even in the sunroom that ran the length of the back of the house. He was upstairs where the bedrooms were.

Jenni hadn't planned on going upstairs, hadn't wanted to. From what she'd already experienced since she'd walked into the house, she was damn sure that her bedroom wouldn't be as she had left it.

She hesitated, but couldn't bear to leave Aric alone with her family's things. Slowly she took the stairs to the second floor. They creaked beneath her feet. When she turned right at the top of the landing, shadows laddered the hallway. The dim light let in by the window at the end was watery—like tears instead of rain.

The hall was full of silent squares of closed white doors, except one. The door to her parents' room was open and Aric stood as if frozen outside it. She thought she saw a silver glinting line on his cheek.

"What are you doing here?" She'd wanted her voice to be strong, to snap, but it was barely a whisper disturbing the silence.

"I never got to say goodbye to them, either." Aric's words fell stark.

Something inside Jenni just shattered, tearing her patchwork heart back into bits. A liquid cry escaped her, she staggered back and hit the wall and slid down it, dropped her pack as she curled into herself, and wept. Wept like she hadn't since her family had died.

Before she knew it, Aric sat beside her, gathered her into his arms, next to his warm chest, holding her, shaking himself.

They were my good friends, too, all of them, and I didn't get to say goodbye, he said mentally.

Guilt ate at Jenni in fat, greedy, bloody bites. She sobbed, but managed a coherent thought or two aimed at her former lover, who had failed, also. *I was too late to save them.* Finally, finally she could expose the depth of her guilt. *They all left an hour and a half before the circle dance to open the portal, early, like I was supposed to do. But I stayed with you.*

CHAPTER 7

ARIC SHUDDERED. "AND WE MADE LOVE AND the Lightfolk moved up the ceremony to open the portal and the Darkfolk attacked."

"I sh-sh-should have b-been th-ere." Jenni spoke through wet gulps.

"If you had been there—if *we* had been there—we would be dead, too. You would have stepped from the misty interdimension when your mother, the anchor for the great spell, was killed, just like the rest of your family. Instead we arrived after the first fighting, and you had the chance to help Rothly keep the balance of elements, contain the uneven powers so that we all didn't perish."

Aric paused and stroked her hair. "I thought of what you said yesterday. You were right. If you and Rothly hadn't managed all the elemental magic your family had summoned, the portal would have collapsed. The older two couples wouldn't have made it through to their new world. If the dimensional portal had become unstable, it would have killed many. If you Mistweavers hadn't taken the time to dismiss the elemental energies your family had gathered, *they* would have killed us." His inhalation was audible. "I reminded Cloudsylph of that after you… left."

Some of the guilt she'd punished herself with for so long had leaked away with her tears.

Aric shifted and rubbed his chin on the top of her head and new tears welled. They'd sat like this before and it felt too damn good. His tone was softer when he continued. "Those of us fighting didn't see you and Rothly working so hard, doing such dangerous duty in the gray mist. We didn't think of how our lives were in your hands. The Air King realized that, so did the others of the Eight. Eight Corp has transferred five million dollars to your account."

Jenni yelled in outrage, tried to pull away from Aric's embrace. "You think I care about *money!* We didn't do the mission for money." She thrashed, but Aric set his large hands on her biceps and rose with her.

"No, I knew your family didn't accept the mission for money."

"They—we—they only wanted to be respected in the Lightfolk community. Half-breeds aren't."

Aric flinched. "They weren't. Now that Eight Corp has been established and the Lightfolk are moving more into the human community, able to merge magic and technology, you are more valued, I promise you."

"Huh." Once again Jenni pulled away and this time

Aric let her go. She pulled a tissue from a wad in her coat pocket, wiped her face and blew her nose.

A distant roll of thunder sounded through the window, a brief flash of lightning illuminated the hall. It looked just as she had remembered except it was dustier. And she'd never remembered it dim. The overhead lights had always been on, doors had remained open with cheery yellow light pouring from the rooms.

Cold and wet and dark and late winter in Northumberland—winter had always been *outside* the house but not inside, where warmth and laughter and family filled the rooms.

How long had Rothly lived in this dim silence? Enough to feed bitterness.

Jenni walked unsteadily toward her parents' door, the only one open, bracing herself with every quiet footfall. One pace away, she hauled breath into her body and stepped from dark shadow into gray light, pivoted to look into the large room that should have gleamed warm wood and rosy chintz.

It was blue and gray with shadows and dust. Pain caught and strangled in her chest, along with breath and voice.

Aric put his arm around her shoulders and squeezed. Then he entered the room and marched through the thick layers of dust, his face set. When he reached the bureau against the wall and the many tarnished-silver framed photos he stood, hands fisted at his side. A fine tremor shivered up his body and pain flashed across his features. Then he scooped up two pictures, turned, scuffing gray globules of dust, and returned to the threshold where Jenni hovered, breathing shallowly.

As she'd watched him, she'd become aware of a scent... not just her mother's fragrance of heat and perfume, but the air element that her father had mastered held his scent—and the smell of them together. Parents. Love. Home. She barely saw Aric through renewed tears.

"Here." He handed her a frame crusty with grime, and she glanced down to see a photograph of the whole family—all her sisters and brothers and her parents. It had been taken a year before she'd lost them.

In the picture, Jenni sat cross-legged on the floor between her sisters, her arms around them, grinning cheekily. Her parents sat on a plump love seat behind them, her mother's head tilted against her father's shoulder, obviously both loving and beloved. Rothly lounged against the right arm of the love seat, lanky as he'd reached his final inches. Her second brother, Stewart, leaned against the left arm in a mimicking pose. Her oldest brother stood behind her parents. Lohr had looked the most like their father, the half elf. His smile was shy and proud.

Jenni clutched the picture to her chest, wailing breaths pounded her body. Again Aric was there, arm curving around her, gently moving her down the hall. They passed doors on the right and left that belonged to her siblings—rooms that Jenni was glad were closed. She yearned to open them, but knew the pain would be beyond bearing.

They stopped at the landing, and Aric pressed her to descend, but she balked.

"Come, Jenni, enough of memories. We have work

to do. We must find Rothly's notes." Aric had tucked his photograph into a large pocket that had appeared in his coat, then vanished.

"No." She pivoted in the circle of his arm and paced away to the door at the far end of the hall and the little room—the smallest in the house, as she'd been the youngest—and stood there. She steadied her breath and her emotions, once again groped for the mass of tissues that Hartha had put in her coat pocket. Foresightful brownie.

After cleaning herself up again, she stared at the door. "I need to do this," she said in a cloggy voice. "H-he— Rothly—threw silver and salt at me."

"At us, and he was wrong." Aric laid his arm once again across her shoulders. "We did nothing to be made dead to him."

Jenni shrugged off his arm. "I didn't get to the ritual dancing circle to open the portal on time."

"You didn't get there early," Aric corrected. "As your family did, and they didn't call you when plans changed. We would have been on time. But the Lightfolk moved the opening of the portal up."

There was the faintest note of cool satisfaction in his voice that reminded her that he'd been her family's guest for the great event. He wasn't anywhere close to being high enough status to have been invited on his own. No, he wouldn't have been late for the dancing circle to open the portal.

Unwanted shades of memories flitted near. She didn't intend to take a closer look at them. "They opened the portal while we were having sex."

"While we were enjoying each other. None of that is a reason for guilt."

Jenni blinked away sticky tears that clung to her lashes, peered at him. He sounded completely reasonable. He didn't feel any guilt—hadn't ever—about being in bed rolling around with her having sex when her family was being cut down by Darkfolk.

She didn't want to think of memories, so only stared at the barrier to her old room. She couldn't bring herself to touch the knob and open the door. Aric reached around her, twisted the knob and flung the door open. Her room was empty and painted a white as stark as clean bones.

Air whisked from the place into the hall, carrying a faint searing scent. Jenni knew in that moment that Rothly had called on his djinn fire nature to flash-incinerate everything in her room, including the bed that her grandfather had made for their mother when she was a girl. Jenni's breath was stolen again and she rocked back. Aric's arm curled around her waist and he drew her against his body, pulled the door shut with a slam. He inhaled a lungful of air. "Rothly burnt your things!"

"I know," she said thinly.

"He's your brother."

A terrible smile formed her lips. "No. He threw silver and salt at me, disinheriting me, making me dead to him. Since he's older than me and so the head of the family, he made me no longer a Mistweaver."

"You will always be a Mistweaver." Aric's hands curved around her shoulders and he gave her a small shake. "The Air King was angry with you yesterday when you baited him, but I double-checked the official lists. You and Rothly are still both listed as Mistweavers."

Jenni just closed her eyes, and went dizzy as Aric swung her up in his arms. He took her back to the landing and clomped down the stairs. "And you can still move into the gray mist, the interdimension, and weave elemental energies to make the land and Folk more powerful. That makes you a Mistweaver." He set her on her feet with a little jolt, handed her pack to her. She was glad to be back in the light they'd left on the ground floor. "Let's do what we must do and leave this sad place," Aric ended.

Her chest hurt and breath came short from all the emotions pressing inside her—grief and anger and guilt. She slid the photo into her backpack. With even steps she walked to the center of the entryway and raised her arms above her head, called on her djinn nature and fire. She *could* do something else here for Rothly—more, for the memory of her parents. She could send a cleansing wind through the place and remove every particle of dust. She tapped her foot in the right rhythm, conjured the sound of finger cymbals, a thumping drumbeat began and she saw Aric tapping both hands against the sturdy wooden stair banister. "I helped your mother occasionally," he said.

He had. As Rothly's friend, he had come to stay now and again.

Jenni nodded at him, started the nasal chant, then began to spin. Soon the room was only a blur, as she gathered air and fire around her, then let it go with a spell and the snapping of her fingers. The fire-wind whistled from her and shot up the stairs, doors opened and closed, the whole atmosphere of the house vibrated and by the time Jenni crossed to the stairs and sat down to rest a little, it was done. The house was clean.

Aric sat beside her and it was almost companionable.

He took out the other photograph he'd chosen from the top of her parents' dresser, leaned his arms on his knees and they both looked down at it. Another jolt through her chest into her heart.

He'd chosen the picture they'd all had taken before the mission in the elegant clothes they'd purchased for the event. Aric himself was in the picture, arm in arm with her, smiling with easy charm. He really was photogenic.

Another frisson slipped through her. She looked as if she'd been in love.

For a moment she sat frozen. Why had Aric chosen this photograph? Because he was in it? Because she was?

"I didn't get to say goodbye to them." His voice had the native lilt of a Treeman. He used his sleeve to clean off lingering dust. "And there was that party the night before the portal opening." He smiled and it was beautiful and almost like an old one that she remembered. Surely he'd lost that original smile as she had most of hers. "We all got a little drunk on mead."

She remembered. She'd stayed to the end of the music, but retired before he, knowing that he would come. They shared a room in those days. When he'd arrived later he'd been singing some Treefolk song that she couldn't understand. They'd loved then, slept in later than they should have, and had loved again...until they'd heard screams.

Jenni rose. "Let's see if Rothly left any sign of his exact path." She grimaced. "Though I still think that the Eight could find him if they tried. They are, after all, the most powerful beings on Earth."

Aric didn't defend them. He stood, looked down at her with an inscrutable face, then moved from the stairs down the main hall and turned toward her father's study.

She glanced upstairs, wondering if she could face the second floor again.

"I examined Rothly's bedroom." Aric's words carried to her through the echoing house. "Nothing there."

Nodding to herself, Jenni snagged her pack, then joined him.

The den was different than she remembered. The overflowing shelves were gone and Jenni understood with a shock that her father's friends and colleagues would have wanted some of his collection. She vaguely recalled her parents joking about making wills, but hadn't considered any legacy she might have until this moment. A grudging anger at her brother took more edge off her grief.

She shook herself from her thoughts to see Aric leafing through one of the opened books on the wide desk. He glanced up at her, tapped the book. "Atlas open to Yellowstone, Wyoming, but no papers showing Rothly's exact route." Aric's green gaze glanced off hers. "But we knew he'd gone to Yellowstone."

"We did?" she asked, but not in as neutral a tone as she'd wanted. She recalled her recon mission to find Rothly. Northwest of Denver. Yellowstone, it fit.

"No notes," Rothly continued in a steady voice. Then

a corner of his mouth lifted. "If it had been you, I'd be looking for electronics, but there isn't any kind of computer here."

He was right. Jenni scanned the room. All of them had grown up with books, of course. Books and family journals and personal papers. Her parents had been reluctant to take up electronics, as was her oldest brother. The rest of them had enjoyed the new electronic toys, including Rothly, but there was no sign of his personal computer.

Naturally he'd taken it with him. But would he only have one? Jenni had three herself, all state-of-the-art, not counting the little one she carried in her pocket. "He must have backup drives somewhere." She'd never go anywhere without leaving saved information behind... and uploaded...and emailed to someone. That just wasn't her personal procedure, it was the whole family's. Her father had been a scholar, studying Lightfolk magic, elemental energies and the Mistweaver gifts in particular.

He'd taught them all, as he'd been taught by his parents and great-aunt, that records of every experiment, every passing notion of an idea regarding elemental balancing must be kept.

Jenni bumped Aric with her hip to make him move aside from the middle of the desk. She checked under the books—no papers. The piece of furniture was full of secret cubbyholes. Closing her eyes, she tried to visualize Rothly here. Her throat tightened and the damn tears threatened once more as images of her father, mother, various siblings, showed up as memories.

Rothly! An older, crippled, bitter Rothly. One who

couldn't naturally balance the home and the land just by his presence. One who had more of an air nature than fire. One who disliked being human and wanted to only embrace his Lightfolk side.

A flash of Rothly as a boy came, lifting the right edge of the desk, putting a pocketknife in the small space. Jenni circled the desk and lifted. There were several drives. Whipping her personal computer from her pocket, she linked them. Before her eyes rolled pages and pages of ancient journals, all scanned. Her heart started thumping hard. She'd thought that she would have to take all the books, read them. Here was the wealth of her family!

As she watched, red markings came up and she stopped the scrolling, magnified. Rothly's notes...among others. A sigh escaped her. Her family heritage that she hadn't understood how much she'd missed and yearned for until now. She scooped up all the drives, hesitated. She shouldn't take all Rothly's stash. What if something happened to her, too?

Turning to Aric, she said, "What kind of personal computer do you have?"

He dug into his coat pocket and pulled out a sleek device, smiled slowly. "Not yet released."

Greed rose in Jenni. "I can see that."

"Eight Corp got prototypes. *And* it has been modified to run on ambient magic."

"No way!"

"Yes. Absolutely no recharging needed." He handed it to her.

She turned it over, felt the hum of magic in it, swept

her tongue across her lips. It felt like Aric, solid native Earth Treefolk magic. The rest of the elemental energies were nearly equal in balance—someone had done a good job. Now that she held it, she could also *feel* the little device absorbing magic from her hand in tiny molecules, and from the atmosphere around her. She wanted one.

Aric had moved to the desk, opened a secret panel he'd obviously recalled, gestured to it. Ancient "floppy" disks were inside, marked with her brother Lohr's name. Jenni swallowed. Would Rothly have included everything her family had on elemental balancing in his own drives?

She would have. And she'd bet this house and the land and all her shares of Fairies and Dragons that Rothly had been studying everything he could get his hands on for years to try and regain his magic, or find a work-around.

They didn't have time to search everything.

Aric took his device from her and picked up a couple of the miniature drives. He plugged one into his computer and linked them, loading the information. He glanced at the clock ticking off the seconds of copying, placed it on the desk and began to scrutinize the bookshelves.

The first drive had loaded onto Jenni's pocket computer, and she switched it out for the second. She gulped when she saw her father's very old-fashioned handwriting and the faded ink. These were his earlier journals when the family had first moved to Northumberland from France several centuries before. Then the scrolling went faster and cream-colored pages blurred by.

"All your father's reference books on elemental energies are here. I think most of the more esoteric volumes are gone, though." Aric shrugged.

Jenni joined him, and noticed for the first time in her life she didn't have to dodge stacks of books on the floor...and every step in this house caused pain to grind within her at the memories.

Her pocket computer pinged and she sighed in relief and returned to the desk, swapped out one drive for another and placed the first back into Rothly's hidey-hole. Then she slid down against the desk until she sat, brought her knees up and lowered her head to them, closed her eyes.

"I'm sorry this is hurting you so much," Aric said.

"I am, too." She waited a beat, but still knew what she felt the most right now was the pulsing of Aric's aura. On her outward breath, she whispered, "I'm sorry you're hurting, too."

A longer silence, almost companionable, and his breathing slowed. "Thank you."

"Welcome."

"Did you plan on balancing this place before you left?" That sentence should have been laden with overtones and subtext, but was perfectly leached of emotion.

Jenni didn't look up. "Yes."

"Why don't you go ahead? I'll load all this to our computers."

She rose, glanced at him. "Are you going to pass on all the information on your computer to the Lightfolk archives?"

He hesitated.

A corner of her mouth quirked. "I didn't ask you if you were going to give Mistweaver secrets to the Eight."

Inclining his head, he said, "Thank you for knowing you can trust me not to do that. I know you do not want the Eight to know everything. But the keeper of the archives has much secret lore and this memory bit can be bound against opening until your...if you...we...are lost."

"If I die."

"Yes."

Jenni nodded. "I'll say such a spell and you can give the memory bit to the keeper of the archives." She still didn't like the notion that the Lightfolk would have access to Mistweaver secrets. There was little enough for halflings to keep as their own.

"Thank you," Aric said.

All the lost voices of her family seemed to protest as if she betrayed them—again—and this time in their very home. She squared her shoulders and toed the bottom line. Knowledge should not be lost. "I'll be in the sun-room." No sun today.

CHAPTER

8

JENNI STOPPED IN THE KITCHEN TO ZAP A
quick mug of the herbs from Rothly's store, cycled her
energy to the correct pattern.

Sipping the potion she entered the sunroom that ran
the length of the south side of the house. There was the
humid scent of many plants, and whatever she'd thought
of the rest of the house, this area—the sacred space of the
Mistweavers—was as wonderful as it had always been.
Tall plants pressed hard against the windows, but there
was enough light that had the sun been shining, the room
would be gold and green.

Her breath clogged when she saw the wheel engraved
on the floor and her insides wrenched. A wheel with
eight places. Each person of the family with their own
place—including her mother, who couldn't step into the
mist but insisted on being an anchor. Jenni's lungs un-

froze and her breath came fast and ragged and she wanted to turn and run away.

Instead she walked to the circle.

Only faint traces of her family lingered as she passed over them. How hard it must have been for Rothly to be here, to try to practice here! He hadn't wanted her with him, but now she saw that she'd had the better deal. With his twisted and crippled magic, how could he have borne this room? She moved to the center of the wheel, expecting to feel Rothly—and didn't.

She stared, tramped her feet in place. Surely he hadn't stayed in his own place at the northeast bronze diamond indicator? Walking over to there, touching a toe, feeling the surge of bitterness and fury, she found that he had.

Jenni withdrew from the bleakness of his spot. With a last sip of her tea, she set the mug due west, symbolizing water.

Once again she followed the whole of the ritual to prepare herself, hone her skills, though training and tea and spells wouldn't work if a person didn't have the inherent Mistweaver talent.

She crossed to the middle of the circle, did a cleansing pattern of body movement. She bowed in each direction. No matter how Rothly practiced their craft, the place for one person was in the middle. No wonder the house and the land were unbalanced. Rothly's magic was maimed, his emotions even more sour and negative than her own, and he'd stubbornly stayed in his own place.

After the chant, Jenni closed her eyes and took the tiniest step to slip into the gray mist of the interdimension. As she did this more often, she would need less preparation time, less potion and even less of the spoken chant. Soon she'd be able to move into the grayness with only a mental word.

She turned in place to survey the area and saw the dark smudge of Rothly's spot. Something in the grayness fluttered. Tensing her throat and entire mouth against more useless tears, she got on with her task.

The sheeting flames of elemental energies hovered brightly near the house, as if they'd stayed after being summoned for so many years and waited to be gathered and used once again. Jenni smiled and let the *feel* of them imbue her.

Then she raised her hands and called her magic, matching the texture and the beat and the density and *taste* of it to each near element—humid air with a touch of salt and forest and hill breezes; rich hillsides with veins of soil and rock; crackling fire of the hearth, of controlled burns, of holiday bonfires; mist and molecules of water in the air, from the sea and streams and ponds.

Like called to like.

By "pulling" on the elemental energies she drew the amount she needed. It was the work of a moment to gather enough water and earth to balance the energies of the area, and she spread that equalized magic as far as she could reach.

And in practicing her craft, for a few precious minutes, peace came.

When the strain of being in the interdimension wore on her, she shuffled back into evening gloaming and rain splashing against the windows.

A shadow moved…Aric pushing away from the door-jamb where he'd leaned. "Done?" He held her bag.

"Yes." She let out a shaky breath. One session down, two more and she would feel competent to rescue Rothly. "I'm completely done here."

Aric nodded. "Good." He repeated his earlier words. "It's a sad place."

She picked up the mug, emptied the liquid in the sink in the corner of the room, rinsed it out and put it on a shelf.

A harder *splat* came against the conservatory windows and she glanced over to see the wetly gleaming teeth of a shadleech.

She stumbled back into Aric. He steadied her.

Then another hit came. Faster and faster like a hail-storm in the mountains, but…squishy. The things weren't hurt. Harder to hurt since they were more magical than physical. Magic enough to enter the interdimension.

Aric cursed under his breath. "They've found us."

Jenni swallowed. "Guess so."

His hold on her tightened briefly. "We must go outside to enter a tree and the greenspace."

The thought of that made the back of her throat slime with chill fear. "Yes," she said, her lips numbed. She struggled with her pack until he helped, then she picked up her tapestry bag.

"The sycamore, to the east, is closest and it's big." He hesitated. "I'll make it right with the dryad later."

Jenni winced. "You're not on good terms with her."

"Not anymore."

Jenni decided she didn't want to discuss the topic.

"We'll have to run." From one of the magical pockets in his coat, he pulled out a large silver dagger that flamed around the edges. "They react negatively to fire."

"I can burn 'em up if they attach themselves to us."

"Good," he said.

Quick inhale through nostrils, puff through mouth. "You have the docs?" she asked.

"I transferred all the files I could find to both our palm devices."

The thumping on the glass came faster, harder. "The house shields—"

"Are holding fine, as well as anything against shadleeches. If the filthy things are Kondrian's, they'll leave when we do." His jaw flexed. "They seem directed, not random."

The thuds of shadleeches against the glass roof and windows were almost mathematical in their precision— squadrons of the things. Aric gripped her elbow and his fingers went white-knuckled on his weapon. "Ready?"

He didn't look at her. Foolish that she'd wanted him to, to reassure her that they were in this together. But they hadn't been together for a long time.

"Ready," she said.

His fingers tightened, overlapping just above her elbow. They hurried through the house, Jenni said a spell to open the east side door. As she did, she sent a blast of fire in the direction of the sycamore.

The smell of crisped and charring fur accompanied screams. She and Aric ran, and she slammed the door behind her hard. More screams, but no shadleeches had entered the house.

Aric swept the air ahead of them with his knife, and shadleeches died or disappeared. They couldn't attach to his coat, but several dipped under his collar and Jenni flamed them with a gesture of her free hand. She'd encased herself in fire except for the arm Aric was holding. Teeth nipped and tore and fastened, sucking magic. She sent fire to them from her skin to their mouths. They dropped.

Five more paces and Aric propelled her to the sycamore. She sent a last look over her shoulder to her old home. Solid. Empty. Her family long gone.

Aric had left a light burning for Rothly, one yellow glow of hope.

A thump and they were in the tree's greenspace. Jenni heard breaking china, saw a flash of a dryad's tea party and the fem shrieking at Aric in Treefolk. Another tug took her to a different tree with a startled dryad laughing at them, then Aric pulled Jenni from the tree...and into Kew Gardens in London. From a sycamore to a sycamore...easier to do. He must have been shaken.

"Where are we going?" she asked, glancing around the empty park. However cloudy or sunny the day had been here, it was now dusk and the place was closed.

"The Eight are meeting us in the main Earth Palace in the States."

"Which is where?"

"Near Yellowstone National Park."

"Near Rothly, too."

"That's why we're meeting there."

Jenni wrinkled her nose; she knew enough about Yellowstone to understand that if the supervolcano there blew, Denver wouldn't be safe. Maybe the whole Rocky Mountain range would be activated. Therefore... "The Earth Palace isn't near Yellowstone!"

"On the contrary. What do you think helps stabilize the volcanic mantle plume?" Aric said.

"Huh." And the Eight had been keeping their own secrets.

So they walked from the twilight that wasn't much different from the daylight, through a tree and came out in Yellowstone, back into the brilliant and dazzling blue skies and sunshine of a midmorning American West winter.

Jenni blinked, stepped away from Aric and shook her whole body out. She hadn't done tree traveling in a long time. Aric matched her deep breaths for a full two minutes. She lifted her face to the sun. No, she'd never go back to Northumberland, she'd become used to three hundred days of sunshine a year in Denver.

Yellowstone in February was crystalline in its beauty. Ice crystal. Drifts of snow heaped around them, smoothing over the features of the landscape. The odor of sulphur twitched her nose, not unpleasant to her djinn-fire nature. Geysers steamed in the distance and she saw a colorful pool not too far away. "Beautiful," she breathed.

The corner of Aric's mouth quirked. "It is."

They stood for another minute, watching a hawk soar, then Aric gestured her to go back to the great pine that they'd just exited from.

"Why did we stop?" she asked.

"Because it's beautiful."

And he'd felt she'd needed a beautiful moment in her life? She'd forgotten he'd done things like that, little gestures of thoughtfulness that had pleased her.

This had given her a moment of serenity. Once more she glanced at the landscape around her, the blues of sky and shadows, the white of snow, yellow of shafts of sunshine. The quiet of a place with few humans sank into her, sliding along her ruffled nerves, soothing her.

She closed her eyes, and sent her senses downward—into a seething lake of magma far closer than she was accustomed to. It was oddly exhilarating. When she opened her eyes, Aric was watching her with a half smile and something like tenderness on his face as if he actually cared a lot about her. Her heart gave a twinge. He looked so much like she remembered in past shared moments. The sorry past.

She opened her mouth and realized the snide words she wanted to say would destroy that expression of his, this moment, and diminish her, too.

"Thank you," she said, then again as she actually realized what she had done. "Thank you." She had risen above old instinct and grief and behaved well. The sting of doing that vanished, as had some of the memories that smudged her.

Since he watched her with an inscrutable face and penetrating green eyes, she figured that he'd sensed a shift inside her. Like he knew she couldn't hold on to her grief forever? She'd thought the clutched grief had been comforting, deadening her to the too-sharp guilt that pierced her. But a bit of that guilt was gone, too. His acceptance of the past was rubbing off on her.

Jenni rolled her shoulders, scanned the panorama again. "Very beautiful, and the supervolcano heat feels nice against the soles of my feet, but I don't think I'd want to live here. It probably gets as much sun as Denver, but a whole lot more snow, and I like the city." Despite her occasional hermit months.

Aric nodded, his head lifted as he stared in the distance. "Can you feel Rothly?"

Her whole body lurched. She hadn't even thought of Rothly! All her concentration and emotions should have been focused on him! She'd spent too much time blocking out the pain that thinking of him gave her. That was a habit she must break. She *needed* to keep her brother in her thoughts. And she admitted inwardly that the emotions she'd suffered through the past two days had been intense enough to weary her.

Dragging in chill air, she spread her stance, closed her eyes again and *reached* for her brother in the here and now.

He was…not near enough to walk to, but close enough to feel. "Yes," she whispered. "He's in the area. I'll be able to find him, though it will take me longer than a Lightfolk tracker. How much do you and the Eight know?"

"I'll tell you when we get to the Earth Palace." Aric turned and stepped into the tree again. Once more he held out his hand.

This time she had no hesitation in taking it.

★ ★ ★

They exited into a large cavern lit by enough glow lights to make a djinn feel welcome. Jenni glanced at the tree they'd stepped from. It was a huge oak. She got the idea the tree had been grown just for a transportation hub for the Treefolk.

The room around her was like a geode. No huge stalagmites and stalactites, and the floor was of many colored flagstones, but the walls were comprised of large crystals. The multitude of surfaces caught the light and magnified it so the room was almost as bright as outside. Air more humid than expected caressed her skin.

Aric cocked his head. "Not all of the Eight are here. I have been informed that I should show you to where you will be staying and we can have a meal and a rest."

"That's fine," she said, not that she was looking forward to seeing King Cloudsylph again. Or confronting the dwarves and merman who'd sent Rothly off on a fatal mission.

Aric waved toward one of the four doors in the room and she wondered if the palace was divided into quarters by magical element. He took her elbow again and they strode to the southern one. Halfway there he coughed and Jenni recognized it as embarrassment, as his skin took on a ruddier tint.

"What?" she asked.

"We're going to the female halflings dormitory." He paused. "So you'll feel more comfortable."

Jenni was pretty sure all the halflings in the palace were servants. She snorted. "So much for my upgrading to nobility and princesshood."

Aric turned redder.

"Yah," she continued. "I know. I haven't completed the damn mission for them, whatever it is."

He stopped and bent until his gaze was level with hers. "The whole magical community needs you, Jenni. Not just the Eight, *all* of the Lightfolk. Believe me."

She did, but hunched a shoulder. "Maybe."

He nodded. He must continue to see deeper into her than she wanted. He opened the door, and waved her through to a long corridor with doors on either side.

Immediately there were more people—beings. Jenni saw halflings in variously colored liveries. There were well-dressed Lightfolk nobles, full-blooded djinns and djinnfems, dwarves and dwarfems, a multitude of brownies scurrying.

Aric had removed his hand from her elbow and was dusting off his trench coat, gray ashy flakes of shadleech drifting from the leather. Everyone around them wrinkled their noses at the new smell.

A djinnfem turned into their corridor from a cross hall. She was taller than Jenni and more voluptuous. Her skin color was a true, bright copper, her hair bronze curls with a hint of metallic shine. Jenni squelched her first reaction to fall back into the shadows as she'd been trained as a half-breed human. Instead she stood her ground and lifted her chin.

Right now, in this matter, she was more important to the Eight than this pure djinnfem, whoever she was, though the nearly visible waves of magic emanating from her aura proclaimed her as royal blood.

With a narrowing of her eyes, Jenni scanned the

female, opened her mouth the slightest to draw in the tang of her. A princess indeed, one of the daughters of the King and Queen of Fire, who had left Earth through the portal fifteen years ago. She'd stayed when her parents had left. Probably one of the highest status princesses around.

Even if Jenni accepted a title conferred upon her, she would never reach the rank of this one.

The woman halted in front of Aric, gave him a brilliant smile showing gleaming white teeth, more pointed than those of humans. "Greetings, Aric, flame of my heart."

That endearment jolted through Jenni. "Flame of my heart" meant that there was some formal bond between Aric and the female—not a phrase that would be used by casual lovers. All Jenni's slight yearnings that she and Aric might become intimate again wisped away like a droplet of water hitting a hot grill. Even as she stiffened, took a step away from Aric, putting more air between them, she caught the sound of the quickening of his blood, saw the slight tint of flush redden his skin.

"Greetings, Synicess," Aric replied. "I thought you were in the Middle East."

The djinnfem's nose wrinkled, her upper lip lifted in a sneer. "Humans have befouled the area beyond belief. It will take firestorms by a dozen of my kind to remove the stench of them." She tossed her head. "I'll welcome an order from the Eight to scour the land of them to return the area to a place where magic can thrive once more."

That was horrific enough to have Jenni fading back

another step, away from the being whom she sensed held a deep reservoir of flaming anger. Jenni felt the searing heat of Synicess's stare. There was a hesitation then the female said, "Ah, this is your little half-breed. The sister of the cripple. You wooed her to the commonweal. Good job." Her aura brightened until there were no shadows in the rough rock hall except harsh ones thrown by the three of them.

Keeping her anger tamped down, Jenni sucked in a quiet breath of the hot, metallic air in the corridor and stepped forward, nodded to the female as if they were equals. "Jindesfarne Mistweaver, here to manage what the Eight cannot do even as a team. Just as we Mistweavers provided enough magic for the portal fifteen years ago."

Synicess hissed and fire licked Jenni's skin, hot, hotter, until she would burn in two more seconds.

CHAPTER
9

ARIC STEPPED IN FRONT OF HER, THE BULK of him shadowing her like the redwood he came from. Jenni watched, eyes widening. She didn't think he had the power to stand up to a full-blooded one-elemental Lightfolk. His aura wavered and Jenni got the impression of wide boughs and thick needles dispersing the heat aimed their way.

He, too, set into his balance. Then the slightest of breezes, made from all their exhalations, further wafted the heat away—Aric using his elven air nature. Jenni was reluctantly impressed with the man.

"Synicess, I will meet you later in your chamber. My duty is to see that Jindesfarne eats and is shown to her room."

Both sentences hurt Jenni. How stupid she'd been to think that she was more than a job to him. That he cared for her. That he'd ever cared enough for her that such an emotion might tip into love. That he wouldn't have found other, more satisfying lovers after they'd broken up.

Her female human part had blindsided her. Her softer, weaker, mortal nature.

Though as they passed Syniecess, Jenni figured she'd rather be human than the full djinnfem whose seething mass of anger within would take eons to work through.

Jenni also thought that Aric's taste had definitely gone downhill.

She and Aric walked through several corridors before the coolness of stone once more closed around them and shadows again pooled under a jutting outcropping here and there.

"She is your wife?" Jenni asked. She'd definitely been stupid.

"No."

Since he said nothing more for several steps, Jenni let the quiet gather like the shadows. From the additional tension in Aric's body, the lengthening of his stride that she had to stretch to keep up with him, she knew he didn't want to talk about Syniecess. Curiosity slid through Jenni, prodding, but she kept her mouth shut. In two days already she was maturing.

Growing hadn't been easy, and keeping her snide comments to herself was hard because the Lightfolk still irritated the hell out of her with their treatment. But this was Aric and they were bound together by past events and she discovered she still liked him. He was intriguing and he stood seriously firm when before he'd have made a light comment to deflect. That battle had changed his life as greatly as it had changed hers.

A few more turns later, they reached a broad and well-traveled hallway. Aric stopped at a door and opened it. The dining room was large with a buffet at one end. A rumbling, rough sigh came from Aric, and as he ran his fingers through his hair, the piney scent of his sweat came to Jenni's nose.

He shook his head, managed a smile. "I don't know if my stomach wants lunch or dinner or brunch." His smile was easy now. "The palace is on a full-day rotation schedule, of course, so there's food for all times."

"Right." Didn't look to her like this was a noble area, more like servants. Since Aric's steps had hesitated, he must not eat here often. For halflings, of course. And no one else was in the room.

But the hours' events and emotional traumas began pressing upon her and she found she was as hungry as if she hadn't eaten in days...and emotionally battered.

She saw pancakes and headed toward them. Now she'd had a little respite, her bruises were coming to her attention...where the shadleeches had gnawed on her, where she'd slammed into the alley...and even where a dish from an angry dryad had hit her midback. She had barely noticed at the time.

"Pancakes sound good." Her words slurred. She hadn't gotten much sleep the night before, too wound up.

"I'd like quail," Aric said and headed in another direction.

Jenni sat at a nearby table and Aric joined her. They

ate in silence. For herself, Jenni was enjoying her meal. Exist in the moment with good food.

Aric was eating with enthusiasm, but a line had dug between his brows and Jenni decided he was mulling over how to explain events to the Eight. Good luck to him. Better him than her.

She rose to get some scrambled eggs and bacon, ate those, too, and found herself full. As she put her tableware down and looked around for a dish bin to place her dirty dishes, Aric spoke again. "Just leave the dishes. Brownies clean up."

"After halflings?"

Another shadowy smile from him. "I think the halflings treat the brownies with great respect."

"Which they don't get from Lightfolk nobles." Jenni made it a casual statement, rubbed her eyes to stay awake. "I think I need that nap." She was realizing that all the time she'd been waiting for the Lightfolk to contact her again had worn on her, too. And the brownies had reorganized her life. Pleasant, but wearing.

Aric inclined his head. "It would be best if you were fresh for the meeting with the Eight."

"Instead of being fresh with the Eight."

He looked confused and she understood that he hadn't gotten the human slang. "I'll try to mind my manners."

Tilting his head, he said, "You never were so contrary."

"No, I wasn't with you. Before," she agreed. "I was a happy child secure in the love of my family." She glanced away. Liquid was pressing at the back of her eyes *again*.

She flopped her hand in a gesture. "The battle and the loss…" She shuddered. "Such sudden change and re-versals made it all the worse." She knew she'd behaved badly but she wasn't going to apologize. Not to Aric and not to Cloudsylph. She wasn't healed enough to be magnanimous.

She stood and pushed back her chair. "Let's go. I'm tired."

His face cragged into concern…new lines and planes she hadn't noticed even the day before. Maybe the events had worked on him, too. Being the Eight's man couldn't be easy. Yes, he was maturing, no wonder he'd gone looking for a mate. "I'll show you to the dormitory."

"Fine." That irritated, too, but weariness enveloped her like a fog, seeping into her pores, infusing her.

They walked to the door, and Jenni sensed whisking motions behind her, turned to look and their plates were gone, the table was damp with cleaning. No sign of the brownies. The nobles and royalty probably liked them to be so fast as to be invisible.

"Thank you." She projected her voice.

"Thank you," Aric echoed.

No more than three minutes later, he was standing on the threshold of the empty female halfling dormitory and Jenni was scanning to find her bed. It was about ten beds along the right wall, just before the entrance to the common shower, and she didn't know whether that was a prime space or not. A shower sounded excellent. She set her bag on the carved wooden chest at the end of the twin bed and began to strip, then a strangled sound came from Aric.

Huh. He'd seen all of her—more, felt and tasted—before.

The skin over his fine cheekbones was ruddier than ever. His green, green gaze met hers. "I'll be back in four candlemarks to escort you to the meeting." That was about the same time she'd met with Cloudsylph the day before. Must like midafternoon meetings.

"Fine," she said, then couldn't prevent the words. "Enjoy your time with your lady."

His smile appeared more like a grimace, but that might be hopeful thinking on her part. He ducked his head and closed the door.

Once again Jenni turned thinking off as she enjoyed the hot shower, and dried herself with a huge fluffy bathsheet, thus conserving her own energy. She wiggled into a large cotton T-shirt that was so old it was softer than silk. Sliding between four-hundred-thread-count sheets, she fell down the hole of sleep.

A shake on her shoulder woke her up and she saw a halfling—earth-dwarf and human—looking down at her, pleasantly ugly. "You only have enough time to get dressed for the meeting with the Eight." The woman's voice was low, raspy and, again, attractive. She was really short, though. "We let you sleep as long as we could."

Jenni must've looked terrible then. She sighed. The woman stepped back and Jenni saw a multitude of rounded eyes on her. She tugged at the tangle of her hair. "So, skirt or trousers?"

"Skirt!" They all sounded shocked she would even ask. Not one of them wore pants.

Shrugging, Jenni tried not to notice as everyone

watched her dress. She'd grown up with two sisters and wasn't modest.

She'd just finished draping a paisley silk shawl around her shoulders—arty again—when a knock came at the door. A mob of women rushed to her, surrounded her and Jenni felt the glimmer of balanced magic enhancing her looks.

"Thanks," she said as she walked to the door.

"Welcome," someone said. "The rooms feel better since you've come."

She'd passively balanced the elements already? Must be because there was so much magic around. That reminded her and she hurried back to her tapestry bag, pulled out one of the vials of brew and drank it down. She had a feeling that the Eight would test her elemental balancing.

That would be good for another practice session—or two.

Aric knocked again and she crossed to the door, opened it and saw that he wore dark green silk trousers with his lighter green silk shirt. No tie. Not looking like a human at all. His deep auburn hair was combed behind the pointed ears he'd received from his father. Aric offered his arm and Jenni took it. Old habits. Maybe she could dredge up old feelings of awe and her old manners to get her through this next bit before moving on to her future.

"Good luck," more than one woman whispered.

Again she and Aric walked in silence. They had too little—or maybe too much—between them to talk about.

They came to a wide corridor of pale brown marble floors and walls that emanated a glow that lit the hallway. Two old dwarfmen stood on either side of smoothly carved pillars of alabaster framing a large, square door of solid gold.

As Jenni and Aric approached, the dwarfmen gestured and the door split into two and opened outward. A breath later she and Aric were in a room, opulent beyond Jenni's imagination.

They faced a glass wall showing a massive aquarium, with a luminescent garden of plants gently waving in a mild current and colorful fish swimming. To the left was a fireplace carved into stone that could have held a dozen people. The soft rippling of a thousand chimes sounded and Jenni looked up to see the ceiling that was nothing but strips of metal and glass in various sizes, hung from thin wires of silver and gold and copper.

She could only spare one glance for the chamber and its furnishings before her gaze went to the Eight, who sat on intricate thrones to the right.

Aric pivoted and bowed deeply.

Jenni curtsied, though not quite as deeply as Aric. Her glance slid over the perfection of the kings' and queens' faces, then focused on the tapestry of an elemental wheel over their heads. She didn't dare meet any of their eyes.

The Kings and Queens of Water and Fire sat on each end with Air and Earth in the middle. The only time Jenni had been in the presence of such power was when she'd arrived late at the portal opening and fought for her family's and her own life. She hadn't paid much attention to them, only caught a glimpse of the four who had passed through.

Those before her had been fighting. She recalled the flash of the silver blades of the elves of air, the flaming blades of fire. The dwarven earth couple had wielded glassy shards of obsidian, thrown darts of other metals, even silver, at the Darkfolk.

She recalled the scent of violent death, of evil that stained the ground with acid blood, with smoking mucus...

"Oh!" A liquid gurgle came from the Water Queen and she rushed to Aric. She was smaller than Jenni and lush with curves accenting the pale green skin encased in fronds of seaweed. The queen reached up, setting her fingertips on either side of Aric's jaw. "You are hurt, Treeman. Too dry. Seared by djinn anger." She looked disapprovingly at Jenni.

Left over from this morning or more recently? Jenni raised her brows. "Not me. One of *your* kind." She glanced at the seven intent upon the scene of the queen and Aric and Jenni. "A full-blooded Lightfolk royal djinnfem."

The King of Air frowned. "Synicess?"

"So she was addressed." Jenni thought it wise not to mention the woman's name.

"Rough sex, then," the Water King grunted.

With soft, susurrating sounds like waves lapping a gentle shore, the Water Queen sent liquid to Aric. Jenni could almost hear his cells being plumped up with vital water.

"There," the merfem whispered and returned to her

throne, leaving damp footprints in her wake. Again Jenni caught flashes of her beauty from the corner of her eyes—a wide forehead, pretty nose, full, plump lips. Eyes of a deep green that would enchant even immortals.

Aric had told her that Water and Earth had sent Rothly on his ill-fated mission. Jenni was sure, now, that this woman had nothing to do with that. No, it would be her mate. He was a large-boned man who took the queen's hand in his. He had green-tinted blond hair and beard, and was strong-featured. The aura of his magic was gigantic—power that had rested on his broad shoulders for a millennium, since the last portal was opened for the previous Eight to leave.

Jenni breathed deeply of the air, let her vision gray as she summoned her gift. The elemental energies in this chamber were close to being balanced. It must be a room the Eight often used.

But the energies weren't *exactly* balanced. Some individuals of the Eight were stronger than others. Some spent more time in the chamber. The room itself, despite the addition of all elements to it, would not have been originally balanced. Who knew what magic—the kind and strength of it—had been done in this room?

Before she'd exhaled, she was in the gray mist, the power in the room was so strong. Now she could look at the Eight and *see* them. The magical beings were like columns of the elements.

Air was a blue-white flame, flickering fast. The Air Queen was the weakest of the Eight, the next weakest in magic was the Fire Queen, a bright torch of yellows and oranges and reds. It wouldn't be long until she garnered enough power to match the older couples. Then came the other newer rulers—the Fire King and the Air King.

In meeting with the Air King, Jenni had been dealing with the strongest person of the two new couples. Huh. She began to believe that this mission was as important as he said.

Jenni turned her gaze on the older couples. Of those, the Earth King, the dwarfman, was the strongest. Instead of the short, thick body that his physical form wore, his power in the mist rose as a strong pillar of a thousand-faceted diamond, stretching beyond the floor into the earth and above the limits of the chamber's ceiling. So many bright angles!

Secondary in power to him was the Water Queen, who'd just healed Aric. She looked like a column of deep blue water showing the froth of sea spume at the edges, with shiny shells occasionally revealed—bits of wisdom, or spells? Then came her lord, the Water King, a tall crested wave frozen at the point of falling, breaking everything in his path? Finally, the power of the Earth Queen stood as an image of the palest pink marble veined in rose, polished and beautiful.

Jindesfarne! Aric snapped at her mentally.

She ignored him, opened her mouth to test the balance of the elements around her. A little too much earth and, of all things, air. The Air King and Queen who had left fifteen years ago had been so strong that sheets of their power still lingered. Yet, had they stayed, their power would have begun to erode, diminishing them.

Jenni!

With a slight shifting of her feet, Jenni balanced the

room, bringing in small sheets the size of bath towels of fire and water to equalize the energies in the room.

Beyond the room she sensed great layers of power she could draw upon to enrich the atmosphere and fuel any spells the Eight might wish to do.

She *felt* mental exclamations from the throats of the powerful beings projecting from the real world to the interdimension. Sighing and straightening her shoulders, knowing she couldn't count this brief trip to the interdimension as one of her practice sessions, she stepped from the mist and back into the room adorned with luxuries of centuries.

"—fascinating," the Air Queen said.

"She is back," the Earth King grumbled in the tones of a deep gong.

The Water King stared at Jenni, his face impassive, but she sensed his impatience and prejudice against her, mixed with a realization that she could be an asset if used well. She swallowed.

He arched a mobile green brow. "I had not realized that this chamber was out of balance in the least." He shrugged, and droplets rolled down his bare arms and splashed on the heated floor where they dried in an instant. A corner of his mouth quirked, but Jenni still felt menace surrounding him. "Interesting."

"It *is*," fluted the voice of the Air Queen. She spread her arms. "I can feel a difference in my power, as if it was refined."

"The elements are exactly balanced," the Earth King said. His dark eyes glimmered above rough-hewn dwarven features and his creviced face. "How long have you...Mistweavers...had this talent?"

Jenni lifted her chin but didn't stare him in the eyes. She'd lose herself under the ton of rock of his will. "Three generations. My grandfather, my father's father, developed it. He was an elf of air, of the Zephyrosa family."

The dwarfman grunted. "Disappeared under mysterious circumstances."

"He got lost in the gray mist of the interdimension." She wanted to add a snarky comment about them sending Rothly to face the same fate, but didn't quite dare.

"Why did you Mistweavers hide this talent from us?"

Jenni's turn to raise her brows. "I was sure that my father explained our powers to you."

The Earth King made a short, choppy gesture. "Only fifteen years ago." His voice deepened further.

"I—we—were always under the impression that half-breeds were not welcome to speak to you royals," Jenni said. "There are plenty of half-Lightfolk half-humans with various powers."

"But you can balance any area for us, enhance our power by bringing more." The Queen of Fire leaned forward, her face broader, her features more sensual than Synicess's. The Queen's brilliant amber eyes fixed on Jenni. She felt the impact. "This is a great boon to us."

Jenni continued, "We were also under the impression that claims of power of half-Lightfolk aren't believed."

They didn't answer and the discussion didn't continue.

Not one soul had believed what the Mistweavers could do until they experienced it themselves.

"I don't think we have thanked you personally for your effort in stabilizing the portal so our predecessors could leave for another world, and giving us more power to do the ritual to summon the portal…and to fight the Darkfolk. You have my thanks," whispered the Fire King in a low rasp, like flames crackling on logs.

Jenni slid her glance across his face and got a shock. His eyes were tilted like her own, like her mother's, and the color was the same, a light brown. She nearly stared too long, got caught in his glamour, but wrenched her gaze away, found she was panting a little.

"I am Cole Emberdrake. My mother is a Desertshimmer," the Fire King said. "You can trace a lineage to her, too."

Jenni reflexively dipped a curtsy. "Thank you for your kind words." She forced a smile, lowered her head. "And thank you all for the funds you transferred to me." Not that she'd wanted them—or even seen her bank balance yet.

"I am grateful, too," the Fire Queen said with a sincere smile.

Jenni curtsied again to her.

"You made our task easier," the Water Queen said.

Another dip of knees.

"But there were eight Mistweavers to do the elemental balancing for the portal," the Earth King said. "Now there is only you for this bubble ritual. Can you do it?"

Jenni didn't know what he was talking about and Aric

moved restlessly beside her. She decided to answer blindly but with confidence. "Yes," Jenni said. "I can." She stared at each of their foreheads in turn. "If I get support of the Eight. If I am not attacked. If I only have to handle the elemental magics that only I can summon." She bit off each word.

"You are still bitter about the portal contretemps." The Water Queen leaned forward. "We were fighting for our lives, too."

"And I and my crippled brother were controlling energies that eight summoned when seven were dead and dying and wounded. I, a half-breed. No one helped me then. No one."

"We have thanked you and we have paid. What can we give you now?" the Water Queen murmured. She sounded soft and sympathetic, but Jenni thought that manner only covered ruthlessness.

"You can't give me what I want. I want my family back. No one and nothing can do that for me."

Aric made a strangled noise and settled into his balance as if hunkering down for a storm.

"We respect you and your gift," the Water Queen said.

"Do you? All of you?" The old wound was breaking open again, pus escaping, poisoning her own breathing air. Jenni was tempted to step into the mist and gather strings of the elemental energies and yank them, disrupting this room…forcing the Eight to work a major ritual to restore it.

Tears boiled away in her ducts before they reached

her eyes. Yes, she was still angry and bitter and hurt, hurt, hurt.

A thick wall of earth magic backed her up a step or two. She looked down to see the broad form of the Earth King, who'd stepped from his throne to stand before her.

CHAPTER

10

THE EARTH KING GLANCED UP AT JENNI WITH ancient, unfathomable knowledge in his eyes. She blinked as she met his dark brown eyes, realizing he was deliberately not snaring her. "You are very young," he said, as if she were a child of two.

He held up a squat hand, palm facing her. "Match my earth magic with an equal amount of fire magic, child." He reached up and linked his fingers with hers and she was hurled down, down, down to the depths of the Earth, where gems glittered like secrets, and streams of gold and silver and copper flowed in thick veins. She fought heavily to breathe.

Give me an equal measure of fire, the Earth King commanded.

On a shaky breath, Jenni stepped partially into the mist, leaving her hand palm-against-palm with the king's. She shouldn't have been able to do that, be only a little into the mist, but even the greatest king could not go where she went. He was powerful enough to keep her hand in the real world.

It was easier to stare down at her feet, avoiding the diamond pillar so close to her. She slid her senses a trifle west, found Yellowstone's fire. She understood its smell, taste, texture, density, then summoned the sheet of red-orange light. As she gauged the king's power she drew more and more to her—to them, watching the fire power flare high.

The rest of the room was still balanced. Jenni wrapped the sheets around them, kept a small line to the magma so she could match the king's earth power down to the last iota. With one last tune humming from her lips, she packed the layers of fire around the king, then stopped, fine-tuned, stepped from the gray mist. Yes! Her skills were coming back!

Her hand against the king's burned with fire power, his cool, solid shape didn't move. One…last…little…bit. There! And fire and earth were equal between them.

A bead of sweat rolled from his temple near his circlet to dribble down his cheek. His grin was red and pointed and fierce. He flung back his head and laughed, raised their linked hands until they hovered an inch from Jenni's nose. "Well done! Dismiss it on three!"

Jenni flung herself back into the mist, counted down and sent the elemental magic back into the restless pool, then equalized everything again as the dwarf locked down his own power.

When she staggered a step from the grayness, Aric curled his fingers around her upper arm, steadied her.

The sensation of his touch zinged through her. She was far too attracted to him. Once again he could become her doom if she allowed it. But her head was muzzy from the effort of manipulating the elemental energies even though fire was the easiest.

She blinked and saw the Earth King back on his throne, dwarven face rocklike and inscrutable. Realizing that her gaze was being drawn to his, she jerked her glance aside, though caught the movement as he inclined his head to her. "I am persuaded that the woman can handle the energies for our ritual. I accede that she will receive a royal title and a stipend—"

"I agree that she and her brother will be formally adopted and acknowledged as our children," the Fire Queen said with serenity. "Rothly, as soon as he is rescued." She sent a stare to the rest of the royals. "For his effort upon our behalf. Jindesfarne soon."

Jenni flinched. She hadn't thought the whole thing through. She didn't mind a title, since it was important to Rothly and it would be a final vindication for her lost parents and siblings, but she hadn't thought she'd have to be adopted! She didn't want such strong ties with the Eight. She certainly didn't want whatever responsibilities they might consider as going with the title. She didn't need another mother.

Once again she knew all too well what she *didn't* want and only one thing that she did. She wanted her brother back and whole again. And she didn't know what kind of miracle that might take.

But the first step was to save Rothly. Jenni swept her gaze across the royals. "I don't know of the mission." She rushed her words so the kings and queens wouldn't blame Aric. "I didn't want to know. It's best if I concentrate on first saving my brother."

Stares turned on Aric. "We were told you agreed to the mission," the Air King, Cloudsylph, said.

"That's true. I love my brother and I am as Mistweaver as he. If you forced a promise from him that Mistweavers would fulfill this mission of yours I am as bound to it as he."

More seething silence that Jenni nipped before it burst into flame. "I don't even know why he is here in Yellowstone."

Cloudsylph tapped a finger on the arm of his throne, a frosty smile curving his lips. "So you didn't listen to Aric just as you didn't listen to me."

He'd probably told everyone of her outburst.

"So listen now," he said in a patient, lecturing tone that still fell on her ears like music, reminding her of her father. "Rarely, once every eon or so, a series of bubbles of pure magic erupts from this planet. The bubble holds within it a great magical creative force."

The king blinked and the glow balls seemed to gather clouds around them. Dark clouds heavy with portent.

"A first bubble came and broke in an area controlled by one of the last great Dark ones." King Cloudsylph's lips folded into a grim line. "Thus those terrible shadleeches were born two years ago. Those things that eat magic and do nothing but harm."

He met Jenni's eyes and she wasn't expecting his glance and froze under his glamour. She'd do *anything* for him.

She could feel the layers and subtexts of his emotions. Anger twisted inside the king that he could not banish the shadleeches with magic, that he hadn't found a way to fight and eradicate them.

Next to her, Aric thrummed with fierce emotion, too. She thought she heard the weeping of dying dryads in his memories as the trees and his kin were absorbed by the evil hive.

"We didn't know such a bubble was coming or had broken until too late." His eyes drilled into her. "Our scholars believe this series will consist of two more such bubbles, each coming exponentially faster and each exponentially greater. They are determining the locations. If we, the Eight, can be there when these bubbles pop, we can guide the creativity of such rich and powerful magic."

Her ears were his, her entire body leaned toward him, but her mind was her own and she figured that the Eight planned on using this new, rich, magical event for their own purposes, as always.

"The second bubble should happen in the next week. We believe you, as an elemental balancer, can augment our power to create something new. Nor is the magic within the bubbles balanced. To maximize that energy, we need you." He blinked slowly and Jenni was able to tear her gaze away. "You could be of great help to the Lightfolk community."

She could speak now. She lifted her chin, pretending her insides weren't quivering. "I've listened and now I know the mission. I'm more interested in my brother. What do you know of him?"

Cloudsylph's nostrils flared as if he realized she had listened but not bought in to the undertaking.

"Rothly was offered noble status, briefed as you have been." The Air King glanced at Aric. "We understand you found that he made preparations for the trip here—"

"Why Yellowstone?"

"We believe the next bubble will pop here."

"Geysers?"

Cloudsylph raised his silver brows. "Magic has rules. The first bubble appeared and burst during a lightning storm. Underwater quakes, tectonic plate action…all are being studied to forecast the last two events."

When Jenni said nothing, Cloudsylph continued, "Rothly took a plane from London to Denver, we provided him with a room here, then a limo to the outskirts of the park. We believe he went on a reconnaissance mission and got…lost in your interdimension."

"He's there," Jenni said. Her palms were damp so she hid them in the folds of her gypsy skirt and wiped them. "And he stepped into the gray mist somewhere in Yellowstone."

"We've sent our best trackers out today to pinpoint your brother's location now that you are here," the Fire King said. "We knew Rothly had thrown silver and salt at you, disowning you. Didn't know you would help him."

Jenni stared at them. Each of them in turn. Four had been rulers since most of the magical Lightfolk left more than a millennium ago. All were older than anyone she'd ever known. Had they lost all family ties? All feelings of family? But she didn't really know how noble Lightfolk families worked. How close they were.

"I love my brother," she choked out. She felt the weight of the Earth King's gaze and it reminded her that he'd called her a child. Maybe she was, to them. "Halflings stick together," she said softly.

There was an exchange of glances at that, as if she'd confirmed information the rulers could use. She stopped herself from rolling the tension in her shoulders away.

A slight cough came from the threshold of the chamber and Jenni turned to see an old friend of her father's. The sight of him rolled through her in a tightness, from her belly to her chest, to her tear ducts. She hadn't seen him for a long time. A month before that last, fatal mission.

He was all air elf, with a feathery cap of silver hair and pointed ears close to his head. There were no lines on his face, but his pale silvery-blue eyes held a wealth of sorrow when she met his gaze.

She was beginning to understand that she hadn't been the only one to grieve for her family. She'd shut everyone out. But no one from the Lightfolk had ever contacted her to comfort, had they? Not her brothers' girlfriends or her sisters' fiancés.

"It's good to see you, Jindesfarne," Etesian said. "Aric." Then the older elf turned and bowed to the Eight.

"We thank you for coming, and for your research," the Water King said.

So courteous to someone who was full-blooded Lightfolk, and not Treefolk like Aric.

"Jindesfarne has agreed to help us," the Earth King rumbled.

Etesian's smile was more a grimace than anything else. His glance briefly met hers, then slid back to the Eight. "Have you located Rothly?" His whisper was so low that had she been mortal, Jenni wouldn't have heard him.

The kings straightened in their thrones, drilled Etesian with glares. Jenni felt the streams of elemental power directed at him. He didn't flinch, his ascetic face tautened into sternness. Silence reigned.

Etesian offered his hand to her and she took it, got a shock. He was still in the early days of his grief for the loss of his friend, her father, and the rest of her family. For him, in his near immortality, the time that had passed was far less, comparatively, than for her. Long-livedness could work both ways...the sense of time passing could be far longer or shorter than for humans.

They connected and mourned together for a moment, then broke contact at the same time.

When Etesian spoke his voice was crisp, and he directed his words to the Water Queen, who stared at him with sadness. "My calculations of the second bubble in the series of three—"

"The earth fart," the Water King snorted.

The rest of the monarchs looked at him. He slouched in his chair. "What? Should I call it a belch instead?"

Appearing pained, the Water Queen twined her fingers with his, said, "It is a potential gift of magic, a force of creativity that we hope to influence for good."

A quick and charming smile graced the Water King's face. "Of course, heart of my heart...but my way is easier to say."

"As I was informing you," Etesian said, "I have a

preliminary time for the second bubble to break. Very approximate, since we are not sure of the exact moment the first bubble came into existence, nor the exact exponential percentage of time, power, location and magic we are dealing with. As I stated before, I am more sure that it will take place here in Yellowstone than I am the precise time."

All the royals leaned forward at that. Whatever other emotions they did or didn't feel, they were excited about this. There was no sound in the room but the faint pulse of water against the glass aquarium wall.

Etesian continued, "I anticipate the middle...ah...burp will occur within an estimated two days."

"What!" The Air Queen's voice was nearly unmusical. She turned her head to look straight at Jenni. "We must prepare. Immediately." She turned to the Earth Queen. "Have you crafted the dancing ritual?"

The dwarfem Queen of Earth's lips thinned, her eyes darkened. "I have a draft."

"Any idea how it will manifest?" asked the Water King. "A geyser?"

"An upsurge in the restless magma from the supervolcano," said the Fire King.

"Steam, superheated air," added the Air King.

"Any or all of those," Etesian confirmed.

The Air King tapped his fingers. "Will it be an actual bubble? Take a spherical shape?"

Etesian nodded. "From reports of a millennium ago, it will be an orb full of a mixture of elemental energies, ready to be guided for a purpose." He glanced at Jenni.

"It's unknown what measure of the four elements will be within it, but it is certain they won't be in balance."

"Thank you," the Earth King said in a dismissive tone.

Instead of leaving, Etesian remained with Jenni and Aric. "I prefer to hear you brief Jindesfarne so that I can amend any of my calculations to include her, and, perhaps, Rothly."

The Water King shifted as if uncomfortable in his throne but again none of the Eight kings and queens said anything. Suffering the consequences of their own behavior—sending Rothly to handle the bubble when he was crippled.

"The event is imminent, then," the Air King said.

Etesian bowed in affirmation.

Jenni looked straight at the Air King's beautiful forehead. "I am less interested in this event than I am in Rothly's location and condition." She continued coolly, "I will, of course, be there to draw additional sheets of elements from around the area as needed *after* I save my brother. When do you anticipate the report on his precise location?"

"The bubble must be our priority. We will free Rothly afterward," the Water King said.

Jenni wiped her palms again, lifted her chin, shot out her hip. "You Eight like to move up timelines, don't you? Change priorities for your own benefit and to hell with halflings? No."

The Water King rose and the unheard pressure of a thundering tsunami rolled through the room. "You *will*—"

"No!" Jenni shouted. "The bargain with your rep—" she glanced at Aric "—was Rothly's rescue first. Do you hold to your honor this time?"

CHAPTER
11

THE EARTH KING'S WHISPER WAS THE ROUGH slide of gravel at the start of an avalanche. "Despite what you might think took place fifteen years ago, we held to our honor then. Your family agreed to move the portal opening up due to the sighting of Darkfolk. We compressed our dancing ritual. All was as agreed."

Earth and water thunder filled the room. Jenni's body trembled. Her mind and emotions held firm.

The Earth Queen rose and angled her body to face Jenni. She was the shortest person there, more squat than her mate—the oldest royal, if not the most powerful. "The original estimate for the rising of the second bubble was next week. Thus the reason we sent Aric to you this week. We all agreed on that." She spoke to Jenni, didn't look at anyone else. "My draft of our dancing ritual is not complete. I will finish it by sunset and give it to the rest of you for input. *We* will be prepared tomorrow morning with a complete dancing ritual for the bubble event." She paused, tilted her head as if listening, then continued, eyes as piercing as a diamond drill. "We have been informed mentally that Rothly Mistweaver Emberdrake has been located. You, Jindesfarne Mistweaver and Aric Paramon, have two hours to rescue the new Fire Prince. Do so." She walked to the door and it split into halves and opened before her.

Aric's fingers clasped Jenni's and he dragged her along, slipping through the doors before they closed. "Change into something for a Yellowstone winter, fast."

Jenni ran to the dorm, heart pounding in her ears. Had she mastered enough technique to pull Rothly from the interdimension? Maybe, maybe, maybe. The well of her magic had filled in the presence of the royals. She'd followed the rituals twice in the last twenty-four hours, had more tea. She didn't think she could use Aric as an anchor, though, didn't know him well enough.

Could she rescue Rothly? Ready or not, she had to try.

The only women in the dormitory were sleeping. In five minutes she'd flung off her clothes and gulped down another vial of the family brew. She could squeeze out one more little session. Three times would be good—three times a charm.

She took a small step into the interdimension to check on Rothly, cast all her senses toward her brother. When her mind formed an image of him, she gasped. He didn't look human.

Instead he appeared like a gray lump with bulges of fluttering leeches coating him. Dire straits.

Rothly! she called.

She thought the lump twitched.

Rothly, I'm coming! Hold on. I'll be there!

She heard the faintest mind whisper. *Late as ever.*

His sneer arrowed through her and she flinched, but she wouldn't be pleasant if she were being drained of magic and life.

Better late than never, she returned. *And I'll save your ornery hide this time!*

She thought she heard the tiniest mental snort, saw a brightening of his aura, and was encouraged. Maybe sheer bloody-minded stubbornness would keep him going. He'd sparked with fire and the shadleeches reeled away. Jenni tried to pull more fire to him, send him some love and energy, but didn't know if that worked. She'd be there soon.

She stepped from the mist and shook herself, glanced around. If any of the women had awakened, they didn't show it.

She hesitated, then drank another potion vial, worrying about the last thing she'd seen in the interdimension—a strange pulsating of the mist. She didn't think that they had two days to the next bubble event. And Rothly seemed to be right on top of it.

Then she gathered as much magic as she could to seep into her pores, top her energies off after that quick session. She drew from the amount the Eight had generated, from the palace itself, even stray bits floating around the dorm.

A faint knock came and she hurried, moving quickly

in jeans and boots, and opened the door to see Aric and a dwarfem.

"I am here to lead you to where we believe Rothly Mistweaver to be," the dwarfem said. She wore a shearling coat and hat.

"Trackers followed the shadleeches and found traces of where he might have entered the interdimension," Aric said.

"Shadleeches!" The dwarfem hissed nearly as well as a djinn or merfolk. A shudder rippled through her like an earthquake.

Jenni went light-headed with relief, clutched Aric's solid arm. "Then I should be able to go directly to him and get him out." She wouldn't have to attempt to travel in the gray mist and get lost forever. "I'd hate to step from the interdimension into a geyser."

Aric set the arm she was clutching around her waist, surprising Jenni. She looked at him with wide eyes, decided to speak to him mentally. *Your lady will not be pleased if she sees us like this.*

He hesitated, then replied to her telepathically and with finality. *I will not speak of Synicess to you. Just as I did not speak of you to her.*

Jenni caught the undertone, the wisp of information that the full-blooded djinn princess had pressed him, and not only about his previous relationship with Jenni, but also about Jenni's abilities. The hair rose on the back of her neck. *Fine,* she said, trying to make the word casual. Since he relaxed a little, she thought he'd succeeded.

As they walked, the tunnel dimmed and the ground smelled of sulphur strongly enough for her to set what fire magic she could into her lungs to protect them. She was sure the heat and acid air would get worse. The magic was nearly half earth and half fire with only a trace of air and water—and more fire lay ahead.

Aric slogged on, face grim. Treemen didn't like fire. Jenni wondered that he was courting a djinn princess. Jenni'd thought she'd fascinated Aric with her own fiery nature, but that would be nothing compared to a full-blooded royal djinnfem. Weren't any elffems or merfems available for him? Or was his ambition such that he wanted the highest ranked woman?

Shaking her head, Jenni slipped her arm in his, found that he was using much of his elven air nature to purify his breath. She added a slight atmosphere around them, like a filter, burning some of the bad gasses before they reached them. He nodded thanks.

They walked through heated rock, and the cashmere Jenni was wearing was soaked with sweat as the temperature became hotter than her own magic could disperse. She withdrew her arm from Aric's and panted with each step, let him keep to the middle of the wide tunnel alone. Though she could only see the back of the dwarfem, something in the set of the earth-being's shoulders made Jenni think she was snidely amused with her charges.

Soon the tunnel angled up and away from the fire, light coming from ahead. The path cooled rapidly and a whistling wind sent gusts of icy air toward them. Jenni's skin dried quickly and she condensed the moisture in her clothes into a small patch of water energy and sent it away. As the light became stronger, Jenni was aware that the tunnel was actually open to the outside.

The dwarfem stopped at the bottom of a vertical shaft. Jenni looked up and saw some brush covering the opening. When she squinted she thought she saw a magical barrier that would act as an alarm for the dwarves. There was no way up.

"Elf!" the dwarfem shouted in common Lightfolk speak, though Jenni couldn't hear all of the layered tones—dwarf tended to be below her hearing range, elf above.

There was a cascade of chiming metal, a streak of blue, and an elf stood before them, dressed in leather the blue-gray of snow shadows. His hair was a mature silver and his face unlined, but his blue eyes had darkened over the millennia until they were indigo. This was an old elf, maybe even one who had been old enough to pass through the first portal when most magic Folk left Earth.

He wore wrist bracers of the silvery metal elven warriors preferred—osmium. The sheaths on each of his hips were of gray suede and platinum. Jenni was sure the hilts of his swords were osmium, too, since the metal gave off a faint odor. The elf himself smelled of the most delicate of tundra blooms and the rich air magic surrounding him had Jenni leaning forward before she understood what she was doing and yanked herself back.

"Mistweaver, Paramon." The elf actually inclined his head a quarter inch, a sign of respect that had Jenni's mouth falling open until Aric nudged her.

He was at the portal opening, saw us fight, Aric explained.

Jenni didn't remember the elf, but she didn't remember many of those that day. Her family, Aric, the Eight.

The elf stepped forward, curved his long-fingered hands around one of Aric's biceps and one of hers. His potent magic made her sway. Before the gasp escaped her lips they were swirled up and away and shot through the air, then they drifted down to shadows between tall pines.

"There," said a dwarf, pointing a gnarly finger. He was half the height of the elf, but fully as broad and wore dark gray leather and two swords with dull black hilts. His salt-and-pepper hair and beard were neatly trimmed.

Aric muttered a tree-groan swear word.

"Ah, you see them, Paramon. Lady? Gotta look sharp."

Jenni squinted, following the line of the dwarf's brown finger, Aric's green gaze. Across the wide and rolling drifts of unblemished snow there was the faintest of movements against the bright blue sky. A flutter, another. Gray shadows flapping like strange, airborne manta rays. Shadleeches. She sucked in a breath.

An electric-blue lightning-shock speared the sky from the elf's finger, killing several of the evil creatures. He made a disgusted noise, loosened his sword in his hilt. "Like most magical beings, they are better off killed with metal."

"Guns?" Jenni murmured faintly.

Aric cast her a look. "Times haven't changed that much. Tech doesn't work well."

The dwarf snorted. "Explosive powder don't transport well."

Not by magical travel. Nevertheless, Jenni would have liked a flamethrower. Not that she could use one, but...

The earth trembled beneath her.

Aric set a hand against a tree, swore longer. "What is going on?"

Loosening her knees to sink into her balance, Jenni probed the energies. Rich air and earth—the elf and dwarf, spots from their waiting going down into the earth and spreading a couple of yards, but below that...

A roiling, surging wave of elemental energies...and in the midst of them an oddness. A spherical oddness.

Blood drained from her. "The bubble is coming."

"Now?" The dwarf goggled.

"Now!" She lurched forward.

Aric's fingers closed around her wrist. She glanced up at him, saw the forest-green depths in his eyes that he got when upset. "Wait one instant."

A Treeman's instant wasn't the same as a human's, so she pulled at her hand. "Let me go!"

"Jenni...you're special—"

The dwarf snorted. "Not now, lad."

A tremor passed through Aric's large frame. "We'll talk later. The Fire Princess and I—"

With a bump of his body against Aric, the dwarf sent Aric stumbling and he let go of her. She shook her head for focus, the odor of sulphur rolled through her, the elemental energies flared around her. She bolted toward the shadleeches. There was a stream, a mudpot pond. Snow was up to her waist, she sizzled it away with fire and fear.

Then she was scooped up by the elf and deposited on a small patch of ocher land that trembled and cracked. The dwarf was there, sunk into the land up to the tops of his ankles, holding her. She tried vainly to wrench away. "I have to go to the interdimension."

Without a word, the elf sang his blade from his sheath, hacked at shadleeches, which turned and attacked. Aric pulled his own sword, stood his ground and fought.

The dwarf's fierce gaze speared Jenni. "On three I let go."

She nodded.

"One."

Jenni began chanting fast, weaving powerful words with unvoiced prayers.

"Two."

Rothly, I am HERE.

"Three."

She bit off the last spell rhyme and stepped into the gray mist.

Rothly was there, covered in shadleeches. Gray streaks of goo dripped down his face, hands, clothes. Gray goo that would be bright red blood in the real world.

No time. *No time.* NO TIME!

With a whisk of her arms, Jenni called all the elements to her—steam fire water mudpot minerals wind. Sheets wrapped around them and the shadleeches cried with glee, flung themselves into the elemental energies to feast, abandoned Rothly.

Jenni reached out, grabbed him, pulled him to her.

So light! He had little weight, emaciated.

She pulled his arms around her, the thin, sound one,

the bent, crippled one, and held him tight and listened
to his fast heartbeat and he was hers, her brother, her
Rothly, her *family,* and she stepped with him out of the
mist.

Just in time to see the top of a bubble a yard wide rise
above the mudpots. "Quick!" she said, grabbing the hand
of the dwarf, one of Aric's hands. "Link!" she ordered.

Rothly still leaned against her, his arms around her
waist. The elf lifted his brows, set his hand in Aric's and
the dwarf's. Power snapped through her and she arched.
Such power. Too much. Her mind whirled as she tried to
balance it. Rich, ancient air and earth, her and Rothly's
small fire, an additional bit of air and *greenness* from
Aric.

Sucking in a breath, she *pulled* fire and water from the
mudpots, watched with horrified amazement as the pool
dried before her eyes.

The bubble still rose, now halfway out of the former
pool, floating from cracked dirt. Inside was a shimmer of
colors: a great deal of blue-green water, some gold earth
energy, some silvery-blue air, streamers of red fire. She
thought her eyes wheeled in her head as she tried to *see*
the amounts.

She stretched her senses, felt the ground beneath her
all balanced, began to let water energy trickle away. The
bubble encased mostly water.

Dwarven words rumbled from her left in some ritual
pattern. The elf sang, luscious notes fell around her,
bringing tears to her eyes.

But as the bubble rose farther and farther from the
earth, large enough to encompass a compact car, her

breath came shorter. Only the simplest prayer broke through her fearful anticipation. "Water, air, earth, fire, bring to me my heart's desire." A child's charm, but she focused all her will, all her talent, on the bubble, minutely adjusting particles of magic to cling to it, to match all the energies within.

"Water, air, earth, fire, bring to me—"

Pop!

Energies poured out, balanced with others, spread.

"For *GOOD!*" The elf's voice was a smack of lightning.

"For the Lightfolk!" The dwarf's was a rock avalanche.

"For the dryads!" Aric boomed like a redwood falling.

"My heart's..." Jenni whispered, awestruck at the colors, textures.

"PLEASE HELP ME!" cried Rothly, flinging his crippled arm to the sky.

Energies fell upon them and all Jenni's senses were swamped in a psychedelic cloud. The only thing she was aware of was Aric's sustaining hand and the dwarf's twisted one. The strange atmosphere engulfed her for an eternity, sinking into her skin...cold, hot, purple, pink, salty, peach blossoms. Clogging her lungs.

Vision returned first. Blue, blue sky, white vapor, geysers and clouds.

"What is *that?*" screamed a woman—a human.

Jenni's gaze seemed fixed so she turned her head, saw a tour group staring openmouthed at them. Her own jaw slackened.

Then the atmosphere wavered as if heat waves encased them, and the dwarf pulled on their circle and they sank into the dry mudpot spring, then down and sideways and back into a large cave.

Their physical link broke and Jenni gasped, crumpling to the cavern floor. The damp rock smell filled her nostrils. Her cheek was squashed against the ground, she became aware of moaning...little sharp ones from herself, a mumbled groan from Aric and harsh sobbing breaths from Rothly.

Rothly!

CHAPTER 12

HER BROTHER WAS ALIVE AND HERE IN THE real world. Jenni craned to see him and her limbs flopped around. Feeling revived as they struck the floor, she yowled, thrashed again and crawled over to an unconscious Rothly. He was very thin, his skin pale with red marks. She put her hand on his forehead and it was damp with sweat under his lank, dark hair. Lines grooved his face.

Closing her eyes she *felt* him. Still half human, half Lightfolk, but there was a swirling mixture of energies inside him that weren't just quarter-elf, quarter-djinn.

The bubble magic continued to work on him.

She shuddered and fell back, looked at his arm. It didn't seem as crippled, but she couldn't really tell.

"He needs to go to the Earth Palace," the elf said.

Jenni glanced up at the elf and stilled. His eyes were no longer indigo. They were the blue of Yellowstone sky, a blue he would have lost centuries ago. What did it mean? Hesitantly she stretched out her senses...and they *zinged* to him, scanned him in an instant and informed her that his magic was as strong as ever.

"What's wrong?" the elf said.

The dwarf stumped over, set his hands on his hips and looked up. "Your eyes are lighter."

The elf became a perfect statue. He scrutinized the dwarf. "And your fingers are straight."

After a hard swallow, as he stared at his hands, the dwarf said, "Huh." He shrugged, walked over to Rothly, picked him up and handed him to the elf. "Let's go."

Aric crossed to her and lifted her to her feet. She tried to dust off the grime of the cavern but ended up smearing it on her clothes.

A thunderous sound echoed and Jenni looked around, then realized many, rapid, *angry* footsteps headed straight toward them.

"The Eight and their horde," the dwarf grunted again. "Let's get out of here before they find us."

Lips curving in an elusive smile, the elf nodded. The dwarf grabbed Jenni's elbow and Aric's hand and once more there was darkness and humidity and dust and the feeling of rock closing around her lungs.

Then they were in a richly appointed room.

"This is Rothly's," Aric said.

By the time Jenni felt able to breathe again, the elf and dwarf were gone. She wobbled and Aric put his arm around her, steadied her as she walked to the door, pulled the heavy thing open and stuck her head out into the corridor. "I need a healer here!"

One of the women from the dorm squeaked and bumped against the wall, her tray of fine china rattling. "What are you doing here? How did you get here?"

Jenni just smiled. "Magic."

The other scowled. "Plenty of that going around but elemental balancer or not, you're still a halfling who can't move through the earth like Lightfolk." She went on with her task.

Rushed steps announced four healers, one from each element.

"Thank you for coming so quickly," Aric said from behind Jenni, opening the door wide. "Jindesfarne, these are the healers assigned by the Eight. They are the very best."

They'd already passed her and gone to a grubby Rothly, murmuring among themselves. Jenni slumped in exhaustion against the door. The bubble event had been wondrous, but draining—all that cycling of great and ancient dwarf-and-elf energy. She slid her gaze to Aric. He looked revved, healthily flushed.

His eyes sparkled as he caught her gaze. He pried her fingers from the door, sent her enough fizzing energy to have her tiptoed with tingles, then kissed the hollow of each palm.

A bubble just for five of us! A blessing. I prayed for help for the dryads against the shadleeches. I know it worked!

Jenni blinked heavy, gritty lids and couldn't figure why he thought that. Didn't have the optimism that infused him.

"Excuse us, Aric, Jindesfarne, but it is best if we tend

to Rothly without any distraction," the dwarfem earth healer said.

"The poor thing has been through a great ordeal," the merfem said, stroking Rothly's pale forehead, which was beaded with sweat, while the elffem air healer held his hand and whistled a low spell.

"Of course," Aric replied. Picking Jenni up, he inclined his head to the healers.

The djinnfem fire healer rose from the large orange-yellow chair. Her skirts swished like hissing flames as she crossed to them and opened the door for them. With brows lowered, she scanned Jenni in Aric's arms, pushing her lips in and out.

"Thank you," Jenni said, trying to pretend Aric was a prop instead of a live, virile man. "I'll be back to sit with my brother after I've cleaned up."

"And eaten," Aric said.

"Rothly needs to be clean—" Jenni began.

"He needs healing first," the dwarfem said. "And I'm sure the Eight wish to speak to you."

The humming, nearly threatening buzzing of magical atmosphere outside the room enveloped Jenni. Consequences of her actions zipped through her mind. The Eight had anticipated using that bubble magic, bending the creativity to their will.

Instead the wishes of five directed it: for good, for the Lightfolk, for the dryads, for Rothly. For Jenni's heart's desire? She didn't even know what that was. But she'd taken something the Eight had figured would be theirs.

Big trouble.

The djinnfem said, "You brought him out of that strange place *they* said you can go to?"

Sounded as if the woman meant *hell,* but Jenni kept her voice even. "Yes."

The fire woman's sniff was more like a hiss. She cast a glance at Rothly, her full lower lip curling. "He's in terrible shape. Especially for a quarter-fire being."

"His elven air nature was always foremost," Jenni said.

"Maybe once," the djinnfem said with scouring scorn.

Had Jenni seen Rothly twitch? He didn't need any more negativity. "Humans have determined that unconscious people are aware of their surroundings and conversations. Please be more upbeat."

A gurgling, steaming sound came from the djinnfem.

The earth and air and water healers had stood and were pattering their feet in place, ready to dance a spell.

Aric said, "We're going now. We'll return."

But the fire healer got the last word just before the door closed. "Pray you brought back all of him."

Jenni had never considered that. Usually it would be impossible to leave any part of Rothly in the interdimension, but if the shadleeches had torn his spirit... She stiffened in Aric's arms, but forced her lips to curve and felt the wetness of blood as they cracked from the dryness of being too much in earth. "Until later, ladies."

Before she'd finished, Aric was out the door and striding down to the dormitory.

"Don't mind the fire healer, she's a friend of Synicess." He hesitated, his arms around Jenni tightened. "Synicess and I are no longer...together. She is angry."

Another shock to leave Jenni's head reeling. The Eight were after her hide, she suffered a gnawing ember of doubt that she might have left some of Rothly in the interdimension and Aric was now…free? Not free, he was the Eight's man, but…unattached. She found herself gasping for air as her mind sparked with competing thoughts and fears.

One pressed against her lips and shot in words from her mouth. "We're in trouble with the Eight."

"Perhaps," Aric said, but she still felt his optimism. Frowning, she thought back over the last couple of days. He seemed more lighthearted now than any time since they'd met. *Why are you so cheerful?* she asked mentally. Had it just been his relationship with Synicess depressing him? He was a guy, Jenni didn't think so.

His green gaze focused on her face and tiny jolts breezed through her like a swirl of leaves.

He replied, *Because I've had to rely on the Eight's goodwill and my services to help the Treefolk, protect the dryads from the shadleeches. Now the bubble energy will bring something positive for them…all of them across the world.*

You really believe that?

I felt the power of the magic—the elemental energies you balanced. It will make a difference to me and mine.

Jenni just shook her head.

A few minutes later he set her on her feet in front of the dormitory door. *I will see you in a half hour. We'll eat.* He bowed and hurried away. Probably to check on the bubble magic somehow, talk with Etesian. She missed the solid comfort of his strong body. Bracing herself, she opened the door.

Twenty chattering voices stilled.

Jenni walked slowly through the room, but all was quiet except for her odd mud-encrusted footsteps and the small *phtts* as caked dirt and grime crumbled from her to hit the floor. Everyone watched her, but she was too physically tired and mentally upset to care. She stopped by her bed, stripped and went into the common shower in silence.

As the hot water pounded over her, she let the steam of the shower help her transition into the gray mist. She'd balanced this cavern earlier, there was plenty of ambient magic, all of the Eight remained on-site, and she'd been stepping into the interdimension often over the last day. Enough to give her a bit of energy to do what must be done.

She sent her senses in the direction where she'd rescued Rothly. Brightly colored energies hung in the mist in the distance, some were even spherical. The signature smears of cast-off energy from the old elf and dwarf showed.

Tentatively she quested for shadleeches, felt nothing. Not one was anywhere in the place between worlds. Could they only enter if there was something to eat? Some other physical presence? Or were they not interested in the place unless there *was* something to drain of magic?

No smidgen of Rothly remained in the mist, not even a bit of his blood. The fire healer had induced false fears. But how could Jenni have known—any of them have known—what might happen with the new shadleeches on the scene? Had Rothly studied anything about them before their attack on him? Had *he* known they could follow him into the other dimension?

Too much thinking. She stepped from the mist and flailed, not coming out at the same spot as she went in.

Screams erupted and she lit hard on her rear on the damn tiled floor. Other women were in the shower.

"You weren't *here!*" one said.

"How did you *do* that?" said a second.

"She has a fricking invisibility spell!" one with the pointed ears of an elf said.

The women's shrill voices bounced off the rock walls. Jenni struggled up, slipping and sliding and bracing an arm against a smooth wall until she stood. She shook her hair back and wiped her face so water didn't drip into her eyes.

Standing tall and refraining from rubbing her aching butt, she said, "I am an elemental balancer and do much of my work in a different dimension."

"Like the dryads' greenhome?" asked a woman with a greenish tinge to her skin.

"Not that dimension, but something like. I'm sorry I chose a common area to do this, and I'm sorry I scared you."

The wary expressions were fading. Jenni eyed them. The Eight had shown her what they considered her, a servant like these women. Rothly's room was one for a Prince of the Lightfolk.

She raised her palms, gathering gazes, as others had come to stand in the wide doorway. "Since I work with elemental energies, I can tell you that you are *all* strong in magic."

"We are halflings," said a woman.

"You're strong enough to make a good living with magic outside of this cavern."

"Like you do?" someone sneered.

"I came here to save my brother, Rothly," Jenni said flatly.

"Rothly," more than one woman said, and some glanced at each other. Obviously Rothly had made an impression, but Jenni couldn't tell what kind.

She went on. "And I *do* use magic in my own work with computers. I don't know how long you have been here, but human technology and magic are merging enough that they can be used as one energy source."

There were frowns and confused faces. Jenni gestured at the lights in the ceiling. "These lights are powered by magic spells that drain a little power from all in the cavern and from the cavern's energies themselves. In the human world lights are powered mostly by electricity. The Lightfolk are beginning to integrate magic and electricity."

"Eight Corp has its own generator in the bottom of that building in Denver," a woman said. "I helped build it."

There was a lopsided smile and a gleam in another's eyes. "I wonder when the humans will deduce that places are going off the electrical grid."

Another frowned. "And what they will do about it. Assassins—"

Jenni thought she had too vivid an imagination. "The Lightfolk are stronger than humans."

"But we are fewer. The transition to meld—magic and

technology—will have to be handled carefully or there could be a great economic crisis," said another woman. She stepped to the threshold and reached for a towel from the stack there. "I'm good at financial management, I bet I could…" She hurried into the dorm.

Once again, Jenni glanced at each of those around her, meeting their eyes. "You are very strong. Think about your strengths, what you really want to do."

The woman who'd spoken of assassins, short and squat with evident dwarven blood, said, "I like being here."

"Then that's your choice," Jenni said. "And your vocation. Good."

"Yah, and the Eight are looking for you."

Jenni walked to the towels, dried herself vigorously. The steamy shower had helped her regain her energy. Still, all in all, she was more human than djinn—just like everyone else here. She entered the room to find women had congregated around two beds at the far end of the room. Ah, *that* was the status area.

Smiling, she went to her bed, suppressing a hitch in her stride from her sore backside. She wasn't too surprised to see that her clothes and the mud drippings had vanished. Brownies.

Nor was the smear of her passage across the room evident, though she thought the women had taken care of that themselves. "Thank you for cleaning up after me."

She got a few passing glances and nods but the dorm was noisy with brainstorming and career planning and Jenni liked that. Life options should be considered every now and then…not that she'd done so lately. She hadn't even known that magic was infusing downtown Denver.

More halflings should be claiming their place in the world, proud of being Lightfolk and human. Again, as she had *not* been, but she was learning.

Her feeling of satisfaction had faded by the time she'd donned a formal gown and left the dorm. She opened the door to see Aric, also dressed formally in a silk tunic embroidered in gleaming green thread and black raw silk trousers, leaning against the wall.

Though she sensed his body still hummed with energy and his underlying optimism remained, his face was impassive.

She adjusted her shawl over her shoulders. "We're in trouble, huh?"

Aric stepped close, fiddled with her shawl himself. "Probably. The Eight don't care to be thwarted and they wanted to experiment with that bubble. Time to pay for our actions."

Jenni blew out a breath. "I didn't call the bubble."

Framing her face in his big hands, Aric stared into her eyes and she felt as if she were stepping into a deep and ancient forest...with pockets of secrets she'd never been aware of before.

He spoke to her, mind-to-mind, his words all the clearer because of their connection skin-to-skin. *But I think the magical elements, the bubble, came to you anyway. For once, you sped things up. I FELT your desperation to help Rothly, and the bubble did that. Somehow. I had my own desperation. To make things better for the dryads and greenhome.*

His fingers stroked her face and the remembered touch,

echoing all the tender loving in the past, whispered through her, bringing tiny yearnings for the future.

Jenni, I have been so lost without you, without your family. Praised by the Eight, all I knew was to strive to please them. I had no balance. Everyone else around me was also determined to serve the Eight—advance their careers, forward their own goals.

Then, the shadleeches began to hurt greenhome and the dryads and I thought I was in a position to help with the Eight. I DID help...but not enough. Until today. Today I was desperate for the greenhome and I know the bubble will help. Because of you. In just a day, you have realigned my thinking.

He was moving closer and closer until his mouth was touching hers. He kissed her. The press of his lips, inhaling the scent of him—his breath, his body—whirled her mind away.

Only the feel of him existed, the solidity of him, the shape of his aura as it blocked everything else, seeped into her. Magic. Acceptance of her uniqueness, of *her* as a woman, individual from all else. His woman.

His hand slid from her face to her hip, squeezed, and she leaned into him as his arm came around her back, pulled her into him.

A harsh, rocky cough hit her ears...with the punch of magic behind it. Jenni shuddered.

"The Eight are waiting for you," a dwarfem said. She wore the colors of the Earth Palace and a golden chain around her waist with three dangling keys, but Jenni didn't know her status.

"We're on our way," he said to the dwarfem. *We'll face them together.* He tugged on her hand and Jenni knew he spoke the truth. The bubble magic had worked on him, too. She wondered how it might be affecting her, but couldn't separate it from all the other events of the past few days.

Several minutes later they were standing before the thrones of the Eight again. Etesian, her father's friend, was there, but he wasn't talking much and didn't seem to be in trouble. But then he'd only given his best estimate as to when the bubble would arrive and burst. And he was a full elf.

The Water King made a disgusted noise that Jenni thought was aimed at her, so she stiffened her spine. This had not been the right moment to be distracted.

The merman leaned forward, smiling enough that Jenni could see his sharp green-yellow teeth. "Perhaps it was the arrival of the halfling and the Treeman that accelerated the rise of the bubble."

With glinting eyes, the Earth Queen said, "Maybe so."

No one else spoke. They all frowned. Jenni went very still. This was not going well.

The door swung open and there was an outcry from some of the Eight that abruptly stopped. The elf Jenni had met in Yellowstone glided in. He walked to her, inclined his head at her and Aric a quarter-inch, then faced the eight thrones. "The Mistweaverfem and the Paramon comported themselves in an excellent fashion." He turned on his heel and left.

Jenni heard the veriest whisper in her mind from her father's friend, Etesian. *A guardian who watches the royals…*

"I think he said enough," the Water Queen said.

Jenni stood in silence, slid her eyes to Aric, who had relaxed into his balance. So the old elf was one who watched the kings and queens? How much power did he really have? Enough to shut them down in mid-rant.

"Welcome to our family, Princess Jindesfarne Mistweaver Emberdrake." The Fire Queen swept to Jenni, took her hands, even as Jenni was instinctively and blank-mindedly sinking into a deep curtsy. Warm lips brushed one of her cheeks, then the other. "Welcome." The Fire Queen cast a glance over her shoulder to her mate. He glanced at the rest of the Eight and stalked to her. To Jenni's surprise he hugged her, smelling a little like lava. "Welcome."

When he stepped back, he took his lady's hand.

The Water Queen was there, too. "I think you would like to see your brother again?"

"Yes." Jenni's voice was strangled from too much fluctuating emotion. "I'd like to sit with him."

"It will be interesting to see how the creative elemental energies that were released from the bubble affected him. You may go." The Water Queen gestured to the door.

"Yes." That was a safe enough word.

Aric opened the door and held it for Jenni, then followed her out.

Princess Jenni.

Just what she always wanted? So very much no.

But now she needed to concentrate on Rothly. He'd probably wake soon, and what would he say? What would she?

CHAPTER

13

AFTER SHE AND ARIC WERE OUT OF THE door guards' view, Aric let out a long sigh that would have fluttered leaves throughout a grove. He kept her hand in his, steady and solid, all the way to Rothly's door.

"Do you want me to come in, or do you want privacy with Rothly?"

Jenni winced, shrugged. "Seeing us together…"

"Are we together, Jenni?"

She swallowed. "I don't know."

A corner of his mouth kicked up, his eyes lightened from deep to misty green. He shook his head, bent down and brushed his mouth against hers. "We have come a long way already…in a few short hours. I can wait." Squeezing her hand, he straightened.

"Aric, the Eight want to 'debrief' you." The same dwarfem with the keys was there again. Her mouth went sour at the "new" word, and Jenni felt a density from her that told her the woman was old...older than the combined ages of Aric and Jenni.

Aric's eyes flashed green with irritation; he inhaled deeply. "I am the Eight's man." He kissed Jenni on the forehead. *For now. We shall see how much they support the Treefolk.*

He turned and strode back down the corridor and Jenni watched him. That was his priority now, the Treefolk. She couldn't fault him for it, but how far would he go to save them?

She glanced at the door to her brother's room. She'd gone far, far to save her brother. Left her home and job. Accepted the pain of her childhood home and being with Aric again. Begun to put aside the bitter grief and guilt at herself and Aric. Far.

But as she put her hand on the door latch, she was pretty sure that even with the trauma he'd suffered, and her rescue, Rothly hadn't forgiven her. She opened the door and went in.

The room was warm, and a small browniefem sat unhappily in the corner. Probably ordered to watch Rothly. Jenni crossed to his bed and her breath stopped and throat closed and eyes stung. He was so thin! She stroked his hair, then his face. He had no beard, a lucky chance from his djinn-elf Lightfolk heritage.

"He stinks," the brownie woman said, scowling with disapproval at Rothly's tattered dress shirt and cords.

Jenni sent her a cool glance. "You wouldn't smell so good, either, if a shadleech had feasted on you for two weeks."

The brownie's ears rolled down tight against her head, her hands came to her mouth. "Is that what happened to him?" Her eyes were so scared that black leaked into the usually brown pupils.

"That's right."

"I didn't know." The browniefem's mouth flattened and she twisted her hands in her apron. "We had heard that the crippled Mistweaver had returned, but not what had happened to him." She ducked her head, but studied Jenni from a sideways glance. "You brought him back here?"

"Yes, I'm his sister."

"Jindesfarne Mistweaver."

"Yes."

"The halfling who gave houseroom to Hartha and Pred."

"Yes."

The browniefem sniffed. "They have boasted of your house, of how it is a magically balanced place. Like *this* place is now. You did that this morning?"

"I did."

"Pred says he's made a beautiful gathering hall under a cul-de-sac for all the inhabitants of the wheel of houses."

Jenni winced.

"Ah!" The little woman pounced. "I knew he was wrong to do so. Humans don't like Folk messing with their cities without a lot of rules."

Feeling like she should defend Pred, Jenni shrugged. "Most people in the cul-de-sac have magical blood, and even the humans are open-minded." She considered the browniefem's words. "I never thought of the cul-de-sac as a sacred wheel…a wheel of houses."

The brownie nodded. "You thought of it as a sphere."

Jenni wasn't sure of that, either, but it seemed to resonate.

Rothly shuddered and moaned. Jenni touched her lips to his forehead and he subsided. Studying the small woman, she said casually, "Hartha and Pred are honored by me. I am fond of them. But my brother is all alone and I visited his home and he needs—"

"No." Shaking her head, the browniefem continued. "He is a very sour man. No brownie would like to live with him. He has a bad reputation." Once again she sniffed, then whisked to the door. "I will let the brownie-men know that he needs bathing."

"And feeding, he needs feeding," Jenni said.

Now the woman looked sympathetic. "He does." She shuddered. "Imagine surviving shadleeches draining you—and you saving him. You must be very courageous."

"He's my only family."

"I'll bring his food after the healers inform me of what his diet should be." The browniefem walked through the rock wall.

Jenni stared at Rothly's filthy clothes, frowning. The interdimension wasn't dirty…though you could certainly sweat in it, of course, if you were working hard. She picked up his hand and turned it over, examining it. You could bleed in it, too.

The shadleeches had feasted well on Rothly's blood

and magic. She glanced at his other hand, the crippled hand and arm. His fingers weren't the red and shiny skin with dark patches that she remembered. The bone didn't look warped by Darkfolk magic.

She stared and her heart started thumping hard in her throat. He didn't look crippled. She leaned across him, picked up his arm, ran her hand up and down the ulna and radius. They felt straight.

Rothly snorted, woke, looked up at her. "Enjoying the view of what you did to me, sis," he taunted.

Jenni flinched. His acidic words seared and burned all the way to the bone. She dropped his arm, forced herself to meet his eyes. Hot, angry blue eyes that matched his words.

He looked ugly, his warped emotions twisting his face. Yet a trace of the haunting of his eyes, the bitterness, Jenni had seen in her own. Was she that ugly, too?

She tried to speak, couldn't until she'd cleared her throat. "Yes, I'm looking at what I did to you." She grabbed his arm again, ran her fingers up and down his lower bones. "They're *straight*."

Shock came to his eyes, he struggled up, stared at his arm, ripped vainly at his filth-encrusted sleeve. Jenni pulled the cuff open, popping the button.

"Your arm is healed," she repeated.

Rothly shook his head as if disbelieving, then she saw memories filter into his head, his eyes. His nostrils flared, he tilted his head arrogantly, enough to look down his nose at her. "You didn't do this. I did it *myself*. I asked for help and it was granted to me. *I* mended my life that you wrecked."

Jenni stood. Hearing guilt thrown at her like mud and vitriol, sticking and boring into her, guilt she'd used as her own whip, sickened her. These came from outside her own mind and they were as ugly as Rothly. Did she still deserve so much hatred? From him as well as her own self? She didn't know. She *did* know that she didn't need to sit here and take it.

Standing, she said, "You're welcome for the save, bro." Staring at the pitiful man, she wondered if his magic had healed, too. She curled her tongue to taste his magic.

"Don't you do that to me! I threw silver and salt at you and you are dead to me. You are nothing to me, and I don't want you here, anywhere near me. I don't *permit* you to test my magic."

Permit or not, she'd done it. She trembled, but answered him. "I don't know what kind of gift you have now, but it isn't elemental balancing." She curled her lip. "Your magic seems strong enough, not crippled—except by your own attitude. I wonder how much more that will taint it. Goodbye, Rothly."

Her whole body ached from holding it so stiffly.

The door whooshed open as the browniefem entered, followed by six other brownies carrying a huge wooden tub and a naiader—a minor Waterfolk man—who sauntered after them. He'd be providing the water to fill the basin.

The browniefem stared at Jenni. "I told you he is such a one that no brownie wishes to live with." She waved to the center of the room, the carpet rolled up and settled itself against the wall under a lush tapestry and the browniemen put the tub down.

As Jenni left she caught a glance at Rothly, who'd flushed an unbecoming red, making him even uglier.

She walked unsteadily down the corridor, her legs weak with reaction, but her mind busy with fleeting thoughts of how negative emotions—guilt and grief— could work on the attractiveness of a being. Guilt and grief were useful now and then, but even with her long life, fifteen years was probably too long to spend flagellating herself. Time to let them go. If she could. But she knew all too well that deciding to do something with her mind didn't always mean it was easy for the heart to follow through.

Jenni stopped at a cross-corridor, blankly staring at the rock walls. She was lost, wasn't sure where the dormitory was.

Once again the dwarfem with the keys whisked up, frowning, as usual. Her breath snorted from her nose in a huff of dust. "Come with me to your new quarters."

Unwilling to argue, Jenni accompanied the woman in silence. She was led to a small, windowless room. Her bag and backpack huddled in a corner. Jenni didn't know whether her poor accommodations were because she had encouraged the dorm women to leave the Earth Palace and strike out on their own, or because the Eight were angry about missing the second bubble event.

Sure didn't look like a princess's room to her. She sat on the lumpy mattress atop a cot and stared at a drip running down the opposite wall. Suddenly everything was Too Much. "Why should I stay?" she asked the air, pretty sure that her words would be heard. "I've rescued my brother. He's not likely to change his feelings about me. I've accomplished what I wanted. No one has bothered to tell me any more about the mission and the third bubble event, so I am thinking my help isn't needed. Especially since the Eight didn't appreciate what I did with the second bubble. They probably want to handle the third bubble completely by themselves."

She stood. "This room sure isn't any indication that my input is valued. Obviously, I am still the dissed halfling. Seems like others' promises aren't being kept, either. No reason to follow up on my statement to see this through—a statement that was made when I was desperate." She shrugged elaborately into her backpack, fastened it around her waist, thought about how she could leave. One last irritated murmur. "May as well take off. Not needed here. The Eight have enough power to handle that last bubble."

The Earth Palace must have a sacred space. If she went there and concentrated hard, she could probably draw enough fire through her to be able to lightning away. If she had the energy, but she'd have to leave her belongings. They should be safe in a sacred space.

Aric...well, she thought he'd help her get home, or bring her stuff to her.

She did need rest first, and sure wasn't going to get it here, but figured she could crash in the dorm.

When she opened the door, it was to see the Fire Queen. The royal lady looked into the miserable room. "There has-s been a mis-stake." She hissed it with such power that three small fire sprites popped into existence to circle her head. A brownie in the hallway disappeared into a rock wall, and a round dwarfem with *five* keys strode into view, her black hair in meticulous sausage rolls down her skull.

The Fire Queen turned to the housekeeper. "What is the meaning of this lodging for my kinswoman?"

Curtsying, the dwarfem didn't glance at the room or Jenni. "I will investigate the slight."

From her peeved tones, Jenni understood that the chatelaine really would.

"We need a suite." The Fire Queen gestured with a graceful hand.

"A suite!"

"A suite with a sitting room, so that I might sit and speak with my kinswoman, Princess Mistweaver Emberdrake."

"Of course." The dwarfem held out her hands to each of them, seemed to brace herself. "With your permission I will transport you there."

Through rock. Making a moue, the royal put her hand in the dwarfem's. Jenni did the same. The next moment they were in a magnificently appointed living room done in light blue and silver. A fire roared in a lapis lazuli fireplace. The opposite wall had a huge window that appeared to be very fine rock crystal instead of glass. Jenni caught her breath at the frozen waves of white mountain peaks tinted gold and pink by the sunset. She yearned to study the view. There was a door to a rocky outcropping that might be a disguised balcony.

"Please sit, Jenni. May I call you Jenni?"

Jenni turned and curtsied, but didn't meet the queen's gaze. The dwarfem had already gone. "Yes."

Queen Emberdrake sank into a wing-backed chair

with wooden arms, crossed her legs gracefully. Jenni sat, too, sinking into a feather cushion on a love seat with the thought that she'd have to thrash around to get out.

"The years since the ambush at the dimensional portal have been hard on you," the Fire Queen said sympathetically. "You lost your family. Your brother...was not wise enough to share his and your grief, support and succor each other."

"No," Jenni whispered. She risked meeting the melty chocolate-colored eyes of the queen. No glamour snagged her. It seemed at least one of the Eight would be straight with her...or at least not bespell her.

Raising her hands palm out, the queen said, "I do not manipulate my kin."

Jenni didn't believe that for a second.

After a small hiss, the queen smiled in a way that made Jenni miss her mother. "Very well, not quite the truth, but I do not entrance and bespell my kin. You should never fear that." Her voice rang with promise.

There was a little silence as they measured each other. The queen spoke first. "We all—the Eight—heard what you said. I understand your discouragement. I have heard Rothly is not behaving well." Another few heartbeats of quiet. "Indeed, Rothly has been difficult since we contacted him."

Jenni felt a smidgen of pride in her brother, yet wanted to defend him at the same time, then the implication of the queen's words actually sank in. Blood drained from Jenni's head. "You were part of the plot to send him, crippled, to deal with the bubble event."

"But, no! That is not what I was speaking of. I meant

when we first rewarded him with all we could after the battle. He was very much less than gracious."

Jenni could understand that and words began welling into her mind and left her mouth low and rusty. "You moved up the dimensional opening." She hadn't been there, and that had been the basis of her guilt, why she couldn't forgive herself.

The queen's fingers clenched into the grooves in the ends of the chair's arms. Jenni thought she saw steam rising from the djinnfem's fingertips. Her voice, too, held more fire and the emotional hissing. "You understand that neither I nor my mate were party to that decision. We were not of the Eight. We were only the prospective Fire King and Queen, nor was the present Queen of Air, the elffem, consulted."

Keeping her eyes on the queen's face, seeing blue flame dance in the woman's pupils, Jenni nodded.

"But had I been asked I would have agreed with the decision." She inhaled and her expression smoothed as she controlled any emotion. Jenni fought memories and hung on to her temper by a fingernail.

"We'd just heard the Darkfolk were preparing an ambush. All of the Eight had arrived, the Four who were leaving were anxious to be gone. I must admit that I was impatient to become the next Fire Queen. We were worried about the stability of the portal, how much power it would take to open it, how long we could keep it open to ensure the safe passage of the Four to a new dimension." The queen's wide mouth twitched up. "Cloudsylph, the current King of Air, who was then the head of the warriors, wanted all done as quickly as possible. He cut the ritual—the pomp—to skeletal necessity. Your family assured us that they could gather such magic as to accommodate us, provide us with rich elemental energies to carry us through the situation. Not all of our retinues—those strong in magic who would support us—had arrived, including you."

Jenni shuddered, bit her lower lip to keep her mouth clamped shut as she recalled running flat out toward the portal and her dying family after she'd heard her mother's scream. The day in France had been lovely, the sun had shone from a soft blue sky, wind had ruffled the vibrant green grass setting the colorful wildflowers nodding.

Then there'd been the stench of Darkfolk and blood and death. Sweat beaded at the back of her neck under her hair just thinking about it.

"We had no sooner gotten the portal up than the Dark-folk attacked. They broke our dancing circle! Blurred the lines of the wheel. We fought. My mate, I, the warriors who were there." A wintry smile. "Not all the warriors were there, either. There had just been a shift change, and some lingered. Lucky. Especially since some showed up early, an hour before the ceremony." Her blue-white gaze shifted to Jenni. "Like your family."

Jenni flinched.

"What saved us all was that the Darkfolk were not organized, as usual. Some of the minor fiends attacked before the five remaining great Dark ones ordered the charge. Cloudsylph had a few minutes to form our strat-egy and defense. The portal held as the Four leaving rushed through, draining much of our energy and power. I, my mate and the elves claimed our magic, but it was not as much as it should have been. We were distracted, fighting, focused on surviving, not becoming royal." The queen's voice had become an edgy drone. Neither did she have good memories of her ascension to the throne of fire. "Then the portal began to waver...." Another slide of the queen's flame-blue stare to Jenni. "Your family was in trouble."

An understatement, they'd been dying. A wave the color and scent of blood rolled through Jenni, tinting her vision from the inside. All she saw was red liquid dripping.

The sound of the door opening had her blinking and blinking again. Aric walked in, aimed a short bow toward the queen and came to sit beside Jenni. She wanted to lean into him. She didn't.

The queen watched her with eyes cooled to her regular brown. "The portal was wavering, then it vanished. The earth bucked under our feet. Fighting became vicious as the Darkfolk poured onto the field. Magics were flung. More warriors, guests, Lightfolk joined the battle."

"Then...?" The queen lapsed into a silence that stretched and stretched and Jenni surreptitiously moved her fingers in a spell to stop memories from coming.

"Then?" Aric prompted.

CHAPTER
14

A TREMOR WENT THROUGH THE QUEEN. "Then there was more elemental energy, magical power around me than I'd ever felt. I had a surfeit of fire energy to work with, funneled some of the magic that could overcome me to other djinn on the field." The queen looked down at her hands, flexed them, and her smile grew wide and sharp. "I had the pleas-sure of des-stroy-ing one of the remaining five Dark ones-ss mys-self. I soaked up all the magic I could, everyone did, especially the new Four, but I feared for my life. There was too much energy." She inclined her head to Jenni. "You know."

"Yes," Jenni whispered from a throat that felt seared. "You came, ran into the mist."

I will not remember, Jenni chanted mentally.

The queen continued, "We fought with wild magic all around us, both Darkfolk and Lightfolk, spells and weapons conjured that I'd never seen before, never imagined. Even the slightest finger-flick reaped death." The djinnfem leaned against a wing of the chair, her voice lowered to a bare whisper. "I've never seen anything like it. Those of us who survived did so because of luck, of fate…except we Eight. We survived because we were the best."

"And the elf and dwarf guardians helped," Aric said. "As did I and others, putting our bodies and magics and lives between you and the Darkfolk."

The queen sat straight again, frowned at Aric, let out a hissing sigh. "That is true." She turned to Jenni, dismissing Aric. "Now you know how it was, from my point of view. Do you wish to interview the other kings and queens? I can arrange it." An undertone in her voice screamed warning to Jenni and she wanted and feared to say yes. "No," she forced from her dry and hurting throat.

Aric relaxed next to her.

"Everyone at the portal opening, the ambush and battle dictated or wrote our accounts…except you."

Heat of humiliation rushed to Jenni's face, but she kept her gaze level with the queen's. A dwarf scholar had come to Jenni soon after the event and she'd sent him away. "I lost my whole family. My sole remaining brother disowned me." And none of the kings and queens had offered support.

The queen tapped a finger on the arm of her chair. "We have Rothly's record of what happened when he was in the interdimension. We believe his account is… unreliable. Only you would be able to correct that."

Curiosity pulsed from the queen—and the very walls. Others were listening.

"Would you like to see the archived stories of the ambush and battle during the dimensional portal opening?" the queen asked.

"Yes," Jenni said.

"And perhaps you will add yours."

"Perhaps."

"There are, of course, scholars studying the event." The queen waved a hand. "All aspects and from all the major Folk—djinn, elf, dwarf and mer."

"Scholars will study it forever," Aric said. He wasn't looking at Jenni, but at the queen, and had shifted closer.

"Also true." The queen stood.

Aric did, too, taking Jenni's hand and pulling her up.

"I will have the volumes of the records brought to you." The djinnfem inclined her head. "A gift."

Jenni was torn between gratitude and dread. "Thank you."

"Perhaps now that Rothly's arm and magic have been restored, his memory will be better and he can amend his record, too."

Aric jerked beside her and Jenni sensed that he hadn't heard about Rothly's magic. She didn't correct the queen about Rothly's talent.

The Fire Queen gazed down at Jenni. "I would like to extend an invitation to you—" her gaze flicked to Aric "—and Treeman Paramon, to dinner tonight. Informal, in our suite. We dine late, in three hours." Her gaze flicked toward the huge window and the dark sky of full night.

Jenni seemed stuck to the floor, her feet wouldn't move. She didn't want to go to dinner, but she sensed the queen hadn't actually discussed what she wished. Another thing that Jenni didn't want to do that she would. So many in the last few days!

She'd been reacting a lot, been manipulated. But now was not the time to dig in her heels. "Very well." She forced the words from her mouth. The day had already been too long, but she could nap again.

The queen nodded and glided from the room.

Staring at the door, Jenni stiffened her spine. She'd not only reacted, but had *acted,* too. She had freed her brother...*she* had formed a circle and influenced the second creative bubble, had used her gift, had said good-bye to her old home—all actions she could be proud of.

Aric squeezed her hand, then dropped it and moved to the center of the room. There he began a slow-moving dance involving wide gestures and stamping feet. The atmosphere seemed to thin and clear. She could almost feel listening spells sliding off the walls.

She scrambled to think of other spells she could add to safeguard the place from words wafting through the cavern to waiting ears, images coalescing in the flames of the fire and being shown to watching eyes. Nothing came to mind. She would have to rely on Aric.

Something else she'd been doing the past two days.

Her life had changed and with all that had happened to her, it seemed like hours had lengthened into weeks.

She was out of her home, her sanctuary where she'd lived with her guilt and grief. Now forced to interact with those who knew her, her family, her history, her brother. Those who had lived through the same frightening and wrenching event.

The queen hadn't said, but Jenni knew to the last drop of magic in her cells that the djinnfem had lost friends she'd cherished during the ambush, maybe even family...as had the other royals. A fact that Jenni should consider.

"Done, now," Aric said, and came and drew Jenni into his arms.

Startled, she looked up, only to see his head bend, his deep green eyes glitter with intent. His lips touched hers, pressed, and she opened her mouth on a gasp and breath passed between them, infusing her, touching her with nearly unbearable tenderness. The deliciousness of his magic, his power, his virility.

Then his tongue slipped between her lips and greedy craving tore through her like a firestorm. All the past and present need for this one man coalesced in her. Her arms came up and wrapped around his shoulders, she leaned against him until she could feel his every hard muscle. His body was tougher, more honed than when she'd kissed him last. Incredible. Wonderful. Fabulous.

His arm was a bar behind her waist as he curved her into his body, bent her back. There was nothing but the sensation of the kiss, heat warming her from her core to every nerve ending as her body readied. He tasted of wild forest, deep woods where anything could happen. Where they'd made love the first time.

The door slammed and the chatelaine with five keys marched in with a stack of books. She let them fall thumping onto a sturdy table.

Dazed, Jenni's arms dropped and Aric took a pace away from their embrace, looking amused.

"Written and translated to *English*." The dwarfem tapped five large, leather-covered volumes. She slid the five aside with easy strength, then curved her fingers around five much thinner books. "Spoken word, with a spell for *English*." A sniff.

Jenni blinked at the final books, much thinner, before she realized they appeared like a Lightfolk version of video, only insert and bound like books.

Sure enough, the woman said, "Video."

Were they 3-D pages? Projected holograms? Jenni wasn't sure she wanted to open one and find out.

"Thank you, Druka," Aric said, bowing.

"Thank you, Lady Chatelaine Dwarfem of the Granite family." Jenni hastily remembered her manners and bowed deeply, too, a little more deeply than the chatelaine's rank demanded, but Jenni was sure that she didn't want to make an enemy of this woman.

One more sniff, then a smirk and glinting brown eyes at Aric. "Regarding the princess's previous lodging. A brownie was suborned to carry a message to one of my assistants. The message stated Jindesfarne Mistweaver should be put in the weeping-wall cave. Some like that ambience." The housekeeper clucked her tongue and her round cheeks hardened, looking menacing instead of cheery. "The brownie has been dismissed and banned from working in any palace...."

"What?" Jenni asked. That sounded bad.

The dwarfem ignored her, still focused on Aric. "The brownie was bribed by the djinnfem Synicess," she said with gleeful malice. "Word is that djinnfem princess is not happy at being abandoned. Again."

"Again?" Jenni frowned.

"Her parents were the old fire royals who left for the other dimension."

The chatelaine turned and her long skirts twitched as she headed for the door.

"A second, please!" Jenni said. "What was the brownie's name?"

"Fritterworth." One. Last. Sniff. "And he lived down to his name."

"Names are powerful things," Jenni said, but the dwarfem was gone. Running her hands through her hair, Jenni scanned the room for a crystal-ball communicator. She didn't see one and an itching between her shoulder blades told her time was important—and short. She strode to the center of the room, where a wheel was woven into the thick hand-knotted silk rug, and flung out her arms. "Hartha!"

The brownie woman popped into existence, frowning. "And what would you be wanting with me that is so urgent that you must call me so rudely?"

"A brownie has been dismissed and banned from the palaces. I want you to take him under your wing."

"I am not a wretched sprite. I don't have wings to travel quickly, I have to come through earth and use much magic to do so." Hartha's arms were crossed, then curiosity shone in her eyes even as she frowned. "Which brownie?"

"Fritterworth."

"*Fritterworth!*" Hartha rolled her eyes and threw up her hands. "*Fritter worthless,* more like. What did he do now?"

"Please, Hartha, he needs a home, like you and Pred did…." Jenni hesitated. "And a new name."

"I'm not naming any browniemen. You name them and they are yours." Her chin jutted. "And you can't name him, 'cause you don't know him, and can't meet him here."

Jenni glanced at Aric. He shook his head. "No. I do not care to be responsible for the creature."

Hartha sniffed. "Creature."

Jenni said, "Take him home. Chinook can name him."

"Chinook, the cat!" Hartha laughed. "Fritterworth owned by a cat." She grinned.

"Please tell Chinook to be kind, to give him an honorable name to live up to. Maybe you could suggest one?"

Hartha was shaking her head, still smiling, but Jenni knew she'd get her way. She lowered her voice. "And maybe, if all goes well, I can name him something even higher after all this is done and send him to my brother Rothly."

"You are one optimistic fem," Hartha said, and Jenni understood that the brownie woman had already heard about Rothly's healing and his continuing grudge against Jenni.

"Fritterworth, hear me!" Jenni shouted, hoping the brownieman could.

Aric moved over and joined hands with her, squeezed her fingers. "Say again."

"Fritterworth, hear me."

"I hear," sobbed a small voice. "I was wrong. I did wrong. I didn't think. I threw the gold away. Bad gold."

Hartha flinched at that. Minor brownies or major dwarves, Earthfolk hated losing gold.

"I give you conditional house space in my home," Jenni said.

"Who?" The voice sounded perkier.

"Jindesfarne Mistweaver."

"Oh! I accept." There came a short pause and the joy in the voice soured as if the impulsive brownie had recalled something. "Hartha."

"That's right. You will be renamed. Hartha will join you and show you the way."

A huge sigh. "All right."

"Fritterworth!" Hartha said sternly.

"Thank you," said the brownieman.

With a huff of breath and a scolding glance at Jenni, Hartha said, "I hope you don't regret this." Then she vanished.

Jenni stumbled back and sank into the plump love seat. It had cost her power to call Fritterworth, and both Hartha and Fritterworth had used some of Jenni's magical energy to transport themselves.

Aric was watching her, head tilted. "You have grown... matured...and are not as bitter as I'd thought." He ran his tongue over his lips. "Not as sweet as you were, but some sweetness left…spicy…nutmeg and raw sugar."

A ripple of sensuality flickered through her. She lifted her chin. "We've just seen the consequences of being together. We've made an enemy of a royal djinnfem."

"Say thank you to the compliment, Jenni."

"Thank you. But I don't think—"

He sat down opposite her, lounging against the corner of the love seat. "Let me worry about Synicess."

Jenni stared at him—he was revealing that same manner he'd used when she'd met him. Was the sympathetic and tender man his true self, or the more confident warrior-businessman?

"The consequences—"

"You were slighted and given a poor room." He lifted and dropped a shoulder.

She narrowed her eyes. "Slighted enough that I considered abandoning this stupid mission."

He sat straight at that, his hands clasped between his knees, and leaned toward her. "How can you say that? You experienced the bubble event yourself."

She'd been too focused on herself and Rothly to ask about his family. She clutched Aric's forearm—it was ridged steel. "Your mother?"

"She has survived." He shrugged again with a casualness she knew he didn't feel. His feelings for his family had always been mixed.

"And your sisters?"

"Which ones? Of my three full sisters, one is missing. Who knows? Of my twelve half sisters, three have lost trees and have pined to death, one fought the shadleeches and lost and she and the tree are dead."

Jenni gulped. "You tried to send the creative elemental energies of the bubble to the dryads and redwoods."

His hand fisted. "Someone has to do something. I have been talking myself green to have the Eight act for the redwoods." His lip curled, he shook off her hand, stood and paced. "Just like the human logging situation, no one acts, not soon enough, not directly enough." His gaze bored into her own. "Do you think I like working at the beck and call of the Eight?"

"Yes."

His head tipped back in a laugh that released some tension. "Perhaps you are right. I like the favor of the royals. The work is interesting." He sent her a look under lowered eyelids. "Especially this mission...and the Meld Project."

"The merging of human technology with magic?" she asked.

"Quantum physics. I don't know much about that."

Neither did Jenni, but she'd seen for herself that it worked, had had a brief hand in developing a storage battery spell. Even that few minutes had given her a taste for it, an itching to get her hands on one of those magical computers.

He stopped and stood in the middle of the floor, hands on lean hips, and stared at her. "No one thinks of the dryads—silly dryads, thoughtless dryads, heedless dryads—but without the dryads the forests of Earth and all they support, *including* Lightfolk, would be worse off than they are. No one gets that." His smile was grim.

"I want to be able to change that. To be able to say send resources here, to the redwoods—there, to the spruces on the mountains…and to do that, I need the ears of the Eight."

"I understand."

"Do you?" He looked at her and she felt his concentration. Now his smile held the faintest edge of ruthlessness. Jenni wasn't proud that she felt a flicker of attraction. She'd been playing too many computer games where males were action heroes.

"I want to have control of my own life, and I want it to be a life worth living," he said.

"You've developed expensive tastes? And most lives are worth living."

"That's where you're wrong, Jenni, still-optimistic Jenni." His tone was a caress. "Most people have little control of their lives…they work for someone else in a job they endure. Lightfolk and humans alike. *You* don't, you enjoy your work, don't you? You are very valuable to your game developers. I want my life to be the same, under my control, with power enough to save what must be saved, what few others cherish."

"You want to be a noble of the Lightfolk."

"I will be."

"Which is why you courted Synicess." A thought that had occurred to her slipped from her lips. "And do you want me more than Synicess now because I'm a princess, too?"

He glared at her. "I have some honor."

"But that *is* a consideration. We have a history. Maybe you think I'm easier to manipulate."

He snorted with amusement, holding his stomach until huge laughs rolled from his mouth and he stumbled to a chair and fell into it. "Jenni…Mistweaver…easy…to… manipulate." He gasped and hooted.

Jenni glared at him.

"You are sitting in the finest guest suite in the Mid-North American Earth Palace because the Fire Queen, your kin, needed somewhere to talk to you, to convince you that this mission is important."

"Which she didn't."

"Yet." After dragging in a deep breath, he stood. "But you should know that this mission is very important to me. I convinced you to accept it."

"You blackmailed me into it."

He waved a hand. "I told you of the circumstances of your brother."

The anger that the Eight had sent Rothly rose, tasting like ashes in her mouth.

"I knew you wouldn't let Rothly die." Aric walked over to sit next to her again. "And you were the only one who could save him." His gaze, when it met hers, was sincere. "We might have tried, but no one else can go into the interdimension."

"No one else?"

He shook his head. "The elemental balancing gift has not been found in any other lineage, any family, any individual, and believe me, the Eight searched. The Eight themselves can adjust and balance the energies of an area…like this palace, but not calibrated to the exactness that you did this morning. Though now since Rothly has healed…"

Jenni studied Aric and decided to tell him her conclusions. Word would get out soon enough. "Rothly doesn't have elemental balancing powers anymore."

Aric's eyes widened. "But he was healed. I *felt* some of the creative energies flow through him, changing him."

Jenni hadn't paid much attention to the different aspects of the bubble event. When she had a moment alone, she'd try to remember everything, moment by moment. What had Aric experienced? And the guardians? Aric might actually tell her if she asked. She filed away the topic for later. "My brother's magic is not as fractured as it was. He may have another strong gift, but I don't know what it is except that I doubt he'll ever be able to access the interdimension."

Again the ruthless smile curved Aric's mouth. "Then perhaps I should pass the information on to the Eight that Rothly's magic should be tested." Aric stood and crossed to the door.

"Rothly won't like that."

"Being treated as if he were a young child? But he's acted as such for a long time now," Aric said and Jenni wondered how old she'd been acting, how old Aric thought she'd been acting. That didn't matter.

He bowed to her and Jenni thought there was just the faintest hint of mockery in his action, but couldn't call him on it. "I will be here at eight forty-five to escort you to the Emberdrake suite." His gaze slid over her, from head to toe. "The queen said informal, but I doubt you have a gown in your bags, you might want to contact your Hartha for that—and you should take advantage of the bathing pool."

"Are you saying I smell?"

He kissed his fingers like a chef. "Essence of Jindesfarne. I've always appreciated the scent, but I'm not sure of others."

Leaving her speechless, he opened the door and walked through, then closed it softly behind him.

For a suite decorated in air colors, it had a large bathroom dedicated to water play. The tub was more like a spa pool and of gorgeous blue tile with flecks of gold. Jenni chose the shower stall with three jets on opposite walls, stood in the center and let the water pound her and steam rise, until every pore felt clean. Then she dressed in clean, comfortable clothes—red cashmere sweater and thick black sweatpants of heavy cotton, nice soft socks—and went back to the sitting room to stare out the window. It rose from floor to ceiling, and was not symmetrical, but roughly a half circle. She wondered what mountain it was a part of, and what range it looked out on. Surely well-disguised to mortal eyes. Aric was right, the suite was magnificent, no doubt usually housing guests of much greater magic and rank than she.

She glanced at the books on the coffee table. The day had been too stressful for her to want to open them. Besides, now she was warm and safe and clean, sleep was dragging her eyelids down. She crossed to the buttery leather couch facing the window and sank onto it, plumped one of the accent pillows under her head, pulled a down comforter—surely priceless elven work—over her. She stared at the dark skies bright with constellations she couldn't see in Denver until her eyes closed and she fell asleep.

And the memories she'd been fighting for the last two days attacked her.

CHAPTER 15

SHE KNEW SHE'D BEEN CATAPULTED INTO THE past, knew she dreamed, but her innermost self wouldn't let her wake, forced her to relive the worst moments of her life.

The dream started soft and mistily and wonderfully, as if all around her was an impressionistic picture painted with joyful brush strokes.

Just as the past morning had begun, but now dread was in her heart, in every droplet of blood.

Aric's lazy voice said, "Stay with me." As she looked at him, redwood-skinned against the white sheets, her heart thumped with renewed desire. They'd loved most of the night, slept little, and now the sun was up and it was time for her to meet her parents to prepare for the Lightfolk ritual in an hour and a half. She hesitated.

Aric sat up, took her in his arms, kissed her, and the feel of his body against hers increased the longing to find ecstasy again. Surely she'd dance a ritual better, draw the sheets of elemental energies faster if she were happier. "My family is expecting me."

He raised his head, grin flashing, eyes crinkling. "Your family is always early for everything." He tugged her back down.

"Supposed to be there an hour early...uphold halfling honor..." But she gave in when his lips closed over hers and his mouth explored her own and his taste, the taste of lover and love, exploded through her. Then she nipped his full lower lip, fisted her fingers in his long and silky hair and moved over him. "We'll be fast."

He laughed. "This time. Later—"

She stopped his words by sliding onto him.

The sweetness of loving blurred fast in her memory, the pleasure of the day squashed beneath the heavy weight of all the rest.

She'd finished smoothing her underwear when fear struck her. Her mother screaming, injured! Grabbing the first clothes at hand, sweatshirt and jeans. Sliding her feet into shoes, flinging the lodging door open, she ran.

Fire magic pushed her fast. She didn't recall her feet hitting the ground, more like skimming over the grass.

Horrible sounds came—clashing swords. Terrible smells—blood and death, human, Lightfolk, *Darkfolk!*

She ran toward her mother's screams, saw Four walk through the summoned dimensional portal from the corner of her eyes. A line of skirmishing in front of her. A gap...near her mother. Red blood. A final gurgle, and death.

Time slowed and each running step of hers lasted way too long, minutes, maybe hours. Too late!

Most of her family—save Rothly and her sister Nettie, stepped from the gray mist. Armed *things* swooped upon them, and they fell. The shock of their loss, their deaths, swept through her like icy hail, chilling her. She screamed and bolted forward, more guards swarmed into the area, around her dead and dying family. She dodged left, right...saw her mother dead, her torso slit from neck to crotch. Wrenching her eyes aside, she saw two brothers and a sister in a heap of glittering colorful clothes stained with blood.

"Jenni," her father whispered.

She stared at him, his long and scholarly face gray-skinned and pale. He was on the ground, holding his side where blood spurted. "Go, Jenni, into the mist. Help Rothly and Nettie." His smile had turned faint, his eyes had dulled. "I love you. I love you all."

Jenni had stood until her sister Nettie had popped out of the interdimension, taken a look around her at her dead family, the fighting, and gone into hysterics—then was blasted by a bolt of dark lightning that shot to her center, blackly boiling away her skin. Killed by a great Dark one's magic.

Mewling escaped Jenni and she doubled over. Aric ran into her line of sight. He scooped up a long elven blade from a fallen warrior, rushed to the new King and Queen of Air, fought, even as Jenni called to him, mentally and with her weak voice. If he'd heard, he hadn't answered. He fought.

A desperate Rothly had managed to *half step* out,

something that shouldn't have been possible. He'd been holding all the magic the whole family had gathered, letting it slip trickling from his grasp so there would be no explosive release. He'd grabbed Jenni. *"In!"*

She'd flung off his hand, shouted the spell to enter the gray mist, saw a black and bloody knife coming toward her and jumped into the interdimension...catching sight of a bolt of dark oily purple magic hitting Rothly's arm, twisting it, *bending* it like malleable plastic.

Then she was in the gray mist with huge sheets of flaming elemental energies on the verge of enveloping all. Sobbing, she concentrated on controlling them. Taking what she could from Rothly, who was now entirely in the mist, but shaking wildly, his aura broken, Jenni set her feet and unwound and released the powers her family had gathered.

Then a long, flashing time of effort, sweating and swearing and hoping that the energies wouldn't escape her grasp, slip from her wet palms and limp and disoriented mind. Explode and kill all. She couldn't see or hear Rothly, he was more than a pace or two away. Finally the massive sheets of energies drifted away, Rothly exited the interdimension. She swayed. She didn't want to step from the mist into a hideous reality. But Rothly needed her, and she needed him...so she emerged from the interdimension into a beautiful summer afternoon and bloodied and blackened earth and broken beings.

The battle was over, and the Lightfolk had begun to take care of those lost to death.

Jenni stared at a freshly turned area of earth. A large headstone with the names of her family was already there.

A fluting, elffem voice said, "This is my land and they are resting and will be honored forever."

That was no comfort.

Her family was gone and she hadn't been there to help. She had failed them.

"I'll take you to Rothly." Soft fingers closed around her arm and she was led away and minutes passed and she was next to Rothly's bedside and he was spitting at her. Throwing salt and silver, casting her out. "You weren't *there!* You failed us, failed me. You were with Aric, weren't you? Having sex, instead of helping your family."

She couldn't deny it. Couldn't speak at all. Was hot and cold and hurting and numb.

Rothly's gaze went beyond her. "Aric, you betrayed me, as well." Another handful of salt and silver was flung. "I disown you as a friend." His lips twisted. "You both are dead to me. Go, and never let me see you again."

Her eyes blurred with tears and the heavy scent of despair and blood thinned, replaced by the fragrance of the high country in winter. Fresh snow, pines...and sulphur.

It's Fritterworth! The mental scream of terror jolted Jenni from her doze...where nightmares waited at the dark edges of her mind.

Mistress, help! Help me!

Shaking her head to vanquish the dreams, she called mentally, *Fritterworth?*

Out here, I'm out here on the balcony. Open the door.

She rubbed her temples, his desperation speared pain

into her head so she couldn't think. Jenni stumbled to the door. *Hartha took you to safety.*

Your cat died and they wouldn't keep me.

"What?" Not Chinook. How could that happen? Her hand was on the crystal doorknob. She flung it open and stepped onto the high ledge. Cold. There was a small shadow perched on the outcropping and she blinked to clear her vision.

Jenni! It echoed in two voices. The brownie transformed into a shadleech, then a gray-colored crow, beak clicking. And in the air before her hung the Dark one. All blackness and white, sharp teeth dripping...something.

"You are mine now. Outside the Earth Palace. The shields up here thin enough for me to call a halfling." Rich satisfaction laced his voice.

She couldn't move. Was aware of piercing cold.

He drew closer, hovered over the ledge she stood on, lifted her arm and set her wrist to his mouth of many teeth. Bit down, hard. Needles of slicing pain became shards, became *teeth*. It took her breath, took her strength, and she fell, her arm ripping wide. He let her, stayed over her. This time it was her blood dripping from his teeth.

Her blood, her energy, her magic was *pulled* from her as if one great nerve was unraveled and stretched and grabbed and slurped.

Agony.

She cringed. Found she could curl herself into a ball. His pleasure at the taste of her blood and being whipped her like nettles.

Couldn't think much, pulled against him and tautened the link between them and he cackled.

She rolled to the edge of the ledge…no rail, but a deadly fall would be better than this! She bumped into a magical shield and the energies flared huge and colorful and screamed in a thousand earthslide, wildfire, flood-water, tornado sounds—pounding through her, giving her enough strength to jerk away—or maybe it was the shock of the alarm that loosened the Dark one's hold, but she rolled close to the edge.

And sobbed.

Her body shook and she gasped and fell off the ledge.

Gasped again as shadleeches followed her and attached to her wounds and feasted. She *yanked* at the nearest sheet of energy. Fire. Wrapped it around her and sizzled the shadleeches and soaked it into her skin and got enough firestorm to lightning away home.

Crack!

King Emberdrake caught her in the middle of the air, pulled her from lightning-form to Jenni. Naked and panting.

Dizzy, her head lolled and she saw a midair battle…. Lightfolk warriors, the three other kings and Queen Emberdrake, flying. Aric stood, sword dripping ichor, on the rocky ledge outside her window.

Cloudsylph cursed, his words mixing with hisses from the fire royals. "He got away! Kondrian!" But the thing's name did not draw him back to the fight. The Air King slammed his sword into its sheath against his thigh, look-ing as ugly as an elf could in his rage.

"Bring her to me." The Water Queen's voice was low and lovely and soothing, her arms were outstretched. Jenni hiccupped with tears.

She was placed in the woman's arms and the pressure on her body made her scream and she was gone.

Jenni awoke surrounded by liquid. She shouldn't have been able to breathe, but she could. Slowly she uncurled. The sphere holding her was huge, about fifteen feet in diameter. Peering through the greenish wall, she saw a room just large enough to contain it with a few feet on each side holding a couple of chairs. She thought the floor and the walls were tiled…easy to clean up when the orb popped, she supposed.

She looked at her arm. The torn and gnawed flesh still gaped but there was no sign of bone, an improvement.

A movement caught her eye and she swam—with ease, with no pain, whatever this liquid was, it was great—to the bottom of the globe to see a brownie. The woman who had watched over Rothly hopped from a large wing-backed chair.

Thank you for caring for me, browniefem, Jenni said.

The woman peered at her, eyes wide. *You are welcome, Princess.*

Jenni found herself shaking her head, her hair waving, tugging at her scalp. *How is my brother?*

The brownie lifted her lip in disdain. *He is healing and unpleasant.*

Oh. Jenni wiggled and it affected her whole body. The water was soothing. She licked her lips, as if she would be speaking aloud instead of mentally, and projected,

The Dark one told me my cat was dead. Do you know if that is true? Even her mental tones were pitiful.

The browniefem tilted her head. Jenni could only pray that she was consulting with Hartha at home in Denver.

The cat is well. Lively. She likes having a brownie to tend her. The small woman shuddered.

And Fritterworth? Just thinking the name brought back the horrible ordeal of nightmares and the Dark one.

There is no such brownie called that. A brownie has been renamed "Crag." Even through the distorting liquid inside the bubble, Jenni could hear the small woman's snort. *A stupid cat-name. Who would call a BROWNIE a crag?*

He's bigger than she is, Jenni pointed out. *And the name has a certain solidity.*

The browniefem dipped her head. *That could only help.* She motioned with her long four-jointed fingers and Jenni swam closer, until her head touched the odd liquid plasticity of the sphere. The minor earth woman placed her hand close to Jenni's forehead. *Sleep and heal!*

And Jenni's consciousness floated into the darkness.

When she woke up again, Aric was in the chair, relaxed but not asleep. *Aric?*

He glanced up at her, stood and shook his limbs out. She noticed he had a broadsword tilted against the chair arm. Walking close to her globe and shaking his head, he said telepathically, *It isn't often that a halfling gets to swim in the primordial waters of life. Never that I heard.*

Well, the Eight need me. Looks like the Darkfolk are interested in the creativity bubble, too.

Aric's smile was sharp. *The Darkfolk love power and that bubble should grant it.*

Power for the Eight.

For the whole magical community. He raised a hand, palm out. *So they say, and I believe them.*

Jenni kicked and swam the short circuit around the bubble. *Shortsighted of Kondrian to eat me instead of use me as the Eight are, to balance the energies during the bubble event.*

The Darkfolk like immediate gratification of their appetites.

Jenni ran her hands through her hair, let it separate and wave around her. The natural curl was suppressed so it was much longer than her shoulders. *How long have I been here?*

Five nights and four and a half days. It's about noon. The dwarves are working on replacing the ledge of your balcony before humans can notice that it was gone. The Air couple state that no satellites got photos of the unfortunate contretemps—the Air Queen deflected any surveillance. The Fire couple insist you need fire healing, too, since you're floating in liquid. They are appalled. So be ready to be baked.

Now that he mentioned it, she was feeling a little waterlogged. *When can I get out of here?*

His eyes took on a gleam and his lips curved in a smile. She thought he saw all too well into her globe. She shrugged and her hair floated and her breasts bobbed— and his smile got wider. *They said that by the time you would ask such a question, you would be healed as much as necessary.*

Jenni frowned, looked at her arm. The skin had closed, but she wasn't sure all the tendons and muscles and nerves were aligned properly.

Swim to the top of the orb. There's a porthole.

Huh. Up she went. There was a tiny two-inch slice of air at the top of the sphere, but she didn't see any porthole. Then Aric's distorted face was over her and he tapped a small circular spot that could be a plug. It was about an inch wide. Jenni stared in disbelief. He tapped it again in a deliberate fashion. *Open it like that,* he said mentally.

So she tapped and the plug opened like an iris, continued to widen until it was her size. Jenni didn't see where the liquid went, it just...vanished.

Aric stood on a mobile wooden staircase. He leaned down and lifted her by her waist, swung her up in his arms and descended. Plucking a thick red robe off a peg in the wall, he stood behind her as she slid into it and tugged it around her. Wonderful thick fluffiness encompassed her. She examined her magical energy and decided against a drying spell.

Aric reached under her collar and drew out her hair, his hand stroking her head. "Jenni," he sighed. Then he wrapped his arms around her, stepped close so their bodies touched. "Jenni." His voice was thick, like fog in a forest.

"You didn't suspect he'd come after me?"

He stiffened a little behind her, but his lips went to her neck and he inhaled deeply. "No. I didn't think of that, either." He hesitated, said, "Though naturally I did tell them that Kondrian had threatened you."

"Naturally." She tried not to sound bitter, but something leaked through.

He turned her around, grasped her by her shoulders and gave her a little shake. "Jenni!"

"You weren't almost eaten by the damn Dark one!"

Fear flickered over his face, then it set back into exasperation. "Who opened the door to Kondrian and his leeches, Jenni?"

She grimaced. "I did." She tried to free herself from his grasp but was hauled against his chest. He smelled great, rich earth turned from winter's frost to spring's welcoming redwood needles. That nearly distracted her. "I opened the door, but he got to me first, affected me mentally." She hadn't sorted out whether her nightmares were her own or the Dark one's fashioning. She trembled against Aric, drew his scent into her lungs to steady herself. "Kondrian said that the shields were too weak to protect me." She didn't know how that could be, she'd been in a damn mountain.

"Thick shields diminish the view and your suite usually houses elves."

"Not a halfling like me."

Aric stroked her back. "I'm not sure that the Eight knew that Kondrian was in the area or would attack you. I don't think they set you up."

"Then they were there awful fast."

"We've learned how to deploy rapidly."

She leaned back, looked at his face. Battles were in his eyes. That would definitely age a person. She glanced at his sword, she could see the whole hilt projecting over the arm of the chair. "How much have you fought?"

"I'm well trained now. I caught the eye of Cloudsylph during the portal battle—"

"He was in charge of the warriors."

"Yes. I trained. I fought. Other Darkfolk both major and minor, shadleeches. Only in the past two years, when the Meld Project was initiated, did I move from a soldier to a liaison with halflings."

She didn't know quite what to say. He hugged her, then lifted her again, went to the chair and sat with her on his lap.

There was an almost silent *whoosh* and the healing orb deflated into a nearly transparent sac hanging in midair. The atmosphere was heavy with liquid for moment, then that vanished, too, maybe into the walls and the floor, though Jenni couldn't see it. She leaned against Aric, listening to his slow Treeman heartbeat. She wasn't sleepy or hungry, and she liked the feel of his arms around her.

"I'm to debrief you," he said, and rubbed his chin against her head. "Tell me everything you can about the attack."

She started slowly, speaking of her dreams, then the fake call from "Fritterworth." There wasn't much action to tell of after that, just suffering. She hadn't even seen the royals or Aric arrive.

"The Dark one was wounded," Aric said roughly. "I don't think whatever he got from you remained with him—not the magic or the energy. He spent more trying to escape. I got the big shadleech myself. That seemed to diminish him some, too."

"Kondrian took my blood," Jenni said in a small voice. "I'm not sure what that means."

Aric cuddled her close. "We'll find out."

They rested in silence together. Together. It felt nice. Silence, no need to talk, as if all the flickers and flames between them that had been extinguished were growing from embers into a fire. How large would that fire become? Could it become? Campfire, bonfire blaze, wildfire that ate up acres?

A knock came at the door and Rothly entered, sneering. "How cozy."

CHAPTER
16

ARIC STOOD WITH JENNI. HE SET HER ON HER feet on the far side of the chair, so it was between her and Rothly, near his sword, as if he were protecting her. "I don't like how you are speaking to your sister."

"She's no sister of mine. Nor are you my friend."

Jenni cinched her belt, circled to stand at Aric's left. She saw Aric's brows rise. "Not your sister? You have both been adopted into King and Queen Emberdrake's family. More of her doing than yours."

"And here you are, ready for sex with her, as always. I heard you were engaged to Synicess. But she's a difficult djinnfem, isn't she? Jenni is much easier to be with and, now, almost as high in rank."

"Nothing is higher than a born royal with no human blood," Jenni said.

"Still believing his lies?" Rothly said.

Aric literally crackled beside her, as if his skin were going to bark…in anger or protection.

"Aric's never lied to me," Jenni said. Her voice was quiet, her *emotions* were quiet. For a fleeting second she wondered if the healing liquid had helped her guilt. She tipped her head, staring at her brother, too thin, but dressed elegantly and well. His arm was straight.

"I never lied to any Mistweaver," Aric gritted out. His fingers touched her back, lingered, and Jenni thought that he might want to put his arm around her waist, but instead he put his hand on her shoulder. "What are you doing here if Jindesfarne Mistweaver Emberdrake is not your sister and I am not your friend?"

Rothly took a step back, bumped into the doorjamb. "I wanted to see-- Rumor has it that you came to the Earth Palace via Northumberland. What did you do to my home?"

"Well, now, I cleaned it," Jenni said, hurt seeping into her at Rothly's manner. "And I balanced it."

He shook his head and his light brown hair flipped out of his eyes. "What did you take? I'm sure you took something."

Jenni lifted her chin. "I took portions of *my heritage*. Copies of the journals—copies—"

"You stole my work!"

"I copied your work, and I haven't had a minute to look at it. I also took some tea." She hoped the coldness of her lips translated to a chilly smile. She stared at his mended arm. "I suggest you send the rest of it to me at my home in Denver. You'll be having no more use for it. You can't go into the mist again."

Pain twisted his features and a raw sound escaped him. Jenni caught her breath. She hadn't meant to hurt him. He'd miss the interdimension? She hadn't…not so much that she couldn't go years without visiting it. Maybe it was the fact that he was shut out of it forever, no longer a Mistweaver in the truest sense of the name. "I'm sorry." She heaved a sigh, rubbed her hands over her face. "I'm sorry. I didn't know that would hurt you."

"You bitch," Rothly said.

"Don't apologize to him," Aric said at the same time. He stared at Rothly until her brother shifted feet. "You haven't been half as mean to him as he has been to you. Haven't been half as bitter or hysterical, either."

"Hyst–hysterical!" Rothly sputtered.

"Go back to your home and your hermit ways, Rothly Mistweaver Emberdrake. I don't care to call you my friend, haven't for years. The lady standing beside me will finish the mission that you were foolish enough to agree to."

Rothly whitened. Pallid didn't look good on him.

"I'm sorry you're so unhappy," Jenni said.

Her brother stared at her with wide and painful eyes and she realized she'd phrased the statement like her mother or father would have. She drew in a breath, decided to go on in the same manner. "What can you do to make your life better?" She opened her hands. "You have power again, find your new talent."

He hissed at her and she managed a lopsided smile. "Your fire nature is more prominent than your air now." She swallowed. "Please get well, Rothly." One more deep breath. "What can I do to help you?"

"You've taken on his task, you've given him kind words, you've tried to send brownies to him," Aric said. She ignored him.

Rothly stepped back into the hallway. "Nothing. *Nothing!*" He slammed the door.

"Oh," Jenni whimpered. She turned to Aric and looked up at him. Strong and stable…and hurting at the sight of such a changed Rothly. As she was.

She went into his arms and they closed around her. She stood with him for a long while, until a brownie came in and told Aric that the Eight wanted to speak with him. He left for another conference. Jenni was led from the water quarter of the Earth Palace to the fire area and a desert sauna room to bake the kinks in her magic…and her tears away.

Later that afternoon, Jenni planned a dinner for Aric and herself. Even as she selected the menu and smoothed a sky-blue tablecloth shot with silver over the dining room table, she knew that Aric would stay with her and they'd make love in the night. She wasn't completely sure of her feelings for him, but the feelings of guilt that she'd had, and the blame that she'd assigned to him for the loss of her family, had fallen and been washed and seared away.

She stared out the huge arched window overlooking jagged, peaked mountain ranges, one rising behind another. All white with snow with blue reflecting the sky and gray with rock. The view wasn't as clear. If she narrowed her eyes, she could see the slight waves of the thick magical shield that would protect her from any Dark one's influence.

But she didn't think that the nightmares of the past had been totally from Kondrian. She'd had them before, though not so vividly for a long time.

If she wanted, she could let guilt and bitterness eat into her heart again. But now she knew she'd made a choice before. Yes, she'd been late to join her family an hour ahead of time at the portal. To show the Eight their honor at being chosen to work for the royal Lightfolk.

What would have happened to her if she'd been on time when the Lightfolk moved the ceremony up and she'd entered the mist at the same time as the others? She'd have been killed and eaten by Kondrian. Hadn't she run immediately to her mother when inundated by terror? Hadn't Jenni felt her mother's wounding and death? Yes.

As for Aric... If she let it, her fragile new relationship could break against the mountain peaks like an egg. Yes, he'd chosen to pick up a sword and run to Cloudsylph and his warriors and defend the royals. She could continue to hold that against him. But he hadn't been well-trained in warfare like Jenni's brother Stewart, who had been the first of her family to fight and die. No doubt being with other warriors in the mass around the portal had saved his life, too.

She could continue to blame him, or accept that he'd made a quick choice—for his kind instead of his friends. No. That way lay bitterness, and she didn't want any more anger at the past between them. She chose to nurture her relationship with Aric instead.

She went into the bedroom and plumped up the pillows. Blue silk bedspread and pillowcases. The entire suite was a luxury she'd never experienced.

That had come with a cost. She'd almost died!

Jenni shivered as she felt the cold wind of her fall. She *wouldn't* remember the horror of being drained by Kondrian and the shadleeches. That way lay panic and madness.

He was still out there...somewhere. She'd been told that he'd been wounded, but she wasn't sanguine enough to believe that the wounds would hamper him. Before he'd fled too far he would find innocents to eat. Hell, he'd probably eat his own shadleeches.

Her imagination was too vivid. So she lit large pillar candles crafted by fire sprites and djinns and smelled spring. The magic of blooming and becoming. Of trees waking up from the winter's cold touch. She wasn't sure what she felt for Aric. Wasn't sure what she'd ever felt for him—real love or infatuation.

But the sharing of selves and passion would be exquisite.

Wandering back to the sitting room, she stared out the window wistfully. The sun was beginning to set and she longed to see colored rays against the snow.

There was a tapping at the door. "Please come in," Jenni called.

A smaller-than-usual browniefem entered carrying a huge tray of domed food above her head. Jenni would have offered to help, but knew it would insult the little woman...and the brownie was stronger than she. Though a minor Earthfolk, the brownie was all magical. Jenni gestured to the cherry sideboard and the brownie efficiently set the dishes out on woven hotpads.

The smell of food filled the air, and Jenni's mouth watered and her stomach rumbled. The small woman curtsied.

"Wait!" Jenni asked.

Twisting her hands in her apron, the browniefem looked down. "Yes, Princess Jindesfarne?"

"Just call me Jenni."

The woman flinched, and Jenni ignored it. She gestured to the window and the ledge beyond. "Is it safe for me to go out?"

"Course. Dwarves fixed. Shields strong. You fall, no. You seen, no."

Ah, the browniefem didn't know English well, probably never served a halfling or a human. Jenni held out her hand. "I'm still a little scared, and would like to go out on the balcony. Would you go with me, hold my hand?"

The brownie's large triangular ears trembled in surprise, quivered at the tips. With small steps, she joined Jenni, placed her hand in Jenni's. She sighed—she'd been afraid that the brownie would curl her hand around one or two of Jenni's fingers, which would be embarrassing for them both.

They moved with tiny steps to the door. Jenni hesitated before touching the knob. But she liked this suite. Wanted to see the view. Would not let her fear get the better of her. She opened the door and stepped out on the ledge. It seemed exactly as it had been before...not that she'd seen much of it.

With another sigh, she stepped farther out on the ledge. The brownie flattened herself against the short rock wall between the door and the window.

"I'm so sorry!" Jenni said. "I didn't know this would be an ordeal for you, Madam Brownie." She considered letting loose of the little woman's hand, decided that would be worse for her. So they scuttled back through the door and Jenni closed it. She released the brownie's hand.

The woman's eyes bugged out more than usual. The tips of her ears rolled down and up repeatedly. Then she vanished.

"That was really well done, Jenni," Jenni said aloud. The view still beckoned, and she wished the brownie were here to give her courage to face it again. Sunset colors smeared outside her window, bolder than the night before. Golden, nearly neon pink. With a big breath, her palms dampening, Jenni opened the door again and walked out onto the ledge.

There was still a waver to the air, but not as much as over the window. After all, her sleeping mind wouldn't be vulnerable out here.

She walked to the rim of the ledge, felt the warm press of magic...air elf and some fire djinn. For an instant she considered stepping into the interdimension and bringing elemental energies to balance the shield and make it stronger. She shrugged the thought aside. She'd want to make tea before she went to the interdimension again, and most of the time she'd spent there lately had been under emergency circumstances. Maybe all of the time. She'd been worried about Rothly...last night fearful for herself. But she'd let go of Rothly earlier in the day. Let him chart his own course without her. She couldn't long for his forgiveness anymore. His grudge wasn't hers and she wouldn't let him foist guilt on her anymore. She'd grown.

She grieved for the brother he'd been, for the bitter man he was, but she couldn't change his mind. She'd changed her own and that was all that was in her power.

In any event, she was committed to fulfilling his word and the mission.

She looked to the sunset painting the mountains gold and pink, casting lavender shadows, and let the colors soothe her mind and spirit. She calmed her mind, sank into a serene meditation, watching the colors shift and shade.

"Jenni," Aric said, coming up behind her and setting an arm around her waist, pulling her close to his body and taking a pace back from the edge. She smiled but didn't turn in his arms, wished to watch the sky darken and stars flare into bright points. With city living, she hadn't seen the Milky Way for a long time.

"Jenni." Aric lowered his head, and his breath on her neck stirred her sensually, caused an anticipatory clench deep inside her.

So she leaned back against him. "The sunset..."

"Fabulous," he whispered, as he stood still beside her.

The colors softened to pastels, then to gray. Darkness descended to the rugged thrusting peaks.

Jenni made to step forward to catch the last light of day, but Aric kept her close.

Aric grimaced as he glanced around. "Above tree line."

He was right. No tree could live here. He arched his green brows at her. "You know you can fall and turn into lightning and maybe live. A whole different matter for me. I'd shatter into splinters." He tilted his head. "Though I might have some cones with a few seeds in me."

Frowning, Jenni said, "Your father was air, an elf."

His face hardened. "So I might not smash and I might be able to pull on both my natures to float a little. The food in your suite smells great. Let's eat."

Jenni watched him as he returned to her rooms inside the mountain. She had enough issues of her own to know that Aric would have to work through his. She smiled slyly. He'd prodded her out of her guilt and bitterness, it was only fair that she meddle, too. Not right now, but soon.

The sitting room was so bright it dazzled her eyes. Blue and silver-toned, not real silver, though she and Aric would not be bothered by the pure metal. He was right, the smells were wonderful. Freshly steamed vegetables, tender slivers of meat—quail, chicken, fish, beef—in various sauces. Gourmet cooking. The French had nothing on brownies.

When they sat to ate, Aric had a gleam in his eyes. At his first bite, he closed his eyes, rumbled approval. "Good food." He scanned the suite. "Luxurious rooms, don't care for the colors much, though."

"You should, you're half-elf."

His jaw clenched.

"But we won't talk of that right now. I prefer you in greens and browns, myself." The baby asparagus was fresh and crunchy and wonderful.

"How's the bed?" Aric asked.

Jenni nearly choked, coughed. She smiled at him. "Really nice." She leaned back in the cushioned chair that almost seemed to conform to her body. "It's nice being a Princess of the Lightfolk." One more glance. "Though I don't think this will be my home for long."

"It could be," Aric said.

"No." She forked up some chicken in a delicate white sauce. "I love Denver, and Mystic Circle."

"You've done an excellent job there, balancing the elements. One of the reasons the Eight decided to locate their corporation there, I think. The whole city has felt your influence, is more balanced than any other human city."

"Thank you."

Aric lifted and dropped a shoulder. A corner of his mouth tilted up as he asked, "What do you think of the Meld Project?"

She raised her brows. "You know I find it very intriguing."

"I know." He opened the dusty bottle of fine wine and poured two glasses. "We would be proud and honored to get you, perhaps even put you in charge of the project.... You'd like to work on it."

"Yes."

He hesitated, and huffed a breath. "You can talk to me about the mission."

She stirred the food around on her plate. "I've been

unconscious and I'm sure calculations have been revised for the next—last—bubble event."

His body relaxed. Must be difficult for him being her liaison, torn between the Eight and her—his soon-to-be lover again. And even if that relationship was what he'd hoped for, even if that was what the Eight had planned, it wasn't easy on Aric. She could see that.

"The experts think that the last event will be within a month." He gave her a steady look over the wine. "And if you visit the area, balance near where we believe the bubble will be released, the bubble might arrive sooner." His mouth quirked as his eyes warmed and he lifted his glass to her. "It all depends upon you," he said softly.

CHAPTER
17

HER CHICKEN NEARLY GOT CAUGHT IN HER throat. Her life hadn't been boring…precisely. But now that she was working on this mission—a *real* mission as opposed to those she wrote for Fairies and Dragons—it was exciting. Between the terrifying moments.

She was now a Lightfolk Princess and respected. Who'd have thought it? She took her own wine, let the taste lie on her tongue. The thought of being important in the Lightfolk world was sweet. Something her family had always yearned for…and if things had gone right during that last mission, something her family would have received. Fifteen years overdue.

But she was only important for the moment, and wondered how often she would have to prove herself. She drank and cleared her throat. "Where will the next bubble appear?" She wasn't as casual as she sounded and

Aric's eyes sparkled, making him look like the young man she'd known.

"Northern California."

"Earthquakes."

"That's right. We believe…I have been informed… that the event might take place at the Mendocino Junction."

"Huh?"

"It's where three tectonic plates rub together."

"Oh." She frowned, trying to visualize the Northern California coast. She'd been to Aric's sequoia home, but the geography was all jumbled together in her head. "Near you?"

"Close enough," he replied with the same false note of casualness that she'd used.

"Why are you so excited?" she asked.

He tilted his head, glanced around the suite. "Still clean of any listening spells, though the dwarves stated they should have some here in case Kondrian returned."

Jenni leaned forward. "Tell me."

His smile widened and he leaned over the table, too. "You saw how the main bubble exploded and some smaller ones floated away." He lowered his voice. "Those would be special and precious, too. Who knows what blessings such small ones might contain? Perhaps they could be directed to help my Treefolk."

"Who knows how strong they are, how long they last?"

"But the general area out there—" he gestured toward Yellowstone "—benefitted from your balancing, from having the sheets of elemental energies summoned, from the bubble that popped. Sure, most of the energies were split in five directions, but not all the magical particles were caught by our various wills. There was plenty of ambient magic remaining even that night to convince the human tourists that they witnessed nothing extraordinary. It took only very minor magic to bend their minds, much less than usual."

"Oh."

"So the area will get magic, spreading out, even if the Eight perform a ritual to direct it."

Jenni winced as she recalled the Queen of Earth creating a ritual that didn't happen. "Uh, how is the writing of that ritual going?"

Aric raised his brows. "I am not fully in the Eight's confidence. But the Mendocino Junction event may be at sea. So the Water Queen is crafting the ritual."

"I like her," Jenni said, dishing out some more vegetables.

"Everyone loves her, and she's very strong, which is why her consort is such a jerk."

Jenni choked, looked around the suite again. "You're sure we can't be heard."

"Pretty much." He stared at her some more, said, "Ah…"

"Yes?"

"We have been asked to visit the Lightfolk who holds the estate where the bubble is anticipated to burst."

"Holds how?"

"Owns. She owns the land and strip of rocky beach fronting the ocean. It's part of the lost coast of California. Eighty miles of country so rugged that there aren't any roads close. She has a helipad for the ridge house, but probably has an underwater palace, too."

"A merfem?"

"Yes."

"And we've been ordered there. Me to check out the place and balance, and you to recon the area for a good place to do the ritual dance?"

"Yes."

"What's the weather like there?" Jenni asked.

"Cold and rainy. Mud."

"Can't be as bad as Northumberland."

"No." Now Aric cleared his throat. "I should tell you that Rothly has left the Earth Palace, returned home."

Jenni should have felt her brother absenting himself, but hadn't. The Eight probably sent him home because he wasn't of any more use to them. She sighed. "Oh." Then she shrugged and sighed again. "Not my problem... anymore."

Aric reached out and took her hand. "I'm sorry he continues to hurt himself and you."

"I am, too."

Aric lifted her fingers to his lips. "I'm very glad that you are...reconciling with the past."

"I am, too." She met his eyes. They were the dark green of the deep forest. She inhaled. "But you have not reconciled with yours—the emotional aches of your childhood."

He dropped her hand, bristled. She could imagine pine needles quivering with affront. "I have."

She propped her elbows on the table, put her chin in her hands. "I had a happy childhood, but since then

I've been through a lot." She looked past him at a huge tapestry showing flying horses dancing in the air, tried a smile, but it was more sad than happy. "I'm working on forgiving myself...and you. I think there will always be a piece of guilt-grit in me. And you've dealt with the events of fifteen years ago at the portal opening very well. Much better than me." Another deep breath and she met his eyes again. This time they were more brown of anger than quiet green. "But you've never dealt with your childhood."

"I beg your pardon. I've come to accept my mother, the flighty dryad."

"But you've never released the anger and resentment of your father's abandonment."

Aric stood. "I don't need to hear this."

Jenni snorted. "We've exchanged places." He was irritated enough that he was heading for the door. So much for sharing sex and loving tonight.

He stopped with his hand on the knob. "We'll leave for California in the morning."

Putting her napkin on the table, Jenni stood and nodded. "Fine."

Once more he hesitated, Jenni was feeling an inner pull from him to come together, maybe he was feeling the same.

"My father was not a good father." Aric's jaw flexed, and Jenni realized that he was a mixture of two natures, facile air elf and solid dependable Treeman...and the "flighty dryad" contributed to his character, too. When he was younger he'd been so much easier in manner. He continued his explanation, and his knuckles had stopped being white on the doorknob. "Many elves raise their sons. Many are not ashamed of them."

"Many Folk—human and Lightfolk and Treefolk—don't know how to relate to or raise children."

"Unlike your parents," he said. The wistful look on his face caught Jenni, had her throat closing. Another old expression she'd seen time and again when he looked at her parents, her family.

"Yes, I had a loving family from the day I was born. They died a terrible death, too soon. I hope they would be proud of me now. They would not have been proud of me last week, but they would have understood. Perhaps if more of us had lived we could have helped each other better through the grief." She shook her head hard enough that her hair was flung in her face, and she had to smooth away the strands. "But they died and never saw me as an adult." Not that she felt too mature. "They died and years of love and understanding and disagreements and arguments vanished. But your father is still alive. Perhaps you could relate to each other better now, as men."

Aric's face clouded, set into a hard carving. "Jenni, the elf loves nothing and no one but himself."

"You're wrong."

Aric's face cracked into shock.

Jenni shifted her balance. She felt as if she were walking on the crusty ground near one of Yellowstone's hot pools, any minute she could fall through and be boiled. "He's a well-known bard." In fact, she thought the elfman had adapted well enough to the current era that he had works

out from the old wax cylinders to the latest music tech...
under different names, of course. "He loves music."

"He lives for admiration."

"He loves music."

Aric's jaw and fingers tightened, but he hadn't opened
the door. "He lives for admiration and loves nobody but
himself."

Jenni let her breath sift from her. "Maybe that's true,
but when was the last time you saw him...spoke to
him?"

"I saw him about seven years ago and turned and
walked away before he saw me."

"Aric," Jenni said softer than human ears could hear.
"You helped...are helping...me understand and get
through the events of the worst time of my life. Let me
help you." She moved her hand in a tentative gesture.
"You aren't whole, aren't the entire man you could be
without reconciling your feelings about the elfman who
gave you life."

Aric grunted. "You're right, his seed produced me,
that doesn't make him a father."

"No, but you are still being hurt by him. It's a splinter,
a thorn, in your spirit." Her smile was grim. "You've
been making me pick out my thorns to heal."

They stared at each other.

Chimes rippled through the air and Jenni blinked away
first, scanned the room for the crystal ball.

"*Calling Princess Jindesfarne Mistweaver Emberdrake*,"
said a female voice as rippling as the chimes, with an
extra lilt of joy.

Aric's shoulders lowered, releasing some tension. "Mother. She always had good timing."

He moved away from the door and waved toward an étagère that held art…and a glowing ball that Jenni hadn't noticed before. As she walked to it, Aric's mother began to hum, blithely anticipating that Jenni would answer her call. Jenni had never had a call from her before, only met her about three times.

She shouldn't have been nervous, tree dryads were about the easiest beings to be around, but this was Aric's mother and Jenni had lived in the human world a long time. She tapped the ball that was at eye level and stared into Leafswirl's greenly smiling face.

"Hello, Jenni," the dryad caroled.

"Hi, Leafswirl."

She beamed. "It's so *good* to see you!"

Jenni figured Aric's mother wasn't sure how long it had been since they'd interacted last…about sixteen years.

"My son is with you? Of course he is! I'm so pleased that you're a princess, Jenni! You deserve it."

Leafswirl had no clue. People she liked deserved the best from life and that was that.

"Thanks."

"And how is precious Rothly?"

"He's healed." At least his arm and magic.

"How wonderful! May I speak with Aric?" Leafswirl's gaze went past Jenni as Aric stepped near.

"Darling seedling!"

Aric flinched.

Suppressing a snicker, Jenni walked away from the

ball…and caught the tiny browniefem whisking away the remnants of dinner. She smiled. "Thank you."

The brownie bobbed and the dishes continued to be stacked on the tray faster than Jenni's eyes could follow.

"And thank you for helping me get out on the… balcony."

"Ledge!" the woman squeaked. The tips of her ears quivered again.

"Ledge," Jenni agreed. "It was very gracious of you."

For the first time there was a slight clatter of china. The browniefem looked appalled, whipped her hands up to cover the whimper coming from her mouth. She'd made noise! And when someone was conversing on a crystal ball. Her whole body shook.

Jenni went as close to her as she thought the woman would allow, made her voice the soothing of slow flames in a low, comforting fire. "You must know that I am a halfling, and not accustomed to having a personal brownie look after me."

"Hartha, Pred…" The browniefem had stopped trembling, glanced at Jenni sideways.

"I think of them as belonging to my house…or the house belonging to them." After their first night, Hartha and Pred had proven to be strong and practical Folk. "I'm glad you're here, and that you helped me." More and more Jenni figured that the browniefem wasn't usually assigned to the suite.

"Mud clothes on you." She began whisking the plates around again.

One of the brownies who served in the halfling fems' dormitory? "Thank you for that, too," Jenni said. "I'm glad you were here to care for me."

"Halflings good!" The woman's dark brown gaze was defiant.

"Some of us."

"Thanks to you, too. Even short time here in suite me rises status." The dishes, serving domes and brownie vanished.

Courtesy done, Jenni hesitated, wondering if she should let Aric and his mother have some privacy.

"...and Brightacorn had a lovely dwarfling child!"

One of Aric's sisters. Apparently he was hearing news of his family.

"That's nice," Aric said.

"And since you and Jenni are coming to California, I want to see you! It's been ages!"

"It's been two months."

"And there's news! Somehow the shadleeches can't enter the grove anymore!" The dryad twirled around, dancing. Her long leaf-hair swung with her, filling the crystal ball. Then her happy face was there again. "Somehow you did it, didn't you? My clever son!"

Aric grunted.

Leafswirl tilted her head in a mannerism that Aric had gotten from her. Her lips curved slyly. "And the Eight would like to know how a grove is protected from the shadleeches, wouldn't they?"

She'd gotten him there, Jenni figured.

He ran a hand through his hair. "Yes."

"Well, I won't tell you. You have to see for yourself.

Come to me tomorrow!" Again the chiming note in her voice and the crystal ball merged as she ended the call.

"Congratulations," Jenni said. "Results from the bubble here in Yellowstone already."

Aric stretched, releasing tension in his shoulders, shook out his arms. "Seems like." He glanced at her, but didn't meet her gaze. "And it seems like we should visit my mother. Midmorning tea time?"

Dryads loved their little herbal tea parties. Jenni had nearly forgotten. No dryads in the game she worked on. She crossed to Aric and touched his arm. "Sounds lovely. You should be proud."

He grunted again. "I am proud." But his voice said he was resigned. Since they were now dealing with his maternal parent, Jenni decided that the issue of his father had been tabled—for a while. Maybe even until after the California bubble event. She actually had a sense that her relationship with Aric might last a while. That would be good. For both of them.

If they survived. The shadleeches had reminded her. "Kondrian will show up at the third bubble event, won't he? And probably not only him. Other great Dark ones."

Aric's arms closed around her. "Most likely. You heard my mother. She already knows we were on our way to California and that was determined this morning. What the dryads know, the leaves whisper."

"All around the world."

"Yes," Aric agreed.

"How many great Dark ones live?"

"Four."

"None have been destroyed in the fifteen years since the portal opening?"

"That was the last time they massed, and we haven't been able to pick one off since. Dark ones raise armies easily. And they're slippery. Sometimes literally."

Jenni rested against him, the lightening of her mood from Leafswirl and the browniefem faded to a low-level fear. Opening a portal to another world so four royals could go through was supposed to have been a joyous event. The ritual dancing had been planned to be cheerfully abandoned. All had turned horribly wrong into death and battle. After the bubble rising here in Yellowstone, she'd thought the next event would be a celebration, too. Not going to happen. Aric had probably deduced that right away…everyone but she, and no one had bothered to tell her.

"I'll be there to defend you." He smoothed her hair, tangled his fingers in her curls, gave a slight cough. "So will the guardians—the dwarf and the elf. You can't get better bodyguards."

"Guess not. Guess this mission is really important."

He tilted her chin up with his fingers. "More than anyone knows, I imagine. Magic was draining from Earth. We think this is a way to increase it. A blessing from the core of the planet to replenish what the Lightfolk community needs."

"If the Darkfolk don't get to it first."

"They won't. Not this time. This time we'll be ready."

So there were plans for more than a dancing ritual. Battle strategies. She didn't want to think of it. She closed her eyes and let her other senses soothe her. Candles she'd lit when she'd thought this would be a night of seduction still burned—adding the fragrance of spring blossoms as if there were trees blooming in every corner of the suite. There was the slight smell of chocolate...dessert? She'd like to taste chocolate from Aric's lips. His scent mingled with the rest to please her, and his heart beat beneath her ear, and his arms were around her....

And his hands were sliding down to her butt. Felt like they might end up in bed after all. Little thrills slipped down her nerves, also pleasing her. She sighed and stepped back. His arms tightened around her, then loosened.

"Let's have dessert. Chocolate."

He was at the table before her, grinning. "Chocolate mousse, made by the elf chef."

"Oh, yeah!"

Then he was seating her and she was lifting froth to her lips, letting the spoon hover before her mouth so she could enjoy the smell. Chocolate.

Aric finished first and eyed her plate.

"You know, living in the human world gives a person greater access to chocolate," she said.

He smiled a warrior's smile. "So it does. You've profited, I've been deprived. I should have more." His fingers crept toward her plate where a puff remained. She scooped it up in three spoonfuls and swallowed fast.

Aric shook his head and looked mournful. "No way to treat good chocolate, not to let it linger on the tongue." He stood and was around to her, pulling her from her chair, before she put down her spoon. "Now I can taste Jenni and chocolate."

His fingers sifted through her hair first and the sensual tingles went from her scalp to the soles of her feet, curling in her core and igniting. He knew she liked her hair stroked. He knew so many things about her, physically and emotionally. If she fell for him again and hit the ground it would be like jumping from the ledge outside the window. There wouldn't be much left of her when she hit bottom.

She sank against his body, uncaring of the past or the future, living in the wonderful, sense-sizzling moment. He was strong…and aroused—that inflamed her.

CHAPTER

18

SHE NIBBLED AT HIS JAWLINE AND HE TURNED her head to fuse his mouth with hers and she *did* taste chocolate and Aric, and it was the best taste in the world. Stupid tears burned at her acceptance of the lost loneliness of missing him so much for so long. Her tongue rubbed along his and he groaned, set his hands around her butt and pulled her tight. Oh, yeah! She rose to her toes to rub against him.

With a grunt, he swung her up, broke the kiss so he could glance around the room. His eyes were dilated, looked glazed. He panted. She did, too. Before her breath steadied she was set on her feet and his hands were roving over her…to the bottom of her shirt, pulling it over her head. His fingers touched her bare skin and the noise he made was a sensual hum that she recalled.

She remembered much…the dance of their loving.

How their magic twined together with each brush of fingers, each slide of skin against skin.

The air thickened with heat, with the scent of him. His hands trailed up her skin to her bra and he pulled it over her head, letting the relief of cooler air caress her. Then her bra fell to the ground and his palms covered her breasts.

They stood there in silence. Blood pumped through her veins until she looked up at him. His eye color was so dark a green it was nearly black, and there was a crystalline edge around each pupil as if she were looking at rare emeralds…a mark of his elven heritage.

Her breasts went heavy, her breath came faster. She reached out and slipped her fingers between buttons of the placket of his shirt, drew her hand up and felt the buttons slip from the holes, felt his light chest hair, the well-formed musculature of his chest. Her gaze dropped and she saw his pulse throbbing in his neck at the collarbone. She leaned forward and licked him there. His whole body tensed as if wound tight…. She smiled—she would love releasing that spring.

She finished opening his shirt, her fingers feathering down his body. His stomach drew in as she reached the top button of his trousers and undid it. A raw sound came from his throat and his hands dropped to her waistband and her jeans and panties were ripped from her. She gasped. She'd forgotten his strength.

Then she was lifted, then falling, landing softly on the thick down comforter covering the down mattress. Her skin was hot, got hotter, and she knew her eyes went blue flame as she watched him undress. He tore off his own clothes. His skin had turned brownish-red all over, a beautiful color. So much more fascinating than her paleness. He stood, looking so magnificent that she whimpered.

She'd had sex before she'd loved Aric—with halflings and even an elf. She'd had sex after him, with humans. Aric had always been her best, the man closest to her heart. The man her body yearned for, the man whose magic entwined with hers. She could barely breathe, the sight and scent of him, the knowledge that they'd soon join, clogging her lungs. Magic bloomed in the air, doubling and redoubling, accentuating all she felt. She licked her lips, lifted her arms, called his name, "Aric."

He shuddered. "No one says my name like you do. Missed. You."

And he was on her and energies enveloped them, flaring green and gold and blue and violet—a rainbow of flashing colors. That didn't prevent her from seeing his narrowed eyes, his rapt expression, as their lower bodies brushed, as he entered her.

For a moment she hung in exquisite pleasure of being with him, only him, as if she'd waited centuries for him to return to her, as if every cell in her body expanded with the delight of him.

They sighed together. Then they climbed high and soared until they burst apart in a million fragments of living flame.

Soft music brushed against her ears and Jenni understood it was layers of wind outside her room, something she couldn't hear herself, but Aric's hand was on her

stomach. He'd slid into sleep, and she was close. She tried
to listen, since she knew the music would be gone when
she woke, she wouldn't be so connected with Aric...the
lingering of magic after sex. As the wind songs lulled her
to sleep she wondered what benefits he received from
her magic.... Someday she would have to ask.

Morning arrived all too soon and it was cold and gray.
Jenni rose from bed reluctantly, lured to the sitting room
by the scent of coffee. Outside the huge arch of the
window was a white blizzard. The weather had been
clear most of this winter, days Jenni thought of as blue
and yellow. Startling blue sky and yellow sunshine.

Obviously that had changed. Just looking at the sideways wind and ragged snowflakes made her cold. She
cradled her hands around a mug of hot and sweet coffee,
heard Aric pad in from the bedroom. "How are we going
to California?"

He grunted and she heard the slosh of liquid from
carafe to mug as she continued to peer out the window,
trying to see the peaks of the ranges she knew were there.
No good. He joined her, wearing a dark green robe, and
grunted again. This time the sound was more disgust
than acknowledgment. "Tree."

"Good thing there's a tree inside here."

"Yeah."

She turned to give him a kiss, saw him streaking his
free hand through his hair.

"What?"

"I need to report in to the Eight."

Jenni choked on a mouthful of coffee, stepped away
from him. When she got her breath back, she said,

"What? On our lovemaking?" All her doubts about him rushed back. His ambition.

His expression turned appalled. "Of course not." He drank deeply. "But the Eight are my employers. I check in with them every morning and evening."

"Ah." They kept a real eye on him, then.

He grimaced. "If one of them is in the same location I am, they prefer that I report in person."

"Huh." She glanced at an antique grandfather clock and blinked. The time was going on 9:00 a.m., later than she'd thought, though there was no way to gauge the hour from the snowstorm out the window. It was lighter than night, that was all. She took another sip. "So you don't have to, uh, check in at any particular time?"

He rolled his shoulders. "They know when I wake, of course…telepathically."

How wonderful. She shifted. The Eight could probably tell when she woke, too. Something she had never considered. She swore inwardly. Great.

"Mental activity," he said. "I informed them a few minutes ago of Leafswirl's call and that there was some new development regarding the shadleeches."

"Uh-huh. How long is the personal report going to take?"

"I believe that the Eight will be eager that we are on our way. We will go to Leafswirl's tree. The royals want her information, so we have permission to visit her."

"Nice," she said, but he was already moving away from her to the bedroom and it occurred to her that he might be going to get dressed. In what? "Do you have rooms here?"

Aric stopped, glanced her way, his lips quirked in an ironic smile. "A room. In the Treefolk section of the Eight's management level. A brownie moved my things into one of the bedroom closets here last night."

Of course Jenni hadn't seen that. She nodded. "Okay." She looked around. "Though I don't know as I'd want this place permanently."

"It's the closest palace to Denver."

"Eight Corp is established in Denver but the Eight don't have homes there?"

"Denver is too crowded. But..."

Her skin prickled with atavistic anticipation. "What?"

Another sidelong glance from him. "There's a mansion at the top of Mystic Circle."

Yes, there was. Sometimes it was heavy with magic, but usually Jenni thought it was empty. Certainly no owner had ever come to their neighborhood meetings or get-togethers.

"Mock Castle. Yes?" Her voice was sharp.

"The Eight are aware of the house. Perhaps they own it."

"Perhaps?"

"They don't tell me everything."

She didn't believe they told him enough.

He drained his mug and stretched his arm to set it on a wooden sideboard. "I think the Eight keep that place as a guesthouse. That it's belonged to them for a long time. Maybe you were even subconsciously guided to Denver and Mystic Circle by the royals." He went into the bedroom and Jenni hurried over to the sideboard and picked up the mug in case it might be too hot or wet enough to damage the wood. But it wasn't. Aric was careful of wood.

His words echoed in her ears, her fingers trembled as she moved the mug to a marble insert. Could she have been "influenced" to settle in Denver after the disaster of the portal battle?

Easily. She'd just kept moving westward. From France to England to Ireland to the eastern part of the United States...traveling, not spending much time anywhere until the sunshine of Denver seemed to bathe her and a piece of land in the city called to her—the Mystic Circle cul-de-sac. Several of the homes had been vacant and she chose the Victorian of golden brick and fanciful round windows.

Mystic Circle hadn't been balanced then. The elemental energies around it had been primarily air and fire, with some earth and a trace of water. She had forced herself into the interdimension for the first time since her family had died. But when she'd stepped out, the house and the land had felt like home. Putting food out for the feral cats had brought her four, and they were good company on a cold winter night, piled on her bed. Yes, a Lightfolk dwarf had visited her asking for a record about the battle. She'd sent him away. Some elf had come for some other reason, and she'd dismissed him, too.

She'd gotten the job with the devs—developers—of online games that had eventually brought her the Fairies and Dragons gig. Staring down at the dark dregs of coffee in Aric's mug, she considered whether that had been of the Lightfolk's doing and figured not.

The Lightfolk and the Eight had left her alone after that. Eventually she opened up to some of her neighbors of Mystic Circle. Her friend Amber, who lived next door, was of gypsy ancestry with a trace of Lightfolk and some sort of odd magic Jenni didn't recognize. They didn't speak of magic. No one really spoke of magic or the mansion, but over the years they'd become a loose community.

For a minute the yearning for home and Chinook was so great an ache that Jenni wrapped her arms around herself. Would she ever see the place again? She didn't kid herself that the new mission wouldn't be hard, standing up to the manipulations of the Lightfolk, the threat of death or worse by the shadleeches or Kondrian or some other Dark one.

The contentment she'd felt the previous autumn seemed like paradise. Though she'd yanked out the thorn of guilt and shame.

Aric walked from the shower and she scanned him for changes. He had the frame and muscularity of an active man. He had scars. He moved differently, more decisively. He chuckled when he found her watching him dress. Flexed a little. She smiled.

He came to her and kissed her soundly, patted her butt with appreciation. "Dear Jindesfarne." He glanced out the window where the blizzard still howled and swirled with snow and ice. "We'll leave when I return. You should repack. It's good that we are together again." Another good kiss and he strolled from the suite.

Maybe having Aric back in her life as a love was worth the vanishing of her old life.

Maybe.

Jenni packed, but Aric didn't return. He sent the dwarf-fem halfling she'd met in the dormitory to lead her back to the oak in the center of the Earth Palace. The woman had chattered cheerfully with Jenni, informing her of the changes she'd helped along...several of the women had left for work outside the palace. Most were acting as liaisons between the Lightfolk and humans. For more money, and, it seemed, more respect. The dwarf halfling herself had been "persuaded" to stay—for more pay and an upgrade in the dorm.

Jenni *did* notice that more Folk smiled and nodded to her as they traversed the corridors. Djinnmen and fems were either nicer—because of her new rank—or surlier, because they were friends of Synicess. Though Jenni wouldn't have thought Synicess had friends, and that was just catty. But Jenni was human and even a little female cattiness in her thoughts felt good.

Surprising Jenni, the halfling hugged her goodbye with a "Thanks for coming. Good to know you."

"Look me up anytime." The offer escaped her without thought, but it was genuine.

"You live in the renowned Mystic Circle. I might do that." She smiled and seemed a lot prettier than Jenni had thought upon their first meeting.

Aric took Jenni's tapestry bag from her, and kissed her now-free hand with a courtly bow. His eyes were serious and his smile lopsided. "And we are off on the mission again."

"To your mother's first."

He hesitated.

"No?" Jenni scowled, crossed her arms and felt the weight of her pack shift on her back, like it was composed of the burdens ahead of her. "You don't have to always wait to tell me bad news. Just spit it out."

He snorted, shook his head. "The Eight are interested in Leafswirl's findings, of course."

Ah, there was a note of anger in his voice. Jenni guessed it was because the Eight were shuttling the Tree-folk down the priority list as usual.

"But?"

"But they want you—and me—to take another look around the area of the Yellowstone bubble event."

Jenni shifted on her feet, stuck a hand under her back-pack and eased it. There were two books about the battle in it. She'd taken them out and left them on the table, but by the time she got back to the pack, they were in it again.

Aric continued, "You haven't been to the location since it happened and they want you to check out the elemental energies…see if the area is still balanced, or if some of the smaller bubbles have lingered." He waved a hand. "Whatever."

"You'd think they—"

His large hand pressed against her mouth. She'd forgotten. All that she'd said since she'd left her room would have been monitored.

"But it's a blizzard out there!"

"Not so much. Just gray and snowing. The blizzard is at the top of the peaks."

"Humph." She worked her shoulders again, said, "All right. How long is this going to take?" She started to turn toward the door they'd gone through the afternoon they'd rescued Rothly, and Aric tugged her back toward the tree.

"I don't know how long it will take. You're the expert," he said mildly. "But I do know the tree closest to the area. We'll go that way."

"All right."

They stepped into the dead tree and the greenhome, through the far side into the space of a tree that Jenni sensed was smaller. The air was colder and laced with the scent of snow. "No dryad here?"

"No."

"Ah."

Aric's fingers rubbed over the back of her hand. Without any words, he knew she wanted to linger here. She only hoped he didn't know why. That was a jolt of shame to mix with her fear.

She was afraid to go outside.

CHAPTER

19

AS SHE HESITATED, ARIC TUGGED HER FROM the greenhome in the tree. She gritted her teeth and moved through her fear, glad she was holding his hand. That helped.

The real world revealed fresh snow and gray sky. The mudpots from which the bubble had arisen were plopping cheerfully. A sniff told her that some Waterfolk had rehydrated it.

"A team of naiads and naiaders had fun the night after the bubble event," he said, smiling. "I saw them when I had to speak with the tourists and smooth things over." Now his smile turned ironic. "I posed as a geologist and Etesian gave me a script to follow." Aric squeezed her fingers. "It went fairly well."

"If that woman who we shocked was there, I'm not surprised." Jenni stopped to kiss him on the cheek. "You're a charmer, you are." She used her old British accent that she'd had when they'd been together before. The past and present of Jenni and Aric were merging, and not too roughly.

"It was a small group, and luckily no human scientists were there to question my simple explanations, though we've been monitoring the rangers and all human communications. They have noticed 'anomalies' in the area and have sent for some experts. Etesian assures us that anything regarding the bubble event is rapidly dispersing."

"And to verify that is why we're here today."

"Yes."

They'd reached the edge of the path, close to where Jenni had gone into the interdimension and the bubble had risen. Neither she nor Aric were strong enough in magic to survive if they stepped off the walk and the earth crumbled beneath them.

She extended her senses to check on the amount and composition of the elemental energies. The area where they stood was almost evenly balanced, with just a trace more of earth energy. A result of her time in the inter-dimension. She didn't know if human scientists could discern or measure a magically balanced area.

She strained to feel any of the smaller bubbles that had been born, but none were in the area. They might have popped or drifted away. She wasn't even sure how many there had been, or how strong they'd been. Too much had been going on. But she figured she'd better be ready for any that occurred during the last event. The Eight would want to use them, too.

The first rustling caught her by surprise, then a whirl

of shadleeches attacked. They were fat on magic. Jenni froze, opening her mouth to scream. Only mewls came from her. Aric whipped out his knife and started swinging. Shadleeches screamed as he cleaved them. They fluttered to his exposed head, hands. One bit his ear.

A whistling cry escaped her.

"Get into the gray mist, Jenni," he ordered.

She chanted in her head. Stopped. She couldn't leave him here.

Go to the interdimension.

"Won't." The word rattled in her throat. And since she wouldn't, she'd better *move*. Teeth scraped her cheek. With a flash of fear and panic she burned it. Sucked in a breath, radiated heat around her. The things dived to avoid her.

One step, two, toward Aric. A shadleech flung itself under his collar, latched on to his throat. Right at Jenni's favorite place. She couldn't *stand* that. She jumped forward, *grabbed* the thing. Slippery, not furry like it looked. Sent a bolt of fire and it fell into flakes.

Aric clamped her to his side, whirled them around like branches whipping in a strong wind, his sword struck again and again. Using her magical senses more than her physical, she aimed, sent lightning from hands to shadleech. Burn!

A minute later Aric and she were alone and panting on the walk. Streaks of blood were on his face, on hers. One of the damn things had nipped at her hand and it ached all the way up to her shoulder.

Most of the shadleeches—twenty? thirty?—were gone. Incinerated by her or dead and vanished somehow. Aric kicked the corpse of one off the walk and sent it flying—right into the mudpots, where it dissolved on contact.

Another touched the ground and disintegrated.

"Appears sulphur isn't good for them," Aric said with satisfaction. He plunged his blade into the ground next to him and it sank to the hilt.

Jenni squeaked.

"Magical knife," he said with a warrior's grin. He pulled it from the earth and it was clean and sparkling.

"Uh-huh." The shakes were coming over her, but that didn't prevent her from digging a handkerchief from her pocket and reaching up to blot the blood from his throat.

"You didn't go into the interdimension." His tone was so even she couldn't tell what he was feeling.

"I don't desert my friends during battle," she said.

His breath hissed in. He turned his back on her. "You mean like I did long ago? I think you should have a different liaison."

"Wait, wait." She stumbled to him, put her arms around him and her cheek against his back. His trench coat smelled of leather and Aric and shadleech. "I didn't mean that as a slam against you." She tightened her hold as his muscles flexed beneath her. "It's just me. I go with my instincts and that's to protect those I…care for. I don't think in battle."

"Not like your brother Stewart, then."

"No. I'm not a trained soldier. Not something I want to be." Though she'd always done better in games than in real life. Crap. Deal with that failure and move on. She was a virtual warrior. Didn't seem much from there carried over to here. Too damn bad. "I don't want anyone else as a liaison."

"Good," said the Earth King, the ancient dwarf, who rose from the ground, sword in hand. He leaned on it. His nostrils widened and he sniffed and clapped his hands, and said a spell. The ground trembled outward in a wave. "Magic enough to muddle any watching humans' senses."

He nodded to Aric and Jenni. "Very good outcome all around."

She wanted to glare at him, but averted her eyes so he couldn't snag her into a trance. Words spewed from her. "This was a setup."

The Earth King's wide lips curved into a rubbery smile that didn't match the granite of his dark eyes. "We wanted you to know that our man Aric can and would protect you."

"You also wanted to see me in action."

A dip of the king's head. "That, also. You did... relatively...well. And your conclusions regarding the elements in this area?"

"This location is balanced." Jenni wanted to close her eyes to study the distance, but didn't dare have less than all her senses alert. "Within about half a mile, in a circular pattern."

"Half dome," the king corrected. "The balancing also affects the earth in a half sphere beneath us."

She should have felt that—had felt that—but hadn't paid attention. She nodded.

"But the air does not hold the same amount of magic."

"No," she said.

"I do not sense any remaining minor bubbles?" the king asked.

"No," she said again.

"All is well, then. We will have one of our halfling scientists assigned to the human team to study the recent changes here."

Neither Jenni nor Aric replied. She wasn't quite sure what her lover was feeling. He'd shut down his emotions. A good thing to do around the Eight. Something she needed to practice sooner than later...if she continued to work with them.

"Thank you, Princess Mistweaver Emberdrake, for your insight." The king turned to Aric and inclined his head. "Well done, Aric."

"Thank you, sire," Aric said.

"Any comments?" asked the dwarf.

Aric said, "The shadleeches weren't Kondrian's. They didn't have his smell—a rather sweetish odor."

"Stale bubblegum," Jenni said and both males stared at her. She lifted her chin. "Well, it's true. He—and his shadleeches—smell like old bubblegum." She sensed that both of them were too proud to ask what bubblegum was and suppressed any hint of a smile.

Aric continued, "The shadleeches were also fat. I believe they were relatively local creatures that were drawn here by the magic of the bubble event."

"Yes," the king said. He glanced idly around the panorama. "No sign of Kondrian. We believe that he has returned to his estate in eastern Europe. Until he heals." He scanned Jenni and Aric. "He will no doubt be well enough to attend the last bubble event, even if he has to decimate his peasants for energy."

Jenni wondered what the dwarf meant by *peasants*. But the Dark one didn't seem like the most modern being, either.

"Best be on your way," the king said. He gestured to the tree they'd exited before. "We'll see you at the ceremony when the bubble arises." He stared at Jenni. "Be sure to notify us immediately if you sense the event occurring in an untimely fashion."

Then he was gone.

Jenni and Aric walked back toward the tree, and she noted their footprints in the snow, wondered what humans would make of those. What would she have thought a couple of weeks ago?

She looked at the skinny pine, the tracks, the walk. Despite most of her life and her time with Aric, she wouldn't have thought of the Lightfolk first. She'd have thought someone went to lean against the tree for a photo.

Eventually the fact that there were Lightfolk would leak. The "meld" of technology and magic would ensure that. So would interacting with humans, but the Eight weren't ready yet. She'd bet Aric's meeting with the humans after the bubble incident had faded from their minds.

At the tree, she turned around, gave Yellowstone a last look. She'd have liked a blue-gold day, but what she had was gray...and the scent of sulphur...the hint of fire energies around them. Once she stepped into the tree she would be away from mountains and headed—in a few steps—to the west coast, California and the Pacific Ocean. She hadn't seen an ocean in fifteen years, but soon the sound of surf would be dominant, not the smell of sulphur. Not the light of days living in Denver, the Queen City of the Plains.

"Let's go," Aric prompted. He tugged at her hand and she wasn't quite sure when he'd taken it, holding hands with him seemed so natural.

They walked into the spruce again and into the greenhome—the sense of interconnected plant beings all around them, throbbing with life in various rhythms. This spruce was younger, its sap faster than a larger pine yards away. The nearby brush was quick. There was the sense that roots knew spring was only a couple of months away.

Aric's arm came around her waist and he urged her into the green-black and they crossed into light—brownish-green light and the squeal of delight hit Jenni's ears.

When her vision sharpened, she saw that they'd entered a large space and the table was dressed for tea and visitors.

"Aric!" cried Leafswirl, and then moved with the grace that gave her her name.

She was much smaller and much greener than Aric. Her hair was the spring green of new needles of the coastal redwood that she lived in. The dryad—appearing younger than her son—hugged him tightly, then stepped back, with a delighted smile. "My son. My one son. You are such a beautiful male."

Aric's skin turned a deeper copper and Leafswirl patted his cheek and spun away. Jenni's gaze followed her and it seemed as if her surroundings exploded into sight. Leafswirl liked pastel floral patterns, and they were everywhere—on the tablecloth and the china set. Even the round walls of the room were papered in pale yellow with pansy clumps. Jenni blinked and blinked again.

"I have tea prepared!" Leafswirl sang.

"I've never known dryads *not* to have tea prepared." Aric glanced at a regulator-style clock. "Early for midmorning tea. Late breakfast?"

"Brunch. I'm sure you can have a little nibble. There are eggs and potatoes." Dryads survived mostly on the nutrients their trees shared with them, with the occasional vegetarian meal. "I have cookies." She gestured and a multitiered tray appeared. There were cucumber sandwiches, maybe the red stuff was even sun-dried tomatoes and—

"Hummus. Cracked pepper," Leafswirl said.

Yes. They were in California. Jenni took a deep breath and it smelled of redwood with a hint of sea spray. The ocean was within forty miles. "Thank you for inviting me into your lovely home, and for tea."

"You're quite welcome." Leafswirl did another spin, this one in place, and Jenni thought the circular room expanded a few feet in circumference.

"I could eat some of your basted eggs and toast," Aric said, putting Jenni's bag out of the way under an occasional table. He sat on a small stool that turned into a chair and enlarged under his muscular butt, opened up a dome that held exactly what he wanted and dished four eggs out onto his plate, emptying the serving dish.

"That sounds wonderful," Jenni said, sliding her

backpack off and stowing it with her tapestry bag. She sat on another stool and became enfolded in a cushy armchair of a dusty blue with pink cabbage roses. Leafswirl giggled and took her own seat, which transformed into a curvy café chair with a pink seat cushion.

Jenni got an English muffin from the toast rack and put it on her plate, lifted the dome where Aric had taken the eggs and there were more, of course.

The three of them spoke of light topics—Leafswirl gave another rundown of Aric's sisters and nieces—and ate. Jenni complimented the tea and food lavishly and often, which dryads seemed to need. Jenni's father had been of the opinion that the Treefolk had come late to hospitality and hostessing and wanted to make up for lost time. At the end of the meal, the utensils and the crumbs on the tablecloth disappeared. The table itself moved to a side of the room, where a china lamp sprouted upon it to give mellow light. Leafswirl put a finger to her lips and gestured to the right and above them. Wooden steps extruded from the wall and spiraled upward.

"My friend Lightleaf is upstairs—sleeping. I want you to see her. She was caught on the edge of the forest when the shadleeches came." For once Leafswirl was serious. She'd never shown her age, Jenni rarely even saw maturity in her eyes.

Leafswirl leaned forward, lowered her voice to a whispering of redwood needles. "She *survived* the shadleeches. And she's not the only one. The last two incursions... the creatures have been stopped!"

"Stopped how?" Aric rumbled.

"That's what I want to show you!"

He stood. "Fine, let's go."

"She's sleeping," Leafswirl warned again.

Nodding, Aric crossed to the stairs that widened for his feet. He gestured to Jenni to come, so she rose and followed him. The stairs didn't creak under their weight, but Jenni was so close to the outer—real?—tree wall that she heard wind soughing outside. As she took each step, she discreetly tried to gauge the elemental magic of the area. A great deal of earth and air, water was good, too, but fire was scarce. Not surprising. Dryads were terrified of fire, and those in California even more. There were few dryads living with humans in the south, but this was now a protected United States national forest.

The second floor was wider than the first, more magical greenhome than tree. A hallway bisected the space, and Jenni figured that at this moment there was a bedroom on each side. If she and Aric stayed, this level would gain more space or— She glanced up. The stairs continued, looking like pegs until they were needed.

Greenhome was endlessly charming.

Leafswirl moved as quietly as an autumn leaf drifting to the ground. Aric's feet weren't quite touching the floor, as if there were a pad of air beneath his soles. He was using his elven air nature. Jenni's footsteps were quiet but she felt as if she clumped along in clogs.

The arched door on the left opened silently at the touch of Leafswirl's fingers. Jenni was glad to see that there was a thick rug of green-gray patterned ferns on the floor. They went over to the four-poster bed and stared down at the girl there. She was shorter than Leafswirl, and more slender, though Aric's mother wasn't voluptuous by any standard. The young dryad's hair was streaked red-brown and green, which seemed natural. Her skin was paler than Jenni thought it should be.

Lightleaf's nose twitched and her mouth puckered before a slight, fearful whimper came from her.

"Shh," Leafswirl comforted, then said softly, "turn over, my dear." Magic filled the air at her quiet command.

Stretching and stirring and moaning a little more, Lightleaf rolled over…and a pattern of a dark green spiderweb stretched from under her hair at her temple to angle slightly across her cheek.

Jenni's breath caught. Holding her eyelids shut on a long blink, she sensed the mark on Lightleaf's face was pure magic…and a magic of balanced elemental energies…and permanent.

Leafswirl stroked the younger dryad's head, then waved Jenni and Aric back.

Aric didn't move. He stared down at Lightleaf with narrowed eyes and considering gaze.

Jenni touched his elbow and his glance shifted toward hers, slid back to the hurt dryad and he gave a little nod. Jenni wanted to clamp her fingers around his elbow and draw him away and that flare of emotion made her feel stupid. He didn't seem interested in Lightleaf as a woman, more like a problem. Jenni had no reason to feel he'd be attracted to the dryad, but an atavistic possessiveness flickered.

When had Jenni come to believe Aric was *hers?* Stupid. Who knew if their relationship would even survive after the last bubble event, even if they lived.

She strode to the door, through it, and circled down

the stairs, inwardly scolding herself. He was his own man, more now than he had ever been when she'd known him before. He had his own goals. He hadn't ever lied to her, hadn't been in love with her as much as she had been with him before. She should remember that, and recall that no matter how much they had changed, he was the Eight's man.

Somehow Leafswirl made it down the stairs before Jenni—had she floated down?—and now sat at a smaller table in the middle of the room, set with another teapot and plates with a variety of cookies.

Jenni needed a cookie.

She sat and held out her cup so Leafswirl could pour.

Then Aric levitated down and Jenni watched the stairs vanish into the wall until they were just a set of ascending knotholes. He came over and took his stool-chair again, selected a chocolate chip cookie and munched, staring past both women.

Jenni, irrationally angry at herself and him and even Leafswirl, took a pecan-shortbread cookie and crunched.

"I like you so much better than that nasty fire djinn-fem, Synicess," Leafswirl said.

Jenni nearly dropped her cookie. She swallowed hard. Aric had jolted and sat stiffly wary. Sipping some tea, Jenni let the liquid sweep crumbs down her throat. "Ah," she murmured. "I'm part djinn, too."

"Yes," Leafswirl said serenely, "but you are mostly human. A native child of our beloved mother Earth."

"Um-hmm," Jenni said, taking another cookie, this one without nuts.

"About Lightleaf..." Aric said, obviously not wanting to touch the topic of Synicess and Jenni.

"You should remember her, Aric, she's only a half century younger than you."

"Yes, ah, well. What happened?"

Leafswirl filled his cup, though he hadn't asked for any tea, topped off her own, lifted the thin china mug to her lips, hiding her smiling mouth but not her twinkling eyes. "Isn't it obvious? I believe that new tracery on her cheek protected her."

CHAPTER

20

"THE SPIDERWEB?" ARIC ASKED.

His mother sipped, nodded. "Yes, that magical design. And the new addition to the forest. Spiders."

"Spiders?" Jenni and Aric said simultaneously.

Leafswirl's eyes got large and her voice hushed. "They are something...different...like the shadleeches, they are not wholly of this world, but are magical, too. But they seem to be *good* while the shadleeches are evil." She lifted her hands and wiggled her shoulders as if trying to produce sensible words. "But they are native to earth magic, like we Treefolk." She glanced around her home. "Not like most of the Lightfolk. And I think they, the spiders, don't last very long. After they weave their webs, they, uh, pop with a teeny sizzle and go away."

Jenni frowned. "What are they living on, then?"

"I think they are living on the teeny tiny bad things."

That made no sense to Jenni. She looked to Aric.

"Pollutants," he said.

"Oh. All to the good, then."

"Yes, we think so...and Lightleaf isn't the only one that this has happened to. Others have survived unharmed... except for that mark. Lightleaf is concerned about the tracery of the web on her skin."

"She shouldn't be," Aric said. "It's very attractive, tell her that." He studied Jenni and the weighing in his eyes had her pausing with a cookie lifted to her mouth.

Her heart gave a huge thump in her chest. "No. Absolutely not."

"It would protect you from the shadleeches."

"Who knows that? It protects *Treefolk* from shadleeches. The spiders or webs or whatever could kill me."

"Any regular humans stumble in and get hurt?" Aric asked his mother.

Her brows knit. "It's not the best time for tourist season. Gray and rainy this year with occasional clear days. Very humid. But...I think so. Let me talk to my friends." She leaned back in her chair and closed her eyes. Within a second her mouth was curving at being linked in mental conversation with other dryads.

Knowing how long they would "talk," Jenni looked at Aric. "*If* this appears to be something I...could survive..." She swallowed and lifted her chin. "I'll only be out in the forest being spider meat if you're with me."

"Done." His smile was wide, his eyes sly. "You'll look hot with a spiderweb tatt."

She rolled her eyes. She didn't think so.

They sat for a while, the sole noises the click of their

teacups on saucers, the pouring of tea and the stirring of sugar into their cups. They liked tea the same way and the small commonality touched Jenni beyond reason.

Aric snared her gaze and said, "We only had that one night in the bedroom in my tree."

"Yes."

A side of his mouth lifted, then he drank his tea. "When I knew you, I wanted to be around your family more than at home in a tree." He drank, set down his cup, rolled his shoulders. "I'd had my tree for over two centuries, but it was…empty." He glanced around the room that was as crammed with stuff—female knick-knacks—as any Jenni had ever seen. "I didn't know how families lived." His voice became cool and precise. "I didn't know how *males* lived in a home. Not until I met your brothers and your father and your family."

"Ah." So her brothers and their easy camaraderie had snared him, then her father's gentle and scholarly and loving and honorable nature.

"So nice," he murmured.

"It was," Jenni said, thought back to her childhood home, the love of her large and rowdy family.

His nostrils widened as he inhaled. "We can stay in my tree tonight." He met her eyes with unusual intensity, then glanced away. "I want you there."

She had to bite her tongue to stop from asking if he'd taken Synicess there. That was before. Jenni had started to resolve so many personal issues over the past week, was shedding the grief and guilt that had lived in her like thorns for so many years. Why did Aric's time with

Synicess bother her so much? Maybe because Jenni was tentatively planning on Aric being in her future.

That didn't mean she needed to know about his past, though, or he needed to know of her other lovers.

Leafswirl stood, nodding to some unknown comments in her mind. Then she stood and spun, dancing like her name...like a leaf on a spring breeze, smiling and humming. When she stopped she had tree needles in her hair.

"Dear children! We have all talked about the spiders and webs and anyone caught in the forests when the shadleeches came."

"And?" Aric prompted.

She settled on her stool and it changed into a different chair than Jenni had seen before—cream-colored upholstery with red poppies, fat arms and a soft, cushioned seat. "The shadleeches *do* feast on humans...suck out what little magic they have. But we think that the humans aren't too harmed and their magic returns over time."

Jenni and Aric stared at Leafswirl.

"Researchers, campers...over the last two years," Leafswirl said. She wriggled a little. "As for halflings...a couple of rangers are halflings and they have more trouble...or did. Sungreen's lover is a ranger—quarter dwarf and quarter elf and half human—who now has a very interesting spiderweb on his butt." Leafswirl grinned. "They had already decided to test the spider theory."

Aric snorted.

"Sungreen didn't tell me where *her* web impression was."

"So the result was..." Jenni said.

"Both Sungreen and her ranger were safe in the forest after being marked by the web. She *did* think she saw a shadleech caught in a spiderweb, but none reached them." Leafswirl poured more tea for herself, looked up with a serious expression. "The shadleeches most like attacking near dawn or twilight, when they can't be seen easily and the magic of the change from night to day, and day to night, occurs. We'd stopped going out then much." She glanced at Aric. "Even the rare Treeman—a dryad's son, like Aric. The horrible creatures aren't good for any of us, not Treefolk or Lightfolk." She trembled. "Then, just a few days ago, the spiders and spiderwebs came from dusk to dawn and..." She frowned, swooped her free hand. "There was an immediate feeling of—of...niceness. Or maybe a return to how the forest felt before shadleeches." A smile came and went on her face. "I don't recall that much."

Dryads were famous for living in the moment.

"Anyway, we noticed right away that everything felt *better*. And there was more magic around, too. As if the shadleeches hadn't fed on the trees—or anything else. Then we noticed the webs—particularly at night—and the spiders, and you know the rest." She sipped just once before she fixed a stare on Aric. "You did it, didn't you? Something you did saved us." Her voice was low and lilting.

Inside Jenni winced. During the Yellowstone bubble event she'd been selfish, concentrating on her desires. Aric had *helped*. He'd thought of his mother and sisters and the Treefolk.

He placed his hand over one of his mother's that rested on the table, looked at Jenni. "We did it." Shaking his head, he nabbed another cookie—a shortbread bar. "I can't believe that it's already paid off."

"What?" asked Leafswirl.

Aric leaned forward and said, "It's the bubble event—"

"No!" Leafswirl threw up her hands. "Too complicated for me. I don't need to know." She sighed and shared a smile between her son and Jenni. "I'm just glad the shadleeches are gone. There will be a great celebration on the spring equinox."

Jenni froze. The equinox. Of course the last bubble event would happen then. The changing of the seasons, the rotation of the Earth. This was all about the Earth and magic rising from the core of the planet.

She stared at Aric. He raised his brows in question. Did that mean he'd already figured the timing out, while the penny had just dropped for her? Probably—the Treefolk were aware of the slant of the sun, as Leafswirl had just demonstrated. Why hadn't Etesian named the date of the event as the spring equinox? Because he would not commit to only *one* day. But the time period he'd quoted bracketed that day. Maybe because when she went to check out the energies near the location she might speed things up or slow them down.

But she would bet everything she had that the last bubble would rise on the spring equinox.

"So you see," Leafswirl was saying, "you can test it yourself if you want. But you both should be able to get a spiderweb for your protection." She wrinkled her nose. "I suppose I'll have to go out sometime and get marked."

"Yes. You must," Aric said. "The girls?" he asked.

Leafswirl nodded. "I just spoke with most of them, and those who weren't connected will hear from the others." Her smile was back. "We will all be having web traceries on our bodies." She tilted her head. "If I must, I must, but I think I would like it on my shoulder...." She sighed. "I will have to find a pretty one to mark me, that's important."

Aric hid his smile with his teacup.

His mother pursed her lips. "It will be the new fashion."

"So, Jenni, where do you want your tatt?" he asked.

"Yes, where, Jenni? What do you think would be a good place?" Leafswirl asked.

"I don't know. Did Sungreen or your friend upstairs say whether the mark had any other effects? Like the shadleech specifically avoided that area in particular?"

Leafswirl looked surprised. "I don't know, and I don't think we talked about that. Hmm. Maybe Sungreen's lover has given that some thought. I think I'll go ask her." The dryad waved her hand. "Be at home."

Jenni got the idea that Leafswirl wanted to consult with her dryad friends more on "fashion" than anything else.

Patting Aric's head and with an absent smile, Leafswirl stepped through the wall and disappeared.

Aric put his cup down, shoved away his plate. "She'll be back, later. I've had about as much tea as I can stand." He stretched and his shoulders popped. "Let's take a walk outside." He took her backpack and bag and shoved them into greenspace. She figured he'd pluck them out later.

Jenni hadn't missed having a window to look out until then. "What of the rain?"

"The fog has burned off and the clouds have cleared," Aric said. He'd know the weather from his magic without seeing it.

The forest was gorgeous, of course. Towering trees with dew on their bark, the ground underfoot thick with fallen needles and leaves from brush and ferns. Jenni inhaled what she could only think of as the scent of primeval *greenness*. All of it seemed to echo Aric, though she knew it was the other way around—everything in Aric resonated of this forest. Even his elven nature whispered of the sighing of the air flowing through the great trees.

Then she began to notice the shadleech depredations. Many of the huge trees showed a shadow where their dryads had been killed. The trees seemed to be grieving. They would survive, but wouldn't thrive as much as if there were a dryad living within them…and there were occasional sobs of dryads inside the remaining trees that twisted Jenni's insides hard.

At these, Aric would step up and place his palms on them, tell them of the hope of the spiderwebs and to contact his mother. There would be the silence of someone listening, then a *pop* Jenni felt inwardly and the dryad would be gone…probably to the dryad meeting place.

"It's wonderful," Jenni said, in a voice pitched lower than she would use with humans. "But sad."

Aric took her fingers, squeezed them. "It will get

better, and the forest will endure. It has managed to survive through the worst of human logging." A ripple passed down his back and Jenni realized that he'd been around to see that—fight that?

"Look." He pointed to where weak sunlight filtered through the trees, catching on tiny threads of a filmy spiderweb disintegrating as they watched. They hurried over just in time to see the whole thing collapse into a few filaments. Aric bent down and poked the small dust-bunny-looking thing and it wrapped around his index finger. He sucked in a sharp breath, lifted his hand as if to fling it away, then set his teeth and drew in noisy breaths for a minute or two as the thing sank into his skin.

"I thought it wasn't supposed to hurt," Jenni said. "It does, doesn't it?"

With a short jerk of his head, Aric answered, "Yesss." There was a hit of whistling air from his throat. "Guess it's because I'm not all Treeman. Wonder if the dryads asked any *males* about this."

Jenni cleared her throat. "There was that dryad's lover."

Now Aric laughed with true humor and Jenni was glad to see that whatever pain he'd experienced was gone. "A guy with a spider tatt on his butt. I don't think he was paying much attention to the web." Aric frowned. "And how did he get something on his butt anyway?"

"I don't think I want to visualize that," Jenni said with a small, prim sniff.

Aric slid a gaze to her and grinned. "But I'll do my best to ensure that you don't feel a—"

Shadleeches struck!

CHAPTER
21

ONE LATCHED ON TO JENNI'S CHEEK BEFORE
she saw it. Sharp teeth bit and she flung up her arms. Too
late. It wrapped its stingraylike wings around her head as
if to smother her. The scent of old bubblegum enveloped
her and she choked. Her magic began to drain. *No!* She
ignited flame inside her, shot it to her head, her cheek,
incinerated the thing. It died with a whimper, and fierce
gladness followed the warmth of her fire throughout
her body.

She used some of the fire energy to force out the pain,
meld the muscle and skin together, she hoped.

She turned to see Aric slashing with a sword in his
right hand, cleaving the evil magical creatures into bits...
that vanished. The infestation wasn't large, about a half
dozen. Then there were three. Aric flung out his hand
with the silver-green tracery of the spiderweb on his

finger. A shadleech tried to back-wing, but Aric's finger pierced it and it screamed and vanished.

Jenni clapped her hands together, focused hard. She could do this, could send controlled fire spearing into one. She'd had enough practice with her magic lately. There! It burnt the shadleech to ashes. Now there was one left and it threw itself at Jenni, but Aric and his sword were before her and the thing was dead.

Panting breaths shook Jenni's chest. Aric appeared imperturbable...so impassive it looked like he might have rooted in the forest. When he raised his feet slowly from the ground, shaking them, Jenni figured she'd been right.

The shadleeches had surprised him, too.

"All we've heard was that they don't like daylight."

"But they've attacked me during the day before, Kon— The great Dark one's shadleeches, those that were created on his estate. I know these were sent by him, they *smell* like him."

Aric stared at her. She looked around for some piece that was left, nothing. Setting her hands on her hips, she scowled. "Not only do they have a geas on them to continue attacking me, but another spell to make sure they disintegrate when defeated."

"I think you're right." Aric inhaled deeply, tilted his head as if cataloging all the scents that came to his nostrils. Well, he'd know this forest. Another deep breath that expanded his very nice chest.

"The Dark one didn't die," Jenni said—she'd been hoping—at the same time that Aric said, "The creature isn't as hurt as I'd believed." Aric's lips tightened.

"Though there are ways for a great Darkfolk to get magic and energy and life force."

By killing others—humans, some of the minor Lightfolk if he could get his hands on them...or his tentacles or whatever he had. Jenni shuddered. She didn't mind imagining such stuff for the game, but real life...no, just no. Too damn sad.

Like her parents and family. The fact that that thought came *second* to the worry of present unknowns actually comforted her. She was placing the event in the past. Never to be forgotten, always to be sore, but not guiding her present. She sent a small mental thanks to God.

Aric was studying his hand. The spiderweb on his finger was now a shiny silverlike scar tissue with a faint outline of dark evergreen.

Jenni smiled. "Interesting look."

His gaze lifted to her. He frowned, strode the two paces forward it took to reach her, touched her cheek. "Faint bite mark here."

She winced. "Really?"

"Yes, but I don't think it will scar." His fingers trailed down her neck, sending tickles of awareness of him as a man deep within her and she reluctantly stepped back.

His eyebrows lifted and dropped. "And I looked...but perhaps I didn't examine you closely enough." He came close to her, bent his head and touched her lips—gently, tenderly. With affection and maybe something more.

Emotions welled within her, yearning for this man's touch, not just sexual, but loving. How long had it been since she'd had loving touches in her life before he'd returned and shaken her from her rut? How foolish of her to have closed herself down, away from loving. She didn't want to think that it was only Aric who could affect her this way. Surely not.

But he was the one lover she'd had who had known her before and after her family's death. That was major.

She put her arms around him and leaned into him for an enveloping hug. He felt good. He felt…almost…like home.

They stood in the quiet of the forest, with birds returning and calling, small creatures rustling around them. The breeze, which had vanished with the shadleech attack, now sang in the treetops far above them.

Aric gave her a last squeeze, then took her hand. "I want to speak with my mother and the other dryads, but it would best if we did that from my place. Will you come home with me?"

"Yes."

He turned to the closest tree, one that appeared to have lost a dryad, bowed and asked permission to use it for travel. Jenni heard no response, but Aric smiled and bowed again and they stepped into it. This time there was no sinking into the greenspace between molecules. The tree was naturally thick enough to hold them both.

"Jenni, the tree is a little cold, can you send warmth through it?" Aric asked softly.

Jenni trembled. A real challenge, to warm the tree with her fire magic without harming it. But it was a beautiful tree. "Absolutely," she said. She disengaged her fingers from Aric's clasp. Maybe he thought she could heat the interior just standing there and expanding her magic and warmth around her—something her mother or sisters had done—but not Jenni, after so many years.

Delicately she placed her hands on the inside of the bark, felt the coolness of the pulp.

The tree grieved, too, for its lost dryad. The magical woman had been with it for a couple of centuries. Jenni matched her emotion to the tree's, sensed the excruciatingly slow pulse of its life. Decreasing her own metabolism to the minimum, she knew she must be very careful. Fire magic moved fast. She dripped a particle or two into the tree, they cycled quickly and the tree seemed to shudder, but to Jenni the coldness of the rainy spring, the deep chill of grief at the loss of its dryad decreased as comforting warmth—even to a tree—spread through it. To Jenni's surprise the small amount she'd given the tree moved quickly through it, then was absorbed by it.

"Just enough," Aric was murmuring when Jenni rose from her trance. He was stroking the inner wall of the tree. "Just warm enough, comfort enough, soothing enough."

Jenni *felt* gratitude from the tree, like a slow drop of honey onto her head, sliding cell by cell into her. This time she bowed. "Thanks to you, too."

Aric encircled her with his arms. "I think it's time to let the dryads know that this tree is prime for another companion." They walked forward, this time into the greenspace that flashed around Jenni in tones of green and redwood, then were in a tree so huge that there was little greenhome space.

He smiled, set an arm around her waist. "My sequoia. It's one of the greatest in circumference in the forest, though I've made sure that it has been magically protected from being discovered by humans since I first moved in."

The floor was redwood-colored "planks," with oriental rugs in a deep blue. The circular walls were a pale sage-green. A bit of white caught Jenni's eye and she looked up to see the blue dome of the sky, complete with clouds.

He left her for a moment as she studied the sky, returned and put a Treefolk-mossy-herbal poultice on her cheek. "It's looking okay, but this should finish off the healing."

"Thanks. Pretty sky."

Aric waved a hand. "Illusion." But his expression was proud.

"Wonderful," Jenni said.

"I have several stories." Another gesture and Jenni saw the pattern of wood knots that would extend into a staircase on the far wall. Aric continued, "But this is my main living space."

The furniture was curved, but looked familiar. The style of frame and cushions was close to what she'd grown up with. The walls were painted with landscape murals of panoramic vistas—a beach, the view of the front range mountains from the high-rise in Denver and a view of the eastern plains from the same building. There was a magical window that looked out on the forest. "Nice," she said.

"Thank you." He led her to a love seat and sat next to her. With a flick of his fingers, a bit of wavy air appeared in front of them, *not* a crystal ball. Jenni looked around and saw a large one tucked in a dim corner nook.

"You do use your air magic for communication."

He hunched a shoulder. "Yes, some."

She patted his hand that lay on her thigh. "Thanks for including me, I know that you can speak to your mother mentally."

"To her, not necessarily to all the other dryads, and I want them linked together for this. I am *not* putting you at risk. Having the spiderweb might help you, but not if it pains you." He flexed his fingers.

"How does it feel now?" Jenni asked.

"Good, a little humming below the surface of my skin, but I sense that will be temporary." He glanced at the large patch of shimmering air. "Mother!" he commanded. He called her three more times, the last using her full name and the name of her tree before she answered.

"Yes, Aric?" She smiled, as if he hadn't been irritated with her.

He held up his marked hand.

"Ooooh!" She cocked her head to study it. "Interesting color, but I don't think it would suit me—"

"Mother! The color wasn't my choice."

"Wasn't it?" She let a pause hang and Jenni thought it was because Leafswirl was reminding Aric of his nature, of what he suppressed or ignored, or...

"I like the pattern, though. You were lucky to find one during the day."

"It hurt, Mother."

"Oh! I'm sorry." Now her expression was that of any mother comforting her child.

"I don't want to put Jenni through the same pain."

"But Jenni accepts both her natures," Leafswirl said.

Aric's teeth snapped together. Jenni leaned forward to catch Leafswirl's eye.

"Leafswirl, do you know *any* halfling who has received the tatt besides the guy who was having sex? Can you check with *everyone?*"

Leafswirl squirmed a bit. "Well, the phenomenon of the spiderwebs seems to be only here on the California coast."

"You have friends everywhere, check and get back to me, please," Aric said.

"I will." Now looking uncomfortable, Leafswirl whisked herself out of sight.

Aric let the molecules of the air communication patch disperse, sighed and leaned back with Jenni. "Let me hold you a bit before I have to get up and report to the Eight about Kondrian's shadleech attack on you."

Jenni kissed his jaw. "All right." She picked up his hand to study the spiderweb marking more closely. "It did protect you. None of them got to you."

"They didn't get past my sword."

"But they like to swarm a person in three dimensions. They didn't get you."

"They were aiming more for you."

Jenni kissed his finger. "Face it, Aric, the spiderweb worked." She touched his cheek so he'd look at her. "*You* caused this benediction for your Treefolk. *You* saved them from the shadleeches."

"So far."

"So far. That's something to be proud of, and something to report to the Eight, too."

He slanted her a considering look. "I asked for help for the Treefolk, Rothly asked for help and he was healed. His arm was straightened and his magic returned."

"Not Mistweaver magic."

"But some unwarped kind. That's how it seemed to me, what about you?"

"Yes."

"Both the guardians might have put a little more power behind all of our wishes—the elf wished for *good,* and it's good that the dryads now have some protection against the shadleeches. It's good that Rothly is healed. The dwarf formed the intention that the creativity of the second bubble be used for the Lightfolk." Aric shrugged. "Who knows how that is manifesting, but the dryads and Treefolk support Earth's natural magic and the Lightfolk, so helping the dryads also helps the Lightfolk, and Rothly is half-Lightfolk." Aric curved a hand around her face. "As you are. What did you wish for, Jenni?"

"Didn't you hear me?"

"No. Everything happened too fast." His jaw flexed. "That's where my natures of air and Treefolk clash. I don't always comprehend events and act quickly. What did you ask for, Jenni?"

Jenni's face heated from embarrassment, not her fire nature.

His turn for his fingers to ask that she would meet his eyes. "Can't you tell me?"

She felt her lips clamp together before she opened

them, stared beyond his shoulder. "It was that little childhood charm."

His eyelids lowered. "I don't know human or halfling childhood charms."

Sighing, she did look into his beautiful green eyes. Now she and he were in his native forest, in his very tree, his eyes seemed to have picked up a shade of hazel, a touch of brown, and made his gaze more intense. She glanced down and saw his web-marked hand. On a huff of breath, she said, "Events and emotions were moving fast for me, too. All I could think of was a little charm we learned as girls. 'Water, earth, air, fire, bring to me my heart's desire.'" Without looking, she could *feel* Aric's slow smile.

"Your heart's desire. What is your heart's desire, Jenni? Jindesfarne Mistweaver Emberdrake?"

The name struck at her, reminding her of all the changes that had occurred in the last week.

Aric's head had lowered close enough that she could feel his breath on her lips. "What do you want most, Jenni?"

"Family..." The word fell from her lips and he shuddered, jerked back.

She blinked sudden tears away. "Oh, I know my old family is dead, but I want family. I want Rothly back as my brother." She wasn't quite ready to say that she wanted Aric as her lover and husband and man—was pretty damn sure that he wasn't ready to hear those words, had no idea how much he might care for her or commit to her and her "heart's desire." She drew in a steadier breath. "I want a loving family, good friends."

Aric nodded, smoothed her hair. "You have me as a good friend. Forever."

That was something, she guessed. When she looked up, his eyes were only that deep, dark green.

"Thank you, and thank you for making me think about what I want." Her smile was wobbly. "I didn't know until you asked. Now I do." She shook her head, felt the mass of her hair gone fuzzy in the humidity. "I only hope the creative energies of the bubble that felt *my* forming intention understood what was inside me."

"Magic seems to do that," Aric said. "As my mother implied with regard to my nature."

Jenni said carefully, "I think that your air and Treefolk natures are more integrated than she believes."

"I hear a *but,*" Aric said.

"But you need to accept your father."

"Right." He rose from the love seat. "We've had this conversation."

"Right."

"Let me show you the rest of my home." This time there was little pride in his voice and Jenni wondered if she'd stolen pleasure from him with the mention of his father. She suppressed a sigh and followed him up to the other stories of his tree.

Just above the living room was a floor with a half-circular small dining room big enough for six and a tiny kitchen. Aric said, "I do most of my cooking in the greenhome."

Jenni wasn't quite sure what that meant, but since the emotions between them had cooled, she didn't ask. Above the dining room was an office. It had modern equipment—two small computers and an all-in-one printer-fax-copier, along with a crystal ball. Jenni was pretty sure that there was no electricity to the tree, but one of the computers showed a screen saver from Fairies and Dragons, and was humming quietly.

His bedroom was a wonder and took Jenni's breath. Here the walls were a pale wood-paneled wainscoting to about the height of her waist, the rest was "open." She wasn't sure how he managed the "windows," whether it was Treefolk magic or Lightfolk, but it was like being in a summer pavilion—up about forty feet. Again the ceiling of the room showed the sky, with graceful rafters rising to a dome, as if there was no rest of the tree above them. Maybe there wasn't, maybe they were anchored somehow in the greenspace.

Slowly, Jenni turned in place. The bed was huge so Aric wouldn't be cramped. It took up a lot of the room, but there was plenty of space around it for the curved built-in drawers and the shining polished counter atop them that ran a third of the room. Then there were a couple of large chairs—recliners!—and a love seat. Once again Jenni wondered if he'd ever brought Synicess here.

Swallowing hard to force the lump in her throat down, Jenni kept her face clear of any doubt of him as she met his eyes. "What a wonderful place."

His stance relaxed and his gaze slid along her. "It is wonderful, Leafswirl saw a picture in a magazine and wanted to try it out on me, first." He waved to the two fluffy comforters, the bottom one in a pale beige, the top in bold colors in an abstract pattern. "Too many pillows, though."

Jenni lowered her lashes, tilted her head, let a smile bloom on her face. "You think so? Maybe I can show you what to do with some of those pillows."

"Yes." The word was rough, and then a nude Aric stood before her, definitely ready for pillow-sport. Gorgeous man. Wide-shouldered, muscular. Thrilling. Jenni melted. Her clothes vanished, too, and he reached for her, covered her breasts with his hands.

Jenni thought no more.

They fell on the bed and rolled and wrestled and played with the pillows and each other, celebrating life.

Aric was snoring softly and she was nearly asleep when the crystal ball pinged with eight notes—two each of earth and water, air and fire. "Your attention, Paramon," the King of Air, Cloudsylph, snapped.

CHAPTER

22

ARIC HAD TAKEN THE CALL FROM KING
Cloudsylph, of course. Since Jenni didn't care to listen
in, she found the amazing bathroom off the bedroom,
this area definitely in greenhome, the inner dimension
that the Treefolk used and moved through and loved. She
spent a long time in the half-round, glassed-in shower
area, letting streams of steamy water hit her from multiple
jets. Long enough that she would have drained her water
heater at home. Then, feeling cleaner and better than
she had in weeks—this place, at least, was not under the
Eight's rule—she dressed and took her pack and wandered down to Aric's office.

The day passed with Aric in consultation with the
Eight and Etesian, and Jenni reviewing and transferring
the old Mistweaver family information to her own new
computer that had been delivered by the Eight Corp fire
sprite. Jenni even managed to squeeze in a telephone call

to the developers of Fairies and Dragons, who reported that the buzz about the short March leprechaun event was great, people were anticipating the roll out in two weeks and making green costumes. From comments on the game's forums, the fan base was enthusiastic about including flying horses in the autumn update. The devs wanted Jenni to write several story arcs for that.

Near dinnertime, Leafswirl popped in and ate steamed vegetables while Jenni and Aric munched on lightly battered chicken fingers with a variety of dipping sauces.

The dryad had a story about a halfling being marked with the spiderweb, a half merfem, half human. The woman had told Leafswirl *personally* that the marking had hurt, but she had cried and cried—using her merfem saltwater nature—on the spiderweb on her wrist and the pain had subsided. Then the shadleeches had come, but avoided her! Leafswirl remarked that the pattern was very pretty and a lovely blue-green color.

Aric's mother had lifted her green eyebrows at Jenni and told her that she was much more tolerant of pain than a wishy-washy merfem halfling. Jenni had nearly choked on that, but set her teeth together, put on a sickly smile and aimed it at Leafswirl.

Aric had covered her free hand with his and said, "We'll be heading out tonight, then, to get Jenni's protection."

Leafswirl had nodded and mentioned that there would be groups of dryads out that night in her area of the forest—south—to brave the webs and do the same. Her friend Lightleaf was now considered a heroine for being the first to experience the spiderweb and had risen from

Leafswirl's extra bedroom to bask in her celebrity. With a flashing smile, Leafswirl warned Aric that *he,* too, was a hero, the Treeman who'd brought this relief from shadleeches to the dryads.

He flinched and Leafswirl vanished in a dancing step through the wall, with a last, lingering comment that everyone was *very* grateful and he'd have lots of visitors in the next week.

"I'll be mobbed, you mean," he called after his mother, and Jenni could sense he was talking to her mentally, too. "But Jenni and I are leaving tomorrow on a mission for the Lightfolk."

Leafswirl popped back in. "You won't be here for the spring equinox?"

Aric rolled his shoulders. "Doesn't look like it." He wasn't meeting his mother's eyes. Evidently he didn't want to tell her of the great Lightfolk ritual, or the bubbles or anything else about the mission.

"Is this dangerous?" Leafswirl demanded.

Then he sighed and shrugged again, shook his head. "Of course it's dangerous."

She flung herself on him and hugged him tight, spun and threw herself into Jenni's arms, squeezing her, too. "Come back, both of you come back…or…or…I'll do *something.*"

Then she was gone again, leaving the scent of her green freshness in the air and the feeling of her—a strong and supple body with a mother's warmth and concern—in Jenni's memory.

Jenni sank down into her chair and Aric cleared the plates and stepped out of the room to some other

greenhome with them. When he returned, he and the
dishes were wet and smelled of another country. Jenni
stood and grasped his biceps, drying him.

Glancing out the window, she saw the sun had left the
forest in the deep shadow of evening.

Aric drew her into his arms and once again they stood,
two together against the problems of their lives.

They left the warm light of his tree for the dimness of
the forest in the dusk and Jenni shivered.

"Wait, I have something for you," Aric said and turned
back to reenter his home, his trench coat flapping.

Jenni stood, rubbing her arms, curling her toes into
her shoes, hesitating to draw fire energy to heat her up.
Aric would sense that and it would make him nervous
for the forest.

Then he was there, draping a coat around her shoulders. It smelled of leather and the finest wool-silk lining.
The bright color caught her eye. A red trench coat!

A noise of delight escaped her and he took the gar-
ment from her shoulders, held it so she could slip her
arms in the delicious heat. The trench fit better than her
old one. She looked up at Aric and caught a tenderness
in his eyes, around his mouth, and her insides softened.
She was going to get in too deep with him again, going
to let him break her heart. She shivered and he folded
the coat around her, belted it.

His smile was full when he stood in front of her, adjusted the lay of her collar and lapels. "This coat really
suits you. You look great."

She slid her hands up to catch his, her heart did a little jump at the contact. "Where did you get it?"

Bending down, he kissed her soft and sweet, withdrew. "I asked Hartha to make it for you. She was glad to oblige." Aric took her hand and started walking. Jenni kept up. "She said your yard was a disgrace."

Jenni winced. Her yard was scruffy. "We must be getting warmer weather in Denver."

"In the sixties," Aric said, just like he'd been following it. "No more snow on the ground, even in the shade. Hartha wondered if she could put in a garden."

Aric's hand tensed slightly in Jenni's. He slanted her a look. "I told her that you like herbs...and roses."

She did, and had never put in an herb garden, had only admired and sniffed her neighbor's roses.

After clearing his throat, Aric studied the narrow path ahead of them. "I told her to go ahead and do what she wanted. As a thank-you, she made the trench coat."

"And I'm blessed thrice, by herbs and roses and the trench coat. Wonderful. Thank you."

He relaxed. "Welcome."

They didn't talk, but walked, the shadows gathering deeper, and Jenni thought of a sunny herb garden in her backyard. Thought of the plants Hartha would put in. Would she try to grow some of the ingredients of the special Mistweaver tea? A couple of the plants didn't do well in zone five, but if anyone could keep them alive with pampering, it would be a brownie.

Then the shadows deepened and Jenni crowded closer to Aric and he put his arm around her waist. "I don't like being afraid of dark shadows."

"The shadleeches would make anyone afraid." The edge to his voice told her he wasn't feeling casual toward the usual dimness of the forest, either. His breath caught and he stopped.

"What?" Jenni asked.

"Look." He pointed and Jenni saw tiny spiders weaving webs between several trees. Her eyesight wasn't that good, but the spiders themselves appeared like sparks when she used a bit of her magic. She realized she'd had all her senses on alert, magical and physical.

"Should we check out the patterns to see if they are beautiful enough?" she asked.

Aric grunted, looked at her. "It's a little cold out, for both of us." He grimaced. "Unless we want our spiderweb tatts on our faces."

"You plan on getting another?" She looked at his hand, the silver of the tatt showed a slight luminescence.

His smile was grim as he flexed his fingers. "Good that it's on my sword hand, but it was shriveled. Maybe I could use another."

"That's not the real reason."

"No," he agreed. "We're in this together." He reached up and sifted his hand through her hair. "I think you should put it up."

She stared at him. "What?"

"I'd like to see a spiderweb tatt on the back of your neck. And, after this is all over, if you couldn't see it, that might be a blessing." Again his fingers twitched.

"You don't think the shadleeches will be around after everything is all over?"

"I don't know, but I've never heard of them breeding."

He stared in front of them and Jenni followed his gaze to see more webs between trees. "I don't think the spiders or webs will hang around after the shadleeches are gone, either."

"You're the Treeman."

"Yes." He lifted their linked hands and kissed her knuckles. "And I want you to be protected—and I don't mind having another mark on my body." He smiled and his teeth were white. "Especially if you continue to pay attention to them during loving."

He'd called it *loving,* but then, he always had with her.

Heat flushed through Jenni. "Uh-huh. But if I get the tatt on my nape, that means I can't put my hair up again, or cut it, either."

"It will be beautiful."

"The tatt will probably be red."

"Probably—maybe some silver like mine—"

"And whatever color human skin makes the tatt," she concluded.

He walked her over to a web, stared at it, shook his head. "No, too high, you'd only get a few wide lines of the pattern."

"So we won't be having sex. Somehow I think we're the exception to the dryad parties tonight."

He rubbed his fingers against her cheek. "I enjoy sharing loving outdoors with you, but at this temperature...I don't want you undressed and vulnerable."

She didn't think he wanted to be in that state, either.

His hand went to the hilt of the long knife he'd strapped to his thigh. "Even though I can handle shadleeches."

Another glance to her. "As you can." He'd always been good at thinking them equals. One of the reasons he was so attractive.

They walked closer to the webs—beautiful, intricate— and oddly enough Jenni *did* begin studying them as patterns that might be marked on her skin forever. "Hmm," she said.

"What?"

She tapped her bicep. "A rather common place to have a tatt, but maybe that's all to the good. I can take off my coat and unravel the seam of my sleeve...."

The spiderwebs gleamed like silver floss. Would the shadleeches see them?

They sure would see Jenni and Aric. She suppressed a shudder. Fighting them twice in one day. And how had the dryads—all the Treefolk all over the world —coped with infestations twice a day? Not to mention the other magical Folk.

Aric replied to her comment about her shoulder. "Pedestrian, and you aren't."

"What about you?" she asked.

He shrugged. "I'll take off my shirt." His smile quirked. "We can keep each other warm."

"You don't mind if I call fire energy?"

"Energy isn't the same as flames. As long as you don't burn anything, I'm fine with your using the elements. You were careful enough this morning. Excellent control."

She nodded. "Thank you again."

He squeezed her hand. "I trust you, Jenni."

He seemed to be waiting, so she responded with the truth. "I trust you, too."

"I know. We've faced the shadleeches and fought them together."

This time she couldn't stop the shiver at the memory of how they'd feasted on her. Her face throbbed where she'd been bitten this morning and she touched it. There was no scar because of her fire magic and Aric's Treefolk poultice.

Her throat went tight. "You think the shadleeches will come tonight."

Again his fingers tightened on hers in reassurance. "We took out some of Kondrian's." Satisfaction laced his tones. "But there are local ones. They love dryad magic."

Jenni thought of the brownies. "Any magic."

"I think they like Treefolk more than Lightfolk. Tree-folk and shadleeches are both born of the Earth."

"Huh. What about exotic taste?"

Aric's smile was quick. "I sure like the taste of fire Lightfolk."

She refrained from saying anything about Synicess. They walked in quiet for a couple of minutes with only the sound of night animals and bird noise around them. There were spiderwebs everywhere, with sparkling spiders busy, then vanishing with a *pop* when their artistry was finished. Jenni studied them closely and the little magical creatures did get bigger as they spun their webs, as if they were eating. She got the idea that when they vanished, it wasn't death, but going to live in the greenspace.

She followed Aric, using her magical senses to see well enough to keep on the path.

He said, "I'm taking us to the edge of the forest, where they like to enter. We'll pick out our spiderwebs there."

"Fine," she said, then stopped.

Aric quirked an eyebrow at her, but she pulled some hair clips from her jeans pocket and arranged her hair in a bun high on her head. He smiled again and stroked her cheek with his marked finger. Jenni's neck felt bare and vulnerable. She wondered how much it would hurt. Not as much as a shadleech bite, not as awful as feeling herself being drained.

A few minutes later, Aric made a low humming noise and pointed to a tiny web that the spider had just abandoned, complete with a couple of dewdrops —already there was enough moisture in the air to gather on such webs. Sure wasn't Colorado. Probably still had frost on the brown grass in the morning.

"That one for you. Gorgeous, lacy, unusual."

Sure didn't look like standard free clip art of spiderwebs that Jenni had found when she'd surfed the Net on Aric's computer earlier. Denser, more delicate. If she had to have a pattern… Stiffly she let Aric turn her around so he could guide her backward into the web.

His fingers slipped around her neck, gathered a few tendrils of her hair that he stuck under a clip deftly enough that no more strands fell.

Jenni braced herself.

"You need to dip your knees a little, walk backward no

more than three steps." His brows came down. "Should wrap right around the back of your neck perfectly."

"Urgh," said Jenni.

He pressed on her shoulders until she was about the right height. She bit her bottom lip and he tapped it. "Don't do that, you don't want to bite through it."

"No." She sucked in a breath, thought about breathing through pain and took three steps back.

Fire! Ice! Acid! Jenni's scream got trapped, her eyes watered. Aric jerked her close and held her. She writhed, not in a good way. One breath in, and, "Uh, uh, uh!" Her knees went out as the fire raced up and down the lines of the web searing her skin. She didn't fall because Aric's arms were wrapped around her.

"Use your *magic!*"

More fire on her skin? She didn't think—

He shook her and her head went back on her neck and she cried out. *"Use your magic!"*

She summoned it, hot, hotter, hottest. Maybe hotter than that which ate her skin. Pushed it out, along the tracery she *felt* on her neck.

Relief. She turned her head against Aric's solid chest and wiped her tears away. Then she just trembled in his more relaxed grip, gulping air. Glad she hadn't peed herself.

"Shh, shh," Aric soothed.

More than a minute passed before she felt she could stand on her own two feet. The real pain had subsided, but left a stinging. She could deal with it.

"Let's take a look," Aric said.

Jenni's breath broke on a cracked laugh. "Not like you

to be impatient." Now that his arms weren't clamped around her, she dug into her left jeans pocket for a nice large handkerchief and wiped her eyes, blew her slightly runny nose.

He let her stand by herself, cupped his hands and a greenish-gold ball of light pulsed into being. "Turn around, lovey, let me look at the pretty tatt."

Jenni grunted, but did as he said. "Don't touch it."

"I won't."

"I think it would have been less painful with damn needles."

"Mmm-hmm. Very beautiful. Tiny lines of silver outlined in red." He kissed it, but instead of feeling more hurt, the touch of his lips brought balm. He'd put his mouth on the complicated center of the tatt and ease radiated out along the previously aching lines.

"It doesn't hurt anymore! You helped. Thanks!"

When she turned back, his eyes were dark and serious. "Kisses can be magic. I wondered if one might help, backed by intent...." He paused. "I plan to always help."

That had her shifting feet, scuffing the thick bed of needles.

"Your turn," he said lightly.

"What?"

He jutted his chin to several webs strung between trees and began unbuttoning his shirt. "Find a pattern you like for me."

The odd tension of increased intimacy settled on Jenni. Yes, they were doing this together, and the more adversity they faced as a couple, the more they bonded. *Was*

Aric her heart's desire, or a part of it? Was she being stupid again to fall in love with him? Would he do the same?

She walked away in a hurry, scanning the trees. Now that she'd survived the tatt, she'd use a bit of her magical energy for a lightball. When she called her glow globe into being it was yellow-orange and much brighter than Aric's had been. Of course, she used fire energy, not plant energy, and the basis of Treefolk light was the luminescence of mosses and mushrooms and the like.

"Pretty light," Aric said shortly, and she knew he'd tensed, too. He wasn't looking forward to being marked again, either.

"You don't have to do this. Certainly not for me."

"Yes, I do."

She didn't know whether he was answering one or both of her statements, but she knew from his attitude that she wouldn't move him.

"All right." She could feel the creeping edge of exhaustion, but if he wanted a partner, she wouldn't disappoint.

Scanning the webs and the trees, she looked for a small spiderweb. An image of one about three inches large by Aric's shoulder and under his collarbone had come to her as pleasing. She spotted one. Simple, a few lines, and wisps. "There." She pointed.

His face changed and she wasn't quick enough to read his expression. "Not this one?" He flicked a hand at a huge drape that would cover his chest.

"I wouldn't put you through the pain of that!"

"No?"

"Ar–ic."

"I'm just wondering how you feel about me."

"I care. And the wondering's mutual. I wonder how you feel about me," Jenni said, heart thumping hard.

CHAPTER
23

ARIC ANSWERED, "I CARE, TOO. MORE THAN
I should."

That eased Jenni's emotions a little—at least about
their relationship. "And I'm sure I don't want to talk
about this. Particularly not now in a deep and gloomy
forest at night."

"You're sure you don't want the big spiderweb to mark
me?" But his gaze was examining the smaller web she'd
chosen, his pecs flexing as if already feeling the sting.

"If the big one would protect you better, then maybe.
But we don't know that, do we?"

"We know very damn little."

"More than we do," said a new voice.

Jenni didn't jump, and neither did Aric, as the guardians
walked into the small clearing. Now that she thought on
it, she'd sensed the potent magic of the two guardians.

Aric bowed. "Greetings."

The dwarf snorted. "You don't have to be courteous. You don't want us here."

"Not much," Aric admitted coolly. "But you're here for a reason?"

"Yes. The Eight heard of this protection for the dryads against the shadleeches."

"I told them myself," Aric said. He glanced around. "Did they send you to check it out?"

"Not quite." The dwarf's laugh was the low rumble of settling rock.

The elf bowed to Jenni. "Princess Mistweaver Emberdrake."

She inclined her torso. These two were completely out of the status game, beyond noble rank. "Greetings."

"The Eight didn't 'quite' send you here?" Aric pushed the question.

"We go as we please," the elf said.

Jenni didn't completely believe that. She figured that what spurred these two were responsibility and curiosity. Good qualities in guardians.

The dwarf went over to a low stump and sat. "Though they do believe halflings tell the truth most of the time, and they've seen your skill…" he nodded to Jenni, then looked at Aric "…and should know your magics, Paramon, the Eight sometimes don't appreciate how important information from and about halflings can be."

"We do," the elf said. He made a casual gesture. "They are wrapped up in discussions of the ritual for the bubble event, what they want to do with the energies, how they

want to shape the creativity." He smiled and stopped
Jenni's breath at the beauty of the expression.

"Politics, maneuvering," the dwarf grunted. He looked
around, pulled a face. "Pretty forest but the trees are too
big."

"Thank you," Aric said.

The elf waved and a good-looking staff appeared in his
hands. Jenni thought that it might have even been part of
the forest around them, but now appeared polished and
just the right size for him. Of course. This was a being
who had more magic than any she'd ever met—including
Kondrian. Despite the guardian elf's charming ways, she
should remember that.

"We are interested in this shadleech protection."

"We are interested in any armor against any Dark,"
the dwarf said. "Tell us all about it."

So Aric did and when he was done, the guardians
scrutinized his thumb and the back of Jenni's neck and
stared at the spiderwebs around them.

"No idea what the effect of such web-etchings have
on Lightfolk, huh?" asked the dwarf.

"Leafswirl didn't mention any full Lightfolk who have
been marked and tempted shadleeches," Aric said.

"Why are we always the first to try something new?"
the dwarf said.

"Because we are." The elf went up to a web. "I think
this tiny one would suit you." He cut the web with
such skill that it suspended from his blade in a complete
pattern.

"Huh." The dwarf stripped off a couple of layers of

armor and shirts. He looked at Aric. "Were you going to do this, or not?"

"I am." Aric smiled. "It hurts."

"You said that. Both of you." The dwarf bobbed his head at Jenni. "And it's a pretty forest with too-big trees and close to the damp ocean in *March*. I'm cold. Let's do it." He glanced up at his companion. "And why am I always the one of the two of us who goes first?"

"Because you're tougher."

"Huh."

"And I have a bit of healing."

"Jenni?" Aric called her attention back to him. His smile was easy, now. He trusted these two.

Well, with all they'd done for her, she trusted them, too. She only wished they'd arrived before she'd had to back into the web herself. She turned to the web she'd chosen for Aric. It had lost a little definition in the middle, but was still beautiful. Linking arms with him, and bringing the lightball closer, she said, "I think we can angle you just so." She positioned him so that the web would hit the top of his pec under his collarbone, near his shoulder.

"Ready?" she asked.

"Yes," Aric said. His chest rippled.

"Try not to tense." Though she knew that was easier said than done.

The elf brought the dangling web toward the dwarf's hairy shoulder. "Ready?"

"Right. Lay it on me."

There was a sizzle and a yelp. Dwarven curses.

Aric turned to look at the two and Jenni gave him a

little push into his web. His cry of surprise turned into pain and heavy breathing. As soon as she saw the thin silvery lines sink into his skin and leave equally silvery scars, she placed her lips on the design and kissed him.

He sighed, put his hands on her shoulders. "Thank you." He closed his eyes and his magic rose and traces of blue-green outlined the delicate silver.

"You aren't doing that to me," the dwarf said to the elf. He shifted from foot to foot, not quite hopping.

"Summon your own magic to deal with it, then," the elf said. Then he clapped a hand over his friend's shoulder and the dwarf shouted—but cut off his yell with a huffing sigh.

"All right. I'm good." His lips curled as he slanted the elf a glance. "Your turn, and I think you should have a nice line down your manly torso."

"What?" the elf asked.

"A pattern down your side. Strip." Stalking away, the dwarf plucked a long web from a branch, whisked it around once so that it doubled and redoubled into a few inches wide.

"Ouch," Aric said and Jenni kissed his shoulder again. He smiled. "Thanks, but that's not what I meant." He nodded to the elf, who stood bare-chested.

"They're good companions," she said.

"Partners, but not lovers."

"No. But such friendship is rare."

There came a long, hissing sound and the air around Jenni's ear shuddered with oaths beyond her hearing.

"Kiss me again, Jenni," Aric said.

She looked up at him and his gaze was quiet, his lips

tender, and she knew she'd fallen in love with him. Again. Perhaps had always loved him since her brothers had brought him home and she'd seen him that first evening. Stupid. But she kissed him again.

She sank into the kiss, quietly inhaled his scent that matched the forest, but had an extra little spice that she recognized as his elven nature. His lips were soft and when she opened her mouth and his tongue touched hers, all of her inflamed.

The kiss lasted an eternity of seconds and she thought she saw magic bloom in the darkness of the forest.

Aric broke their embrace. His smile was lopsided and his hand slid from her shoulder to link with her fingers. He turned and they looked at the guardians. The elf and dwarf were studiously watching a white, sparkling spider ·spin its web and vanish.

"Maybe you should tell your mother about the kiss thing," Jenni said, trying for lightness.

She saw Aric shift into mental-communication mode, then grin. "She—they—all the dryads know."

Jenni frowned. "I bet we didn't get the full story on that butt tatt."

"Nope," Aric said as he donned his shirts.

The elf glanced over his shoulder at them. "This forest is well-protected." Jenni couldn't see his eyes, but his manner was measuring as he looked at Aric, then his lips curved in a slow smile again, and Jenni was glad it wasn't aimed at her. "But then, you, Aric Paramon, Treeman, asked for help for the dryads, your mother and this forest, didn't you?"

"Yes," Aric said.

"And you got it," the dwarf said. "Looks like a good job."

The elf chuckled, patted his companion on the shoulder that didn't carry the tatt. They were both clothed again and Jenni was trying to forget how well they looked without their armor and shirts. Not as good as Aric, but really good.

"And we aren't as fussed about the next bubble event 'cause we've already participated in one," the dwarf pointed out. This time he made a full bow. "Thanks to you. And we are grateful for that and won't forget it." He touched the line of a broken web and didn't flinch, Jenni couldn't tell if he felt pain at it or not. "If our wishes are fulfilled like yours, we will be well pleased."

The elf cocked a brow at Aric. "Though we made sure to phrase our intentions as generally as possible. It didn't take very long for the sweep of magic from the Yellowstone bubble to make it here."

Aric didn't move beside her, but Jenni sensed his discomfort. His chin jutted. "The dryads need help. Some of the drain in magic and power you Lightfolk have felt over the centuries was because of what was done to the Treefolk and the forests."

"Can't argue that," the dwarf said. He'd found a faint track and started walking.

The elf made a sweeping gesture to them to fall in behind the dwarf. Aric tugged on her hand and she reluctantly went with him. "Where—"

"To the most open area to the outside. Now we wait," he said.

"We wait," Jenni repeated as dread curled inside her.

"For the shadleeches." Aric loosened his long knife in its sheath. Neither the dwarf who'd become a barely visible moving shadow ahead of them, nor the elf behind them, made any noise, so it was as if they were alone again. There was no more smile from Aric. His lips had firmed. "I want to make sure you're protected. We all do."

"And there's only one way to find out," Jenni said.

"Yes."

She wanted to cling harder to his hand. Her own palm had gone sweaty, but she kept her fingers loose. "I will point out that you now have two tatts."

His smile showed briefly. "As I said before—if you want another…"

"No, thanks!"

"All right, then." He dropped her hand to touch her nape and it tingled. She knew she'd always be extra sensitive there. Not something that had occurred to her earlier. Was the back of her neck an erogenous zone? She thought so. It was now, anyway.

Had Aric wanted her tatt to be on an erogenous zone? She should have thought of *that* before, too, and figured out somewhere she could have asked him to do the same. But he was soft inside for her, she could tell. Because she didn't want him to hurt from a big spiderweb. Fierce and protective on the outside. From the little she knew of warriors, that was the best kind.

Soon they reached the edge of the forest and the moonlight illuminated more paths that appeared to be human-made instead of by wildlife or the dryads. Jenni let her lightball fade.

The dwarf settled in the low crook of a tree, leaning rather than standing. The elf chose another tree, half in shadow, half in moonlight, and seemed to disappear. She was the odd one out in this little adventure, with no forest craft or background. City girl.

Aric reached into his coat and pulled out a dark tarp that he spread between the wide roots of a tree, dropped down onto it and drew Jenni after him. She shouldn't have been surprised at the cover's softness, but she was. He leaned back against the tree and spread his legs so she could sit and spoon against him. Lovely.

After a minute, the dwarf said, "Shadleeches." Jenni thought she heard him spit. "It goes against grain for me to stand here and wait for an attack," the dwarf said through gritted teeth, as if every word were a curse.

The elf sighed. "It's not going to be one of those waits, is it? The kind where you talk my ear off?"

The dwarf said something in dwarvish that sounded derogatory.

Aric said, "I don't think the shadleeches will be put off by our talk. Likely, they'd hone in on us as food."

"My thought, too," the dwarf said sourly.

"An elf, a dwarf, a Treeman and a half human, half Lightfolk. A banquet of tastes for the discriminating shadleech," the elf said.

Jenni muffled a snort.

"What?" asked the elf.

"It just sounded like the beginning of a joke—an elf, a dwarf and a Treeman walk into a bar..."

The dwarf groaned. "Please, don't encourage him.

He has thousands of those jokes, and he accuses *me* of nonstop talking."

"Jokes, songs..." the elf mused. "Reminds me that I saw your father, Aric, and he sends his greetings."

Suddenly Aric wasn't so nice to rest against. Every muscle behind her tensed. "You can give mine back to him."

The next silence was weighted as if the elf or dwarf intended to say something. Jenni could almost feel the mental communication between them. Finally, the elf said, "You are a man a father should be proud of."

Aric grunted and no one said anything else.

Soon the animals they'd disrupted with their talking began to move around again and Aric eventually relaxed behind her. Tension crept through Jenni, tightening her nerves. Waiting in the forest for shadleeches to attack was one of the worst things she'd ever done.

She didn't know what the others were doing, but all of her magical senses were extended to the fullest. She wouldn't be able to keep that up long, but a twitchy feeling on her neck warned her that the shadleeches were coming. She shifted time and again, and Aric closed his arms around her.

I've got you, you're safe, he sent her mentally.

He wasn't even on his feet! Though his sword was right beside her.

Are your tatts tingling?

He stiffened a little, then raised his hand with the spider mark on his index finger. The silver tracery had darkened until it was black.

Lean forward, Aric said in her mind.

She complied. *Early warning system?* Jenni asked.

Looks like, Aric agreed. *Your spiderweb is no longer silver and red, but black against your skin.* For an instant he brought her close, held her. Then lifted her and set her on her feet, rose himself.

The new mark on my shoulder is itching, the dwarf said matter-of-factly, using whispery mind-speak, too.

Mine feels like a breeze is brushing it, the elf said.

Both Jenni's and my tatts have turned black, Aric said.

The dwarf and elf released identical grunts. There was a sense of slight movement as if they readied themselves to fight. Jenni drew her coat close, buttoned and belted it, wrapped her arms around herself. She should turn her back to the entrance, prominently display her tatt protection, but she couldn't stop herself from watching.

Shadleeches zoomed through the trees low and black and nearly unseen.

The first few hit the spiderwebs. Instead of bulleting through, the web blanketed them and they fell to the ground with an awful shrieking that died as they did. Those behind the first wave flew straight for them.

The elf stepped into their path. They dived for him, but couldn't quite connect. As soon as they were close, they slid away.

With his sword raised, the dwarf joined the elf. The shadleeches swarmed him, too, hit him, then fell to the ground, twitched and died...at least those the dwarf didn't stab first.

Much as she really, really didn't want to, she walked into a flurry of shadleeches. They stunk of caves and dead things. They grazed her. One or two tried to bite, then were deflected, whimpered and flapped away from her unevenly as if hurt...to turn around and try again.

Aric stood stoically as they rushed him, circled, couldn't even get as close to him as the elf, and they squeaked distress, abandoned him for the others.

"Now!" ordered the dwarf.

Blades gleamed in the moonlight, flashed, struck. One shadleech escaped and shot toward the path to the open, got caught in another spiderweb and died.

"All done," the elf said cheerfully. His sword was clean and back in its sheath. He rubbed his hands. "And well done. These spiderweb marks *do* protect." He rubbed his side. "Though I don't think they shield the Lightfolk as well as Treefolk."

"An' I don't think any of the Eight will put themselves through the process and be marked and shielded. They'll rely on their magic," said the dwarf.

More fools, they, Aric muttered mentally and privately to Jenni.

The guardians looked at them sharply and Jenni deduced they could hear any mental communication.

"But maybe the rest of the major and minor Lightfolk will be smart," the dwarf said. "The minor Folk, especially—brownies, naiads and naiaders, air sprites—"

"Not air sprites, they aren't plagued by the shadleeches," the elf said. "Air sprites can outfly them or just translocate, and fire sprites can burn the shadleeches up." His teeth gleamed in the moonlight. "Shadleeches don't like fire sprites."

Rubbing his short beard, the dwarf said, "Not sure how long the shadleeches will be around."

"Maybe they won't last." The elf touched his side. "But I've got a feeling my spiderweb mark is permanent."

"The shadleeches have done too much damage already," Aric said. "Any more was unacceptable."

"So you sent the bubble creative force to change that," the elf said softly, and nodded. Then he shifted his blue gaze to the forest floor, toed a streak of black that was shadleech remnant. "Appears like it worked."

"Thank God," Jenni said. "The forest and dryads needed it." She looked at the elf, a master of communication. "How widespread are the spiders and webs?"

"Here, mostly, but I'll wager they will be global soon. Traveling west to east." His gaze landed on each of them for a considering moment. "Four natures. Four different results. But all protected."

"I'm gonna have bruises," the dwarf said.

"I don't think so," the elf said. He nodded to Jenni and Aric. "We've learned what we came for."

"Had a little fight," the dwarf added, putting his weapons back. "Too short, though. Not much challenge, either."

"Fine by me," Jenni said. She'd had nothing to defend herself with except her power.

"You need a knife," the elf and the dwarf said at the same time, and two blades appeared in two hands. Neither of the knives looked like they were the ones the guardians carried, but surely the weapons were from their private arsenals. Jenni was touched.

"Take 'em both," the dwarf said. He was smiling and it looked odd.

"Thank you." She did.

The dwarf ducked his head. "'Til later." He vanished. The elf smiled and disappeared, too.

"Well." Jenni was left with Aric standing silently beside her and well-balanced knife hilts filling her hands. One was lumpy with what she thought were jewels, but still provided a good grip, the other felt as if it was wire wrapped around leather. "Well," she said again.

Aric swung her up in his arms, nuzzled her neck. "Yes. Very well. A good night's work. Now let's go to bed."

CHAPTER
24

THEY HAD BREAKFAST WITH LEAFSWIRL, WHO glowed with satisfaction and sported no spiderweb tatt that Jenni could see. She didn't doubt that the dryad had a beautiful one. After the meal Leafswirl kissed her son and Jenni, sang a little blessing and disappeared.

Aric readied his pack, then they stepped out of the tree to a wet and rainy morning. They walked through the cold and dripping redwood forest. Now and then they'd take a shortcut a few miles by moving through one tree to another farther up the coast. Jenni had a hard time keeping track of their location, but she had complete faith Aric knew where they were going.

Midmorning they came to the end of their journey and exited a pine sitting in a deep crevice between rugged hills on the coastline. There was some scruffy vegetation, and a thin strip of beach.

"Like I said, the lost coast of California, no close

roads," Aric said. "Diamantina's home is up there." He gestured to blocks of red-brown stone atop the rock cliff.

It took Jenni a moment of blinking to see the shape of the house, it blended in so well. She frowned. "A merfem living in a stone house?"

"I think her main dwelling is under the sea. There are several passageways from the house to the ocean."

Jenni's frown deepened. "She lives under the ocean so close to tectonic plate activity?" She stared up at the house again, shook her head.

"Denver, too, has had earthquakes."

"Yeah, yeah. But not since I've been there." She flipped a hand. "No accounting for taste. Stone."

"She is a merfem of the sea, they don't tend to trust wood," Aric said drily. "They think of the waterlogged timbers of old wrecks in the oceans."

"Huh." Jenni couldn't help it, she slipped her arm in his. "Brick houses are nice, but wood..." She sighed. "Wood is the best."

He smiled.

"Diamantina doesn't sound like a mer name," Jenni said.

Aric shrugged. "She probably changed it a long time ago, I think she might be distantly related to the King and Queen of Water, the Greendepths."

"Oh."

"Diamantina is an oceanic trench off of India."

Jenni frowned. "I don't think I knew that." But Diamantina sounded hard and Jenni pictured a thin and whiplike merfem.

Aric swept his arm toward the ocean. "Etesian, the elf scholar, thinks the bubble will rise from under the sea floor."

They both looked at the gray waves with white crests. Jenni moved her shoulders. "I want to check for it, but I'm...wary. I did that at Yellowstone and it was rising."

"If it was already rising from the mantle, then you didn't speed it up. It would have happened at that time whether we were there or not," Aric said.

The words sounded as if he'd repeated them often. She leaned a little into him. "Thank you."

"I wasn't the only one to point that out." His hand came up to slip under her hair and trace a pattern on her neck that she didn't think matched the spiderweb. When he spoke again, his voice was rough. "I wish we could have spent more time at my home, but the Eight are nervous and want us here, though everyone's sure the last bubble event will be on the spring equinox in three weeks."

Her own throat was thick. "I don't blame them for wanting us here." Echoes of the time when she wasn't where she should have been flashed through her. That would never happen again. She cleared her throat. "Did they give us any instructions in case the bubble rises before—"

Aric shrugged. "Yes. I have a sheet of a spell they'd like us to memorize, just in case."

"Oh."

He turned to face her, pulled her so they were body-to-body. You'd think they would have had enough of each other in the past couple of days, but Jenni could feel her passion rising. He didn't kiss her. "I had hoped for a few days with you with no distractions."

"On a mission for the Lightfolk?"

Huffing a breath, he rubbed his face against her hair. "All right, a delusion." His arms tightened so that she could barely breathe. "But you aren't anymore, Jenni. A delusion, illusion. What we have isn't."

"No." The nearby surf wasn't louder than her heartbeat.

"Ahem."

They both jerked. Jenni looked toward the sound, saw a merfem walking out of thrashing waves. Unlike the Water Queen, she was plump, not voluptuous, using fat for extra insulation in the water. She was "dressed" in a few strategically arranged fronds of seaweed. Her face was heart-shaped and pretty rather than stunning, though Jenni was careful not to meet the woman's beautiful turquoise eyes. Her skin tone was that of an Indian Sea merfem of high status, green-gold.

She beamed and her fluting, musical voice cut through the sound of the crashing ocean. "Welcome! I am Diamantina. You must be those sent by the Eight. I received a message that two would arrive." Her gaze lingered on Aric, then she winked at Jenni and smiled, gestured to the house on the steep hillside. "We can have coffee and speak of what you need from me. Would you like a pastry or two? I have chocolate croissants."

Jenni's mouth watered and she heard Aric gulp. He bowed. Unlike Jenni, he could look the fem in her eyes and did. He showed exactly the amount of appreciation that was proper. Since Jenni was brought up in the

Lightfolk world and her mother had been much the same shape, she understood that the woman was very attractive to other mers...and Lightfolk in general. She felt too skinny. "Thank you, that sounds wonderful."

"I'll meet you at my house." The woman ran fluidly to the ocean and dove in, vanished under the waves.

"Do you know Diamantina?"

"I haven't met every noble in the States." He began to lope up the trace of a path to the top of the ridge. Jenni drew a little air energy to her to make her weight a little lighter and her mass easier to move.

The house was unexpectedly charming, reminding Jenni of juxtaposed children's building blocks. It couldn't have been constructed too long ago, thirty years at the most. The front door had copper panels faded to green. On each side of the door were long rectangles of stained glass of blues and greens showing stylized waves or undersea plant life.

Aric swore as he touched the doorknob and an arc of electricity jumped from the brass to his hand. "Damn mer security." He scowled, then glanced at Jenni. "That could have hurt you."

"Electricity, fire? Maybe. Depends on the jolt. Certainly could have hurt a human who tried the door." She shook her head. "Not wise."

"Don't touch..." Diamantina called out, then the door whisked open to show a contrite face. "I am *so* sorry." She grimaced. "We are so isolated and more often in the underwater home..." She sniffed, seemed to scent the slight whiff of seared wood that had risen from Aric's skin. "*So* sorry," she repeated. The merfem stepped back and flung the door wide, showing the entryway floored in large, colorful tiles with a definite Indian influence. The walls were sponge painted in shades of turquoise, mimicking water patterns. Skylights over the entryway made the atrium cheerful, though Jenni found the temperature cooler than a human home.

They walked past a large fountain that took up half a wall as a divider between the entryway and the great room. The living room had a wall of glass facing west, looking out onto the ocean. Again the theme was shades of turquoise and pale green with accent pillows and one fat tapestry chair of deep gold. Jenni headed straight for that chair. Aric settled in a pale green one of watery damask next to it. The merfem gracefully sank into a love seat close to them. She folded her hands on her lap and leaned forward with concern on her face. "Tell me how I can help."

At that moment a clipping sound of footsteps came, along with a jingle. A smaller, thinner minor Waterfolk naiad appeared with a tray holding a celadon china coffee set and a platter of croissants. Her skin was a deeper green with a tint of gray, her eyes more protuberant.

The rich scent of prime roast coffee wafted through the room, making Jenni's mouth water. Her throat clenched as she yearned for the taste after all the endless tea of the dryads. The naiad placed the tray on the coffee table between them. "My companion," Diamantina said and picked up the platter. The naiad, in her jingling sandals, walked away. "Please, stay," the merfem said.

"Rather not," the naiad said as she turned a dimmer corner into the house.

Diamantina sighed, then chuckled. "Courtesy is not as valued by the younger generations as it was." She took a croissant and bit into it, passed the plate to Aric, who poured some coffee for Jenni and handed her a cup and saucer, then a chocolate croissant. That left four croissants for him. He ate two in a few bites. Diamantina smiled at Jenni and winked again. She patted her mouth delicately with a napkin and leaned forward. "How can I help you?"

Aric swallowed and cleared his throat. "I don't know if you have heard of 'bubble events.'"

For a moment the fem appeared confused, then her brows dipped and she said, "I think I did..." She dimpled. "Centuries ago."

Jenni had bitten into her croissant. The powdered sugar on top mixed with the flaky pastry and the chocolate—which must have come straight from Mexico—exploded in her mouth, delighting her. Incredible. "Wonderful croissants." She sipped some coffee. The drink had definitely been brewed from prime roast beans. "Fabulous coffee. Thank you."

After the next croissant disappeared into Aric, he added his thanks. "A bubble event is upon us," he said.

Jenni decided to cut to the chase. "The Eight believe that the last bubble of this series will rise and burst near here."

Diamantina sighed. "Plate tectonics. It's been a fascination of mine, and interesting to watch, but there's no denying that it can be dangerous living in the area." She sounded as if she'd moved in a year ago, not going on two centuries. Her eyes sharpened. "The *last?* Don't they come in series?"

"Yes," Aric said.

"I haven't heard anything of previous ones in the series."

"Ah." Aric had his impassive face on that showed he was uncomfortable under it. How often had he confronted Folk on behalf of the Eight? "Such magical events are a release of creative force into the world. The result of the first, two years ago, was the shadleeches."

Diamantina paled. "Filthy things."

"Yes. They originated in the area of the Darkfolk. The second bubble burst not too long ago in Yellowstone, Wyoming. The results of that occurrence are still being studied."

Jenni said a swift and silent prayer for Rothly's health, putting her croissant down and taking a sip of coffee. Then she stared at Diamantina and shook her head. "I would have thought the Eight would have briefed you by now. Told you all this."

Rolling her eyes, the merfem snapped a piece of croissant off with sharp, greenish teeth and chewed. "I would have thought so, too, but they didn't."

Jenni took up the tale. "The bottom line is that the Eight want to do a ritual, here on your land, to shape the elemental energies that will be released by the bubble into providing a better life for the Lightfolk." Such a stream of creativity should also influence human affairs for the better.

"Here?" Diamantina gasped and her hand fluttered to her bosom. "*Here?* On my land?"

"That's right," Aric said.

The merfem's eyes rounded and went moist, a sign of excitement. "Oh, my."

He continued, "The ritual dancing circle will be large, of course, since the anticipated magic to direct will be great. The Eight would like permission to stay here, and do the ritual at a place to be determined. They will be asking some of the stronger nobles to attend such a ritual. You, of course, will be included."

Diamantina's panting had a slight sucking sound as if she needed more humidity in the atmosphere or wanted to breathe water. "Oh, my!" She clapped her hands sharply three times and the next minute two naiads and a naiader stood dripping on the marble floor before her. "The Eight are coming, and other guests. We must prepare all the rooms, including the caves below. Mers can take the wet and damp ones, but make sure the dry, sandy ones are well readied for dwarves. All must be perfect."

The tallest naiad, who had served the croissants and tea and now had her thick green hair braided with pearls, said, "When?"

Diamantina opened her mouth, shut it, looked at Aric.

Jenni answered. "The anticipated ritual date is the spring equinox."

"Of course, of course," Diamantina said.

"Ritual date," said the naiader.

Diamantina flicked that topic away with a gesture. "We must prepare. I will move from my suite in the underwater home and give it to the Water King and

Queen." She glanced at Jenni and Aric. "My rooms have tunnels to this ridge."

"The vernal equinox is in three weeks," the first naiad said. "Plenty of time."

Diamantina pouted. "Everything must be perfect. Call in your relatives if you need help."

Jenni said, "I am here to balance the elements. That will give you more magic to draw from. If you're going to be using a lot of water energy, let me know and I will summon more of the elements to match."

All three of the minor Waterfolk stared at her with fishy eyes.

"Will you be staying?" asked the naiad in charge, studying Aric.

"We have been requested by the Eight to do so," he said.

The naiad with pearls stiffened. "They watch *us!*"

"I think they are less sure of us than of you, and want us on site for the ritual," Jenni said. The chocolate had turned bitter in her mouth.

"Of course," said the naiad. "Ritual?"

Aric glanced out the window. "I'll let the lady Diamantina explain that to you. There will be rain soon. Do you have a ritual space large enough for...ah...a hundred?"

The naiader goggled at him. "A hundred?" He turned to his mistress. "We can't house a hundred, not even using the water home."

"They'll bring tents, too," Aric said. He frowned. "I was sure they would have already contacted you by crystal ball."

"They should have," the pearl naiad said tartly. "Not leaving it for you to tell us. Our lady is a relative of the Greendepths, the royal water family."

"Since your household is small—" Aric's glance took in all four of the Waterfolk "—I'm sure that you have a personal and private ritual dancing area."

"Underwater," the naiader said stiffly.

"Of course." Aric inclined his head. "I need to scout out the best place for the royal dancing circle." He glanced at Jenni. She ate the last bite of her croissant, savored the swallow of coffee on her tongue and rose. Once on her feet she dipped a curtsy though she wore jeans. "Thank you for the wonderful coffee." She met the eyes of each naiad and the naiader, cruised her gaze over the lady's pert nose. "Thank you for your hospitality."

"You are very welcome." Diamantina stood, too. "I'll have some rooms prepared on this ground floor, looking landward for you two."

"Thank you," Aric said in a neutral tone.

Jenni said nothing. The best rooms would be either near the ocean or on the third floor, and definitely facing the ocean. Despite all her courtesy, the merfem didn't think much of them. As Jenni followed Aric to the door, she glanced back to see the lady's brow puckered and her mouth set in dissatisfied lines. Her eyes had deepened to a dark green with mysterious depths. Jenni thought she saw a flash of calculation.

CHAPTER
25

"JINDESFARNE?" ARIC PROMPTED. HE WAS holding the door open for her.

Lengthening her stride, Jenni passed him and walked out into the gray March morning. Aric closed the door behind them and joined her. Hands on his hips, he scanned the wooded area. "Before anything else, I need to make sure that I know every tree on her land." He grimaced. "First just the ones around her house." He bent and gave Jenni a quick kiss. "I'll be chain traveling now, be back shortly." With that he stepped into the nearest eucalyptus.

Jenni let out a breath she hadn't known she'd been holding. She was alone. All by herself. The minor Waterfolk or the merfem might be watching, but she was in no one else's company for the first time in a week. A few breaths of freedom until Aric stepped out of the tree. She walked closer to the cliff and stared down at the beach.

Wherever the ritual would be taking place, she should be on the beach, close to where the orb might appear.

She settled into her balance to check the magical elemental composition of the land, feet wide, arms spread. Another sighing breath escaped her, then she drew in one damp with humidity, the taste of the salt of the sea and cold. She curled her toes in her shoes, opened her mouth and tasted magic. She closed her eyes for a better focus.

Overwhelming water energy. Not surprising. As she parsed each bit of energy for the house and the immediate bluff she sensed Aric coming closer as he checked every tree.

"Well?" they asked each other at the same time.

Jenni smiled, dipped her head at him to speak first.

He said, "No dryad trees. Haven't been in a long time. I can't tell why."

"Maybe too much water magic? It's about two-thirds here."

Aric frowned. "Maybe. All the trees are acceptable for travel use."

"Good." Jenni didn't much care, she couldn't use them by herself and wouldn't trust many—anyone other than Aric—to bring her through the tree network.

The concerned lines in his face deepened. "I think there might have been some shadleech activity. I found a stump or two of a pine that might have been cut down because they nested there."

Her usual dread at the things trembled her nerves, and she lifted her hand and touched the sensitive back of her neck, felt the protective spiderweb inside and out. Better.

"Your findings?"Aric asked.

"Water two-thirds, earth one-sixth, fire one-twelfth and air one-twelfth."

"Not too odd for a land that has hosted a merfem for a couple of centuries."

"I would have expected a little more air." Jenni rolled uncomfortable shoulders. "Too little fire."

Aric's smile was slow. He reached up and smoothed a curl of her hair that had been dangling by her face to behind her ear, his fingers feathering across her cheek as he did so. "You'll remedy that."

"Yes."

"Then you'll feel better about being here."

Jenni made a moue. "I'll bet you anything that there's a fountain in my room."

He shook his head. "No bet."

A movement caught her eye and she found that the two naiads and the naiader had appeared and were staring at her and Aric.

The merfem's companion said, "Your rooms are ready. Our lady felt you assess the elemental energies of our land. She requests that you don't balance the magic until we have prepared our homes for the influx of visitors. Nor does she wish for you to visit the beach."

Aric's hand came over Jenni's shoulder and the warmth of it made her realize how cold she was. Being inside would be good. He spoke and his voice was as cool as the air. "Doesn't your lady know that drawing on a balanced mixture of energies will make your tasks easier? Your spells quicker and more effective?"

The naiader stepped forward, managed a stingy smile. "We are more accustomed to working with water energy. We ask that the elemental balancer does not alter those energies as yet."

"All right," Jenni said. "When do you think you'll be ready for me to do my work? The sooner this area is balanced, the easier it will be to keep it so, and prepare for the ritual."

"She will notify you," the naiader said.

Jenni suppressed a sigh. "Fine. Can you lead us to our rooms?"

"Of course." The second naiad's smile was falsely cheerful, she turned with every expectation that Jenni and Aric would follow. Jenni did, and as she walked away, Aric's hand fell. By the time they reached the door, the other naiad and the naiader had disappeared.

Well, they were true magical Lightfolk, not halflings.

She and Aric were given rooms at the opposite end of a hallway. Before Jenni could speak, Aric told the naiads firmly that they wanted to share a room. With a curled lip at Jenni, the naiad led them back to the smaller room with the lousier view. "For you, Treeman and halfling."

Jenni stiffened, tired of the whole thing. "It appears that you aren't so much in your lady's confidence. Since she didn't inform you how important this ritual is, and how much depends upon Aric and me."

Now the naiad's upper lip lifted. "Self-important."

"Just important. You may address the Treeman as Sir Paramon, Representative of the Eight, and me as Princess Jindesfarne Mistweaver Emberdrake."

The naiad froze midsneer. "Emberdrake is the name of the Fire King and Queen."

Jenni continued, "That's true. I see you have some tiny knowledge. My brother and I were adopted into the Emberdrake family last week. Mostly because of my import for the upcoming ritual."

Aric pushed away from the doorjamb he'd been leaning against, arms crossed. "And since your lady wasn't briefed by the Eight as I had anticipated, perhaps I should tell you, and you can tell her, that the ritual event may draw some Dark ones, so you should prepare any defenses you might have."

The naiad's mouth opened and closed several times.

"You may leave now. The household has much to do," Aric said.

With a squeal of fear, the naiad ran.

Aric slung his pack on the bed, gave Jenni a smile. His hair appeared greener than ever due to the dull light from two small windows. Heavy drapes covered what Jenni thought was a sliding glass door. "Staying here is fine with me. The bed's large." He winked.

"And we certainly are away from everyone else."

"All to the good. But I really do need to find a good place for the dancing circle. You'll have to balance it."

"I'll have to balance a lot, the area, fine-tune the beach where I'll stand during the ceremony, and the dancing circle. This house."

Aric's smile grew sly. "Why don't you go ahead and balance the room, if that isn't too much for you?"

"Might be a good idea," Jenni agreed. She glanced around the room. "I'll need a hot plate to brew the tea."

His forehead wrinkled. "Tea?"

She took her knapsack and shook it, leaves rustled. "This is a huge deal. I intend to do every single thing right. By the book, our family books."

Aric nodded. He walked up to her and rubbed his hands up and down her upper arms, kissed her. "I understand. I'm with you. All the way, Jenni."

She wanted to believe him. She *did* believe him. "Thank you."

Jenni made tea and heated it in her hands, did her own rituals for entering the gray mist and balanced just the room and attached bath. It felt great—both practicing her craft fully the way she'd been taught by her family, and the chamber after she was done with it. Her magical senses had also been fully awakened and "tuned." She could tell where her lover, Aric, was, and the lady whose house this was.

Aric was concentrating and doing his job. As she scrutinized his aura, she understood that despite what he said about the dryads and his home and his forest being his first priorities, he was content and proud to be the Eight's man. He valued his position and defined himself with regard to it and the Eight. He wouldn't be the same man if he resigned. And she cared deeply for the man he was.

More soul-searching for her, that he was tied to the Eight by his own bonds. She still didn't trust *them*.

And from the chaos in the household, she wasn't sure that the lady Diamantina trusted the Eight, either. Especially not to defend her. She'd called on allies of her own, and some were coming to swell the ranks of Lightfolk, who would dance the ritual and fight any Dark ones who showed up. Jenni got the idea that old, old caverns that the merfolk had excavated in this land when she'd first arrived were being opened.

Dinner was civilized and the naiads—a few Jenni hadn't been introduced to before—were very courteous. Aric assured Diamantina that their room was fine with a stolid, bland smile that didn't reveal he'd understood the insult, but if the lady was at all bright she must have known that he had—he and Jenni had. Or did she discount them as unintelligent, Jenni brought in to do one thing and one thing only and not smart about anything else?

Jenni didn't care, but over the next week, as she became accustomed to the feel of the land, she understood that Diamantina hadn't interacted with humans for a long, long time.

Magical traps were being set around the estate: underwater, on the beach, the cliff faces and steep slopes up the hills, the bluff itself and, of course, the house, though Jenni thought that the lady was ready to sacrifice that building.

And magical shields were being erected to hide any increased activity from humans. There were no roads to the place, not even close, and the only way to the beach was by hiking along it from towns many miles away. But the Eight were being careful.

The Air King, Cloudsylph, had arrived to get the lay of the land and consult with Diamantina. Both approved the large flat area covered with the dry grass of winter with the hint of greenness and tiny spring wildflowers low to the ground.

Jenni was given permission to balance the land, which she did with all the proper Mistweaver rituals, and it went very smoothly. When she stepped from the mist, she saw respect in Cloudsylph's eyes. Later that day, Jenni was led to the main tunnel from the house to the beach by Diamantina's companion naiad, who continued to give Jenni the notion that she was being weighed and found wanting. She'd already found the door down to the beach on her wandering, but hadn't opened it without permission.

This was the way she'd take on the morning of the spring equinox, while the Eight and the great Lightfolk gathered to do their ritual. On the beach, she'd wait for the last bubble to rise from the ocean. The beach was where she'd step into the interdimension to sense its energies, balance what she could in the bubble and the moment it burst, equalize all the energies in the area so the Lightfolk would have the greatest amount of magic to work with to direct the creativity of the bubble.

There were elemental energies around the door, a trap, and she disarmed it by pulling some fire energy and flicking it at the spell, smiling from under half-lidded eyes at the naiad. Jenni gestured with her flashlight, she didn't want to use magic when tech was good enough.

"I'm afraid that I can't reset the trap, and if I have to walk through a tunnel loaded with traps, I'll have to disarm them all. So, if *you* can take them down for the time that I'm on the beach, it would be better." Jenni brightened her smile. "You should have plenty of balanced energy to call on."

The naiad scowled, she'd still refused to be formally introduced to Jenni, so Jenni didn't know her name, not even a nickname that she was called. The woman muttered liquid syllables and Jenni felt pressure beyond the door release as the traps were removed.

Jenni nodded. "Thank you, and you might want to remind everyone in the household that if something happens to me before the bubble event on the way to the beach, the Eight will be displeased."

With a green sharp-toothed smile, the naiad replied, "We won't put the shields and traps up on the tunnel until after you're down on the beach on the day of the dancing circle." She looked down her nose, the nostrils of which were thin membranes that fluttered when she was upset, like now. "One of the lesser naiads will do so then. I will be dancing at my lady's side."

Of course they'd arm the traps behind Jenni, cutting off retreat if the Darkfolk attacked and she didn't have enough energy to disarm the traps.

"Mmm-hmm," Jenni said. "See ya later." She opened the door and went through. She should reach the beach a half hour before low tide.

This tunnel wasn't as pleasant as the Earth Palace ones she'd traveled through. All the walls and the floor glistened with wet, and since Jenni was living mostly in her

magical nature of djinn—fire—the caves were disagree-
able. She worried about slipping.

There was the scent of the ocean, and the throbbing
pound of it, that almost made up for the wet…the Earth
Palace had always had an underscent, and taste on the
back of her tongue, of sulphur. Sea salt now lingered
there and she liked the change.

The angle down to the beach was steep and the solid
rock floor turned to rocky grit, then silty sand, and she
considered each step carefully. When she reached the
bottom, there wasn't much space and she swung her
flashlight around to see a small bulb of a room of dark
stone draped with seaweed. Narrowing her eyes, she
called up her magical sight and found the doorway outlined in blue-green-violet where water and air energy
seeped through.

She could *feel* the great sheets of water energy from
the Pacific Ocean restlessly shifting. Additional air energies rose from the foam of the waves where sky met sea.
Around her was the rock and earth magic.

Jenni blinked and frowned at the cave door, wondering how much magical strength it would take to open
it, and if she had enough natural energy within herself
to handle it. The merfem was a greater Lightfolk, all
the naiads and naiaders minor Waterfolk but completely
magical. It was a good bet that there'd be no physical way
to open the cave and it would be camouflaged outside
from any humans who managed to hike up the coast to
this beach.

Stepping up to the rock wall, she put her hand on the
door, and *pushed* with all her magical strength. Nothing

happened. She wasn't accustomed to trying to influence physical objects with magical energy. Entering the gray mist wouldn't solve this problem in the real world. With a huff of breath, she took a pace back, considered all the lessons she had and the few magical things she could do outside of the interdimension.

She could push and pull air. Though she felt more djinn than elf, her father had been half-elf and she could use that part of her nature with a little more difficulty than her fire side. Pulling air toward her, against the cave door, should move it, she thought.

Or she could ask for help. But if she did that, she wouldn't know whether she could move the door if she had to.

This door was the least of the major tests that would demand all her strengths.

CHAPTER

26

PUSH AIR TO OPEN THE DOOR. RIGHT. SCUFFING sand and grit out of the way, she turned off her flashlight and darkness pressed upon her. No light, no fire. Absence of all light.

Darkness could be a blessing, she knew that. It could be a soft comfort. Breathe and breathe again, listen to the ocean. The human and air portions of her nature loved the steady sound of ocean surf, the fire not so much. There was no storm outside to whisk her away, the beach would be fine at low tide.

Her heartbeat had slowed to regular and she tucked the fire bit of herself that still flickered uneasily deep into a corner inside her, set her feet, gathered all her own personal power and *pushed*. Air sucked out of her lungs, whistled through the tunnel, ground the door open a half inch. Sweating, she panted and wiped an arm across her forehead, dredged up more and pushed again—and fell into the darkness of unconsciousness. Mistake.

She wasn't out long and woke to a bright glow of Cloudsylph's white-violet light. Aric and Diamantina were with the king. Some of the other naiads and na-iaders might be behind them, but Jenni figured that humiliating herself before those three was enough.

Aric must have informed them when he'd sensed her consciousness fade through their bond.

The elf king stooped. "Stand aside," he said to Aric and Aric moved. Even though the touch of the elf sparkled across her senses and he held her as if her weight was nothing, she wished it was Aric. Tilting his head, the king stared at the heavy rounded rock door that was cracked an embarrassing tiny amount. "This door—"

"Is not defective! Especially if Dark ones come." Diamantina's voice was as shrill as the screeching of a shark.

"No, not defective," the king said. "But obviously too difficult for Jindesfarne, and she must have easy access." He tapped it with his toe and it swung open as if a soft breeze had blown against it. The rush of sunlight and sea scent and the deep thunder of the ocean flowed in. On the release of a breath that barely moved his chest, he lilted a few elvish words and the rock door swung back and forth. Envy surged through Jenni and burnt away the last of her weakness.

"I'm fine now, and I'd like to walk on the beach to study where I should stand for the ritual."

She felt the lightest feather-brushes of his great power against her as he verified her health, then he set her on her feet. Discreetly watching each step and trying to appear like she wasn't hurrying away from them, she strode out onto the beach.

To her dismay the others followed—Aric with solid sturdy steps that set footprints in the sand, the Air King and the merfem gliding along and leaving no trace of their passage.

"Do you sense anything of the bubble energies?" the merfem asked. Jenni thought the woman had just battered Cloudsylph with the same question.

Jenni would have been happier to explore the beach and extend her magic without company, even Aric. Too late now. She'd botched that.

"I'll check." Pacing, she studied the water, sending all her magical senses toward the depths of the ocean, where she thought the bubble would rise, walking the tide line until she felt a tiny fluttering that might precede bubble energies. There she stopped and turned to look inland. Of course it was where the cliff had risen up to make the bluff.

Everyone watched her, and again she turned and scrutinized the sea, more with her other sight than with her eyes. She didn't think that the bubble would come more than a couple of hundred yards out in the ocean, easy enough for her to see—for everyone to see. For the Dark ones to be interested in the house on the bluff and the Eight's great ritual dance. And Jenni on the beach.

"Will it be there?" the merfem asked.

Jenni glanced at her to see the slightest wrinkle of her brow, the shift of her gaze toward the south. Ah. Maybe she'd been thinking the bubble would rise directly under her own water home.

Rolling her shoulders, she spread her hands. "I think so. Maybe you can tell if there's a shifting of water energy? Or you, King Cloudsylph, if there is a hint of air?"

All three of them joined her, Aric standing a few more handspans away than the two greater Lightfolk. Jenni took the pace to come close to him, put her arm around his waist, connected with him mind to mind. *There, in the direction of that last spur of cloud ahead.*

He smiled easily and answered, *Asking a Treeman, even a California coastal Treeman, about sensing strange things in the Pacific Ocean is useless.* He smoothed his hand over her wind-tossed hair.

"Nothing." Diamantina pouted. She glanced at the ocean as if she wanted to check herself, hesitated, then inclined her torso toward Cloudsylph. "Do you sense anything, my lord?"

But the king was shaking his head. "Not underwater."

Again his gaze lingered on Jenni and she felt it. "I doubt that the Emberdrakes would sense any fire energy, though it is a quake zone." The tiniest lift and fall of his shoulders, too small to be called a shrug. "The dwarven royals or the Greendepths might be as perspicacious as Jindesfarne."

"You're sure you felt something?" Diamantina persisted.

What if she hadn't? What if she was wrong? No reason to try to save her pride. It had already been shattered. The back of her neck tingled in continued embarrassment. "Yes. Very faint, but...yes."

"But you can't tell us how fast it is rising or when it will appear?" Diamantina said.

"No." Frowning, Jenni wondered if she'd really be able to keep track of the progress of the energy sphere, how fast it rose. Would it be like Yellowstone's or move faster? Not that she recalled much of anything at Yellowstone except that the bubble was *there* and about to break. Maybe she'd be able to give the Eight warning, maybe not. "Surely you who know the land and are more powerful magically will sense it better than I when it's rising." Them doing a lot of the work would be good.

"Of course," Diamantina said.

Jenni studied the rocky angle of the earth up to the merfem's estate. "I can see the area where your dancing ritual will take place. Good job, Aric." She squeezed his waist. "I'll be able to keep an eye on the bubble and the Eight's ritual. When I'm out of the interdimension you can watch me and the bubble." Sounded good to her.

"Yes," Diamantina said. Her smile was sharply smug and Jenni realized why when a cold wave lapped over her feet. She yelped and slogged in toward the cliff.

"Do you know what the tide will be at the time of your ritual during the spring equinox?"

Diamantina raised her brows with another implied *of course*. "Currently the ritual is set for the precise time of the equinox, which is 10:32 a.m. human time. The tide will be ebbing, but not at the lowest. The moon will be waxing but the tides will not be high," she ended sweetly.

Jenni flexed her jaw. Why hadn't she checked the details out on her pocket computer? It would have taken a few strokes of her finger. Then she forced a smile. "Thank you, that's good to know."

"And we should return to planning the influx of the Eight and our retinues and the ritual," Cloudsylph said, offering his arm to the merfem. She took it and beamed at Jenni and Aric, beamed *down* on them as the Air King floated them up to the house. "I will need your input, Aric," the king said.

Aric turned and enveloped Jenni in a hug. "Everything will go well," he said. His mouth came down on hers and she was kissed quick and hard. Then he was loping to the nearest tree in the fold of the earth, then gone.

He was being optimistic again. As for her, if she thought things would go well, she was a damn fool.

The whole household ignored Jenni that afternoon, and she was fine with that. For a couple of hours, she just lay on her bed and stared at the shells encrusted in the ceiling and let the elemental energies wash around and through her. Now and then she would close her eyes and visualize the areas she needed to know.

Earlier on the beach she'd been tempted to enter the interdimension, but decided to limit her time there. The spring equinox was in two weeks. Before that, she'd be balancing the land under the dancing circle, the beach and the house. If she balanced the area, would the sphere itself be drawn in this direction? Another shudder passed through her. She needed to ask her father's friend, the elf scholar, wondered if he would be welcome here. She was sure he didn't have a cell phone…though now that she considered it, cell phones would be natural to Airfolk. Of course the merfem Diamantina would have a crystal ball.

And Jenni had to consider that she'd be spending time in the gray mist for however long it took for the bubble to rise. That was a lot of mist walking.

Everything might not end well, but she was trying her hardest to shape events for a good result, and that included being very responsible.

So she let energy come to her.

The thick "sheets" of the ocean ebbed and flowed like the tide, soothing. There was more fire energy than she expected, but she'd never been in an active earthquake zone and this was close to the Mendocino triple junction where three of the great tectonic plates of the earth's mantle collided together. The magical elemental energies reflected that: shifting and mixing and separating more than she was accustomed to. Those energies were more changeable under the ocean than here on the hill.

Flickering streaks of fire magic rose from the earth's core upward to the ocean, then into the air. Faintly, faintly, she thought she sensed the unique encapsulated energies that might be a hint of the next bubble and shivered. She definitely wasn't ready for that and, looking back on the Yellowstone bubble event, was glad she hadn't been there alone—or even with just Aric—when it had burst. All five of them had formed that creative energy, shaped the force of it and sent it to accomplish different things. She wasn't too proud to admit that controlling the energies within that bubble would have been beyond her. Balancing them with other energies for a while when the bubble popped, yes, she could do that, *did* do that, but imprinting the creativity with a purpose... no.

She was glad that the Eight and their dancing circle would be here to forge the power in the direction they pleased. She gave a few minutes' thought to the spell they were preparing...but their minds, too, were beyond hers. She wouldn't presume to understand what beings who'd lived for centuries might do with bubble energy.

If she continued to sense the bubble energy, she'd be fine. But she worried that tiny indication would vanish under the influx of all the great elemental energies of the Lightfolk who would be arriving. So after everyone had left her alone on the beach, she'd drawn a pillar of flame energy toward her, and attempted to "affix" it to a spot where immense water energy met earth energy and air was churned up. Even in the real world, she should be able to feel the fire energy pillar and know that was the location on land just east of where the bubble might rise from the sea. That's where she would stand to balance the energies as the bubble broke.

But right now there was blessed peace and quiet.

The warm afternoon enveloped her and she drifted off and her thoughts were drawn to her brother Rothly. He, also, seemed to be drifting, alone in a quiet, cold, dark house. She *felt* his loneliness, his grief, his depression. His longing for contact and anger at himself for lashing out at others...and his need to punish himself for his failure at the portal so long ago.

I forgive myself, Jenni said to him, not quite knowing if she was dreaming or not.

Of course you do, he sneered.

Not dreaming, then, just in that half-awake state where almost anything could happen. But his words couldn't hurt her. *I forgive you, too.*

You have nothing to forgive me for!

For not standing by me. For not sharing our grief. Since she was in that mellow state it was easy to let harsh words that might have come to her tongue melt away. She didn't remind him that the basic tenets of their family were loving, generosity, forgiveness. She hadn't allowed herself to remember that for a long time. Her parents would have been grieved at what their children had done to each other and themselves.

No reply snapped from Rothly and Jenni absently decided that was good. *You are too alone,* she said. *Time to enter the real world. I know that.*

He waved his healed arm. *The "real" world. The only world I have now that the interdimension is closed to me.* But his bitterness seemed halfhearted.

Your magic was transmuted by the bubble energies in Yellowstone. You'll find your new magic. Your new STRONG magic. Her vision of him shifted until he was more energy and magic than human. *Yes, strong magic within you.*

He said nothing.

Aric asked for help for the dryads and help has come. You asked for help for yourself and it was granted. Why are you not exploring it?

Again, no answer and this time she was sure he was

nothing but a construct of her mind, her elder brother listening to her as he hadn't for so long. Maybe never.

You are too alone, and the sight of him was thinning, as was the house, and she knew she was retreating from them. *I will send you...*

Send me what? Irascibility.

Let me check on that.... Then she was in her kitchen. Her sparkling kitchen with new and better cabinets gleaming, newly painted in her favorite soft yellow.

Hartha whipped around at her, ear tips curling and tucking a dishtowel into her apron pocket; both were spotless. "What are you doing here, Jindesfarne?" The brownie glanced down at Jenni's feet. "Ah. Astral traveling. Well, spit it out, what do you need?"

"The kitchen looks great." Jenni glanced up and toward the front of the house. Chinook was sleeping in the middle of her bed. Love welled in her, for her cat, the brownie woman who was caring for her, her brother. "What of Crag?"

A lustily disapproving sniff from Hartha. "Not as much of a nuisance as he was."

"I would like you to take him to my old home in Northumberland."

Pointed brownie teeth gleamed in a smile. "You are giving him to your brother."

"I don't think Rothly will mistreat him, now. My brother's changed."

"Huh." Hartha shrugged. "Might be good for both of them. Pred will take care of that today. He needs to get away from this place for a little bit. Brownies can become housebound if we don't watch out and Pred loves this place and what he's doing for the cul-de-sac."

A slight thrill flickered through Jenni, but not enough to bring her from her sleepy trance. "Sounds good. Later."

Sleep claimed her.

Jenni and Aric weren't invited to dinner with Cloudsylph and Diamantina, and that was no disappointment. She'd asked Aric to take her to his home for time away from the water house. She'd been in the dampish room and suffered the slights of the merfolk for a week and wanted a break. Especially since she'd be there two more weeks. Aric refused.

The Eight wanted Jenni on site from now until the bubble rose, not three minutes away by tree-route, because of course Aric knew all the trees now.

Aric's refusal and Cloudsylph's insistence that she remain irritated Jenni and made some of her wariness regarding the Eight return. They didn't trust her, so how much could she trust them? With every minute that passed she sensed that her life would be on the line.

Instead Aric took her to the limits of the lady's land, out of sight of the house, where the beach was a good twenty feet between the edge of a steep hill and the ocean. On the beach was a table that might have graced a five-star hotel. Long, dark green linen tablecloth, with another silvery cloth atop that, draped in swags. Stacks of plates and lines of silverware for courses of the meal that seemed to be arranged on a large silver cart.

Not much of the knot inside her chest loosened at the

sight, though a few weeks back it would have made her sigh with romantic contentment. She felt like a puppet on a not-so-long string.

They walked down the beach and Jenni's hurt wasn't so much that she jerked away when he took her fingers.

"I've never invited any of the Eight to my home," Aric said, as if they were continuing a conversation, though she hadn't spoken to him since they'd arrived on the beach a few minutes ago. "I'm sure they could pinpoint my tree if they wished, but I've never been more than *mind* summoned."

When they reached the cart, Jenni expected him to seat her in the equally plush curved-legged chair, but they just turned around and walked back down the beach. Jenni looked over her shoulder at the food cart. Her stomach rumbled. "No food?"

"Not until your taste buds can appreciate it. I know the sound of the surf soothes you, always did in Northumberland when we went to the beach. Why Denver?"

There was hardly a twinge of pain at the reminder of her childhood home. Jenni shrugged. "I wandered until I stopped. Maybe the mountains soothe me, too."

"Sure." He squeezed her hand and she linked fingers with him.

"I'm hungry and you're maneuvering me."

"Sure." He stopped, which meant they stopped. Turning toward her, he put his hands on each side of her face, made sure their gazes were locked. "I'm the Eight's man, and you're Princess Emberdrake. We're tied to the royal Lightfolk for a long time, and you'll no longer be wholly of the mortal world again."

She wanted to pull away from him, from the feel of his hands that excited her...from all the things that bound her to a new life. And she couldn't. She'd given her word. So they stared at each other and their bodies leaned into each other until they touched all along. They stood, sharing the moment, the lingering sunset, the occasional droplets of spray that reached them.

The rhythm of the ocean pounded until it was part of her blood. Primeval. Essential. She was born half human of this Earth and any ties to another strange dimension were lost in time beyond family memory. Earth, the ocean, the fire beneath the ocean, they were home and so the surf reminded her.

But the sea breeze also carried unique fragrances: the scent of Cloudsylph and air sprites; Aric of the Tree-folk, magical being of the planet; and elf. Spicy with a hint of champagne effervescence; exquisite fragrances of food and a brownie to keep it properly prepared no matter how long before they sat to eat; a brownie to serve them standing beyond the cart, also enjoying the sea. Lightfolk.

"Yes," she replied to the questions between herself and Aric, floating around her mind. "I am human and I am Lightfolk, and I'm currently tied to the royals." A spurt of anger from her heart reached her lips. "But they show me all too often that they are powerful and I am not. I am here on this beach because I am not allowed off site."

"You are here because you gave your word you'd fulfill the mission, and part of the mission is being here."

"True," Jenni grumbled. "But I've been independent

for a long time, and I don't care to be treated like a child who doesn't know her responsibilities. I think I've proven that I am more than that, and I'd like to come and go as I please. I feel like the Eight are assuming I will always be moved where and when they wish me to be, like a chess piece."

"Always someone more powerful than you around," Aric said, then kissed her.

Through his soft mouth came his deep steadiness. His belief in himself and his confidence in her, and acceptance of his fate—their fate.

She wasn't sure that acceptance would rub off on her. But for tonight she let the next ebbing wave take her annoyance out to sea and sink into the ocean, away from her so she could enjoy the moment. Something Aric had once taught her and she'd mostly lost. She was learning to accept that she could only control the present, the past was gone and could not be changed, the future was beyond her shaping.

They sank into the kiss with the knowledge that it was a special moment, that they would enjoy dinner, and that later they would love.

Then a wave slapped hard and Aric's mouth curved into a smile and the kiss broke. He took her hand, grinned with a flash of teeth and shouted into the breeze that was picking up. "Run!"

She didn't think that was exactly good for her taste buds, either, but it fit the moment, so she ran with him.

When they reached the cart and circled the table, the

browniefem gave a little start, as if she'd been mesmerized by the ocean, and hurried to them.

Jenni recognized her as the one assigned to her in the suite in the mountain.

The small woman dipped in curtsies. "Again you help me. Pretty place. Never seen beach. Nice beach." As if she couldn't control them, her feet danced a bit, scuffing up sand...the earth of the beach that the minor earth elemental fem liked. "Thank you for beach time."

"You're quite welcome," Aric said with a serious expression in the face of the brownie's dignity as he seated Jenni.

"I'm glad to see you again," Jenni said sincerely.

The brownie nodded, stared at Jenni. "Cuz you, I get job with high fire lady. Will be to serve here at great dance ritual. Cuz you, I pros-per. I served you, Prin-cess. I was courage on ledge. All know. I am mate-worthy." Her round brown face stretched into a smile, and her large eyes glistened with tears.

Jenni smiled back, pleased with herself, happy that something she'd done had brought good to another. "My thanks to you, too."

With a last jerky nod, the browniefem vanished and appeared next to the cart, returned with a pitcher of iced tea. The meal was exquisite. Salad a mixture of sweet with mandarin orange slices and savory with blue cheese and spinach leaves. The walnuts gave it a nice crunch. The fish was fresh and topped with a light sauce that accented its flavor...and on through several more courses until chocolate mousse truffles for dessert. All became right in the world.

When the browniefem whisked away the last dishes and Jenni felt the slight tremble in the air that she and the cart would soon vanish, she touched the woman's shoulder. "Thank you, again." They'd shared a fear and that was a small bond between them. She realized that this, too, was part of the world of the Lightfolk, bonds with others who were not great lords and ladies, but still magical. She'd have to make more halfling friends, too. Changes were coming.

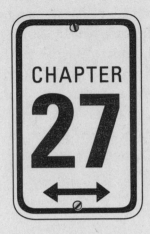

CHAPTER 27

THE NIGHT BRIGHTENED WITH THE FIRST pastel tint of dawn and Jenni left the house, clean, with her hair free and flowing to her shoulders, her heaviest dress substituting as a ceremonial robe. She'd brewed a cup of the special tea to help her step into the inter-dimension and downed it. Now that she'd spent more time with the Lightfolk and Treefolk, she'd gone back to considering nature as part of the timing for spell-work. Dawn was good for elemental balancing, made it a little easier—though the gray mist was the same night or day.

She'd left Aric sleeping, as was most of the household, though she believed Diamantina was awake...sensitive to Jenni's work in her home. The ground was cold under her feet, but Jenni drew fire close, letting flickers of red-orange sink into her, warm her blood, ease her muscles, keep her soles toasty. She hummed as she paced through the misty blue-purple dawn to the ritual dancing ground. Holding out her arms, she turned, getting a feel for the energies around her before she stepped into the mist. She walked to the center, found it radiated too much water to be a good base for her, took a few steps to the west, where the most fire was...down beneath the ocean.

One deep breath, two...and the spell pattern was started, physical reality around her faded, and her words chanted the mist before her. She took a step and she was there.

Again she turned in place, saw the flame on the beach that she'd set to mark where she believed the bubble would rise, long and steady and red-orange-yellow. Sheets of all the elements were around her that she could easily draw, and the ground showed a mixture of more than water, strong earth energy, a lingering of air as if Cloudsylph had infused it the day before.

All looked perfect for balancing the place. She rolled her shoulders, smiled. This wouldn't be too difficult.

So she stamped a complex beat that unfurled her own magic, had energies drifting near her in just the amounts needed and she wove them together in a balancing tapestry of light.

Jenni! Aric's frantic cry pierced her peaceful trance.

Here, she said.

Stay in the interdimension. Kondrian comes!

She tensed, wanted to run. She couldn't, not in the gray mist. She dared not move from where she stepped in. Too easy to get lost, run in the wrong direction, step *out* into the reality of midair above sharp rocks.

What is he doing here! Her mind was gibbering. *I thought he was too injured—*

Only. One. Answer, Aric said. She sensed him swinging his sword. *He. Murdered. Innocents. Used. Energy. To. Heal. Himself. Probably minor Lightfolk. Otherwise, I'da heard.*

She *saw* him—Kondrian, a hideous smear of pulsating, oily black-brown-red. A major Dark one. Found herself breathing fast. Noticed a green-white aura-cloud. Aric!

Biting her lips, she wondered if she could affect the Dark one with elemental energies…draw them to him? Envelope him in them? What would that do? Give him *more* energy maybe.

Helpless.

No. She wouldn't be.

Like the shadleeches zooming toward her, if she could give them—Kondrian—more energy than he could handle…maybe more *balanced* energy than he was used to, wouldn't a Dark be more unbalanced than Lightfolk, evil more unbalanced? Who knew? She could only try.

The shadleeches snapped at her, their white and pointed teeth gleamed, the only hard and definitive quality about them. But their teeth scraped along her skin, doing no damage. Jenni jolted at that. Panted hard. Remembered the spiderweb tracery on her nape and touched it. The mark protected her even here!

I am safe, she called to Aric, pulling more elemental magics from the atmosphere around her. Good thing she'd already balanced the energy where she was standing, that would give her power a boost. Good, good, good.

The evil creatures lunged and lunged again. Kondrian knew they could fly into the interdimension. He'd think they would be hurting her, distracting her, keeping her busy.

With one huge breath, she gathered as much energy as she could, from all four elements. Acting on instinct, she *compacted* them until they were in a sphere—so much time thinking of bubbles—a hard, too-bright-to-look-at ball of pure balanced energy. Bigger than herself. Would it be enough? What would it do to him?

No time for dithery questions. *Throw it!*

She shot it like a bullet at the greasy blob of black-evil.

It didn't seem to hit. Floated near him. She wailed through gritted teeth in frustration.

But...but what? It looked like the sphere of energies was nibbling at the edges of his aura, like a flame flickering at the edge of a wick before it caught.

Whoosh!

The energies smacked him now, flashed over the Dark one as if over a pool of oil.

There was a scream and he vanished...just before the balanced flame of the energies took hold. Argh. Raising her hands and *pulling* fire as she closed her fingers into fists, she flung it at the shadleeches who continued to dive around her. *They* went up in satisfying puffs of black smoke.

What did you do to him? Aric asked, now with a little awe.

Threw balanced energy at him.

Excellent, that helped me a lot. Now he sounded satisfied.

What did you do?

I stabbed him a couple of times with my sword. Are you all right?

Yes. And you? She scanned the green-white flare that was her lover. His aura looked healthy, but she hadn't seen the physical wounds that Aric had inflicted on Kondrian.

I'm fine.

She let out a relieved breath, scrutinized the area and squared her shoulders. The dancing ground was unbalanced again...and she was tired, and had spent nearly too much time in the gray mist. But she didn't want to leave this task to be done once more another time. Especially since she still had the beach to balance.

A headache was beginning to pound in her temples and her mouth was dry, but she could ignore that until she had finished her work.

Much of the nearby elemental energies were gone, but the distant sheets glowing through the mist like the northern lights were still there. She pulled at them, fast. Working quickly but efficiently, she intertwined them in another lovely pattern...two in a row...something she hadn't been able to do for a long time, but practice was renewing old skills. The design was circular, more difficult to make than a square, than just "weaving like a pot holder," which was the first thing a child of her family learned. Yes, pretty, not that anyone except her would ever see it. The pattern was like a seal, on the ground, comprised equally of all the energies.

She dispersed the remnants of the elemental fields she'd summoned and took a step forward…and into the golden sunshine of California. Her knees couldn't hold her and she pitched toward the ground, and was caught by a grinning Aric.

Blood trickled down from a cut on his scalp.

"You said you were all right!"

He rubbed the back of his hand against it. "I am." Inhaling deeply, he set her on her feet, kept an arm around her waist and looked out toward the endless blue-green of the ocean. "Glorious day."

She sighed and relaxed into him, ready to go back to sleep. "It is."

Stamping the ground, his grin widened to show beautiful teeth. "This place is *balanced*."

"Yah."

"You did it."

"Yes."

"And helped defeat Kondrian, too."

"Yes." That dimmed her cheer. "But maybe that was a mistake."

He frowned. "Mistake?"

"Kondrian knows what I…we…can do now, and will be ready for us during the bubble ritual. Was this just a feint, do you think?"

Aric stared down at the beach, his gaze seeming to pinpoint her pillar. The great Lightfolk would be able to see her on the beach—when she wasn't in the interdimension. She didn't know whether that was good or not, either.

"I don't think it was a feint." He let his breath out slowly and his muscles loosened even as her own tensed. "It would be worth his while to take you out before the ceremony." Aric's eyes were deep green when they met hers. "The danger and the fight were real. And, yes, we can expect him on the equinox, too." Aric's mouth twisted. "Probably along with the other three remaining great Dark ones."

Jenni looked at the silent house. "Neither Diamantina nor any of her Folk came to help."

"Kondrian's attack—and that of his shadleeches— occurred pretty fast," Aric said. "Diamantina might still have been sleeping."

"Maybe."

"Jenni, the lady wouldn't want death, or her land befouled by Kondrian," Aric said patiently. "And he'd come after her as soon as he was done with us."

"Probably true."

Aric snorted. "Very true. Best place to ambush the Eight."

"If we aren't being watched, which I doubt. The Eight might have arrived to clean up the mess."

"Wouldn't have been happy with her for losing you." Aric squeezed her.

"Too late for both of us."

"And right now is too late for second-guessing what might have happened." His grip changed to her hand and he laced his fingers with hers and pulled to have her walking back to the house. "I'm hungry," he said.

Jenni was disappointed in herself that she'd irritated him. But she couldn't prevent a black thread of thought of what might have happened to them if she hadn't discovered how to work the elemental energies against the Dark one. She doubted Aric was strong enough to win against an ancient Darkfolk no matter how good of a warrior he'd become.

Adrenaline filtered from her, leaving her tired but wired. She became aware of her pounding headache again.

She stumbled and Aric swung her into his arms. She didn't protest.

As soon as they reached the door, Diamantina opened it, exclaiming, "What happened to you? I was meditating in my ocean chamber and felt this terrible evil, and now look at you!" She scanned Jenni. "You appear tired but unharmed." Her frown encompassed Aric. "*You're* hurt!" She gestured to the tall naiader behind her and he took Jenni from Aric.

"I should have been here!" the merfem said. "I like to watch the dawn from under the waves, but I should not have left you or my home or my Folk!"

"You weren't to know," Aric said.

Jenni had to agree. "No." She hadn't told the merfem, hadn't wanted any interference. A bad call.

The Waterfolk took them to the living room overlooking the ocean. The naiader lowered her gently to a love seat and brought a heavy raw silk afghan to cover her and she realized she was shivering.

Aric was placed on a chair under a skylight that let in the sun, and his shirt was whisked off to show bloody wounds on his torso as well as his face. Wounds—plural—that Jenni hadn't noticed, hadn't tended. Guilt stung her as she watched Diamantina lay her hands on him and close those injuries. She had a small healing gift.

He leaned toward her—unconsciously, Jenni knew—and more than guilt twisted inside her. A fire to a Tree-man was intriguing but dangerous. Water to him was… necessary and fulfilling.

Stupid twinges of jealousy, she shouldn't be having them. Her emotions were too near the surface, she was more exhausted than she'd known. She tried to keep her eyes open to watch her lover and the merfem, but it got harder and harder and she slipped into unconsciousness.

Noise woke her, and she figured she hadn't been out too long—not long enough that anyone had moved her from her seat, though both the guardians stood on each side of her chair. It didn't take ten seconds before she understood that if she'd thought she was watched and on short reins before, it was nothing to what would be in the future.

All the Eight were there. As she watched in tired stupefaction, they marched out to the area she'd balanced and a great hum of approval swept through the open door and broke over her. They even joined hands and did a quick, joyful dance that shot bright and glittering light through the door, too.

Jenni looked at Aric in the chair. She, he, and the guardians were now the only ones in the main room.

"I'm hungry," she said, repeating Aric's earlier words.

There didn't look to be any sort of table with food that had been presented to him. "And I'm tired."

The elf guardian patted her head and the pure strength of him filtered through her, letting her sit up straight. "We've listened to Aric's report."

The dwarf snorted. "I think we need to go through that fight step-by-step again. Aric said that you *threw* energies at Kondrian?"

"Yes, and can't anyone follow him and stop him from...hurting people so he heals?"

Both guardians shook their heads. "He's home by now," the dwarf said. "And his stronghold has impenetrable defenses."

"But he has to feed—"

"He has slaves," the dwarf stated.

Jenni couldn't wrap her mind around that. Slaves.

The dwarf grunted. "Disappearing homeless from financially devastated cities in the east. Refugees moving from one war-torn place to another unaccounted for."

"Humans," Jenni whispered.

"Humans are prolific and he and his sort feed on the humans that no one cares about," the elf said gently. "And he's old, and as far as Aric could tell, he wasn't too wounded."

"Damn! I did my best," she said.

"And you did very well." Another pat on the head sent calmness through her, even though she didn't want it.

"Pearl Wave, we need food here for Aric and Princess Jindesfarne," the dwarf called.

Stomping so that the bells on her ankles made dissonant jangles, Diamantina's companion entered the house.

She gazed at them, sniffed and shut the front door, as if Jenni and Aric were too lowly to see the great Lightfolk as they explored the elemental magics caught in the land that Jenni had balanced for them.

The naiad vanished into the kitchen and came back with two large bowls of oatmeal.

Aric dug into his with enthusiasm.

Jenni hated oatmeal.

Later that week Jenni prepared to balance the beach, the place she'd stand when the bubble rose from the core of the Earth. She went through all her rituals and was unsurprised when Cloudsylph knocked on her door as soon as she was ready, took her and floated her down from the cliff to where her pillar of fire energy was.

Nor was she surprised to see the two guardians and the full complement of the Eight watch her as she summoned the mist—that only she could see—and went into it. The Eight and their great powers added to the problems of balancing the land. She didn't dare draw magic from them and had to continually peer through the mist for more elemental energies, so the balancing was harder and more complex than she'd anticipated. But she was pleased with her pattern. And it was *her* pattern, something that would resonate with her, boost her own energy, tailored to her since she was the one who would be using it. She decided that she'd visit the place every day to feed more magic into the pattern. She wouldn't need a pillar of flame anymore, she'd just be pulled to *her* place.

Blocking all the interest and "whispering" of the

Lightfolk that she thought was going on in the real world, she carefully turned ocean-ward and stretched all her senses to once again see if she could feel the beginnings of the bubble energy underneath the ocean…like trying to search for minute indications of boiling on the bottom of a simmering pot. She believed she could distinguish that, and realized that the Eight, or Diamantina, or her staff or all the other Folk the Eight would bring with them, might try to search for such signals.

They would probably consider her perfectly balanced spot on the beach the place to stand for such a search. They'd muck up her pattern by imprinting their own energy on it. And though Jenni fully intended to fine-tune the pattern the morning of the equinox, she didn't want to do that again and again.

What to do? Shifting her balance, she realized her skin began to go clammy, a sign that she'd stayed in the mist too long.

CHAPTER
28

BUT SHE NEEDED TO PROTECT HER PATTERN. A few minutes now would save her magic in the future, and it was already too late to stop the effects this time. Her body heat had drained.

Ignoring her shivering, she flipped through mental files, decided on a spell Rothly had created. One she'd found on her pocket computer after she'd visited Northumberland.

Stamping in place and shaking out her arms, bringing dry heat to warm her, she crafted a cagelike shield spell, a ward that would keep others from stepping on the ground that contained her three-dimensional magical pattern. And...done!

She left the mist and saw Aric's concerned face. The Eight now stood together, arranged much like they were when they sat on their thrones.

She stumbled to Aric.

"You've been gone a good three-quarters of an hour. I worried." Aric took her hands, dropped them with an oath, watched her from under lowered brows. "You had to summon fire to warm yourself, didn't you?"

"Yes." The word was a croak, and she realized how dry her throat was. If she smiled or talked too much her lips would crack.

The Water Queen hurried over, stood before Jenni and placed her hands on Jenni's shoulders. In an instant, Jenni felt her shriveled tissues plump. She inclined her head. "Thank you."

The queen patted her on her shoulders. "You're welcome."

Someone yipped. Jenni whirled to see that Diamantina's naiad companion, Pearl Wave, was standing close to Jenni's pattern. Too close. The seaweed gown the naiad wore was crispy brown, cracking and falling in pieces.

There was the tiniest snort of laughter from the Water Queen.

Jenni scanned the crowd. "I need to keep the spot where I will work pristine. Sacred. Naturally I set wards."

"Naturally," the Fire Queen said, gliding up to them.

The Water Queen smiled cheerfully, then withdrew to where the ocean could swirl around her calves.

Humming approval, Queen Emberdrake went toward the wards, then ran her hands as if shaping a column. "Very well done, dear."

"Thank you."

Her husband joined her. Nodded. "Yes." He put his

arm around Jenni's shoulder and squeezed. "Proud of you."

Jenni swallowed. These two were treating her as if she were a part of their family and she was still unsure about them, and all the Eight.

"Hmmph!" The dwarf king, the eldest and most powerful, stumped over. He looked Jenni's column up and down as if he could see it easily when it was only a shimmer in the air to her. Jutting his chin and sliding his eyes toward her, he lifted a finger as if to poke, and said, "You permit?"

Surprised that he'd asked, she nodded reflexively.

He touched his finger to the ward, just testing, not trying to get through. If he'd wanted he could probably collapse her shield like a round of tissue-paper cards.

He hopped back, swearing in dwarvish with words that crashed against her ears. His fingernail-gnarly-claw looked burnt. Then he grinned, nodded. "Good work."

Without saying another word, he vanished, as did his wife. The rest of the Eight followed. Diamantina sent Jenni a considering glance, gestured for her companion to leave, then vanished, too.

The only ones left on the beach were Jenni and Aric and the two guardians. Those men circled the column, the elf with his hand on his sword hilt, the dwarf rubbing his beard. They walked to the beach, along the tide line, along the shadowy brown ripple in the sand that marked low tide, back to join Jenni and Aric.

"You'll stand here for the equinox ritual?" the dwarf grunted.

"Yes," Jenni said.

"In the mist, like you were earlier."

"Right."

Another grunt. He circled until he was on the north side of her ward. "Think they'll come from the north if they want Jenni. They'll fly."

"Yes," agreed the elf guardian. "The south has many humans that one must shield oneself from, which takes energy that should be saved for battle. The east will have all the wards that the Eight put up around the estate and any attacker would reach them before Jenni on the beach."

"And me," Aric said, tilting his own sword at his side.

"And us," the dwarf said.

"West is the ocean. Crossing it takes a lot of power, too."

"They'll come from the north," Aric said.

Jenni got the idea that this had already been determined and was being said for her sake. At least none of these males were being condescending.

All three of them stared at Jenni's ward, maybe observed beyond that to the balanced energy pattern. She wondered what they saw.

The elf turned to her. "How long can you stay within the place between dimensions?"

Shrugging, Jenni said, "I don't know. It depends upon circumstances, how strong I am, what ambient energies are around—" She'd made the mistake of looking him in the eyes and the piercing blue of his gaze immobilized her.

When he spoke, it was softly wrapped steel. "You can't be harmed in there. On the day of the ritual, you stay in there." He glanced away so she wasn't enthralled, and she found herself trembling. He didn't want a repeat of the portal tragedy when her mother, who was anchor, was struck down and her family exited the gray mist at her screams.

"Girl child," the dwarf said, jerked a thumb at her spot on the beach. "You stay in there until you'll die with your next breath. Only then do you come out. Got that?"

Icy waves of fear flooded her. Treeman, elf, dwarf. All three men wore identical warrior expressions. They were expecting her to be attacked, anticipating a battle right here. By Kondrian. Maybe even other powerful Dark ones.

She stared at Aric, his face was unyielding. "Stay in the interdimension, Jenni."

She could only nod.

The days between the attack by Kondrian and the spring equinox dragged by with oppressive slowness. The only good news was from her job. The leprechaun event and story line was a major hit. Enough that it would repeat for several years in March. Jenni wondered if she'd be alive next March.

The guardians were often around, though unseen. Jenni got so she could sense them and knew Aric could do the same.

One or another of the Eight was usually on site part of the day, interacting with Diamantina and her staff, chanting or dancing on the ritual area—and if they upset the balance even slightly they wanted Jenni to fix it then and there. When she was within three days of the ritual, she refused, saying she couldn't spare the energy. The Water King was not pleased.

Jenni was both irritated and relieved that she wasn't in on all the war sessions that Aric attended. She wasn't sure she wanted to think of worst-case scenarios, but concentrated only on what she was responsible for, and what she could handle.

She'd decided that she would call her brother every day. He was healed in body and magic—even if it wasn't his former magical skills. Maybe being whole would lead to healing his heart and mind. And attitude. She phoned Rothly and, as usual, had to leave a message. She told him what she was doing and that she'd used his shielding spell to good effect. No answer. The next day she spent a while talking about the spiderwebs and shadleeches and received a rude message in return. "Sounds stupid. No spiderwebs here, you fool."

His continuing bitterness pinched her until she walked in the ocean and let the waves wash over her feet, checked the beach once more, though few people had come down here—Aric and the two guardians, and the Emberdrakes. Jenni could sense that the King and Queen of Water, and other merfolk, had swum down to the ocean floor to check on incipient bubble energies. She wasn't informed if any had sensed them.

The day before the ritual, Jenni watched Diamantina and her household check the dancing circle and the beach, and step out measurements where the pavilions of the Eight and their retinues would camp. She hadn't ever seen the huge and gaily colored tents arrive, but recalled that she'd run past them on her way to the portal during that mission many years ago. She and her family had stayed in a shabby hotel.

Today she watched until she was shooed away. After she double-checked the beach, she went back to her room and called Rothly and told him she loved him.

She recorded the various spells she'd used in the family journal and emailed them to him. Then Aric came in and proposed other, more physical, plans to relieve the tension.

As afternoon cooled into evening, Jenni woke from dozing in Aric's arms when sudden power surged through her as if she were a gas burner being ignited. She sat up at the same time as Aric. His arm around her went hard and she sensed he was mentally cursing.

"What is it?"

"Nothing."

But his tone of voice as well as the change in his aura told her what was wrong. She leaned against him and rubbed her head on his shoulder. "I suppose we should have anticipated that the Eight would have brought an excellent bard or three."

"Hired." Aric slipped from her grasp and out of bed, pulled on some knit sweatpants of a pale brown. His lip curled. "My father, Windstrum, doesn't work for free."

Jenni shoved hair out of her face, watched Aric pace, shoulders bunched with muscle. She wasn't sure what to say. She didn't want to push. Aric knew that she wanted him to reconcile with his estranged father.

He went to the window that looked inland and snorted.

"What?" Jenni crawled from bed.

Shaking his head, a lopsided smile kicked up a side of his mouth. He angled his chin, pointing. "Look."

She did, and blinked. The sight was familiar—sort of. Denver's white airport "tents" were pretty well known by now. The Eight had copied the shape, but the large pavilion sure wasn't white. Peaks were red and orange with flamelike tracings, light violet and the palest shade of summer-blue sky, a mountain of varied-colored browns, deep blue and green with wavy swirls. She laughed and a little of the strain of the anticipation of tomorrow eased. "Nice."

"You would think so," he said, but there was an indulgent note in his voice.

Jenni noted that there weren't any colors of Treefolk— no rich red-browns that mimicked redwoods or greens of spring leaves or oak forests.

Aric put an arm around her shoulders. "We wouldn't want a place with the Eight anyway."

She wondered if that were true.

"And if there are visitors from dryads or Treemen…" He tilted his head and Jenni knew that there were. "They would be using the trees on the land and the greenhome."

"Uh-huh." She wondered if his mother was there.

He turned to face Jenni. "I've asked Leafswirl to stay away. Too dangerous."

Fear painted the inside of Jenni's throat. He wouldn't want his mother to see him dead, either.

"Will you go meet your father?" Jenni asked, and knew at once she'd made a mistake.

"No." Aric's expression set. "He'll be entertaining the Eight and their entourages, busy."

Too busy to acknowledge his son. That had always been the excuse Jenni had heard. Aric didn't want to risk rejection again, who would? And she figured that Windstrum *would* reject Aric...or be more interested in soaking up the effervescence of the Eight's magic, being the life of the party, catering to the great Lightfolk than spending time with his son.

A brief knock came at the door and it opened to show the most minor naiad of the household behind a tray floating with a nutritious but bland meal.

Aric went to take the tray and the anti-grav spell vanished. "Apparently we are eating here in our room tonight," he said.

"All our rooms and dining areas are now full," said the naiad, who then turned her back and hurried away. The door swung shut behind her.

Aric grunted and glanced at the tiny round table that they'd been using as a desk—one at a time.

There was a small *crack* and the browniefem who'd served them before walked out of the wall. She sniffed in disapproval. At first Jenni thought it was because the room was very humid due to the staff practicing their magic to make everything perfect. But then the fem reached up to touch the tray full of food and it vanished.

"Fire lady say your food must good," the brownie said. With a whisk of her hands, the electronics and papers on the table were banished to a dresser drawer that opened and shut in the blink of an eye. A new top was placed on the table to extend the space—it looked to be granite. Jenni touched it and found it heated. Then dishes and flatware appeared on the table, along with food.

Luscious-smelling seared steak made her mouth water. Tender steamed green vegetables along with buttery new potatoes.

"Keep you good for tomorrow." The brownie gave a definitive nod, then disappeared.

Aric bolted toward the table, found "elf and Treefolk" fare—more tubers and roots that he preferred, quail. He transferred half of the steamed vegetables to his plate, half to Jenni's and the moment the serving dish was empty it disappeared from his hands. He grunted again, this time in pleasure.

He pulled out a chair for Jenni, then sat himself and they both ate.

As usual, flavors popped in her mouth and sank into her tongue and there was just enough for her to feel replete but not overfull. She made no comment on the music that drifted to them from the Eight's banquet.

After dinner was done and they moved from the table, everything that the brownie had brought disappeared and the electronics were reinstated in their previous places.

They hadn't spoken much during the meal and now Jenni said, "I'm going to take a shower. I think I'll stay in here tonight." The atmosphere outside was more like a carnival than the eve of a battle—reminding her that it had been that way fifteen years ago, too. The Light-folk, in general, were a happy people. But last time she'd stayed out until the last flute played the final note. Not tonight.

Everything rested on her tomorrow.

Aric's eyelashes lowered, his smile was slow.

Jenni had already taken off her blouse, slipped out of her jeans. At his look, she stopped and held them in front of her. "I don't know if I can. Loving. Tonight or tomorrow morning." Too many memories, too many similarities between this mission and the last.

She'd tried to ignore those over the last days, concentrated on the differences—her own power was greater, as was her knowledge. Her spell technique had refined since she was so determined and focused.

But now all the memories had risen to plague her and anything that echoed of the past resonated to thrum her nerves. She couldn't bear it if she failed again, and that meant taking steps so she wouldn't.

Her emotions churned and she knew he sensed them.

"Oh, Jindesfarne," he whispered, sorrow in his eyes. He stood. "I hadn't considered."

Men. What was so difficult to understand that she wouldn't take a chance on repeating her previous mistakes?

He walked to her, into her personal space, but not quite touching her. She became aware of mass; his height, taller than she, his body wider than hers. The solidity of him, the strength. But he hadn't been strong during the portal mission. He'd been weak, and his weakness had matched her own in putting their pleasure before their duty that morning.

She wouldn't do that again.

CHAPTER
29

ARIC SAID, "WHAT IF I PROMISED YOU THAT we will be on the beach and ready for the ritual to start two hours before it is scheduled?"

An inward tremor had her gritting her teeth. Tears pressed against the backs of her eyes. He, too, had regrets. Maybe he didn't feel the guilt because they'd been "late," but maybe he was as determined as she to make this experience different.

This time he touched her. Fingertips on her cheek, feathering down to trace her lips. He smiled and though the sadness lingered in his eyes, a glint was back. He pressed his fingers to her lips like a kiss, a benediction. Then his hands drew down her neck, and again he barely brushed the sensitive tatt on her nape. Tingles shivered through her, heating her blood, her skin, her core.

His smile widened, but he remained silent. His touch swept down her shoulders, her waist, until his hands settled on her hips. His gaze met hers. "I wouldn't do anything to upset you at this juncture, Jenni." He jerked his head to their electronics on the table. "Four alarms are set." A corner of his mouth twisted. "And the naiad we like least has orders to personally wake us three hours ahead of the midmorning ritual. For breakfast and cleansing and preparation. We won't be late this time, Jenni. I promise you."

He'd changed. The careless young man who'd put his pleasure first was long gone, ground to a sharp blade for the Eight. He learned to put their missions first, and his own Folk, the Treefolk. He'd thought of others first for a long time.

"I trust you," she said.

Closing his eyes, he dropped his hands, his smile dimmed, then kicked up again. "Go start your shower, Jenni."

She rolled her clothes up and stuck them in her backpack—a magical backpack now with a pocket of greenspace provided by Aric. She couldn't reach into such a space, but she could request something pop out. The pack had expanded as she picked up items along the way. Even as she stuffed her clothes in, she wondered if she'd be in any kind of shape to draw them out in the future.

In the bathroom she stripped and put her bra and panties in the laundry chute, again wondering when she'd get them back with all the demands on the household staff.

The bathroom was the best thing about this place, and nearly as big as their bedroom. Each tile was uniquely painted and had a slight texture that made it nonslippery.

There was a freshwater pool-tub set in stone in the floor, with easy steps down and jet options…all worked by magic. An enclosed shower had opposite showerheads on each wall. She stepped in the shower and steamed up the place. Her muscles relaxed and her turbulent emotions quieted enough to be tucked away.

Then the shower door opened and Aric stepped in, fully aroused, and her entire body hummed with anticipation. Again he put his hands on her hips. He said, "Music," and a deep beating rhythm upped the spiral of desire that came as his slick hands roamed her body. He pulled her close and they swayed to Spanish-inspired music that she didn't know he liked. It lit her fire nature, and as his hands stroked and she returned the sensual touch, reveling in skin over smooth muscle, wet, hers, all thought vanished.

They danced, they played, they merged. Him thrusting into her with a pleasure that had her panting, pumping, breaking into shards of deep pleasure. Forming again.

She held on to him as he leaned against the warm wall of the shower, ordered the music and the water off. With barely enough breath to order a breeze to dry them, she enjoyed the contentment of caring that came after sex.

He put an arm around her, bracing her as they walked from the bathroom, where he helped her with the overlarge soft cotton T-shirt that she wore to bed, nuzzling her ear, then tucked her in.

She was sleepy until a wisp of song came from outside their windows and all the responsibility she had tomorrow hit her once again and froze her with icy dread.

Aric was there with a drink, his face austere.

Sniffing, she understood the warm herbal liquid was a sleeping potion without any side effects. With the potion and sleeping with Aric, she might not even wake up in the middle of the night. She took it and downed it, warming from the inside out without using her magic. She settled back into the plump feather pillows. "I take it that this means no more loving tonight."

"You take it wrong." He slid into bed with her. "I need to ensure that you will sleep well. My duty."

"Ah," she said, then she only moaned.

When she woke up, the planet had turned and the sun had risen and it was the day of the spring equinox. The day of the mission. The day that would change her life.

Aric was as quiet as she, speaking gently to the naiad who pounded on the door after they were already awake, the browniefem who'd come to serve them breakfast.

Jenni listened to her blood and body's beat, had done the procedure for entering the interdimension often enough that there would be no hesitation.

She dressed in silk: undershirt and blouse, thin long johns and heavier trousers. All items were woven in different directions—a battle precaution. Aric wore heavier padded silk armor with light chain mail—and spells. He'd also hardened his skin until it shone like polished redwood.

Soon they were ready—or for Jenni, as ready as she would ever be. It was obvious from the way Aric dressed and checked his weapons that he'd fought over the years, while she had avoided her magic and her heritage. The last week had been good. No one had wanted to visit with her, so she concentrated on the mission—and proving herself.

Ripples of chimes collided with piano riffs and an epic music theme as all their electronic alarms sounded.

Jenni chuckled and Aric laughed, rolled his shoulders to settle his armor. "Now we go. The Lightfolk are preparing the dancing circle."

Some of the underlying tension that had imbued her since she'd awakened knowing it was *the day* settled within her, adding energy instead of distracting. These were the great magical Folk. She certainly wouldn't be alone in handling the bubble. Now that he'd mentioned it, she felt the heaviness of magic surrounding her.

She could only do her part and balance the energies inside the bubble and when it popped. Everything after that was up to the Lightfolk.

Aric stopped her when she put her hand on the door latch, turned her around. The feel of his hands on her—smooth and flexible wood, so different!—distracted her mind and body and sent them into considering sex instead of magic.

He tipped her chin up, his eyes like emeralds, crystalline, hard to read. Bending his head he kissed her, lightly, tenderly. The scent of him—sparkling air magic, the secret depths of great forests, redwood, man—wrapped around her until she ached with wanting to stay with him.

Lifting his head, he stepped back. "I love you," he said, just as he hadn't said it fifteen years ago on that lost morning of Before.

She opened her mouth to say it in return, but the words couldn't come out. She couldn't be that vulnerable before this man who had hurt her so, whom she'd believed had betrayed her. Not *this* morning, the morning of the next battle where she might live or die.

He might die, too. "I—I…" But she could only scrape that word from her throat, no others.

Again he gathered her close, rocked her, murmured words against her hair. His hand covered the tatt on her neck and she shivered under his touch. "I understand. This is too much like the time before when you were hurt so badly." His other hand lifted to stroke her hair. "I'm with you all the way today. I won't leave you."

Unless he died outside the interdimension, like the rest of her family had, except Rothly.

Rothly she *could* do something about. She reached for him mentally, it was eight hours later there, in Northumberland, and she sensed it was gray and raining. She almost wished it was gray and raining here, so the weather and the morning wasn't like that last battle.

Rothly, she called mentally. *I love you.*

He was startled.

I forgive you, she said, telling him again in words what had to be said. *I love you and forgive you.* This was the right thing to do.

Her brother slammed shields against her, but she'd done what she'd needed to, a small weight that had burdened her had lifted. She looked into Aric's eyes, found her mouth quirking as she said, "I forgive you, too."

Aric shook his head. "I don't think you do, all the way down to the last flicker-flame of your being, or you'd be able to tell me you loved me." He kissed her forehead. "But you've—we've—come a long way in a short amount of time. We'll get where we need to be."

She hoped so.

"Time to go." He stepped around her and opened a door.

On a shaky breath she left the room to walk out the door for a last check of the dancing circle. To confront the Lightfolk and the full Eight.

CHAPTER
30

NO ONE WAS IN THE HOUSE, EVERYONE WAS outside near the Lightfolk camp...and they all watched Jenni as she crossed to the area that had been prepared for a sacred dancing ritual. Aric accompanied her like the guard he was.

The gazes of the Eight and all the other powerful Lightfolk they'd gathered had weight. The strongest in elemental magic were there to cast the spell that would direct the rich bubble energies for the result the Eight wished. A new stream of change that would affect the entire world.

This wouldn't be an on-the-fly spell like she and Aric and the guardians had done at Yellowstone. Since this was the last bubble, she was sure the event was planned to the last detail.

The Eight wanted that creative bubble force to bolster the Lightfolk so they wouldn't die out, maybe become more fertile. A good plan as far as it went, but Jenni figured any stream of magic infused with hope and creativity would benefit everyone. Not to mention the fact that this new upsurge of magic might very well meld with the evolving tech of humankind and forge something better.

Look how the shadleeches that had been created by the first bubble had been bad for Lightfolk and humans alike, "good" only for the Darkfolk who could use and direct them to do harm.

Her feet tingled as magic from many Folk saturated the ground. Where the Lightfolk had trod now showed greener grasses, and even white crocus in a wide ring, a fairy ring. Beautiful. She stared at the green and the flowers, reluctantly accepting that the Lightfolk, on the whole, were good for Earth…at least better for the Earth than her own human heritage.

She'd even give the Eight the benefit of the doubt and accept that, in this matter, they were truly interested in helping the whole Lightfolk community, all the way down to the weakest air sprite.

Her trancelike state deepened as more of the herbs from her last potion kicked in. The air seemed to buzz around her. She went to the middle of the circle and stood, spread-legged, and lifted her arms wide, opened her mouth to check the magic.

Not. Quite. Balanced. Too many magical people spending too much time here. But it would only take a tweak or two to set all right.

One breath, two, the pattern of the chant and steps and the gray mist formed before her. She took the half step into the interdimension. A night with aurora borealis was nothing like this. Each Lightfolk colored the mist—from the dull gold of the small browniefem who'd taken to providing Jenni and Aric with their meals, to a flaming red-orange that had Jenni frowning at the general familiarity of its superheated flash of blue until she understood that Synicess had been invited.

The Eight were majestic pillars of elemental magic.

It took Jenni only three breaths to gather some of the ambient power and weave it into her previous spell, adjusting the balance of all four elements to perfection. That's what the Eight expected from her, and what she intended to deliver.

Another breath and she backed out of the mist, banished it with a gesture. Sunshine warmed her and she caught a look of surprise on Aric's face. "Done so soon?"

"I don't know how long it will take the bubble to rise from the Earth's crust and float up into the atmosphere to break." She rolled her shoulders, the coolness of the interdimension had slid against her skin, not quite sinking in, and she wanted the warmth. "I anticipate entering and exiting the interdimension several times instead of staying there."

Her father's friend, Etesian, the scholarly elf, hurried up and put an arm around her shoulders, gave her a short squeeze. "Quite so." He stared at the Eight. "You must reserve your skill to attempt to balance the energy inside the bubble."

Jenni nodded, leaned slightly into the elf, who smelled of leather and paper and a spring breeze. "Most of my magic will be joining great outside energies with the bubble magic after it bursts."

The Fire King, Emberdrake, now her adopted father, rubbed his hands, smiling. "You'll give us a great deal of equal magical elemental power to work with. Thank you." He topped off his thanks with a bow.

"You're quite welcome."

"Dear Jenni," the Fire Queen said, smiling. She walked up on a perfumed fragrance of summer blossoms with a hint of musk. "Well done." She took Jenni's hands and leaned over to kiss each of Jenni's cheeks. Her chocolate-brown eyes were warm with pride. "You have been so very sturdy this last week under less than ideal circumstances." She gave the tiniest of sniffs. "Living in a mer-fem's house."

"It wasn't that bad," Jenni said.

Queen Emberdrake raised perfect dark brows at Jenni's lie. Her mouth quirked and she squeezed Jenni's hands. "We'll be ready to drink champagne with you after this is all over."

Jenni could only pray that would happen. She dipped a curtsy and the queen released her hands. The Air King came up and patted her shoulder. "Good job."

"Thank you." Then she faded back to the front porch of the house, leaving the area to the Lightfolk. Not one halfling was there except herself.

They formed a large circle, but didn't hold hands yet to close it. The strongest of all the Lightfolk in the world, about thirty of them, and most of them armed. Jenni wondered if it would be enough against the Dark ones who would show up. And wondered, as all must, how many of the remaining four great Dark ones would come.

The royals, the Eight, entered singly in the order of the strength of their power. Last was the dwarf king, as the greatest of all the Lightfolk. He circled the Folk, as if studying them, stood in the center and stamped his feet as if testing her work. Then his gaze arrowed to her and he nodded. Her held breath dribbled out. First obstacle overcome. The Eight approved of her balancing of their ritual area, even though it changed every instant each person was on it. She'd done her best.

She inclined her head and turned to go back into the house, to descend to her place on the beach. Behind her, she sensed Aric bowing to the Eight.

The house was colder than ever, seemed almost empty since much of the power it had contained was now drawn to the dancing circle.

When she reached the beach, she found the two guardians walking along the shoreline. They turned and greeted her with welcoming smiles. Their gazes slid over Aric, weighing, and he stiffened beside her.

The elf came up and slapped Aric on the shoulder. "You're looking good."

He relaxed slightly, but Jenni thought his anxiety was still there. No matter how much he trained, a half-Tree-folk half-elf could not match either of these warriors. "Glad to see you here."

"For the duration," the dwarf grunted.

"What's that smell?" Aric asked.

Jenni sniffed, there was a faint oily metallic tang in the air.

"Dark ones."

She stopped, yards from her place in the sand. "What?"

"They've been here, scouting." The elf loosened his sword in his hilt, a gesture that indicated a habit rather than need.

"I didn't sense them," she whispered.

"Minor evils." The dwarf showed his pointy red teeth. "Minions."

"Uh-huh." Jenni's stomach tightened. She wished so much this was a computer game and not reality.

Aric's fingers touched the small of her back, urging her toward her pattern. "You'll be safe in the interdimension."

"I shouldn't stay there for long. Only when I need to be there to work. That is…when the bubble bursts and to hold the magics equal for the Eight's spell," she repeated for the benefit of the guardians.

The elf graced her with a half smile. "We heard you the first time."

"Ah. About the Dark ones." She hadn't asked about that, either.

"We don't think all four'll show up," the dwarf said. "Three, max."

She was close to her spot now, could smell stale bubblegum. "Including Kondrian."

"Intelligence has it that he is at full power again," the elf said. "No doubt they'll attack at what they perceive to be the worst possible time for us." He sounded unruffled, though Jenni was nearly panting.

Aric frowned at the air guardian.

"We believe they may work at cross-purposes, as usual," the elf ended.

Notes of chimes and harps and flutes drifted down from the bluff. Jenni looked up to see the circle ceremoniously closed.

"They're starting the preparatory ritual to test their magics and blend them. Though everyone convened once to practice, that was in the air palace, not here, not where they have a completely balanced dancing floor." The elf lifted Jenni's limp fingers and kissed them. "You have nothing to worry about. You'll be fine."

Pellets of sand shot into the air. They looked at the dwarf, who kicked the sand again, scowling at them. "You know I hate when you say things like that. *Hate* that."

Still with the half smile, the elf shook his head, bowed and handed Jenni onto her spot. She took it, and her churning emotions subsided. Everyone was prepared for the Dark ones, for the bubble. She should just concentrate on fulfilling her tasks.

She angled herself until she faced the point where she'd been keeping track of the energy she'd associated with the bubble. There was a little fizz, one she could almost hear. Shaking her head, she met Aric's eyes. "I'm going into the interdimension."

So she breathed and chanted and pattered her feet. Misty and gray, the interdimension rose before her and she shuffled into the different space.

There was a quiet sigh.

Nothing mentally from anyone around her—Aric or the guardians.

Nothing from the Eight and their chosen Lightfolk on the hill above, who had finished their preparatory ritual and were dancing freely, flickering energies.

From deep in the earth, under the ocean, under the crust.

A sense of great magics, encased in a sphere.

Enormous.

Rising.

The bubble.

Her skin went clammy in an instant. The mist pressed against her, seemed to writhe with nightmarish shapes. Her imagination, she knew. But her heart beat hard as she realized that all their timing was off. Again.

The bubble wasn't going to wait for the exact moment of the spring equinox in an hour. If she'd been on time, once again she'd have been late.

She calmed just enough to say the words to make a graceful exit that wouldn't wrench her.

Still, as she stepped back, her ankle twisted and she lurched into Aric's arms. She grabbed him, looked at the guardians. "It's rising. The bubble is coming!"

"At what pace?" asked the elf. His face had gone tight, intense.

"Fairly quickly. Coming through the planet now, I can't tell how close. Except probably will hit within…" She speared her fingers through her hair, tugged at it as if that would make her calculate correctly. "No more than three-quarters of an hour. And it's huge."

"How huge is huge?" asked the dwarf.

Jenni flopped her hands in a wide gesture. "Uh. Could encase a semitruck? At least."

Not a Lightfolk comparison. The three men stared at her. "Uh, hold my house?"

"Full. Of. Magic," the elf said.

"Yes."

"Wild magic, *new* magic, elemental energies straight from the Earth's core itself!"

The Kings and Queens of Earth and Water appeared on the beach. Ringed around Jenni.

"You say the bubble is rising!" the Water King demanded. His green hair moved like waves.

"Yes." She stood straighter, lifted her chin. "It's coming through the crust now." She looked at the Earth King.

His brows lowered but he didn't appear any more gruff than usual. Tilting his head, he said, "Maybe. Maybe." He shot out a stubby finger to point at her. "Go back into that place where you can see such energies and link mentally with us."

She didn't want to, wanted to save her strength. Aric nudged her.

"All right." She rubbed her arms, didn't want to spare any magic to warm herself. Shaking out her limbs, she enunciated her words—Mistweaver spellwords, nonsense words to others—and did all that must be done, and found herself once again in the interdimension.

YOU CAN HEAR ME? The Earth King's voice pounded in her head like a sledgehammer on an anvil.

You are too loud, she replied mildly.

She thought she could hear the rumble as he cleared his throat. *Examine the energies you believe indicate the bubble.*

Since no one was around, she sniffed in disdain. She hadn't entered facing the ocean, but now let the already stronger elemental magic pull her to the right direction.

Pressure filled the atmosphere as if even this space between the Earth's dimension and others' awaited a significant event. She scrutinized moving elements, wrapped in balls, not stretched out in sheets like she was accustomed to seeing. Flashing lightning red-orange and violet-white: fire and air. Thrumming splashes of green-blue, golden brown that moved like earth, groaning and cracking. Near the crust right now. No more than a couple of hundred yards northwest of where she stood. Though deep, it was "visibly" coming closer.

Narrowing her eyes, she focused and projected her magical-sight, hoping the dwarf king—and whoever else might be linked to her—the Emberdrakes on the cliff and Aric could sense what she did.

Wonderful, whispered Aric. She got the impression he was looking at the mist, too. The sheets of elemental magic that flowed eerily in the distance, the flickers of the magical Lightfolk on the ridge that she glimpsed at the edge of her vision.

A hollow grunt popped in her ears. The Earth King. *Eight, prepare for the royal tuning-and-joining ceremony,* ordered the dwarf.

Dark ones sighted in the distance! someone cried.

Fire is MINE! shouted someone.

The blackness of death slammed across Jenni's senses. She crumpled onto the ground of the interdimension. Dared not move.

CHAPTER 31

FIRE WINKED OUT. A HUGE GAPING HOLE appeared in the balanced elements that had glowed around her. Jenni rocked to her hands and knees. Magic lifted her hair, coating each strand with sweat. The King and Queen of Fire had died! Stabbing pain of loss. She hadn't thought she'd bonded with them much. She'd been wrong.

How?

No time, no time. Air and water energies were rushing to overcome all. She reached into the Earth's crust, into the center of herself and *pulled,* grabbing as much fire as she could handle, drawing sheets of the energies to herself, the beach, the area.

Her tears sizzled away as they left her eyes and met the hot skin of her cheeks. Another family lost, ripped away. New mother and father. How? How? How?

Jenni! Rothly screamed in terror.

Here! she managed a faint reply. Forcing the air and water energies back, drawing fire to fill the gap. She couldn't hold it long.

Sister! Hold two minutes. A male voice, but not Rothly. Strained but calm. Who? She strove to think as she wedged raw elemental fire energy into the gap she'd kept open. Let it run wild a little bit, flame the air hot, steam away the encroaching water. Maybe, maybe she had two minutes before the fire burned her up. She took a breath and it seared and she used the fire itself to protect her lungs.

Who had called her? Blinking, an image formed of a man—a full Lightfolk—whom she'd vaguely noticed on the bluff. The Emberdrakes' son. Even as she thought of him, the wild fire was drawn to a new source, tamed. Most of it. Not as much as the older royals could control, but enough to keep all steady. Enough that Jenni could let the reins on it slither away. A new Fire King and Queen had stepped into place.

Rothly pressed again...*Jenni?*

I...am...okay.... She doubled over, feeling aching emptiness, the hollowness of loss, the stone of tangled emotions lodged again in her belly. She—they'd, Rothly and she—had had ties to the Emberdrakes. Distant relatives and adoption bonds that had lain lightly until cut. She didn't know how she could bear it, but she would have to. She had no time to let grief roil through her, she *had* to go on, or all was lost.

Who died? Rothly asked in a small voice and she heard the self-blame in it, the loathing of self that he hadn't been there to help.

The Emberdrakes, she moaned.

The King and Queen of Fire? Both!

Both…both…both…all, all, all.

Sister, we need you! Control yourself! the new King of Fire snapped.

Who the hell are you on our private mental line? Rothly demanded.

I am your brother, Blackstone Emberdrake. Jindesfarne, straighten up and do your job. Desperation seeped into his tones, and the fire was wild again, unconstrained. Jenni snatched more.

How? whispered Rothly.

Betrayal! A female voice hard with anger shouted it aloud as well as mentally. With the whip of words, more fire was gathered from Jenni, shaped into good use. Blackstone's wife. A strong djinnfem. Good.

Betrayal. Jenni finally understood the word. It hit with the force of remembered agony that she'd betrayed her family. She reeled, didn't hold on to the mind-set for the interdimension, fell out, onto the beach where only Aric and the guardians were.

Mistake.

"How dare you say I betrayed!" screamed a familiar voice and Jenni felt a wrenching in the magical fire energies, more immediate here in the real world. A wrenching in her being, too, as her bonds with the other Emberdrakes were skewed, strained. Her gaze went to the top of the bluff where the Eight—the *Six*—had mended the circle and were grimly continuing with the ritual.

Three figures were separate, throwing flames.

"Jenni, get back into your mist!" the new Fire Queen shouted from above. But she wasn't the queen. Shades of magic bathed her. Synicess had grabbed fire energy, was glorying in it, using it as a weapon on Jenni's Emberdrake brother and his wife.

Synicess wanted to be Fire Queen.

Royal status was in the balance. Power.

"I *was* the one betrayed! Me! My parents abandoned me to go to another dimension." Synicess would have frothed at the mouth if her flaming magic hadn't prevented it. "I was *left behind*. They didn't take me, though I begged."

Jenni would have left her, too. Crazy woman.

The crazy-strong-full-Lightfolk-djinnfem turned her copper gaze on Jenni. A shot of flame hit the sand next to her, fusing it into glass.

"Get back into the mist!" her Emberdrake brother roared.

"You betrayed me, too," Synicess said. "You took my man. And there he is, the fool. *Burn,* Treeman."

Jenni stepped in front of Aric, braced, figured they would both die.

The new Fire King slipped behind Synicess, wrapped an arm around her neck and snapped it.

Synicess's body dropped, Emberdrake kicked it from the cliff. It hit a couple of rocks before it burst into flame.

"The bubble!" He met Jenni's eyes and jerked his head. She wriggled to send her senses downward through the sea, found a huge spherical shape breaking from the Earth's mantle and into the ocean.

Emberdrake grasped his lady's hand and they inserted themselves into the circle between the Cloudsylphs and the royal dwarves. The dwarves were moving slowly, too slowly, as if their feet were reluctant to separate from the rock of the bluff. The elves appeared strained, almost transparent.

Energies needed balancing.

Jenni lay encrusted in sand, panting, soaking up sun, scrabbling for her own balance. Everything was too bright, all sensual input from the real world too painful.

The loss of a new mother and father too black.

"And here are the Dark ones," the dwarf guardian said grimly.

A cloud passed over the sun, casting dark and wavering shadows on the ground. People began to curse and Jenni looked up. Not a cloud, shadleeches! Huge, triple the size of the ones she'd fought. Horror escaped her in a cry. She wanted to clutch Aric, but was caught in her ritual. Keep to herself. Even love—given and taken—distracted from the concentration needed to face the interdimension and do a major working in the mist.

Spitting, the dwarf sliced his sword whistling through the air in a couple of testing swings. "Should'a figured that if Kondrian modified his shadleeches to go into the interdimension, someone else might make 'em grow to be better weapons." He moved his gaze from the sky to Jenni. "Better slide into your interdimension, girl."

"They shouldn't be able to follow you, not these," the elf said.

"No," Aric added bleakly. "But those might." He

jutted his chin at a smaller line of grayish dark that flew lower from the north, along with a gray shape that Jenni knew in her bones was Kondrian.

Aric pulled his sword, loosened his shoulders, took his fighting stance.

"Think the great Dark one Demitroland made the large ones?" The dwarf had hunkered down, freed his other weapon, a short axe, from its sheath.

"Probably," the elf said. He still stood negligently, holding two thin and shining blades. "Demitroland likes big." Then his blue, blue eyes met hers. "Go, now."

A few armed Lightfolk showed up. To Jenni's surprise, all of Diamantina's staff—ready to defend her land home. Another surprise was the tall, silver-blond and elegant elf, Windstrum, Aric's father.

Aric sent the elf a brusque nod, turned to stand in front of Jenni.

"Hades, they're not aiming for us, but attacking the *Eight!*" the dwarf said.

Jenni stood, tried to meet Aric's eyes, but he was focused on the enemies. Heart thundering in her ears louder than the wings of all the shadleeches, she began to say the meaningless words in any language but Mistweaver. The words weren't important, the sound of the syllables were. She stamped in place, felt it was better to keep her feet close to the ground. Her eyes sharpened or dimmed or changed…whatever they did for her to see the interdimension. It was here, just a half step away.

The mist formed before her, she hesitated.

The great shadleeches swooped and the Earth King

shouted dwarvish words that *pulled* at Jenni, but she knew the command. "To me. To us!"

The dwarf guardian trembled, then shuddered, like a rockface about to be sundered. "He orders *me!* I am older. I am stronger—" he shouted in outrage. "That dwarf can command me if he pulls earth power." The dwarf guardian was sweating dirt-brown droplets.

"Go." The elf clapped his hand on his friend's shoulder.

"I *will* not."

"Go! Return when you can. Demitroland hopes to divide and conquer. Go!"

With a desperate look at the elf, who grinned wildly, the dwarf vanished.

More screams from the hill, the sound of fighting.

Something brushed Jenni, pulled her attention to her job. One of Kondrian's shadleeches! She stamped her feet and her words, saw more converge on Aric and the guardian, the slash of shining blades. Then Aric's face as he mouthed the words, *I love you.*

She halted for a moment, suspended in his love, in her need for him. She screamed, "I love you!"

His grim expression broke into wonder. He blew her a kiss and she thought it went straight to her lips, filtered down to settle in her heart. Tears rose to the back of her eyes. "I love you." She formed the same sentence with her lips.

He nodded, saluted her with his sword. "Go into the mist!" Aric yelled. "Your spiderweb will protect you from the shadleeches. Be safe."

She lifted her foot, and a bolt of black lightning struck her side, burning! She shrieked, fell.

Aric grabbed her, slapped a hand over her wound that sent pain to every nerve. "Heal, my love!" Her skin twisted, seared more, hardened. She couldn't think, could only gasp. Treefolk healing couldn't affect her. Could it?

"Elf-bright lightning!"

They both had elven blood. That blood seemed to boil and blister and burst around her wound.

"Get into the interdimension!" Aric roared. He shoved and the mist was there and in she went. Again she fell to her hands and knees, moved to her butt, huddled over, focused on what she had to do for them to be together. She'd barely reached her feet before she heard the King of Air, Cloudsylph, order the elf guardian to him.

Leaving Aric alone to guard her. Her heart leapt in fear and her hands went to her mouth to suppress a cry.

She wanted to go help him, but she had her own duties.

Sheets of energies flashed. She cast her senses toward the bubble and felt the roiling of them all inside. If they burst now, mixed with other wild magic, there'd be nothing but chaos.

That the Dark ones could use to their advantage.

She turned her attention to the hill. The Eight, the old Six and the two new Emberdrakes, were continuing with the ritual, others fought. She had to do her part.

So she struggled to her feet.

Two Dark ones attacked the Eight and their people—not the strongest. One held back, seeming to rise on tendrils of smoking evil as if he watched the fight—ready to swoop in if there was an opening for a killing blow, but staying selfishly separate.

Balance the hillside first. She sent great sweeping elemental energies there, all in equal amounts, saw it caught and formed.

They fought around her, she could sense it in the gray mist...so many moving and flashing auras. Deep, dark oily ones of three great Dark ones. The bright pillars of the Eight. *To me!* the Earth King commanded once more. Aric hesitated, glanced her way. He would think she was safe in the mist. Would he go to the Eight?

He stayed.

Not many around her, and Kondrian was committed to fighting her defenders, to wresting the whole of the energies of the bubble from the Lightfolk if possible.

No time to worry about the battle...Aric...anything but the bubble.

Ignoring the tears of grief and pain and fear rolling down her cheeks, she pressed a hand to her side and stretched her magic, herself, toward the bubble...through the thin skin of it, delicately, delicately, to be swept into the swirl of energies.

Fire! More fire to lick at her, her wound, her skin. She pulled it into her, used the energy to heat her, fight her pain.

Water, not much in the bubble, but surrounding it... surrounding her. She filtered some into the bubble. Pulled a matching amount of air from the molecules of the sea. She thought. She hoped.

All even.

Maybe. Best she could do as the bubble floated through the ocean.

She heard a mental cry from Aric, and turned to look at his strong green aura, saw that his father had deserted them to go fight in the mass with the Eight. Relative safety.

Another inner cry from Aric and he swung his sword fiercely at the dark and flitting triangular shapes—shadleeches.

She ached. Emotional pain ripped away reason and rationalizations and mental understanding of why the Eight did as they did, opened old wounds again.

All the bitterness she felt before flooded her again, rising from where she'd quashed it away. Hurting, light-headed, the past and the present merged.

The Eight fought, but they'd abandoned Aric, abandoned her.

Where were her guards? Gone. Needed to protect the circle, the ritual, the Eight. Perhaps they needed the guards, but so did she. She was tiring, would not be able to stay in the gray mist for long, and once she left she'd be killed.

So much for channeling the force of the bubble—a bubble that contained enough power to kill them all.

Six fully powered kings and queens, two new ones, but all older than Jenni. Twenty more full-blooded Lightfolk, and all concentrating on the bluff. None on the beach.

Even if they didn't believe she was important, Jenni knew she would stick to doing her duty, while the Eight ignored what they couldn't see.

She looked down. Her blouse and undershirt gaped,

showing brown-scabbed skin that ached. She had to discount it. Yes, so much for guards.

Her anger, her bitterness, her grief had to be quashed—or more, finally released. Jenni took the whole seething mass of negative and violent emotions within her and *flung* them away toward Kondrian. There was a concussion of magic when it hit the Dark one— the *thing* that was less than a person. Its aura shivered. Flashing green and silver sliced at it—Aric, fighting. For her, for them, for his belief in the Lightfolk, whom she doubted.

Again and again she flung her rage and loss and wailing desperation at the thing and it receded. Then it snapped out a tentacle and shadleeches swarmed.

Toward her.

Instinctive panic that the shadleeches could enter the mist, trap her and feed off her as they had her brother.

She spun around, saw no more flames of elemental magic that would signal any other guards but Aric. Once again she shoved her anger out and away from herself. Betrayed or not, she must keep her bargain.

She coughed, sucked in a breath at the realization that she *believed* in the good of this mission. If the Eight and other Lightfolk could influence the energies inside the bubble for the good of the Lightfolk, create a force for good in this world, any sacrifice would be worth it.

So she pressed her hand to her side even as she fell on her knees and faced the direction where the bubble lifted from the ocean into the air. She *willed* it to rise faster, but it continued to move at a steady pace. She began gathering all her energy, drawing sheets of water energy from the ocean, earth from the rocks and sand, air from the turbulent wind, fire from the very source of the bubble, magma under the earth's crust, close, close.

The Eight's ritual continued. They were ready for the bubble. Good for them.

She'd make sure to do all she could, in memory of her lost families—the Mistweavers and Emberdrakes, Aric, if he fell, even for herself if she did.

Resting on her heels, she studied the glorious pearl that was the sphere—shining with energies moving within it, painting its gleaming surface.

A shadleech zoomed through the mist, another and another. A mass. She wasn't ready for the agony as they bit her and hung on.

Breathing through the pain, Jenni flung her arms to shake off the shadleeches. Didn't happen.

Had they been mutated again by Kondrian? Or was it that the spiderweb tatt didn't work as well in the mist as the forest? But it had been as a protection for the dryads and Treefolk. The first was a shock, and the second and third. Piercing pain as their teeth clamped on her. Terrible lassitude as they sucked her magic before her mind overcame her rioting fear and sent fire against them.

Yet they fastened on her side, slurping her magical energy—and blood. Two others attached to her raised arms.

She wiggled until she buried her knees in rich earth energy, drew that into her body, it came slowly, reluctantly. The Earth King not so supportive in this, either.

Jenni! Jen-gin! Rothly's call touched her mind. She shuddered.

Roth-ly!

I'm here to help. He sounded grim. *Use me and my power, our shared blood-bond.*

She looked around but couldn't see him in the mist. More shadleeches were coming, though, enveloping her.

And energy began to trickle into her. She gasped and felt more power. From Hartha and Pred, from the small browniefem of her suite in the Earth Palace. From Fritterworth-Crag and Chinook and *Rothly.*

I love you, Jenni…I forgive you, and myself, and thank you for forgiving me.

Pulling a fire sheet closer, she drew the energies into herself. Shadleeches flapped and unheard screams rippled through the atmosphere. Some had fried. She found herself grinning, gnashing her teeth as if ready to rip into the things.

Evil hive creatures. She *loathed* them.

And Rothly's energy matched and twined with hers and she *reached* for Aric, found him desperately fending off Kondrian, helped by more Waterfolk. She bonded closely enough with him that they shared magic, and sensations. She *felt* his weary-heavy sword arm swing, and surged fire through it.

Aric lunged with a flaming sword, cut Kondrian's belly open so his putrid guts fell out, and flamed, and he died screaming in an oily spiral of smoke.

"The bubble!"

It was a chant she could hear in the interdimension.

Aric whirled and she caught a glimpse of what he saw—an enormous iridescent bubble full of elemental magic. Breathtaking.

She caught one sentence of the rising chant of the Eight—a triumphant Eight. Understood from Aric that one other Dark one had been defeated and slain.

"Give us what we need, the way to prosper—Lightfolk and human." The words Aric heard reverberated into her ears.

Jenni, the bubble, Rothly whispered in her mind and she turned her sight again to the interdimension, the massive amount of energy about to burst.

The bubble and the forces were just…too…big. She couldn't control all of it, could balance the energies but not control. And she didn't think that the Eight and their dancing could, either. She gave her all, then watched it pop, most of the energy flowed and was directed by the Eight.

Grab some, Jenni! Pull it! Use the bubble magic to become a true Lightfolk! Rothly shouted in her mind. *Become a real djinnfem or elffem!*

He was right. She *could* become a true Lightfolk, a pure magical being.

If she did, she'd give up her elemental balancing talent. She was the last, and she was proud of that talent and being a Mistweaver, a Mistweaver Emberdrake.

She watched the energies of the bubble and the sheets of elemental magic she'd summoned to equalize them meet and merge. Water to fire, earth to air. But not equally—and balancing them was beyond her.

The chant moved over her, but she couldn't hold on, was drained.

Letting go of the last of her own magic, she fell again into the real world, found herself on the beach with water lapping at her.

CHAPTER
32

ARIC GRABBED HER, HIS ARMOR GONE, smelling like sweat and blood.

She leaned against him, feeling scoured out, both tired and good. Finally she had managed to rid herself of negative emotions that had been eating at her from the inside. She glanced again at the wound in her side, healed somehow in the last few minutes to a wide and shiny red scar.

"Jenni. You did it. I love you. We *did* it!" Holding her, Aric hopped to his feet and whirled them around. "Two Dark ones dead, their shadleeches dead, too."

"We did it," she croaked, putting her head on his chest. "I love you."

"I heard you." He kissed her. "I felt you. The most amazing thing. My Jindesfarne."

The elf guardian appeared before them. He had a few

smears of blood and ichor on his clothing. Jenni figured that if his appearance really matched the way he'd fought, he'd have been covered in the stuff, his armor would show rips and blows, his hair would be matted with sweat and blood of his own.

But he looked just a little less than immaculate. And he was smiling—deeply, joyfully—as if he, too, felt an immense relief.

He bowed. "Well done, children." Shook his head at Jenni. "Your skill is incredible. Thank you." Then he clapped Aric on the shoulder, nodded. "You are a man I'm proud to fight next to."

"Thank you."

"And your father, Windstrum, is in the triage tent and has asked to see you."

Aric flinched. "How badly is he hurt?"

"Not too badly, a sword thrust through his chest, but being healed. Fluttering the healers' hearts, of course."

"Of course."

"Go see your father, Aric," the elf said softly.

Aric's brows came down. "Advice. So you're being a guardian?"

"Always." The elf bowed once more. "Again, good job, both of you. I am glad to see the future in your eyes."

"Uh," Jenni managed before he strolled off.

Aric slid her to her feet, but kept an arm around her. She turned her head into his shirt, let it soak up more tears. "I could have lost you," she said.

"We could have lost each other. And not just from battle. I felt that great bitterness you had."

"Gone now. As gone as the Emberdrakes." She couldn't help the tears. "I didn't know how much I liked them."

"You never know how deeply you feel," he said.

"I know that I never liked Synicess."

"She was deranged. And sly. Waiting until the worst possible moment to try and usurp both Fire royals. I'm sure she believed she could win." Aric shook his head. "I didn't realize how angry she truly was until she met you."

Jenni tried to think. "The other kings and queens wouldn't have interfered."

"It wouldn't be the first time violence was used to become royal. Kingship goes to the strongest. Though I doubt Synicess would have held that throne long."

Jenni gulped and clutched his shirt, decided to change the subject. "You have a father, Aric."

"You have a brother."

She sniffed loudly. "And we've made up." His gaze was green and soft when she looked up. "We're good now, Rothly and I. And Rothly and you."

"I'm glad." Aric pulled her along to the nearest tree at the bottom of the hill, they entered, then exited at the top.

The ridge was full of rushing people dealing with the aftermath of battle, or collapsed nearby in sweet gratitude that the fighting was over and they'd lived. The sun was warm on them and Jenni finally smelled their own odor—forest and air and sticky-resin-sweat from Aric. Regular human sweat from herself with a hint of ocean and scorched hair. She released Aric's hand to run her fingers through her hair. Definitely some crispy ends. And why was she thinking about her hair when Aric was having a crisis? She tugged at it.

Because she didn't want to prompt him further to do what she thought was the right thing for him. He had to decide and he already knew her opinion.

He turned and reached up and took her wrists. "Leave it alone, it looks fine." After a breath in and out, he said, "We'd better go see Windstrum."

"Don't do it because of me."

He snorted. "That's what I think I should do. Make my peace with him."

She pulled her hands from his grip, linked an arm with him. "Good idea."

"After all, half of my nature comes from him."

"Yes."

"I was hurt when he didn't come to help us."

"Yes," Jenni said again.

"I know what you felt that first battle. And I'm sorry now that I hurt your feelings then."

"Ah." She wasn't sure what to say. Everything seemed so complicated. She didn't want Aric to mix his feelings about his father and her together. "It's past." As the Emberdrakes were past and her grief was present and would have to be dealt with in the now and the future.

The rest of their walk to the triage tent was in silence. The place was dim, and Jenni's nose twitched at the stringent odor of healing herbs. No one was groaning in pain or despair though, the way it had been during that first battle. The Eight had been prepared this time. Those who were dead had been taken away by their families or the Eight had cared for them. Those who had been deeply wounded had been transferred to palace healing wards. Only those with minor wounds were still here.

No stench of death was here, either, and Jenni breathed easier.

A healer of the minor Waterfolk, a naiad, hurried up, but Aric waved her away. His gaze had already fixed on a raised pallet in the corner of the tent near a light-heat glow globe. They walked toward the elf reclining there, pale and beautiful. His harp and flute cases were beside the bed.

"Hello, Windstrum," Aric said.

"Can't you call me Father?" Windstrum's eyelids were puffy and heavy, but his voice, though plaintive, was still musical.

Aric hesitated, then bent down and kissed the elf's smooth cheek. "Hello, Father."

"So tall and sturdy and strong, excellent," Windstrum murmured.

Jenni leaned against Aric. "I think so."

"A good man. A strong man," Windstrum continued. "I am not much of either." He cleared his throat. "I was not the father I should have been. Will never be the father that I should be." His eyes seemed to burn. "But know that I care for you, and that I think often of you." His breath bubbled on his lips.

A healer hurried over and tsked at them, bending a disapproving look on Aric and Jenni as she stroked

Windstrum's brow. Then her hand went to his chest and pressed. Green healing energy flowed from her hands into Windstrum. He tensed, then went limp, but his gaze was still fixed on Aric's face.

For an instant they looked eerily alike—in bone structure and expression. With a slow incline of his head, Aric said, "Thank you, Father." He reached out and took his father's long and fine-boned hand in his larger one, clasped it between both of his, sent his father loving energy.

The healer hummed approval. "Very well done."

"My son is a better man than I am, and I am pleased with that," Windstrum said on a small sigh. Then his merry smile curved his lips and was reflected in his gaze. "Most of the time I am pleased that he's an honorable man." He fell asleep.

Aric stepped away from his father's bedside, shaking his head as if at a loss for words.

"He is what he is," Jenni said.

"He is what he is, and has never pretended not to be what he is. That's something."

"Yes."

"I do love him."

"Of course."

"I'll never understand him, but I love him."

She hugged Aric. "And he loves you. You felt it when you held his hand, didn't you?"

"There was love passing between us, yes." Aric's voice was rough. He wrapped his arms around her. "He loves me in his own way."

"And it's not a bad way. He wasn't there for you when you needed him. But you found others to help you along your way."

"Your brothers, your father. Etesian, even Cloud-sylph."

"Yes."

Aric sighed, glanced around at the tents. "It's over. Let's get our stuff and leave."

"Fine by me. My pocket computer stated the weather in Denver would be cloudless and in the upper sixties." She rolled her shoulders. "I'm sure the brownies have my yard spick-and-span and maybe there are a couple of lawn chairs out in the back where we can soak up rays." She sniffed and the scent of the ocean came to her as it had so often in the last week.

"I'm invited?"

"Of course."

They hurried to the guest room and packed the few things that weren't already in their bags—Jenni's palm computer that she left on the desk, a sea-stained paper-back book she'd carried along and been trying to read to distract herself, her brush.

"Ready?" Aric asked.

"For sure."

They reached for each other's hand at the same time and Aric smiled. He tugged her to the sliding glass door and opened it and the screen. They stepped from the house onto the hillside and let out pent-up breaths. Aric didn't close the doors behind them as they walked around the house.

"I'm going home with you," he said.

"Yes," she said, then caught the resonance in his words, flashed back to a time long ago after she'd first met him. They'd been in a pub that catered to halflings, and her brothers—his friends who'd introduced him—had wandered off. Jenni had invited him to the house. That had been the first time he'd been to her home, met her parents. She knew now how much that simple invitation had meant to him at the time, outside of the sex that he'd anticipated and they'd had. She also knew now—they both acknowledged—how her inviting him to her home had changed and enriched his life.

She didn't think this invitation could match that.

Hurrying her along, Aric took her to the empty area where the dancing circle had been. Powerful magic thrummed under her feet and the lingering traces of elemental power nearly made her dizzy.

He walked her straight to the center, turned them until they faced the forest south, took her other hand and gazed down into her eyes. Uh-oh.

"Will you wed with me and twine our lives together until we pass to the next?"

She hesitated. Even harder to answer than the *I love you*.

In the aftermath of the victory, of the knowledge that she had completed her mission, she could have let the giddy rush of triumph that still fired her nerves answer him with a yes. But she didn't.

She *had* forgiven him, hadn't she?

He stood there, tall and broad and with a mask of inscrutability on his face and his eyes dark and aching.

She hurt for him, too. Surely that was enough. She wanted him. She treasured his friendship and companionship. She loved him.

Before she could answer, the Eight glided toward her, and she had an instant's revulsion and panic. She didn't want to see them. Not when the faces of the Emberdrakes were new. Be congratulated on a good job when all this still reminded her of the past.

Despite everything, she hadn't forgiven them. Aric was right, she felt deeply and she hung on to those feelings too long.

And despite the true words of love she'd screamed at Aric, she hadn't forgiven him, and wouldn't until she'd forgiven the Eight, and rooted out that last kernel of hard, unforgiving self-guilt.

She had to forgive them all. She had to open her heart and accept that they had all made errors in judgment that had led to tragedy.

She wouldn't be whole, couldn't claim this man who stood and suffered before her, if she didn't forgive. She wasn't the person she *could* be if she didn't forgive. Her parents, her family, had taught her that.

She'd forgiven Rothly, but that was almost easier because he'd been the one who'd been the more bitter of the two of them, and he was a loved brother, not a beloved man that she wanted to spend her life with.

Then the Eight were there, not appearing as sorrowful as she thought they should. But even the younger

Emberdrakes had lived centuries, and known losses before.

The Earth King walked up to her until he was only a handspan away, invading her space. "Well, child?"

"You abandoned me. Without me that bubble energy would have been nothing but chaos."

The king's face was as inscrutable as rock. He inclined his head. "That may be true. As it is true that I believed—" he put his thick-fingered hand on his chest "—that you would survive and triumph, as you did." He stared at Aric. "That I believed our Treeman would fight and not fall. Which is what occurred."

They stared at each other. Jenni and Aric against the Eight.

"Do you take our man from us?" asked Cloudsylph.

"Aric is his own man," Jenni said.

"He is and we are honored to have him represent us," the dwarf king said.

That was something.

"So you feel now, as you have felt all along. Angry at us. Can you not understand our past actions—even those of an hour ago—and forgive us?" the dwarf asked. "We were Six instead of Eight and needed the guardians. Had we fallen, the Dark ones would have swarmed over our gathering and eaten you all."

Jenni shuddered. "I can understand and I can say I will forgive, but feelings don't always follow words."

"For now, the words will do," the Water Queen said.

Many of the circumstances were the same as after that

long, failed mission. But Jenni had changed. Was willing to admit that she'd changed, and she didn't want to hold anger and bitterness close to her, let it poison her life as it had.

"I forgive you, I forgive you, I forgive you." And she continued the magical three-chant for each.

"And you forgive yourself," the Water Queen said.

"I forgive myself, I forgive myself, I forgive myself."

"And now, a boon for you." The Earth King snapped his fingers and held a small crystal sphere. "I captured one of the minor bubbles that formed after the huge one broke. It's yours, to do with as you please." His lips twitched. "I think you will find that the elemental energies are balanced."

When Jenni didn't take it, he lifted her hand, put the thing in her palm and closed her fingers over it. "To do with as you please," he repeated. "To become a full djinnfem or elffem if you please."

Everything her family had ever hoped for was in her hand, but Jenni had learned so much since she was a child, mostly in the last few weeks. Being halfling wasn't as important as being alive and happy with your life—your magic, your future.

She took Aric's hand, gazed into his dear face. "I'll wed with you."

He closed his eyes, sighed out a breath that sounded like wind whispering in pines. "Thank you." Opening his eyes, he kissed her hand. "Thank you."

"And you will work with Eight Corp on the meld project?" asked Cloudsylph.

"Yes. But I'll work with my game, also, and practice my Mistweaver magical craft."

"Good, we need you," Blackstone Emberdrake said.

He was right, and she knew it. She'd remain a halfling, and be proud of herself and her talent that no one in the world could match.

The magical community, the Lightfolk royals, needed her as she was.

She had changed. She was Jindesfarne Mistweaver Emberdrake, and she would shape the future of Lightfolk and halfling and magic.

★ ★ ★ ★ ★

There's more to come in this world!
Watch for Amber's story....

Acknowledgments

California Coastal Records Project, www.californiacoastline.org, for the wonderful images of the Lost Coast of California. The U.S. National Park Service and most particularly the Yellowstone National Park website and online cams, and the cams at Sequoia and Kings Canyon National Parks; the U.S. Geological Survey, and the QuakeWatch iPod Touch application. England's Northumberland National Park and the Royal Botanic Gardens, Kew. My apologies to any other references that I may have lost in my desktop crash (one hard drive of two gone, including internet bookmarks and history), and my laptop crash (motherboard and internet bookmarks and history gone).

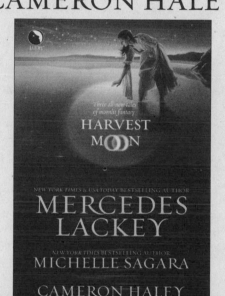